START WITH C

GR McDougall

Long-listed for Gloria Burley Award, Whitsundays Literary Festival, 2024.

Readers Comments
Superbly written! Dialogue moves the story along swiftly and is well written to incorporate Aussie rough slang.

…exciting and mysterious. It has great dialogue, and it's very-bloody-Aussie.

'The warm sunlight ebbed, and a curtain drew across his face. He felt a chill that had little to do with the weather.' This is a wonderful story. You did a great job.

'… fast-paced, hard-hitting and clever. The characters shine through, and the writing is natural and smooth.'

'… now I know Kev well enough to grin at him if I see him.'

Start with C

The inglorious days and nights

of an outback town

by Vick Watson

Pamela Press ©

In Memory of Jimmy Barker (1900-1972), Essie Coffey (1941-98) and Tombo Winter (1938-2004).

My sincerely thanks to Mick Childs for taking me to outback Brewarinna in 1977, and his precious feedback on the manuscript. Thanks also to AIATSIS, Canberra, for access to the Jimmy Barker recordings, Thanks too to Dr Virginia Nightingale and my 'Write-On' critics Helena Ameisen, Stuart Campbell and Sarah Bourne.

* * *

'... figure I'll write a book one day; call it 'Days and Nights' or 'Forgetting and Remembering'

The Two Worlds of Jimmy Barker. (1980)

If memory is a past that becomes part of me, forgetting is a past that's no longer a part of me. But all that's forgotten can again be remembered.

Paraphrased from *The Conversation,* September 2012.

All characters in *Starts with C* are fictional, and any resemblance to others is coincidental, false or imagined.

ISBN:9798345393628

©

Pamela Press

CONTENTS

Welcome

Part One: Bicentennial Trust: Chapters 1 to 14

Part Two: Days and Nights: Chapters 15 to 21

Part Three: Get Rid of It: Chapters 22 to 28

Part Four: It's All About: Chapters 29 to 41

Part Five: Return Service: Chapters 42 to 49

Part Six: Finale: Chapters 50 to 68

Historical Note for Non-Australian Readers

Australian 1980s Common Usage Words and Expressions

The Story Behind the Story

Short Story Bonus: Patting the Dog

Other Works by the Author

Welcome, dear Reader. It's rare for our first-time author to win rave reviews for a novel written in His Majesty's prisons. Rarer too when the writer's experience of murder mysteries was limited to Arthur Upfeild's *Inspector Boney* series.

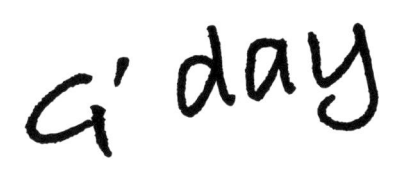

G' day

What good fortune to meet and assist the innocent author in crafting a fine narrative, borne of toil, heart and soul.

At the start of this journey, in the hope of broadening the writer's literary experience, friends gifted him/her Albert Facey's *A Fortunate Life* and a few Tom Keneally, Frank Hardy and Xavier Herbert novels.

The resulting work might have gone unnoticed, except the authorities blocked its publication when it appeared to include the crime that put the author in gaol. The Court decided *Start with C* was evidence of rehabilitation, and contemporary media reports spurred first-edition success. In a heartless act, the Department refused the author's release from prison during a public outcry against parole.

With this release, please be patient for the first few pages as its conventional start soon morphs into a rollicking tale of colourful characters, stirring events and the joyous use of colloquial language. (The expressions common in 1980s regional Australia are listed on the back pages.) As Editor, I admit weeding out most expletives but the numerous brutal, curious and bizarre outback expressions remain.

You will notice the events in our unnamed outback town parallel the infamous Indigenous death-in-custody in outback Brewarrina when Prime Minister Bob Hawke established an Australian Royal Commission. The Commission's Report, featured in *Time* magazine, rocked the continent.

Since then, Australia's cultural catharsis has continued. This might explain why the Author's third-person storytelling breaks into the intensive hues of a desert sunset. Intense, tragic, farcical and comic, it reminds me of the passion and painful honesty of Elizabeth Smart's *By Grand Central Station, I Sat Down and Wept*.

Our *Start with C* detective is Kev, a retired shearer who records his indigenous Gundawarri language for posterity. His people's past exposes what everyone tried to forget: racism, rivalries, misunderstandings and human absurdity in an outback town. Its sorry story is a microcosm of the nation's.

The appearances of the inestimable Cliff Badger, Bicentennial Official, almost steal the show, while the Bolshie legal service rep, Billy, is a picture of contradictions. The personable town councillor Cheryl Sheila and her administrator boyfriend, Humblebum, are town spirits gone wrong. Unforgettable, harrassed Mara, breaks all the rules, and the petty crim, Paddy Bourke and his Hard Boys remind us of outback characters we'd rather not meet.

I'll let you decide who's been murdered, who is the murderer, and who is telling the tale. I sincerely hope *Starts with C* delights you.

G.R. McDougall

Editor, Pamela Press, Sydney.

Part One, Chapter One

Bicentennial Trust

Australia Day, January 26, 1988
Western Plains, New South Wales.

'What a stinker,' said Chief Warren to his junior officer as they halted the squad car short of the water tower. In a burnt, forgotten corner of the town tip, they followed a line of burnt posts and slack wire to the body. Warren scratched his neck as he inspected the blackened, stick-like form, only saying, 'Another murder.'

'Well, there's dead, and there's this,' said the constable, scrunching his eyes to decipher what lay before him.

Warren sweated under his stiff new cap, grimacing at the charred and dismembered remains under the tower, its fixed outstretched arm evidence of the victim's last, agonising moments. After thirty years in the Force, the sight of a body picked over by a dingo forced a flinch. 'Poor bloke's been lured here, set on fire, and found all escape blocked. Some animals had a nibble but the meal ain't tasty enough.'

The young one pulled out a handkerchief and wiped the sweat from the back of his neck. A hot breeze blew a stench his way. 'What a bugger. Who'd do something like this?'

Warren blew his nose and haunched over the corpse. He peered at the water tank overhead, screwed his eyes, and noted the persistent drip from the tower.

Needs fixing, he thought.

Peering at the ragged remains again, he turned his excessive belly eastward, then south, his feet barely moving. Wiping the

back of his hand against the collar, his face twitched. 'Must be that

Bicentennial bloke, Badger. He's been missing a while now. More enemies than a Brown Snake.'

He kicked the dirt if only to draw attention to the ashes. 'Hey. What are you doing here?'

An emu glared at him from the bushes, so he stared back until it moved away.

'It might be a she,' said the constable.

'He. She. It. Who cares? Dumb bastard's been set alight and murdered.'

'What about suicide?'

'Nar. They take sleeping pills or a shotgun. No one in their right mind would do this to themselves in this dump. Some black bastard's taken revenge on that Bicentennial bloke, odds-on. They never liked us celebrating eighty-eight. They've gone too far this time, matey.'

The constable blinked; the corpse so dark daylight made no impact.

'Nothing to say, sonny Jim?'

The young one turned to him. 'Well. It's burnt to a crisp, so we can't make out who it is. Barely smells.'

'Aren't you a bright one?' He grinned. 'Don't worry. Some drunken boong will spill the beans soon enough.'

'I mean, we all look black after this. Could be anybody. Might not be one of us.'

'Not one of us? Of course it bloody well is. Ain't you noticed what's going on?' With a fly buzzing around him, Warren whacked himself on the neck. Taking out the handkerchief, he wiped the muck from his hand. 'Anyway, seal it off.'

The young cop stared at the corpse as the Chief stamped his feet.

'Move, will ya? Fast.'

'Yeah, but what'll I use for tape?'

'Fetch rope from the boot, for God-sake. Knock a picket over here so the whole tower's included. Hop to it.'

A few minutes later, the job done, the Chief tipped his head. 'Let's piss off. We've had our holiday. We gotta get back to the station. Give them Abo troublemakers a warm welcome while the media's not hanging around. Keep your bloody eyes open, or we're toast. We'll shove it up 'em, then drink to the Bicentenary.

The Riot Squad's office at the old police station had scattered papers everywhere, With filing cabinets jammed, scribble on walls, and stained coffee mugs gathering dust and mould, riot gear was left on tables, floors and chairs. So much had been cast aside, and the troops didn't care.

The Chief burst in via the rear door, saying, What a mob out there.'

'The town's gone crazy,' said Hanna, throwing out his hands. 'They're chanting for Kev. What'll we do?'

'Do?' said Warren to his startled men. 'Whatever we have to.'

So much had been cast aside, and the troops didn't care.

The Chief burst in via the rear door, saying, 'What a mob out there.'

'The town's gone crazy,' said Hanna, throwing out his hands. 'They're chanting for Kev. What'll we do?'

'Do?' said Warren to his startled men. 'Whatever we have to.'

'Black, white and brindle outside,' said Cassidy. 'They're as mad as a two-bob snake. They reckon we do the killing around here. Can you believe it?'

The crowd chanted, yelled and heaped abuse on the forces of Order, chairs, sticks and milk crates thrown on the landing, 'roo poop splattered on the door.

Shortie peered through the grill. 'That's the dago, isn't it? Some nurses too. They're troppo.'

'Cops out.' 'Murdering pigs out,' the mob chanted.

Cassidy leaned on a wall. 'I've got some boys keeping an eye on things. The publican's protecting the pub with a shotgun. Reckons the blacks are after his grog.'

Warren held up both arms, calling for attention. 'We've just come from another murder out near the water tower. Those boongs have burnt a man alive.'

A sweaty officer entered from the cell quarter. 'Did you hear what they're saying? What in bloody hell is going on?'

'A fucking rebellion, that's what,' said Warren. 'Told yous it would be on Australia Day. Four dead, and more missing. Grab your ammo. Put on your gear. We're going to teach them abo radicals a lesson. And here's a little tip, boys: if you point the gun straight at their face, they'll shit themselves.'

Several officers let out tribal 'whoops,' though a few others were silent. Warren turned to Chris Hanna. 'Well?'

'You must be … I mean, nurses and shopkeepers and …'

'You're a pansy, mate; been with the fairies too long,' said Cassidy.

Warren sneered. 'This is the riot squad, mate. We gotta keep order out there. No use handing out bloody flowers like Nyngan cop-shop. Grab your weapon, and be prepared to shoot.'

Chapter Two

Sydney, six months earlier.

Cliff Badger sat at the far end of the Steering Committee's table, his fingers tapping the mahogany surface. Surrounded by paper clips, manila folders and cheap, framed photographs of former Premiers, he straightened his yellow tie and nodded to his Rugby mates, Charlie, Harry and Johnno. Principal Administrator to the Bicentennial Council, Edward Percival Fitch, officiated.

Once they settled in, his boss attacked. 'Mister Clifford Badger, State Coordinator. We spied on your Sodom-and-Gomorrah in Kings Cross.' He slapped a report before his opponent. 'We investigated everything.'

Cliff glanced at the boys before dragging the document across the surface, and scanning its title: *Unauthorized Budgetary Allocations and Expenditures, Premier's Bicentennial Standing Committee, July 30, 1987*. He leafed through its pages at a leisurely pace, underlining a phrase or two as if identifying the points of a school essay.

'After your disgraceful escapades, the choice is gaol or a termination of employment,' said his superior. 'The goings-on in and out of work hours, the corruption and theft. Your letter of resignation is here.' He pushed two, typed sheets across. 'Sign, and you are free to leave. Refuse, and you won't land a job from here to Timbuktu.'

Bader picked up the two-pager and read it as slowly as the first.

'Well?' Fitch's lips tightened.

'In such a hurry, Herr Filch. Don't expect me to autograph a non-disclosure clause just like that.'

'Sign, or else.' The boss sat erect.

'What? Accused, convicted and hung already? I'm hurt. What about due process?' Cliff Badger drew out a cigarette and lit it. 'What happened to your darling procedures? I reckon this matter will be in the papers for a year or more. TV too.'

He eyed his three colleagues for effect.

'Enough,' said Fitch. 'This is your deserve for your insolence.'

'Easy now, you're getting emotional. What do the boys opposite say?'

'They have nothing to say. They are here to witness your resignation and uphold Public Service standards.'

'Filch, old man, I had a few nights out. Got a bit plied. So, I used the wrong credit card. An innocent mistake.'

'Don't talk —' His boss buttoned his lips. 'We tabulated everything: twenty-six mistaken usages in brothels. We call that corruption and breach of duty. Quit, or I guarantee a custodial sentence.'

'Look Filch, I guarantee the Premier won't like airing the issues in the media. They'll ask: How is it that a senior public official, that's you, knew nothing about the alleged use of taxpayer funds for almost a year? If only I'd been told earlier. No problem. These are Bicentennial monies, mate.'

His boss gripped the table. Badger grinned. 'Have the boys something to say?'

'Leave them out of this. The charade is over. A public servant involved with prostitutes; you don't stand a chance.'

'I don't make empty promises. I will drag this through every administrative and judicial process at my disposal. Questions in Parliament. Ministers under fire. By the time they've finished, you'll be hailed as the Flinch.' Rocking back against his seat, he winked at the boys opposite. 'Or you could …' he said, hinting at what he already learnt from his Rugby chums.

The administrator balked. His eyes darted to Charlie, Harry and Johnno. His hands pressed against his thighs lest Anglican restraint abandoned him. His three project managers betrayed him; they sat with their hands on their laps, looking straight ahead.

'Why fool around? I won't be signing. I've got a career in front of me. I give as good as I get. Either we go the full eighty minutes, or…'

Fitch's neck stiffened, and his eyes narrowed. As a churchgoer, he was not supposed to hate. The Premier demanded the weeding out of wayward types, so Badger would take his punishment.

Fitch fixed his eyes on Mister Clifford Badger. After a pause, he pulled out a single brown folio labelled *Assignment #5293*. 'Your alternative is this task, with pay docked. He wants you out.' He pushed the folder across the desk.

Glancing at its content, Badger thought: never heard of the place. Outback? Sent to the wing. He shuffled the papers into place. Who cares? I'll leave town for a while. A bit of a break. Let the heat die down. 'I was hoping for old Port Macquarie. You know, a missionary position, with beaches, boobs and bananas.'

Fitch sneered. 'I'll crush you for this.'

Chapter Three

In an outback town the same week, a thin man in baggy shorts and a loose, checked shirt pushed a card across the Post Office counter. The lady glanced at him before turning away and entered a small room near the back door. When she returned, her husband slid a sizable cardboard box across.

'For me?' A bulky package.

The woman scowled. 'Who else?'

With thick bands of tape, wrapping and numerous stamps, his name appeared on the white label.

Maybe, it's …

His arms beside his hips, he wondered how he'd carry it. Needing help, he slipped next door to Marco's Grocery Store. Passing the rows of canned fish, flour, shoe laces and polish, he wheeled a trolley to the counter.

'Marco, can I?' he said, with one hand on the rattler.

'OK for you,' said the bushy-browed shopkeeper, because Kev never gave him trouble. Insisted on paying cash for all his purchases. Never on-the-tab.

'Back by morning. Promise.'

So done, he dragged and slid the package over the polished floor to the post office steps. He loaded it and headed across the road, passing Evans Street's featureless shop windows, cast-iron awnings and tiled frontages. With few cars parked and fewer people walking the pavement, he entered Hook Crescent's tarmac unnoticed. Abandoned rose bushes, grass stubble and rusting gates lined the succession of plain fibro houses on both sides. With his prize on wheels, he imagined townspeople peeping from their curtained windows, asking "What's he up to?" "Is he hauling stolen goods to the river, running errands for drunks?" "What's in the box?"

He crossed Pioneer Park on a worn track, over the barren expanse to a solitary grand gum.

'Watch out,' said a distant voice.

Too late. A station wagon pulled alongside him, tyres grinding the gravel, its deep-throated engine throbbing with disdain. A side window dropped, slow and even, before an overweight cop eyed him.

'Sergeant Farrell,' he blurted.

'Hold up.'

Though he slowed, he continued his walk so the cop's foot was suspended on the clutch.

'What's in the package, Kev?'

'A present from my brother. From the Post Office.'

'I'll check.'

'Yes, sir.'

'Stealing a trolley is an offence.'

'Marco lent it.'

'Who's running grog downriver, eh?

'Don't know, sir.'

Farrell eyeballed him, Kev expecting the usual verbal serve. The copper hesitated as his foot ached from holding the pedal down as the Falcon neared the dirt path that ran down to the river. The vehicle's tinted windows closed. The cop did a swift U-turn, sending up an ominous plume. He coughed in its wake. As the police car accelerated towards the Unity Hotel, he took the lower track beside the bridge, finding Mara behind a pylon.

'Damn, Farrell. Making you eat dust.'

He shook his head before noticing her hessian bag.

'What have you got, Mar?'

'Them toys. Don't have time to fix 'em, m'self. Do you mind?'

He nodded, lips pursed.

The kids at Patchtown's public housing ran 'sister' Mara ragged, so Uncle Kev was useful now and again. Seeing her well-dressed, he smiled like an indulgent uncle as she added the bag to the trolley. She clasped his hands in thanks but dared not eye her senior. Hurrying away, she climbed the slope to the bridge and headed for home.

She's in a rush. There must be something going on.

At his upriver cottage, Kev couldn't wait to unpack his parcel. Removing the crumpled paper, he opened the cardboard flaps to reveal his prize. Pulling the tape deck out, he put the aluminium-clad recorder on the kitchen table.

Reel-to-reel. No one else has one of these little beauties.

Plugging it in, he loaded the tape and reels, gazing at its razza-mataz cladding. Pushing the white lever produced a loud 'clunk,' a small light appearing on the console. The spools turned in harmony, one fast, the other slower, like a waltz.

'Hello. Testing.'

Microphone too.

He took a seat on his lounge and leafed through the manual.

Electricity driving it, copying sound; a bit like the old phonographs. Been fixing appliances for years. Townies chuck them out, I pick them up, and make them go again. But this is new.

He chuckled.

Told Farrell it was a present, like a television. Wasn't a lie. No use complicating matters.

Later, he recorded a few throwaway words and replayed it, the speaker producing a deep resonance like speaking into a well. A high-pitched whine too.

What's that?

Flipping through the manual, a chapter at a time, he stopped at whatever interested him. He covered Feedback, Playback, Rewind and Quality. Another hour passed.

Catherine promised – and here it is.

Last month, a visiting anthropologist discovered he spoke some Gundabarri, the local indigenous language. Leaving town after a week, she claimed she'd send him the recorder, so he could record, though he didn't believe it. Until today.

These Canberra people, giving me this tape deck. They figure the Earth will swallow me up any time now. I am sixty, I guess.

Clunk. The machine came alive.

'This is Kev. Eh, August 16. Before I start, speaking Gundabarri, I'll say a little about my mother's people, where they lived.'

The spools turned, chewed up time, and urged him to continue.

'They lived down Nyngan way. On a mission station, a place called Crooked Tree, on the bend of ...'

Ten minutes later he gave himself a break.

Tiring work, this remembering. All this time forgetting.

Reclining on his old lounge, he stretched out his thin frame, counting his years by the number of aches and pains harassing him. From where he sat, he spied his newly repaired cane chair between the wood heater and umbrella stand, some old river stones at the base.

Barely room to swing a cat.

Grabbing a coat hanger off the string along the wall, he bent it to a hook and inserted it into a small hole in the galvanised iron behind the alcove.

That's better. Right above the shoe box too.

To anyone else's eye, objects littered every shelf and table in his room. Jobs-on-the-go, a kind of home assembly line, including Mara's bag of broken dolls and toys kept by the door.

My orderliness, not Bess', he would say.

He lost her a couple of years back, and the unbearable emptiness had to be filled. Her death left him surprised and anxious more than miserable. He was alive when fellas like Bunny Murrijju and Kenny Coodujah 'went' a few months before her.

Bunny was only fifty-eight. Isn't old.

Despite the days of forgetting, memories of his youth remained strong. Easy recollecting croaking frogs, night eels, darting fish, fluorescent insects, the 'roos moving about at night, a million stars looking on. His brain burst with visions of throbbing billabongs, and camps by the fireplace. Golden nights, away from the mission's sickness and fighting.

'You old chatterbox,' Bess said of him after another of his recollections.

Since he lost her, he busied himself making, repairing and fixing damaged tools, toys and electrical appliances. For years, he turned broken things into working things, repaired them on the landing or around the linoleum table, returning them to their old owners. Sometimes he fetched a few-bob selling them at the pubs.

For the last while, he worked odd jobs at the hospital. With a disability pension, care of the union's support, and a shearer's bad back, he could do favours for anyone he chose, sparing himself tiresome put-downs about 'boongs' or 'aboes.'

When Catherine turned up, she wanted stories and asked questions, so he kept to himself. Around country towns, the police ask the questions, though they are just as good at making up evidence. So, when she asked him …

Perhaps she didn't understand that digging up the past is dangerous.

She asked about the Gundabarri language too. He sent her away.

On her second visit, a few words seeped out. 'I remember some things. A bit.'

She tested him. 'You know, Kurri na?'

'I say, Parri na.'

'Unrunnta ka Parramar?' (What have you there?)

'Parramar. Marri arribree.' (I have brought food aplenty.)

'Excellent.'

On the last day, she came back with a tape recorder, and they talked all morning. Found myself chatting away like a young man flattered by a woman's attention. She promised this machine to me, like a present. Just like them experts, wanting to dig up everything about a man: my Gundabarri, family, the river life, time out bush, in the deserts, on the stations.

'It's important to remember history,' she said, 'or the old ways will be forgotten. No police. Nothing to do with them.'

She made me laugh. Catherine's a sweetie, hungry for stories. Running around talking to us 'elders' and that. Old men, yep. Most of those elders, like Rabbit Burns and Dickie Reilly, they're gone.

In his lounge room, he stirred his sweet, milky tea while he looked out the window, to the bush, the chook shed and the driveway.

Got to take the trolley back to Marco. See Billy too. Write a letter to Danny. Fix Mara's things. I'll help Cheryl tomorrow. Hope Farrell stays out of my hair.

Reaching inside the cloth bag, he pulled out two dolls and three bears, a few smaller toys at the bottom, each one damaged by rough play. A dismembered arm. A torn foot, lost padding or a nasty tear down the back. With a golden-haired, rubbery child's toy on his lap, a job ahead.

But hell, this tape recording is a bigger one. It'll test me. What's worth saying to these people? I'll probably disappoint her. Catherine of

Canberra.

I can't talk about my mother anymore, about her trials and the adults of my early life. Not yet. Guess I'll recall our camps along the river when I was young; how we found his people in the bush, how we gathered bird's eggs, caught fish and collected honey. All those things.

He began recording again that evening, choosing his words carefully, sometimes lingering mid-sentence. Gathering his thoughts. Only when he recalled his mission station years did his voice hollow, phrases tripped on his tongue, choked in his throat, his mouth as sticky as jam. He stuttered; hadn't happened since his younger years.

He possessed more stories but tripped up in their telling, like his first driving lessons, halting, nervous, engaged in the wrong gear, without the clutch, the instructor getting crankier. He talked a little about his years with Bess, in and out of town, and wondered why anyone would be interested.

After another hour, he stopped.

Grand listener, this machine.

Had he said anything useful? What would he say after this, and in what order? What would he not say? Names? Who would he name? Who should he not name? What would his friends say, if they knew? This could be dangerous.

I'll help Catherine. But not like she thinks. I'm Kev. Just Kev.

Chapter Four

Cliff Badger took the new VL Commodore from the Public Service carpool right under Fitch's nose. Waving goodbye to Sydney's youthful body, the harbour's sparkling eyes and its sandstone legs, he dashed across the Cumberland Plain, climbed the misty Blue Mountains and glided over the western slope's sinuous curves.

'Bye-bye, sweetie.'

Immersed in surround sound, he played *Dark Side of the Moon*, Michael Jackson and Neil Diamond, luxuriating on the highway's voluptuous lines, thoughts of passionfruit Pavlova and memories of Melanie's rainbow lipstick.

Hours later, when the lowering hills and grey pastures of the beyond blighted his vision, he spied a glowing red light on the dashboard.

B-Jesus!

His lusty conversation with himself broken, he quickly tamed the speakers.

Need gas.

With straw paddocks, ancient fencing and pale skies as company, he entered the fringe of a one-horse town, pulling into the first fuel station by the highway. Once the Commodore landed beside a pump, he grabbed the petrol holster without a thought.

Then it hit him. At his feet were oil stains, foul asphalt, dirt and dust; in his nostrils, fumes, greasy air and the odours of rotting carcasses. Muck clung to the rusty red-white-and-blue installation with its corroded icon of the Statue of Bloody Liberty.

My shoes, soiled by sheep's dung. My hands – yuk.

With wonky grey telegraph poles, broken concrete, damaged awnings, weeds and languid, stray dogs limping in circles, moderno

Sydney had evaporated. The Blue Mountain's crisp air and ready takeaways only a memory. The rolling hills before Bathurst were more welcome than this. His thrilling journey on Motorway Two's silver-white ribbon was up-in-fumes, and his sense of handsome revenge on Fitch crueled.

After hours of following the curving, tarmacked highway's pulsing white edges, dashing past cattle trucks and caravans, lane-changing on short passing zones, the way narrowed. Brown goo stained the road and dusty side tracks. Lonesome railway crossings and tatty grey poles extended to the horizon. Old things, old ways, run-down buildings, old bosses, grease and dirt; he hated every crusty thing.

His slinky new vehicle with its sonorous stereo system had arrived in a warped, grimy town, its men and women as thick as pickled dills. With vehicles bull-barred like blacklisted bulldozers, their V8s were fueled by country music and bad breath. Dead sheep, rotting 'roos, rusted signs and cast-off radiators littered the highway, as these folks knew how to kill and gut.

And worse ahead.

A real wreck of a woman stood before him. With her weathered face, shrivelled hand and bent body, she wore a plain garment of indefinite colour. In pink slippers and a dirty rag in her hand, she yanked the petrol bowser from his hand, dashing his modest hopes of an outback town with bright-lit poker machines, fine whiskey and a few live wires to kick on the night.

While she filled his tank, he thought, I'll be stuck out here for God-knows-how-long with a bunch of hicks, and more shit work afterwards. Johnno reckoned he did me a favour by getting me this assignment. I've been sent to Bleeding-Coventry.

'It was my idea,' he said. Bloody wanker.

Cliff Badger consoled himself with a Coke and a pack of crisps. Paid in full, the glaring daylight almost blinded him and only the reassuring plastic and leather interior convinced him to continue. He soon turned onto a compacted gravel road with a battered and bullet-ridden sign indicating his destination another two hundred kilometres on.

The land collapsed into miserable mallee and plaintive mulga plains; a grey pall everywhere, in the bushes, at the horizon, extending into the sky itself. On a left-hand track to a property named

Wordsworth, its iron gate was locked and the overhead arch was decked with horseshoes.

And nothing much beyond. Now, that's irony.

Properties around here had fifty-kilometre front yards.

I should have bluffed it. They'd have buckled. Sink the matter in the dark interior of a legal committee. Instead, I'm gonna be Santa Claus of the West.

He gripped the steering wheel. Fitch's instructions: do something useful. Give the local council a cultural centre for some old, indigenous fish traps. Late thought: not enough Bicentennial Abo projects. Get out there and give away a million bucks. Think you can do that?

The hide of the man.

He had never heard of a fish trap, nor did he bother to find out what one was. He only recalled an aboriginal tent embassy parked in front of Parliament House.

They invented nets aeons ago.

He wrinkled his nose like he did before the long-legged whore in Darlinghurst because he liked what he saw and what he smelt. He remembered how she laughed and that made things easier.

I'll play this by ear. Always works for me.

He drove on, noting the long puddles in the side channels. Occupying the road's centre, he passed around an abandoned semi-trailer on the next curve, before a straight section stretched to the horizon. He squeezed the accelerator.

Fitch should show me more respect. Who sewed up the Rugby Internationals for Sydney, eh? Me. Who saved the Premier's skin when the Minister went all Buddhist? And who tied up a Harbour development when the architects were throwing their weight around? Me. Me.

Squeezing the accelerator further, the three-litre engine roared, accelerating to ninety-plus.

I test this machine until it chokes.

A mighty dust plume rose behind, the VL's power surging through his backbone.

I'm all over it, thought Badger, like Fitch, straight and ugly.

Slamming it, the Commodore ripped over the wretched gravel and passed a hundred. A hundred-and-twenty, a hundred-and-thirty, a hundred-and –

Bush. Silver.

One-way, go, go.

A mesmerising surge to the horizon in this brilliant, white flame, his torch of power.

'All the way. All the way.'

The VL rode like a jet boat; it skated, bumped, and cut through the surface. The wheels roared on, a high, dusty cloud rose, and debris struck the underbelly until the steering shook.

'Shit!'

Vibrations seized Badger's arms. His knees tensed and the VL's traction dissolved.

'Arggh!'

Lifting his foot from the pedal, the car floated, drifted and strained. Caught in a side drift.

A short, sharp turn of the wheel. A tearing. Body stiff.

His steed glided into position again, when, over the bonnet – something on the road, rushing towards him.

Slam the brakes!

A lion's roar. Wheels ground and drummed against rock and gravel. The Earth spun.

He eased off, the vehicle righting until he asserted them again, his white-hot flame grinding to a halt.

Extinguished. Exhausted. A huge drift of dust enveloped him.

'Jesus and bloody Mary.'

He poured sweat and thumped the steering wheel with both hands.

Somewhere beneath. Some thing.

His face lifted to the heavens, air pumping from his lungs. His heart raced.

Throwing the door open, he took three deep breaths and shook his head before he struggled for balance and edged past the bonnet. The thing twitched at his bumper bar, rolled to one side, and fell back to the same position, blood on its rear end.

A 'roo. It's a bloody kangaroo.

Truck hit it. Weren't me.

Its haunches had been crushed, a rust-brown lather bubbling from its mouth.

Badger ran his hands through his sandy hair, scanning the Commodore's duco for damage, shaking his head. Returning to his seat, he sat there, recovering his wits. Eventually, he opened the glove box and took out a silver sponge bag. Hopping out, he returned to the car front after another look at the VL's metalwork.

Won't need a panel-beater.

Reaching into the bath pack, he pulled out a revolver. He gripped the leather and steel. Aimed.

'Sweet Caroline. Do your job.'

Bang. The roo slumped.

Always useful in a tight spot.

'Tis a far, far, better thing… or something.'

The gun hung from his hand.

Me and Shakespeare. I better stick to Neil Diamond.

Chapter Five

Cliff Badger got down to business the next morning, pushing passed the revolving door to the Council's fawn-coloured lobby. At the abandoned reception counter, chewing gum and cigarette butts littered the plant pots. Along the corridor, a long, faded roll of carpet led to even-spaced doors painted in primary colours.

Like the set from *Play School*, thought Badger.

Past the secretarial desk, a frosted glass expanse obscured a garden courtyard of unknown dimensions. To his right, a panel door led to the council chambers or the mayor's office, depending on the size of his pretensions. A drab staircase climbed to the administrative offices where staff looked down on their subjects.

Cliff put a fag in his mouth and mauled his nether regions, content to let matters unfold. Within limits.

'Well. If it ain't the Beanbag,' said a familiar voice over his shoulder.

Haven't been called that for years.

He tilted his head to one side and smelt *Kiss* perfume.

Of all the rotten luck!

In her early forties, she wore a tight, cheery dress, with the dark hair and sculptured features of a Greek Helen with claws that scratched out eyes. Unmistakably business, with her hands glued to her hips.

Seen better days, he thought, but said, 'Fancy seeing you here.'

'Sweet. And my day started so well.'

'Yeah. You never disappoint.'

He picked himself up, gave the lady a peck, and peered into those diminutive blue eyes. 'You work here?'

'You might say.'

'What? Planning or –'

'Councillor, actually.'

His eyes popped. 'Then aren't you going to invite me in?'

'Well, you've arrived on Race Day so everyone's out. My place is around the corner. Got all day?'

That old barb. Sad bitch.

Cliff followed his former wife into harsh daylight, kicking dirt along the way, annoyed that his old lady would cramp his style.

Imagine, her living in this shitty little town.

No surprise when he spied her brick-and-fibro house, a plain 1950s bungalow with a sparse array of roses, weeds, grass and wattle.

She used to park our lawnmower outside like a trophy.

Stepping over a tangled hose on the pathway, her fly-screen door squeaked open and slammed shut. In her palace, he threw out his arms. 'How chic it is.'

'Don't bother,' she called from a kitchen stacked with dishes. 'Take a seat.'

'Bloody hell, Cheryl, how did you end up here?'

'Must have been all that alimony you didn't send.' She sat two cups on the table by the TV. 'Or maybe our son's talent for pissing me off; he's a chip off the old block.'

'Sorry I asked.'

He settled on the lounge while she prepared instant coffee.

'All water under the bridge, eh?'

'You asked, Sonny Jim.'

Her ladyship brought out drinks and biscuits, and he couldn't help comment. 'Check this. Still like your Iced Vo-Vos.'

'Yeah, well …'

He sipped his tea and bit into the sweet coconut, jam and marshmallow without a word.

'So, why are you here?' she said. You're a million miles from beach and casino.'

'I'm your witch doctor, baby.' He wiggled his bum and shook his shoulders. 'Bringing a little wet weather to town with my cleft stick and magic mojo.' He jumped up, did a little dance across the room and chanted

'Udiwada, mucho de grasso. Udiwada, mucho de grasso. Grasso, grasso.'

'You been on the weed too long. We could do with a bit of that.'

He took a bow, collapsed to the seat and resumed his position.

'A Bicentenary is coming your way, and I'm raining money. I have business to transact and need somewhere to put the dough.'

'Well, I am on Council. Let me in on it.'

He grinned. 'The Honourable Cheryl Venessa Badger. I like the sound of that.'

'Bullshit. Call me Councillor Sheila at meetings.'

'What? I spared you being called a common Sheila. Come on. What's wrong with "Badger" for a name?'

'Plain Cheryl does me. It goes down well around here. I'm a Main Street landlady so don't tell anyone about our past. Finished, right? Crashed faster than a Spitfire.'

'Fine. Scouts honour.' Badger lounged back and smirked until she picked up the conversation.

'Now that we're past formalities, I'm also your esteemed Anglican counsellor.'

Badger whistled. 'Bloody hell. What's got into you?' He bounced about for a moment like he tested water beds for the weight of two.

'Mind your language. Save it for the fellas in the pub.'

'Yes, Madame,' he said, but shuffled a bit closer.

'So come on,' she said, 'usual bloody Badger: tells you nothing, takes you nowhere, and gives ya bullshit. What's the business?'

'Hey, I've plenty of dollars and sense, blue-eyes. But come to think of it, where are the pleasures around here? Struth; this place is vile. My motel room's a sweatbox. Stinking walls amplify the traffic and vibrate with every passing car. I have drunks talking gobbledy-gook, smashing bottles and rattling their bones. How's anyone supposed to sleep round here?'

'Leave it out, Cliff. This town's been good to me. The business, God damn you. What's the news before I blow your brains out?'

Two hunting rifles hung from her wall so he decided to do her a favour and give her the low-down on his million-dollar mission.

'You see?' he said afterwards, wrapping his muscular arms around her and planting his face on her neck. He whispered something short and sweet and fell back against the lounge.

'Sound alright?'

'Sounds fine. Feels ...'

'Nice and easy, babe,' moving his hands to sweeter places. 'You were always my type.'

Chapter Six

On his recent visit to the tip, Kev scoured the grounds for old and broken radios, tools and electrical appliances before rain or a dust storm consumed them. He found metal files, an electric fan, nuts and bolts, and a red hammer with a split shaft.

Back in his workshop, he examined the tool again.

The head is fine.

Using a vice, punch and chisel, he removed the handle, cut and chiselled a new one from mulga, and sanded the joint for a perfect fit. Secured with wood glue, he completed the job the next day with bee's wax and two nails.

The rubber tubing he recovered was another matter. He wondered why the items were so neatly wrapped. An industrial machine must have damaged them, but they were still useful. Why hide them in the slashed tyres? Secretive, and wasteful.

Yeah, Bourke's Garage dumps broken tools here. Them rasps are in fair condition. Probably been used to rub off vehicle engine numbers. That's what they do there.

He cleaned up the files in an acidic bath and scrubbed the grooves. He rinsed and dried them in the sun, later washing his hands. Next, he set up the tape recorder on the old lounge on the veranda. This way, he kept an eye out for visitors coming up the drive.

They don't need to know about this.

He glanced towards the riverbank and adjacent chook yard, reminding himself to collect the eggs and muck the pen. He made a cuppa, took a sip, and pressed the deck's record button.

C-Clunk.

For Catherine.

'Kev here. Saturday, August 17, nineteen eighty-seven.' He took a deep breath. 'People ask me about the old ways. As a little boy, back in the thirties, the old fellows took me out bush, for weeks sometimes, getting away from the mission station. They were wonderful days. They told me the old stories, what to eat, tracking the roo, goanna, finding and fetching honey, making hop-bush beer.

'Emu is the hardest. Could spear the animal easily enough, but you'd never discover the eggs. You want the bird alive, mostly. They're cunning too. They'll protect them well, circling all day, poking about, appearing natural. If they smell you upwind, they might defend them to the death, hers or yours. Or they'd lead you astray, so you're lost in scrub before you realize. Most of them elders knew how to find them, wily like, stayed downwind, so the nest will be somewhere near the middle.'

The tape turned and wrapped itself around the spool.

'We always loved this walking business. Leaving the sandy scrublands, heading into country, camping under the stars, chanting around the fireplace, hunting possum and gathering honey up those trees. Them old men slowed us down. Tracked every animal from lizard to emu. Talked across the land too. Could tell you what's coming next.'

He paused and stared ahead. The tapes kept turning.

'So many stories. I figure I'll write a book someday. Call it "Days and Nights," or "Forgetting and Remembering." Those times are still in my memory. They are.'

His right hand gripped his thigh.

This is going nowhere. Those spools are burning me.

He took a deep breath. This is harder than I thought.

Rubbing his hands, he pushed the stop button, found rewind, and listened awhile. After sipping his lukewarm tea, he started again.

'I might start with some Gundabarri. How to address people, describe where others are, and what they are doing. So, for 'Here we are,' is 'Mari ibidu', like 'we' and 'are here.' For 'You have arrived,' we say, 'Yaridarra.' Might count as two words or one. So, for 'Come here,' there's 'Yanni idima.' One word or two; I don't know.'

C-Clunk.

He exhaled, glancing at the clock on the fridge.

An hour and a half. Wow. Talking the old language is easier than expected.

By concentrating on the expressions, he almost forgot about the machine. He listened to the results.

Yeh. Much better.

Gundabarri lived. His people's words, their rhythms, tones and pronunciations conjured his youthful campfire nights by the coolabah, the old men's faces in the fire's flickering light, and him, wiggling his toes in the sand. He smelt the burning mulga, tasted roasted possum, dreamt the smoke curling into clouds. He recalled the convoluted tales of stars and travelling spirits, a language of chatter and curiosity.

They rubbed goanna oil in their skins, and their quick-fire re-enactment of the day's hunt, a kind of slapstick that had them rolling in the warm, sandy soils in laughter. It wasn't about memory as the old men held time in their hands. Their facial scars, creased necks and broad noses pleased him.

After the morning workshop, alone on the veranda, recalling and recording, he rubbed the length of his face and breathed deeply.

All this remembering makes a man thirsty.

* * *

As heat blew through the door, he ordered Lemon squash at the Unity Hotel bar.

'Whoa,' came the deep-throated call from fellow drinkers. 'Try something stronger, Kev. Get a charge-up.'

He turned his back to those words, despite familiarity with everyone around him. Yet, from a nearby table, Billy waved him over.

'Bud. Come and have a mag.'

As the Aboriginal Legal Service chief, he often inhabited the 'black' pub, a two-storey edifice left over from the mighty shearing days. Being close to the bridge, park and river, he fraternised with the Service's past, present and future clients, showing his support. He called it his second office.

Acknowledging his friend with a slight turn of the head, Kev carried his drink to the table. He liked him. Nobody gave him lip, not in their right mind. Muscular as well as a wee bit bulky, even the town's three or four hell-raisers steered clear of him.

He drank from the same waterholes as Sydney's big boys, at home making a splash in court with his cowboy legalese. They probably feared him as he'd stare anyone down. No way around it: if they found themselves in trouble, he was their man. All the way: from the cops to the courts, to prison. He ran the Centre with ease and claimed city legal training. Sergeant Farrell called him 'black-snake-Boyo.'

Billy yawned. 'Don't mind them. They should respect their elders. You hear me, Boney Moroney,' raising his voice, 'respect.'

Around the bar came begrudging agreement.

Billy turned to him again. 'So, what's cooking, Kev?'

'Bit of fishing; repairing Mara's toys; handiwork.'

'Heard about that. You've been fixing her veranda too. I reckon Mara hasn't picked up a hammer in her life; probably just as well.'

Kev grinned and shook his head. 'She has lots of kids to look after. Welfare's always at her.'

'You mean big-hearted Connolly? Think she'll tame him sooner or later.'

He took a sip of his squash. 'She needs some help, now and again. They can be scallywags.'

'You're a good man, Kev. No doubt about it. We'll never forget how you rescued the McKenzies.'

'Weren't like that, Billy. They were being a bit stupid.'

'You mean the coppers were. Just because they took the Emergency Services boat for a joy ride, fishing at Yattaladda. No harm done. Bad luck having them catch the lads.'

Recalling the day, Kev advised the boys to apologize to the cops. Show consideration. Understand the outboard's purpose in emergencies. Like rescuing Danny, his wayward son.

High-spirited youngsters can be crazy. Harmless, a man's not a man in gaol.

Billy jolted his shoulder. 'How about joining us? Roo shooting. Come out tomorrow. Me and the fellas got the car, got the fuel.'

'You younger blokes don't need me. You can pick me up, if you're short.'

'You're a fine shot.'

He grinned. 'Once. You fellows should try hunting the old way. I'd like to see that.'

Billy adjusted his hat. 'It's a bit more fun hooning around in the ute. Easier bringing home a catch and collecting a few bucks from the factory. Everyone needs extra dosh.'

They settled in, watching a few kids scurry about the back bar. A group played cards at one table, Draughts at the next, so few words passed men's and women's lips. Billy patted the Unity's adopted canine. No need to hurry on a Saturday.

The pub was quiet most times, especially when the heat kicked in. They couldn't sit in the town's only air-conditioned club as townspeople stared, pushed or cajoled them from the premises. Besides, at the Unity, they got on well with nothing said. Something drew them together.

Minutes later, young Henry Freeman entered the saloon, barely noticed.

'Hey, Billy.'

'Yeah, Hen. How are you, bud?'

Billy's eyes narrowed. This fellow had a habit of upsetting people. Bedraggled Henry's once handsome face still had a cheeky smile. He dressed casually in a dirty, white T-shirt, shorts and thongs. Thanks to his drinking habit, he developed a beer belly by the age of twenty. The pub had no dress code to speak of, but as long as no one smashed glasses, the Marto brothers wouldn't order anyone out. But if someone started a fight, they were barred for a month. If swearing and pestering didn't get cooperation, they'd call the cops.

Kev scoured Henry's unshaven face. A man should be clean-shaven or full-bearded, he thought, so perhaps he'd been drinking all week. A young bloke like him needed no encouragement to start a fight.

'What is it, Hen?' said Billy.

Henry grinned. 'Come here. Come on,' he called, already on the payphone.

Billy stayed seated, Kev seeing Henry dial. 'What's he up to?'

'Listen to this,' said Henry.

The ringing continued, and when someone answered 'Police,' everyone around the bar paid attention.

'Mate,' said Henry, affecting his best cocky voice. 'A bloke's gone and shot Fergus. Black bastard. He's out at the sheds. Gone mad, he has. Can I shoot him?'

Henry put his hand over the phone when the pub broke into laughter.

'Name? I'm bloody Pat Cummings, you dumb-arse. What do I pay taxes for? Cootalong station. Wife's going barmy with this bloke running around. Get yourself out here before I shoot him.'

Henry held out the phone, a finger asking for hush. A sharp voice saying, 'Right? Cootalong, Mr Cummings. Certainly. Only one of them? Hold off. Don't shoot him yet.'

'How long you going to be? I want to kill the nigger.'

'Mr Cummings. We do the shooting around here. In twenty minutes.'

'Quick. Hurry up.'

Clunk.

Chapter Seven

Cliff Badger pow-wowed with the mayor beside the town bridge, upstream from the fish traps. He anticipated a getting-to-know-you affair, a sunshine job, as he called it; a bit of straight shooting; two blokes standing over muddy waters talking, joking and trading favours, ending with mutual back-slapping. A million bucks reckoned they'd be chums before day's end.

But raving drunks outside his room disturbed his sleep, and rumbling trucks taking the corners shuffling in and out of gear haunted him. The Motel manager's midnight rendition of *Love Me Do* massacred music, only reminding him that finding Cheryl in town complicated matters. As crusty as ever, her old wounds persisted, despite his best efforts in the gentle art of schmoozing. What a headache.

Where's my Port Macquarie studio over the beach, and a fat budget for buns, banter and a rosy tart?

After passing Evans Street's shopping strip, he shook his head at the town's sorry excuse for a public park. A few picnic tables, a concrete-and-iron loo bordering the dirt-and-amalgam levee, and a cluster of gums surrounded by tight-spaced rose bushes paralleling the curved road. Imagine entering the place at night, hit by perfume and barbs.

Yet …a Council planting, an opportunity for flattery.

At the far corner, he spied two men and a dog on a leash, a green Commodore parked near the bridge. Under the shade of a giant eucalypt, at the levee's solitary gap, they chatted on the gravel underpass.

Must be him. He and his clerk, an overweight fellow known as "Humblebum," or so the motel cleaner told him, though he noticed Cheryl recoiled at the description. She reckoned both were pet lovers, the mayor keen on canine discipline, his pooch a kind of local mascot. So, having done his homework, he approached them with a pleasant smile, tail up and wagging.

'Good day, gentlemen. Mr Anthony Peake?' He shook hands before the mayor could answer, his grip firmer.

'Thanks for coming,' said the bleary-eyed Chief, hat in hand. 'Trust your journey's been worthwhile.'

'Badger. Cliff Badger. New South Wales Bicentennial Authority.'

'Yes. This is Rodger Clifford, our Town Clerk. Your journey has been …'

'Of course. Like your park roses.'

The councilmen stared at each other until the mayor spoke. 'I've brought you here so you'll see the lay of the land. I believe you're proposing a cultural centre that would be sited out here near the bridge.'

'Who told you that?' said Badger, suspecting Her-Big-Mouth.

'A little puppy dog,' said Peake grinning. Cliff grinned too.

'Bring us some seats, Rodge.'

Humblebum fetched the director's chairs from the car and leaned against the tree within earshot.

'Sit,' said Peake to his powdered pooch before he turned back.

Cliff couldn't grin any longer, so he stretched his neck and winced. 'Our proposal,' he said at last,' is an Indigenous Cultural Centre, or ICC, here, celebrating the fish traps and their long-standing importance as a food source, intertribal meetings and ceremonial site. I believe they are in the vicinity.'

Peake chuckled. 'Them? An old pile of rocks, if you ask me.'

He surveyed the muddy river, and yes, odd rock formations covered its width.

'Hardly Hadrian's Wall,' said the administrator.

Peake adjusted his top hat. His small, bloodshot eyes were open but uncomprehending. With a round, balding forehead and short brown hair slicked down with cream, his arm extended. 'They bloody well blocked the old ferries. This is as far upriver as they got.'

'Not to worry,' said their guest. 'Does a million bucks drive your engine? Think what you can do with the dosh.'

Peake shared a pained expression with Humblebum as Badger added 'It's money in the coffers. New swimming pool. Little gifts before election day makes a man very popular.'

Peake shook his head in disbelief. 'A blackfella museum?'

'One and six zeros. We've mocked up a many-coloured grant application with all the graphs and scenic pics. Sign-off and the funds are yours. Let them rub sticks together for all I care; throw boomerangs, cuddle koalas, whatever.'

'With a Pioneer Centre, people would come in droves. They built this place: properties, ferries, wool, 'roo factory, everything. Progress, isn't that what the Bicentennary's about?'

'World-class, Mr Mayor,' he said, thinking snouts-in-a-pique, Peake-in-the-trough. 'I understand you. I really do. But I am duty-bound to do my master's bidding. They want an Indigenous establishment by next year. If you don't want it, the money goes elsewhere, so we will have our ICC here or somewhere else.' Cliff let his words sink in. 'Up to you, mate. Progress is progress, here or in Gympie, Longreach, Upper Galahganbone. Money flows if you know what I mean. It's in your hands.'

The mayor screwed up his face, patted the dog in long strokes, and stared ahead.

Resembles thinking, thought Cliff.

His po-faced administrator nodded to his boss before the Mayor returned to business. 'Mr Badger. Of course, we'll take the grant. Of course, we'll build a museum. Times like these, every council needs funds.' Humblebum pushed off the tree as Badger sat. 'But we've got a security problem. This town is impossible. The moment these blackfellows hear about the grant money, they'll want it in their hands. They'll want to be on the Council. They'll say it's theirs. Where will we be then?'

Tempted to answer, Badger stared ahead.

'So, you'll put the motion to Council on Tuesday? On the agenda? Table the report. Pass it. It's a case of the quick or the dead.'

Peake's eyes glazed, and his helper encouraged him with a hand on his shoulder.

'Sure.' He dabbed his dainty dog. 'But there could be trouble.'

'You'll have a million bucks and a very smart dog.'

The fellow pulled the leash.

'Roll, Griff! Roll over.'

Chapter Eight

After clearing away his plate, cup and saucer, Kev sat his tape recorder on a bath towel over the kitchen table. He readied with a well-padded cushion on his chair.

No rooster crowing today.

Clunk.

For Catherine. Catherine of Canberra.

'It's August, nineteen eighty-seven.' He took a deep breath. 'In fifty-six, I became a shearer. Strange how it happened.

As a kid, Dad told me to stay away from shepherding. Gets lonesome herding and protecting sheep from dingoes, he said. It's one of the few things I remember about him. He hated being alone at night. Paid ten-bob a month, and only if the manager felt like paying.

He would never have married if he kept the stars company, meaning, no wife, no Kev I suppose. Only met and shacked up with Mum after he left.

"Better off shearing," he said. "Blackfellas can go to work these days. The union's OK with it."

'Anyway, first chance there's a job, I take it. The night before starting, the blokes approached me in the shed, grabbed and pinned me down. I'm a bit worried, expecting a beating or something, like on the mission station. They held me hard, and Artie, the head guy, pulled down my pants and grabbed the little fella. Someone else tied a string to it and passed it to him.'

"You a union man, Kev?" and yanks it.

"Sure."

"One hundred per cent?"

Yank.

"Sure."

"Never rat on your brothers."

I nodded.

"Jimmy. Take one pound and give him his membership card."

He came out of the shadows, shoved it in my pocket, and presented a glass of brandy. A fellow said, "Open your mouth," and poured the stuff down my throat. Damn near killed me. Inside a minute, my legs turned to jelly.

"Welcome to the brotherhood," says Artie. "Present your member's card at every shed. Look after it. Tonight, you were real good."

I was too stunned to say much.

"Sorry about the boys holding you down. One bloke landed a punch on me after our little ceremony. Double spirits slows them down."

Anyhow, a year later his marriage is in trouble. He takes me aside and says, "I'm pissing off to Sydney. It's your job now, Kev."

"Me?"

"You're the best man, and besides, you don't drink. I've seen you keeping an eye on things. Most of these fellows aren't so reliable."

So, I take the job, only temporary like. Artie teaches me the ropes. "Simple. Everyone's union. You get to the property, form a ring and tell them "All-for-one and one-for-all." The cocky bastard agrees to the contract or it's "all out." You only start when the rates are signed off. Any problem, you phone headquarters from the nearest town."

"What if they set the dogs on me?"

"No heroics, mate. Back off and call us. Fixed rate, or all out. Simple."

"What about the initiation?"

He just grinned like a fat cat.

Remembering.

Kev took a bite from his biscuit, watched the reels go around, and heard the tape's soft brushing sound like Bess combing her hair. He bowed his head. Clunk.

A breath. And a few more bites, a cuppa, and check the chooks. C-clunk.

The job lasted eleven years. Nine years as a union rep. You learnt those cockies treat their dogs better than us. Their kids go off to private schools. Some own thoroughbreds and go to the races. Off to society balls while we slept in rusty sheds away from our family. Their dogs had warmer kennels. Better fed and bitter bread we used to say.'

Kev's lips sealed his next words like the lick of an envelope. The spool wound on, once, twice, three times, his face taut and still, eyes closed.

Another breath.

'I don't hate cockies. They have their problems too, like when a drought comes along or when the kids return home and no longer recognize them. Happens.'

He adjusted his pillow. Inhaled.

'My mother was light-skinned. She told me her mum was a white girl living amongst blackfellas for too long. Said she lived away from family for weeks until she became one of the mob; her Irish relations bore too many kids, and the problems that come with it; one less was a blessing she said.

'She spoke Gundabarri well. Mission people didn't, and never took the trouble to learn. Her and the blackfellas would go-bush, living on the river banks and turn up for rations. It pleased them managers, having them off their hands and saving expense. As long as the inspector or district medico didn't come along, they'd pocket the savings.

'Forbidden town visits, when someone died or caught a disease, some of us joined the supply wagon. One time we drove an old Gundabarri called Teddy; gangrene leg, I think. In the hospital waiting room, I read a book with star charts. The nurse told me to keep it.

'Anyhow, some white folk objected to us; said they didn't want blackfellas in the ward. Reckoned we were diseased. Well, Sister gave them a roasting. "One person is as good as another," she said, but in their case, they might be an exception. Blow me down. I'll never forget.

'Had another surprise in town, meeting black fellows on the river. They were not supposed to live there, but some townspeople employed them. Met Charlie Lonergan. He said he met my father. He were cagey though, and didn't mention gaol or courts or anything like that. He said my mother moved out when she found out dad was a Blacksmith, Jimmie Blacksmith's son. Everyone knew Jimmy murdered seven whites in 1900; went completely berserk and slaughtered them, the last black fellow they could shoot on sight.

'Ma didn't want anything to do with them, with him or anybody like him. Must be why she left him. Spoiled my day. Instead of digging around to find out more, I got busy forgetting, reading my astronomy book, and learning about Orion, Southern Cross, Gemini, Lepos and Monoceros.

'Proper forgetting.

'Later, I asked Mum about our name 'before,' because she would never lie to me. She said 'Never you mind,' so I must be a 'Blacksmith.' She was ill, in her forties. I didn't press her then.

'Next month, I asked again. I regretted it because her spirit drifted away.

'She said: "Kev. You mustn't worry. You aren't like that. The Lord will protect you."

'She wouldn't say anymore, except to ask who told me. "Some things are best forgotten."

'But I can't.'

Chapter Nine

'Shoot,' said the leering cop.

Henry winced. His eyes bulged and his heart thumped. Blood rushed from his head.

A deep breath. A gasp. A gun pointed at his temple.

Click.

Click.

'No bullets, mate,' said the constable with a grin. 'Forgot me ammo.'

Laughter all round. Belly laughter.

The town coppers glared at their prisoner recoiled against the cell wall.

Detective-Sergeant Farrell had caught the braggart after he made a hoax phone call from the pub. So they delivered him a well-deserved comeuppance.

He was nabbed a few hours after the smart-ass left fellow cops redfaced at Cootalong station, Pat Cummings was caught with his pants down, amazed and derisive, his afternoon delight on the haystack interrupted.

Farrell's fright on Henry caused the drunken bastard to wet his bed, piss soaking his duds. He stood by, admiring the effect. Well executed, he thought.

'Think we'd waste a bullet on you, you worthless piece of shit?'

The poor fucker curled up on his mattress and sobbed.

'What a Wally! Beats up his wife, takes the piss, and wastes police time. You been caught, mate.'

'Will you take a look at this,' said Farrell pointing to Henry's piss-soaked trousers. 'Like a nappy for that?'

'Jeez, he smells like a dunny.'

'The stupid dog thought I'd shoot him. Would we do something like that?'

'Nar,' said the constable. 'We'll cut off his balls.'

Chapter Ten

Henry James Freeman was dead. *That* Henry. The dumb, half-crazy blackfella hung from a cell window, torn sheets tied around his neck, the bed wet with salty sweat, urine, blood and alcohol, the iron bars making a hanging easy, all materials supplied.

Arrested after an anonymous tip-off, he had argued with his wife and come off second best. He entered the hotel to make his hoax call in front of pub patrons midday. Ejected sometime later, intoxicated and raving, the cops nabbed him in the park and banged him up behind the station.

At dusk, Susan, an English teacher spied Sergeant Farrell scurry from the station, its lights ablaze. Was he checking repairs at Bourkes Garage? Out for a biscuit at Marco's? Nothing worth running for.

'He ran like a thief,' she said to Glen, her fellow teacher. 'Since when do they do more than shuffle papers and hassle people?'

In turn, she spoke to Cheryl Sheila, saying 'Me thinks something is rotten in the state of Denmark,' thereby confusing her. But when she pointed to the station, with no one coming or going, it aroused suspicions.

She and Humblebum phoned the cop shop from the Council chambers.

'Farrell?' he said. Silence. 'Who's there?'

'Yeah. I'm here.'

'Teddy? It's Rodger. What's happening, mate. Something the matter?'

'Christ, Rodge. We've got a dead man here. Henry, frigging Freeman.'

'OK. Calm down. Let's talk this through. I'm coming around.'

Within the week, the *Advocate* gave his death the appropriate treatment:

> Town police are in shock today after finding a local man, Henry Freewood, collapsed in his cell. After only a few hours in custody, the well-known identity failed to show signs of life. All resuscitation efforts proved fruitless. "A magistrate's inquiry will follow," said Sergeant Farrell, "and will adhere to due process. No one should spread rumours or jump to conclusions."

The news of a suspicious death in custody reached Sydney overnight. In parliamentary debate and the national media, suspicions of national police behaviour crystallised. The protester types beat drums, chanted and made a lot of noise in Brisbane, Melbourne, Newcastle and Adelaide, although, amongst local townspeople and shopkeepers, they talked in whispers.

Up to then, Indigenous deaths-in-custody were collateral damage in the Police's difficult and dangerous work; unfortunate events put down to heat, exhaustion and the poor health of their clients. A few statistical characters produced needless suspicions that the practical men of the Force used excessive force and naked violence against the original Australians. Some lofty professor insisted on pronouncing Henry the twenty-third death-in-custody that year.

The Brother police would rather people read their Annual Reports where such numbers lurked in footnotes or not at all. All the better to tell their media friends that a diseased mob of academics conjured doubts infected their work and undermined morale.

Local cops didn't tell Billy about Henry's death, too occupied with paperwork, routine and referring on media enquiries. But when the music teacher told him the news, he stormed the cop shop, demanding access to Henry and the lock-up where he died. His job required hard questions, defiance, and persistence against police and judicial hostility. If necessary, he'd camp on their counter.

For him and Murri and Koori alike, the cop shop was a house of formidable evil with many rooms: a kitchen of fear, a lounge of blue-leather contempt, and a laundry for whitewashing the Law. Within its doors, the cops had their ways of welcome. The wretched and the poor entered as suspects and offenders, in the cop's minds, hopeless cases. Being likely criminals, they needed reasons to dread them and a red-hot reluctance to bring their dirty boots inside the House of the Law.

In the Force's remote regions, they believed their deskbound city officers in air-conditioned offices were beholden to others. If the country brotherhood dealt with the blacks their way, they would do their chiefs a favour.

'Mister William Matchett, Aboriginal Legal Service,' said Billy at the front desk. 'Get him, sonny. I want Farrell, now.'

A disbelieving Constable Darling stood rigid, his boyish face and capped head electric with resentment. But the visitor passed the stark lights outside, ran through the demanding door, and there he was, thumping the counter with both hands.

To such demands, the constable blinked and retreated to the next room. Billy grabbed and slid the red Day Book around, quickly reading the entries:

H. Freeman Drunk and D, 2.30 pm.'

No reference to a hoax call. No one else Monday arvo, so, no witnesses.

Damn.

Poor Henry, a troubled bastard. Good for a joke or two, sentimental, sensitive and prone to take exception to personal slights. Had no chance when three or four cops had truncheons.

Billy could smell police lies, collaborations and cover-ups. Familiarised with statutes and by-laws and the arcane mysteries of administrative policy, he made coppers sweat. He sipped and slurped from the radical's trough, and hung around Redfern pubs and the Louisa Street ghetto talking revolution and fight. Had photos of himself with leaders of the black fraternity fondly framed and displayed on his office wall.

'We know police methods,' Billy told everyone in the pub. 'And they won't learn if we don't show strength.'

He would always defend his people. Law, Facts, Truth, Evidence, Due Process, Torts, and Jurisprudence; all written in capital letters; white man's terms serving white fella's purposes. He reckoned laws were conspicuously, scrupulously, methodically ignored; conventions forgotten, bypassed, misinterpreted and willfully misunderstood.

'Coppers are cogs in a machine, grinding people to little pieces,' he told drinkers in the Unity, 'extracting our juices and sending us to gaol or a grave.'

Their muscular words were lovely, seductive, and illusionary; Billy said they deserved contempt.

Everyone lies. Facts can be hard to come by. It's one man's word against another. 'And who will the authorities believe?' he asked. 'The guy in the suit. The private school bully Uniformed.'

He witnessed evidence cleaned up, invented, rearranged or reinterpreted at police stations and courts far from metropolitan centres.

He said it to the cop's face. 'Due process is a bloody joke.'

Only domination matters; standing up, being knocked down, and lifting again until the bastards drop. It was about carving out territory, putting others under glaring lights, about defending, and offending bodies. Guerilla warfare: skirmishes here and there, a few wins, but mostly grinding out rough justice. The Aboriginal Legal Service would land punches, pepper the community with a cautionary tale, and put some home-grown fools in their place. The cops were the enemy.

For years now, things in town worsened. Bad enough dealing with them, but the old Murri stupor returned after the usual media mix of horror, damnation, a few pints, and do nothing. He enlisted Mara's help sometimes, but these days, she staked her ground with the Patchtown mob. A hundred or more Murris shared the run-down public housing on the other side of the river, far enough from town for each to ignore the others. No one else would live in that place; even the alcoholic river dwellers shook their heads.

She'd sort out the little things. All secretive and uppity these days. Only makes my job harder.

Kev might be useful, being the kindly town black looking for respectability, love and kindness. Prone to help everyone, he'd say thanks very much for anything, so the drinkers and churchgoers took no more interest than necessary.

Council is as useless as ever, he thought. Now this Bicentennial bloke's arrived, offering little rewards for obedient black fellows. He had seen Peake and Badger meet over the fish traps. Not behind closed doors. No, they pow-wowed outdoors, snubbing Murri involvement, rightfully their business. No invitations issued, and no respect shown.

Yeah, it's worse than ever.

'We'll bring them down a peg or three,' he told the Unity mob. 'Tonight.'

Billy weaponised law and politics, assembling opinion, a cynical media and a few whitefella allies. The big men, Charlie Perkins, Gary

Foley, Chicka Dixon and Paul Coe, all wanted him on their side. They gave him respect and he returned it. He could settle things down or stir them up; and at this time, they needed stirring up.

He couldn't speak much Gundabarri but knew "Balli-al-mal." Place-of-the-dead.

Balli-al-mal, the cop shop.

In the old days, the whole country turned into a place of the dead; Murris shot, diseased, and pushed over cliffs. In 1901, they hunted down Jimmy Blacksmith. And bang. Finished. After that, you needed a reason to shoot someone, and it wasn't too hard to find one, 'attempted escape' an old favourite.

Once the cops were obliged to arrest Murri offenders. Taken to the station …

Balli-al-mal.

Blood likely.

Balli-al-mal.

Death-in-custody? How many had there been? When do you start? From 1788? With more ahead.

For Murris, and not only blacks, carried, whacked and dragged across the threshold, but the cop shop promised abuse and oblivion. For police, it meant filling out forms, attending enquiries, writing and reading reports and sometimes swatting the media. More time organising confusion, describing contusions, and creating illusions. The new lexicon included credibility gap, the weight of evidence, toxicology, technologies and grand obfuscation. Public sympathy would be massaged, explained or turned around in a month, sometimes a week. Media and political friends would emphasise the offender's misfortunes and shining character, and soon enough, he'd be handed Bravery awards.

Billy understood how the cops handled the dispossessed: arrest, isolate, humiliate and interrogate. No limit. With the undeserving, an officer of the Law might slip and fall on a drunken lout and burst his liver. After all, accidents do happen, and this way they leave few bodily signs. Isolated in a cell, a prisoner might sleep, and not wake up the next morning. The stupid bugger might slip from his or her bed and break their skull. Others might expire in a paddy wagon's heat. The Murri might be born suicidal. He or she would do-themselves-in while cops are having a quiet cuppa. Without biscuits, someone must pop out to the store long enough for a poor sod to find hanging points for their demise.

'Around here, the cop shop is a death sentence,' Billy proclaimed in the Unity, making Marto nervous for his glassware.

Balli-al-mal.

One way or another you'd get the message: you're a helpless animal in a cage; made a lifeless shell in Long Bay, Maitland or Grafton gaols. Society's prison guards could take you out at any time and any place, in anonymous outback spaces or against a prison's concrete wall. They'd eat you whole; and like the gluttons they are, display their pleasure with a loud belly-burp in your collective face.

That's what provoked Billy. After the hellish sight of Henry's body sprawled and dumped in the cell, he left the cop shop, knowing he must saddle up his disgust and ride into demanding days. Mid thought on Main Street, some be-suited Gubba belched in his face, and he bumped into him. Saying nothing, the bastard offered no apology. He snapped and hit him, fist clenched. He hammered him, the fella reeling against the telegraph pole before twisting to the ground. With one hand on the footpath, the bloke held himself up while the other hand clutched his ribs.

Billy felt better and would have continued down the road except the bloke leapt at him, grabbed his legs, and felled him. Rugby tackled.

'Farrrk!'

Kicking and scrambling away, he put a post-box between himself and the Gubba.

Who is this guy? Round-faced, in stupid city dress. Turned down lips, disdainful eyes. Not a local. Can't fight wearing a suit.

'Who are you?'

The fellow stared back, nostrils pumping and fists clenched. He puffed his chest and pushed hair from his eyes. 'No man decks me, matey, and gets away with it.'

'Coppers do it all the time. There's a dead man in the cells to prove it.'

The stranger's feet shuffled. He wiped the dust from his sullied clothes. Gravel gripped his lips. 'Forget it. OK.'

Billy ran his hand across his face and grinned realising he received a backhand apology. He might have accepted it but the other bloke hadn't finished.

'Listen chum. I'm Cliff Badger, Projects Chief, NSW Bicentennial Council. Don't ever assault me again.'

Cliff made a major mistake: Billy despised pretentious shits telling him to do-this and don't-do-that. Mighty Mr Bicentennial, money-in-hand, money he could give or take away. 'What are you doing here?'

Bighearted Badger smirked. 'Come to the Council meeting and find out.'

'Tell me now.'

'Get stuffed. You can find out tonight, same as anyone else.'

'You're here about the fish traps, aren't you?'

'You're a nosey bastard. We're running a Bi-cen-tenary.'

Billy sneered. This outsider bypassed every aboriginal voice in town, a carpet-bagger, a spiv or a do-gooder; coming here with his beads and trinkets two hundred years after stealing the whole bloody country. After Henry's death, he would give him merry hell.

For the moment he had phone calls to make after offers of radio, television and newspaper interviews. He'd soon deliver full-blooded speculation, rampant suspicions and juicy scuttlebutt; all the free copy and dramatic entanglements his outrage could muster. He needed no devil to excite the media.

Chapter Eleven

The meeting settled down to business, Mayor Peake and councillors sitting around their glossy white table while the visiting journalists and locals assembled to one side. Behind him, Humblebum offered occasional advice, word-in-your-ear style, while Cliff Badger occupied the "special guest" chair at the front of the public area, once removed from his ex-wife.

As the Bicentennial proposal approached, the supermarket owner, Marco, Susan, another schoolteacher and a few property owners entered. A Sydney reporter and photographer also stole in, so, with all chairs taken, late arrivals stood against the wall or behind Council officials. Humblebum blocked their advance to the mayoral space with a stool.

Billy entered in a tatty suit with a large green, plastic flower on his lapel. When another black face followed, another, and more again Peake threw up his arms.

'No more. This room is filled to capacity. Close the doors.'

But a Murri commandeered the entrance, holding the door open for newcomers. Con Demetrios, one of Paddy Bourke's Hard-Boys by day, took the part-time security job to please his Smash Repair boss. He posted surrender rather than earn local displeasure.

Peake buried his head until it exploded, 'Enough.'

'Plenty of room,' said Billy, ushering his allies. 'Where's Mara?'

'Here, brother,' she waved, her mob tightly positioned in a corner.

'This is a Council meeting. You can't come pushing and shoving your way in.'

'What's the problem, mayor, Murri mob not welcome?' said Mara.

Peake turned to Humblebum, and Billy eyed Badger. With other topics swept aside for the Bicentennial matter, he and Mara set about their work.

'We don't want no museum,' she said. 'We don't want tourists coming here and gawking at us like we're in a zoo. Ain't going to help us. Only gets you mob lining your pockets, the coloured shirts pointing, farting and making trouble.'

Not to be outdone,' Billy added, 'Of all the things this town needs: legal service, hospitals, schools and the like, the Bicentenary wants a museum. It's a bloody joke. This Council cottons-on to any hopeless idea. A man rotted in our police cells, another death-in-custody right under our noses. And what do you lot do? Nothing. Sees nothing, hears nothing, does nothing.'

He waved his arms like they were tangled in rope.

'Listen, a man can't find a job around here. So what are we offered? A bloody useless museum, so we black fellows can dress up in paint, dance and pretend to be savages. You can shove it. The Bicentenary's a fraud.'

When Peake suggested the speaker's time elapsed, he continued: 'Here. Take a look at this bloke,' pointing at Badger. 'Yeah, him. You can send him back to Sydney, the arrogant bastard, because if you don't, we will. His kind is trying to buy us off, throwing money so we lick his boots. You know where they can shove it.'

'You tell them, Billy.'

Banned from filming or photographing, *Herald, Telegraph* and *ABC* reporters wrote furious notes.

'If you lot had any guts,' he said over the cheers and moans; 'if this Council showed any respect for the dead, respect for aboriginal people, you'd cancel the meeting. Now.'

'Now. Now,' chanted the crowd. Susan joined in.

The mayor's flint face turned to ash, and some townies pushed back.

'Bugger off, you stupid boong.' 'You mad drunk.'

'Mister Chairman,' said Badger. 'Chair.'

'Right. Give us some bloody quiet,' said Peake. 'Settle down.'

The uproar ebbed and receded to grunts, snorts and whispers.

'OK. I remind those present that our guest of the Shire came from Sydney to address us, so he will be heard in silence. Councillors and visitors will show respect. Please welcome, Mister Cliff Badger from the New South Wales Bicentennial Council.'

Having received patchy applause, he raised himself, puffing out his chest. 'Thank you.'

'Respect. Did I hear right?' Billy gave a queer face, and his supporters chuckled.

Peake grabbed his gavel but refrained from beating it against the table until the laughter ebbed.

Badger's lips tightened, and his eyes darted left and right.

'The Bicentenary. Soon, come January twenty-six, we will enjoy the biggest party this state has ever seen.'

'Over a dead man's body.'

'Blood oath.'

'Shame. Shame.'

'You got no respect,' said a Murri.

Cliff Badger gripped the table with both hands, leaned forward, and rocked back. He sat again as his whiskey-soaked brain ached and his face sweated.

'Mister Chairman: Are you going to put up with this?'

Billy thumped the table. 'We've tolerated you long enough. Here, have a drink.'

His large plastic flower shot out a liquid and splashed on Badger's face and suit. The Bicentennial official recoiled, took a breath, picked up his water, and leapt at him. He aimed to splash the Legal Service rep but the glass slipped from his hand, bounced off the table and shattered on the floor. Badger lunged at him regardless, but other Murris pushed back. When the table collapsed under his weight wood splintered, iron buckled, folders, pens, agendas and ashtrays spilt and scattered everywhere. Peake's fag dropped from his mouth. His hand reached out, spilling his lemonade over the Council papers.

'Stop. Hold.'

An incensed Badger barged on, a councillor and local restraining him before he thumped his tormentor.

'Stone the crows.'

Humblebum's eyes closed. Volleys of Jaffas and White Mints flew across the room. With scrapping furniture, screams, groans and plentiful abuse, people held, repelled or shoved their opponents, yelling, climbing over bodies, scattering chairs and pushing aside tables. While some sought safety at the mayoral plinth, others threw punches or elbowed for space. Badger stared down anyone laying hands on him. Assuming a dignified pose, his eyes fixed on Billy who unleashed a piercing, gargantuan laugh that stopped everyone.

'Look at you,' he said. 'At this. A man's dead. Coppers are out of control, and you lot fight and talk about parties.'

'Order. Order.' said Peake, but his gavel resembled a sponge. No bangs for his bucks.

People resumed abuse after a journalist slipped on pens and pencils and screamed for help. With broken glass on the floor, Susan escaped through the jammed door. Cheryl fell back in her seat, planted her elbows and scrunched her Council agenda into a ball. Placed on the last table alive, she flicked it into oblivion.

Meeting abandoned.

Cliff Badger returned to his hotel room and wrestled with the night's events.

Peake is an idiot. Bloody incompetent, even with his puppet master next to him. A stuff-up. A million-dollar project goes begging. Media everywhere. And that bitch, Mara, demanded money from me, for a dead guy. Where was Cheryl when I needed her? All my schmoozing on a moralising Anglican.

'Quite a display, nincompoop,' she had said.

The hide of her.

'I want you out of here. Stay any longer and I'll bloody well kill you myself.'

So what if things backfired? I'll still succeed. I've struck big deals in my time.

He pushed his motel door closed, switched the lights and collapsed on the bed. Grabbing his pack of Marlborough, he took out a fag, lit it, and sucked hard. That fuckwit Billy. He's the one. If he so much as breathes on me, I'll –

He seethed. The ash tip lengthened and teetered until he stubbed on the tray. He sat up, a tragedy of his own making, his clothes hung on a peg. Snack wrappers littered the floor, cigarette butts in and around ashtrays, and his bed was unmade.

What do I pay them for? Clean sheets. Should be made by now.

On any other night, he'd phone reception and complain about the state of the towels, tissues, soap, whatever. But after the night's events, he held his head and squeezed a thought.

Ah, this mattress is something. He stretched his tired neck. What's Humblebum got to do with Cheryl? Something's going on. I saw the way they glanced at each other.

He threw a packet of matches at the wall and reached for the near-empty bottle of whiskey on the dresser. My precious, the only good thing you can buy around here.

He poured the remaining amount into his glass, and sculled it, reminding him of his grand times with ladies of the night. For the cost of another scotch, I could taste a bit of black velvet.

The firewater soon worked its magic over his entire frame. Muscles relaxed, mind-numbed, the liquid making a hearth and home in his belly. Light-headed and stiff-necked, serene and uncomfortable, he slumped on the mattress and ran his hand over the coarse bed cover and silky sheets. As the bare light bulb shone in his eyes, he groaned at the thought of the night's disaster.

He closed his eyes, rolled over and cosied up to his pillow when a knock on the door disturbed him.

'Piss off, unless you're here to pleasure me.'

The door flew open.

'Oh, Hell.'

Chapter Twelve

A world away from the Council drama, Kev went to bed by ten and woke the next morning when Skipper leapt on his bed and licked his face. He swept him from the bed, the mutt recovering and settling at the far end, snoozing with an occasional growl, it rolled around, leaving black hairs on the cover.

Time to get up. Leftovers for the dog in the fridge. Put on the jug. Collect the eggs. Breakfast, and …

On his way to the chook shed, he passed a sleeper on the landing's sofa, a blanket covering most of him or her.

Hmm. Socks on exposed feet.

After collecting from the henhouse, at the driveway, he set his guard dog loose. 'Fantastic work, mate. You could have at least barked.'

Washing his face at the tank, he returned, the sleeper draped across the lounge with his old blanket, still snoring. Many a feckless townie, relative or buddy landed on his veranda. One of Mara's gang might doss down after a dispute or argument. Or Danny might bed down if he arrived home late, finding his dad already asleep. Kids wagging school might spend time spying on him. If he were in the mood, tea and biscuits would be provided.

Hmm. Feet that size. Definitely a 'him.'

Kev never locked his door, because he reckoned some silly bugger would climb through the window and break his precious soda siphon. Or put their feet through his cane chairs.

Come to think, an adult's form; not a short and thin fellow, but tall, in dirty socks.

Yep. Shoes on the floor, wet, muddy and scuffed.

A beefy brute. Unfamiliar.

The body shuffled and turned, sandy hair showing.

A stranger! The only one about is the Sydney bigwig from the Bicentenary. Is it him? What's he doing here?

At times like this, he prayed. He hadn't seen this bloke before, but word around town suggested an official type, come here in a flash Commodore, offering something-or-another. Throwing his weight around.

He couldn't be sure what the Bicentennial meant; something about history and stuff. Sandy-haired, round-faced, come to buy the place, or something strange. Talking with the mayor, looking at the fish traps.

He came nearer, seeing the fellow's lily-white neck.

Gawd. Make a shearer gawk.

A bush hat lay on the floor.

At least he took his dirty shoes off. But …those bruises.

The sun's rays fell on the blanket. When the cock crowed, the sleeper wriggled and rolled around, but didn't open his eyes.

What if he wakes up, and he's mad as hell? What if he has some crazy idea I assaulted him? The police are only minutes away.

He rescued the boiling water before the kettle's whistle woke the stranger. When his restless sleeper grunted and groaned, he knew he had a short preparation time.

The stranger awoke soon after, stretched and meandered indoors. He walked into the kitchen and sat at the table like a regular customer. Rather than keep him waiting, Kev placed tea, toast and biscuits before him. The stranger wriggled his bum and reached his haunches before sweeping his hair into place. He did not rub his patchy skin or bruised arms so he suspected he suffered, though the fella said not a word. Barely looked at him.

With dark eyes like an Afghan trader, a slashed shirt and bloodstains on his upper neck, Mr Badger looked like some madman he had seen on TV. The bloke glanced at him but concentrated on sipping his hot tea, blowing away the vapour before taking a few gulps.

No acknowledgements. Not a word until he said, 'Where am I?'

Kev spat out some incoherent answer, stammering.

'Where's my car?' said the stranger.

He didn't spy any car outside. It made him nervous.

'Bastards,' said Badger. With a scratched face, he reached to his forehead but withdrew his hand. 'Well, well. Time to get square.' As he leapt to attention, the bread crusts fell to the floor. Clenching his fists, ready for a fight, he stood erect.

Kev kept a careful distance.

'They've stolen my car.'

He peered at Kev, hand to his head again. 'You. How can I recover it?'

It puzzled him at first, but soon replied: 'Bourke's Garage. You could offer a reward.'

Badger gazed skyward. 'This is over. No one's kicking me around.'

The brute sneered, ready for battle, or something nastier. Rubbing his clammy hands against his sides, he turned his gaze at him. 'Tell no one about this, understand? Tell abso-bloody-lutely no one.' He lifted a finger at his face.

'Here's twenty bucks for your troubles.' He thrust a note in his hand. 'Man's word is his bond, right?'

Kev nodded, the big fella stomped out the door, and the fly-screen door slammed behind him. He never saw Badger again.

Chapter Thirteen

A doctor attended the town hospital two days a week so the Authorities kept Henry's body on ice. They flew in a coroner to examine whether his death stemmed from murder or suicide.

With so many accusations flying around Kev couldn't tell how it happened, and he doubted how much those experts wanted to know. Shameful to kill yourself, he thought. Or did they drive him to it? Or do it to him?

Other concerns pressed on him all week. How were the families coping? The river people, Patchtowners and the nurses.

He almost forgot about Mr Badger's visit. But when the Bicentennial bloke disappeared, he understood Henry's death took precedence. People gathered at the town's edge, outside the mortuary ward where the body remained, Mara with Henry's wife before she identified the deceased.

When Billy gained bail, he led the mother, a frail woman named Rose, inside the ward. Other Murris crowded under the old fig tree as blasts of hot air offered no relief. Reporters at the fringe carried microphones with long black cords.

'With ya, luv,' said a Murri friend, one foot against the old fig tree.

'Cops got it coming, Rosie,' said another.

'Chin up, darl.'

When he emerged with Rose under his beefy arm, two journalists sprung forward to ask questions. Positioned between Henry's mother and wife, Billy addressed them in front of his people. 'Yesterday, as your Aboriginal Legal Officer, I met with Sergeant O'Farrell in the cop shop.

'Murdering bastards!'

'I talked with the police –' The young men boo-ed. 'Please. With them this morning, and demanded we inspect the cell where Henry died.' His hand squeezed as the wife stood near. They cheered for him, perhaps for her too. 'They agreed to our demands.'

'Watch them, Billy.'

'They'll admit his mother and myself at noon today.'

'What about Emma?' said Mara.

He leaned to her ear and hissed a few words before addressing the reporters. 'I want everyone to support Henry's family, stay united, back the legal service; stick together in case the coppers get nasty. Let's keep out of trouble because these guys are looking for excuses. We've gotta be strong.' Louder cheers from the mob. 'We got TV, radio and newspaper people here now, and more coming. We sent that Bicentennial bloke packing, and now we'll expel Farrell as well.'

Two nurses stuck their heads out the window, waving their arms and demanding a hush. Mara waved and ushered them further away. Standing nearby, Kev wondered at Billy and her at odds.

He spied Cheryl too, outside a ward in her blue cardigan.

Something's bothering her. Never seen her stand back like this.

When he approached her, she mumbled, 'Pray God finds a way,' her body half-turned.

When Kev returned home, Mr Badger's bedding had been untouched, but so much was happening that he went inside and fell on the lounge.

Billy's sure angry at her, he thought. I mean, they aren't getting on. Henry doesn't deserve this. He could be a nuisance for sure, but this is wrong. Dying in police hands. My son Danny is high-spirited too; this shouldn't happen to anyone.

All this business about putting a building near the fish traps when the town has taken so little interest, and Murris took them for granted. And disrespecting them. That Bicentenary is rubbish, I reckon.

Henry's death he understood; the cops had killed blacks and a few gubbas for many years. But this government man; this museum thing puzzled him.

And finding him on my veranda ... He shook his head.

Kev gazed at his chook-yard.

So, where did Mr Badger go? Billy reckons he's left already. Perhaps he found his car.

He collected eggs and put them in his paper bag.

Ever since this recording business, I've been feeling strange.

Talking into the machine, yabbering about family, he confessed his links to Jimmy Blacksmith. Jawboning those nights around camp with the old men. *Catherine's gift might be bad luck. I should keep the recordings secret.*

He reckoned he wasn't good with words, his mother drumming something similar. 'Don't use language,' she'd say, meaning he shouldn't swear like a camel herder he guessed. He and his kind suffered by giving or taking inflammatory talk, volatile and uncontrollable passions. Better to be silent. If you speak too quickly, words explode in your face. And that meant trouble.

And Mr Badger? He went to Bourke's, but what happened?

Picking up chook feed, he threw a couple of handfuls in the pen.

If the cops ask after him, they'll come here and find my tape deck. They'll say I couldn't own one like that. They'll say it's stolen.

The thought struck him so hard that his mouth opened. Sunlight emerged from cloud and the shifting light washed around him like a twirling baton. Every shiny object on the landing glowed revelation: shovel and spade, spoons, hubcaps and broken clocks alike elevated him to airy Goodness. He felt giddy.

If only you were here, Bess. Then, I'd know what to do.

When the warm sunlight ebbed, a curtain drew across his face; a chill set in, that had little to do with the weather.

I'm a fool. I should never have told him to go to Bourkes'.

Holding his arms against his chest, his fingers dug into his shoulders. His head dropped. A cooling breeze came off the river. A line of ants traversed the wooden deck, pacing back and forth from the kitchen across to the steps. When they reached the glossy ceramic tiles, a gust of wind blew them away.

Down the road, Mara's mob gathered on the highway. Several charcoal children climbed under the bridge, clinging to steel girders, their bare feet eased into the river waters before searching for gudgeons in the shallows. Their gang stood at the bridge's far side where the fifty-metre strip of tarmac dipped to the flood plain, so townspeople couldn't see them. They chatted to each other and sat on old chairs hauled from the roof rack.

'Listen, you mob. When some car comes along, stay seated. Don't move, eh.' A faint nod from all, and the uneasy squinting of weary, sun-ravaged eyes. 'We're gonna collect donations, and give Billy's family a present, like good blackfellas. No one will help us unless we help ourselves. We only got thirty bucks from the Council mob last night.'

Though the young sworn her protection from other's thuggery, they bit their lip and eyed each other, her daughter, Christine, amongst them. Women her age kept close, handsome ones in ragged dresses, barefoot, eyes narrowed, and all wondering what'd become of them when they commandeered money from passing cars.

She carried a little swagger in the afternoon sun. Last night, she confronted the Bicentennial official and all the councillors, demanding contributions for Henry. She received a few bucks and a ton of resentment, although she also discovered the delicious joy of audacity.

Today, she and her mob added to donations by collecting from drivers passing east and west. When they stopped, most of them didn't bother protesting. They donated a dollar or two and kept going. 'For his family,' they were told, so the travellers gave enough to avoid trouble. Everyone knew Henry's death made the national news, and though opinions differed, no one wanted to upset her and her gang.

It was risky for Patchtowners too, already harassed by Welfare. The cops would be out like a flash if they found out. But Mara told them: do-this, do-that, asking for so much of their courage. 'This is for Henry, his wife and them.' And that should be enough. Together, they might perform miracles. With her help, they would do things only Jesus could do.

.

Chapter Fourteen

On the old lounge, Mr Badger's body imprint was deeper where his shoulders rested. His shoes scuffed the landing and dried mud left a crumpled pattern, making Kev again regret recommending Bourkes Garage.

Hostility littered Paddy's workshop like abandoned radiators. They're the meanest mob in town, he thought. They fixed more than vehicles and didn't like people snooping or asking questions.

But given the Bicentennial official disappeared without a trace, he couldn't avoid a visit.

I sent him there thinking they would find his flashy Commodore. Something might have happened to him. What a coconut, I am. They do the stealing and dealing around here. If anything shady is going on they want their share of the action. What if the bloke walked in as angry as hell and found his car being spray-painted?

Paddy's advantages were considerable, the next garage was two hours away if you could drive that far. His monopoly meant he charged heavily for panel beating, repainting, mechanical work and parts.

As most Murris lacked money, they and their mates spent days in mulga country leaning over Holdens and Falcons to change oil filters, revive suspensions, knock dented fenders into shape, spray paint, tune engines and replace mufflers, disc brakes and shock absorbers. Similarly, undergo hot and dirty labour on salvaging car wrecks left in the scrub.

He smiled. Away from local's suspicious eyes and common hostility, they enjoyed outings unmatched since corroboree times. You could talk your head off, test out solutions, take a break for some hunting, and for once, every mistake was an honest one. They always returned home laughing.

When they needed his help, you watched your words. With his short temper, if you were connected to his known detractors, he liked to point out his collection of golf clubs, including a wicked four-iron.

By his reckoning, the Bourkes practically ran the town. When a councillor or cop required vehicle repairs, their amiable, long conversations conducted in his yard, resulted in smiles all around. In the *Advocate*, Mayor Peake's always talked about 'relationship management.'

If a Sydneysider like Badger walked into Paddy's place unannounced and demanded anything, it would upset him. The big, battered bruiser would be overwhelmed when the Hard Boys rallied. Surrounded by grease, axles, chassis, and metal parts, a fight could be fatal.

Holy days! I sent him there. Now, I've gotta discover what happened to him. Difficult with police, newspaper people, and the rumour-mongers all about.

I'll put things right. Find his whereabouts.

Of course! If I locate his car, I'll find him, dead or alive.

He set out the next morning. Made a sandwich and trudged to the Traveller's Motel where the Cliff Badger occupied a room. He figured the fellow would have returned to clean up before going to Bourkes.

Like nosey Inspector Boney, I'll check his last movements.

Peering through the motel's fly-screen door to the reception area, Teddy Smith, his old shearing comrade, read his newspaper with the sun over his shoulder. Kev caught his eye with a friendly wave.

'G'd-ay,' said Ted.

'How are ya, mate?'

'So, so.'

He took off his hat signalling a readiness for a conversation. 'Is there a bloke staying here called Badger? He drives a –'

'Commodore. A Holden XL model, white. Yeh. Air-conditioned, power steering. Huge engine. Got a real hummmmm.'

'That's him,' he said, amusing Ted by pretending to steer the vehicle. 'May I say "Hello" to the bloke?'

'Ooooh. Bit late. Ain't seen him for a while. Must've up and gone;

at least, I think so.'

'I am worried about him. Could we –'

'Take a peep in his room. No problem, cobber.'

His mate led him along the covered walkway to Room Three, keys hanging from his hand. He pointed, 'He parked his car right here' as if he could see it well.

At the door, he struggled with the lock and key before the door gave way. 'Here, take a gander.'

Kev followed him inside. 'Holy Hell.'

The room was a mess; the bed was unmade, bathroom towels were scattered on the floor, the wardrobe was open with clothes jammed behind the door. With lingering tobacco odour, a stranded vacuum cleaner impersonated a walrus.

'Maggie ain't keen on the clean-up. She's preparing other rooms for them media people.'

Kev walked around, eying things. Mr Badger's clothing: a tie, trousers, shirt and underwear. A pack of Marlborough with a few fags inside by the overturned lamp stand. Two glasses in the wash sink. He sniffed them.

'Whiskey.'

'What's going on?' said Ted.

'Did you see him leave?'

Ted scratched and twisted his neck. 'He went to the Council meeting a couple of nights back. Ain't seen him since. In a hurry from what I hear. As long as I know his car rego and license number.' He thought again. 'I didn't bump into him yesterday. The day before, he … I have his American Express card.'

'His credit card?'

'Not the actual thing, but …seen his car coming down the road. In the morning. Can't miss a flash XL in white. Then again, those reporters make me nervous.'

'What?'

'Take a geek, man. Over here.'

Teddy took him by the arm and led him around the corner to suites four to eight. A van with "ABC" written on the door, another, a blue Holden with "Seven", and larger box-like vehicles in blue, probably technical support.

'I'm booked up. Radio, television. A sheila from Bathurst and another from Brisbane. Everyone's here.'

'You didn't see him come in, some time?'

'Could have slipped in. Too much going on.'

'But, you saw the Commodore? Who drove it?'

'The town's seen nothing like this.'

'Who drove?'

Ted raised a finger, leaned to Kev's ear, and whispered the name.

'No!'

Mr Badger's car had been driven around town, and not by its owner. With newspapermen and TV types sticking their noses into everybody's business, snooping, looking for stories, this might be their next one.

The town's already in trouble. Who knows what they'll discover or invent, and turn into a scandal? Mr Badger slept at my place, so I might be the centre of suspicions.

'What do you think? A lady driving his car.'

Teddy, fishing for gossip. When media people filled his rooms, his old mate's attempts pleased him; amongst fellow shearers, exchanging yarns is the stuff of life.

Kev worried. What's going to happen when the city TV and its pollies take a close interest in the town, its people and the goings-on? Townspeople whispered or wept about all their misfortunes, the shady deals, the hidden shame, even a Murri's death, but they also feared being caught like 'roos in the spotlight. Reporters terrorised them when they pointed cameras and microphones at them, demanding words, stories and explanations.

All this media business stinks. When the heat is on, townspeople will regret talking, especially when a Murri's already dead.

So many people were brought down by a few misplaced words, and Murris most of all. Kev knew they were dangerous; sly, greasy, slippery things in other's hands. Words become sentences, fashioned by smart people in courts, newspapers, radio and TV shows. They are written on official forms, company contracts and welfare reports. They tie you down, leave you in knots, twist and distort, bound to the devil's end.

With Blacksmith blood, in the media's hands, it could be a death sentence.

PART TWO, Chapter Fifteen

Days and Nights

Teddy's revelation made his head spin. The car, he thought, as he strode down Evans Street, she drove it through town. As he headed for Bourkes' Garage a weedy, long-haired man in a white shirt and spectacles stared at him. His buddy-in-black held a walkie-talkie, both with fags in their mouths, a third fellow in pressed trousers with an ABC microphone in hand.

'Excuse me, sir.'

Kev turned away, retreating into the Shearers Arms, the town's second hotel, and further to the bistro. Safe.

Not so fast. The door behind flew open, and the white-shirted fellow closed on him. Before he could ask a question, Kev raised his arms. 'No.'

Lunchtime patrons laughed at the sight of their town handyman pursued by the out-of-towners. The thought of wanting his opinion at a time like this.

'Talk to these other blokes,' he said, pointing to others at their tables. The laughter died with his suggestion as no one wanted to talk to the ABC, Seven, Nine or anyone to do with the media. They threw peanuts at them to express their views. Any difficult question spoilt their lunch.

The stranger in white considered settling among the locals but with the patron's backs turned he left. Young Glen, the local High School English teacher, handed Kev a beer. 'Another confederacy of fools,' he said.

He took a sip. Have to be sociable. Need reinforcement if I'm gonna visit Bourkes.

'How about a game of pool?' said Glen. 'Five bucks on it.'

With the sideways tip of his head, Kev declined.

'What about cards? You play poker?'

'Thanks, Glen. But I only want a break.' With two familiar women nearby, he pointed to them. 'Try the girls.'

'Danielle and Susan? Where to start? They'd rather rattle-tattle about death, cops and mayhem.'

'You mean, what happened to Henry?'

'Henry, the media, police, everything. A lot of fuss, isn't it? The way she talks, she reckons there'll be blood on the streets, riots at the palace, fires on London Bridge. Like *Bloody Sunday*.' He swayed and clicked his fingers.

Kev took a deep breath, and refrained from shaking his head at the Brit's strange expressions.

'That's U2, dad.'

'Oh,' said Kev, unsure whether "U2" was a code or an accusation, a film perhaps. It sounded familiar. If it were music, he preferred Country and Western or Tom Jones' *Green, Green Grass of Home*.

'Hello,' said Susan, with a shandy in hand.

'Hi,' added her companion.

Young Danielle was the town's newly graduated social worker in her twenties, with straight brown hair and a fair complexion. The music teacher was a taller woman in her mid-thirties, known for her bright, chunky jewellery, and notorious for her brazen politics. With Glen, these three were amongst the few townies who conversed with Murris, making a closed circle in the Arm's lounge.

Susan thrust her hand out to Kev, shaking his hand loosely. As town revolutionary, the fractious one insisted on drinking at the Unity, befriending Billy, but relishing a Caesar Salad at the Arms. Both pubs had duke boxes, *The Red Flag* on neither, so she settled for beating out Beethoven on her piano after lunch.

She joined the bowling club too, only metres past Bourke's Garage. With the only decent dance floor in town, it once ran separate events for blacks and whites. She made a point of nominating a Murri or two for membership but Kev quietly declined. Every nomination evaporated in Committee. With women only allowed 'associate' membership, and Murris not welcome, rejection was a simple matter of pissing in her beer and laughing at her every sip.

She glanced at Glen. 'Kev. You been talking to this excuse-for-a-human-being. He still pines for swinging London. Thinks a man dying in our cells is a storm in an English teacup.'

'Hold on. I only said, "What's so surprising?"'

'Obvious, what you meant.'

'Be fair,' said Danielle. 'In a town like this, he's got a point. This place is a madhouse. I can't sleep in my caravan for all the drunks. And people here are so boring.'

'Three years in Social Work,' said Danielle, 'you should know better.'

'Jezz, Susan. I thought you were going to help me.'

'I will. But if you're scared of Mara, Murris and publicans, it doesn't mean we are.'

Glen threw up his hands. 'Boring, boring, boring. I've been stuck here for years, care of the New South Wales Education Department's loopy system. One conviction in the Old Country and I'm sent to Nowhereland. At least Danielle can be expelled for soliciting underage boys.'

'Pipe down,' shouted Col, the barman. 'Bloody well shut it or Sergeant Farrell will do something awful to you.'

The four of them searched the bistro, argument silenced until they spied the cop at a table across the room, beer in hand. Susan bit her tongue, tempted to curse and spit venom, though Kev put a restraining hand on her shoulder.

'Behave yourselves, or clear out.'

Colin delighted in rebuking 'chalkies,' and all the blow-ins, black fellows and know-it-alls who drew attention to themselves. As a manager, he enjoyed baring his teeth at disturbing influences; what local patrons wouldn't say, he could. Business as usual was done there, or at the club, only he made more fun with pesky drunks and do-gooders. Their lot received a worse reception further down the street.

Kev peered across the room. At the far end, O'Farrell sat with Humblebum and a formally dressed, third man, a rotund stranger in his fifties. He had chubby cheeks and a balding head with thinning, jet-black hair slicked back against his skull, his upright posture indicating his superior status. Kev struggled to imagine who he might be. Who could be more important than Farrell or Humblebum?

Susan turned her back to them. 'Know him?' Blank faces all

around. 'That is Phillip Bowler, bloody National Party MP.' Kev hadn't heard of him, and neither had the others. 'A pollie, a coroner, a punisher; probably doing Henry's autopsy.'

Glen's jaw dropped. 'Him? Autopsies, and talking to those two.' He grimaced. 'Look at Humblebum. He'll pull out a cigar soon.'

His whistle confirmed the State MP, Police Chief and the Council's Town Clerk shared drinks, potato chips and vinegar with conspiratorial conversation in a public bistro. 'They're getting their story straight.'

Danielle giggled. 'Maybe we should leave.'

Susan held her back. 'It's our pub too.'

'Ignore them,' said Glen putting a hand on Danielle's shoulder, but eying Susan. 'Forget them, and tell me what else is happening, sweetie?'

'Poor duckie here wants to find a way out of town. Our social worker reckons her customers are not to her taste.'

'I'm going mad in this place,' said Danielle.

'What do you think, Kev? What should she do?'

He bit his lip at such a question. He advised Badger badly, and it might have killed him. Trapped here with the youngsters, he doubted he'd reach Paddy Bourke's workshop, or whether he should.

She turned to Glen. 'Our pet is ready to leave our working-class battlers. Reckons this social work game is too hard.'

'Never mind that,' he said, a hand each on Danielle's and Susan's lap. 'You two deserve better. So, how about it? Do either of you ladies want a good time tonight?'

Chapter Sixteen

Kev reached Bourke's driveway, hesitated, and stepped back to Madam's Dress shop's display window where he felt embarrassed. If he went ahead, he confessed that he dreaded a probable eruption. Any dispute with Paddy Bourke had implications for Murris. Besides, his son, Danny home returned soon.

Discovering his Inspector Boney routine more difficult than expected, the next day he turned to the good Cheryl Sheila. In the church meeting room, he kneeled with her, in hope of finding the courage he missed yesterday, but also seeking a bit more than reassurance.

She soothed him, as always, with 'It is God's will we are here, together. With His help, we will find our Peace.'

As the town's de-facto minister, she filled the building with Godliness: a few Holy portraits, some leftover tinsel wrapped around the table legs, and a broad red cape she wore over her shoulders. Transformed from Capability Sheila to Mother Teresa, her public briskness and directness disappeared behind a veil of kindness and compassion that drew him close to her untouchable body.

With much to tell her about the last few days, about anxieties for the future, about Henry's grieving families, and in general, the anger in people's hearts, he feared some of it could infect his son. In his bones, he sensed frayed friendships and future calamity borne from past and present hatred.

Over the last year, Cheryl replaced the assigned minister from Collarinabri to the south, a man who rarely troubled himself with distant parishioners, the two-hundred-kilometre drive delayed by floods, tremors, earthquakes, road closures, CWA meetings, liver problems, school disruptions, elections, alcohol programs and annual dinners.

Called to replace him on an increasing number of occasions, her exposure to desperate townspeople seeking reassurance and ritual led to increased appearances in gowns lengthy quotations and musical backup. She grew into the job, and others accepted it. She had the church keys and administered blessings to everyone in a sanctified manner.

Alone in a pew, Kev wondered how Danny would take the news of Henry's demise. They swum together in the river over the years, around the riverbank and under the bridge, played in the schoolyard and met at the dance hall. He never read newspapers; he preferred mate's talk and handiworks.

With the media attention, passions around town ran high. for Murri, disgraced police who routinely harassed and persecuted them should go to Bourke. Most pastoralists and townies expected Murris to practise invisibility, stay in Patchtown, around the river or confine themselves to the Unity Hotel. They liked a comfortable, wide, white street, and the cop's bad behaviour was excused if it had the desired effect. They didn't want to say so to a media hungry for stories. Other townspeople, unwilling or unable to say what *really* happened, whispered rumours, assertions and denials that were liable to start fights. No town could afford that.

Kev wouldn't stoke the fires by reporting a missing Bicentennial official no one liked. Who would? Talk of him raised disbelief. 'Shut the fuck up,' the more direct types would advise. 'There's enough trouble already', especially for Murris in shock at the death of one of their own.

After he sipped beer with Susan, Danielle and Glen, he set out to find Mr Badger, or rather, locate his Commodore and ask after its owner. But he didn't confront Bourke. He frightened, and talk of town anxieties confounded him. Though familiar with Henry's waywardness, he half-blamed himself for his death. 'l did not bring him to his senses. I only watched.' he said to Cheryl. 'And see what happened.'

He mustn't fail him. With his son's past school troubles, he and Bess won some success in his late teens. When he went shearing, Danny helped his mum. Handy in the workshop too.

Some teachers praised him for finishing eleventh level, but their words lacked conviction. When he left with sketchy hopes and a ticket to Sydney, Kev stayed at home for days. He missed his wife, and after three years without either, his son promised to visit. He doubted his strength in steering him from trouble.

A tear welled from his eyes. 'God forgive me.'

Cheryl knelt beside him, with one hand on his back. 'Let us pray.'

Head bowed and hands cupped, he glimpsed her soft and silky hands as she clasped them together, his own, calloused and worn by many years of shearing and handyman's labours.

'Dear Lord. Our Kevin is your disciple. He seeks your peace in the face of turmoil and hardship. Give him everlasting comfort in thy bosom. Jesus, our time with you is precious when sadness and regrets burden us. Protect us from the vicissitudes and trials of life. Let your light shine down upon him. Forever and ever, amen.'

'Amen.'

'I think you need a cuddle.' She embraced him with both arms, her ample body pressed his. They lingered until embarrassment pulled him away. Their intimacy melted his concerns for Mr Badger.

Later, they sat in the bare church kitchen at the church's rear and sipped diluted whiskey.

'I guess I'm no detective.'

She shuffled. 'What do you mean?'

'I'm curious about this fellow from the Bicentennial, about him disappearing. What's happened to him when Henry...you know.'

'He left the Council meeting in a huff. Around nine-thirty. He put everyone offside with his awful behaviour.'

'He slept on my veranda overnight.' She bit her lower lip. 'Took a beating from someone.'

She faced him, her forehead creased. 'You haven't seen him since?'

'No. And you?'

'Hmm. I bet he's back in Sydney.' She chuckled, 'Running back with his tail between his legs.'

Kev couldn't understand her glee. 'He lost his car. He walked out of my place.'

'No! Without his Commodore?'

She noticed what model he drives? She's never mentioned cars before.

'Tell you what. I'll ring the Authority in Sydney, and see if they've caught up with him.'

'Would you?'

She placed her hand on his. 'Look… the Bicentennial grant will be approved, despite the Council cock-up. Our town's fish traps are too important. So, what do you blokes want? Does anyone want them protected?'

'I dunno. No one would touch them, would they?'

Cheryl never asked his opinion before. Flattered, bewildered and wary he presumed the stone arrangements across the width of the river unassailable. Anthropologists visited the site decades ago, They made notes and disappeared, so no one said much about them one way or the other. When he worked for the union they cared about wages and conditions. Around the properties, they worried about drought and cattle prices; and Cheryl about rent and income. Only Catherine of Canberra took an interest in language, Murri sites and our past. Or so he thought.

'Pay attention, Kev. The council will build an indigenous cultural centre, a museum if you like, beside the levee. It'll bring jobs, and we'll have to give them to Murris. Why don't you take it up? I'll back you.'

'Me? You think?'

'I want this place going ahead. I really do. We can settle things down, and unify the town. I reckon you'd be the best person to run it.'

'Me?'

'Yeh. You're a worker, a shearer. You speak Gundabarri. And you're no stirrer.'

He shook his head like it might relieve him of the suggestion.

'I mean it. When this Bicentennial grant comes on…' She took a deep breath, 'That Badger was hopeless. We can do this, if you support me.' He lifted his head. His eyes locked on hers.

'Well?'

He tipped his head, her purposefulness and determination so impressive.

Accepting his slight nod as agreement, she put both arms on his shoulders, grabbing his attention again. Staring into his eyes, her face burst with faith and optimism.

Kev pulled back. His body bucked like a brumby about to be broken in.

'OK?' She smiled.

He sat still, his lip curling in. He might have bucked and twisted free, but the spell would be lost. Instead, he noddedand grimaced.

'As for the muck flying around, well, there's nothing we can do. Things will take their course, God willing. Best you …, the most important thing is, stay away from trouble.'

She was right, he thought, in a broad kind of way. Henry's death might bring more trouble if they were not careful, Mr Badger's disappearance a terrible complication. His Blacksmith blood too was bad luck. But when Cheryl said 'stay away from trouble,' she meant Billy and Mara.

Chapter Seventeen

When the fly screen door squeaked and slammed, Kev sat up. Could have been anybody but when he turned to see Danny's endearing, naughty-boy face at the kitchen door, he beamed. 'You son of a gun.'

'Yeah, Dad. How is it?'

'Danny. You!'

He held him in his arms, arching his head to the lad's masculine features. At twenty-two, with a winning smile, clear-skinned cheeks, baby-nosed, broad shoulders and curly black hair, he had a life ahead.

'You're early! Should have rung the post office.'

'Nah. Takes too long. Besides, the place is rubbish.'

Living in the city kept him away from home all year. His awkward letters had halting phrasing, events poorly recalled, and his other thoughts scratched out. So much noise in his life, so much about rights and wrongs, blames and claims, incidents and accidents, and things half said. He lived in Sydney's black hotbed, Redfern, doing courier work and probably hung around pubs, chasing women, getting drunk and mixing with the wrong people.

'You're here now, son. Sit down. Have a cuppa.' He slipped into the kitchen, turned on the gas, and placed the kettle over the burner.

Danny called, 'You're coming up in the world.'

Without answering, he finished preparing the tea and biscuits in happy silence. The lad hummed rock tunes, and burst into 'on fire, fire, fi-re', leaning over the new tape deck, examining buttons and knobs.

'Where's the manual for this?'

'Leave it. It'll wait.'

'Yeah, but… can we play *Midnight Oil* on this?'

Danny smiled. His cheeky grin.

Kev poured hot tea into two mugs, added milk and slipped one to hand.

'Anyway, what are you doing with this new machine? Fall off the back of a truck?'

'Of course not.'

'Only saying. You're sunk, man.'

Danny's city talk annoyed him, but he wouldn't comment. Was it the right time to tell him about his recordings, about the Gundabarri language and his past work for Catherine of Canberra. Perhaps he'd understand.

He confided in him. And after?

'Jeez, dad. What are you thinking? You're giving it away, man. Especially after what's happened.'

'So you read about –'

'Henry? Yeh.' His hand fisted. 'It's all over Sydney radio and TV. We're gonna make them pay for this.'

He anticipated Danny's wild talk and prepared some words of reply. 'Danny boy: times like this, we need some common sense. Keep calm about Henry. In town, the media people are everywhere.'

'Is that why the tape deck's a secret?'

'I'm going to give them the true story, not the lies. For Henry, and everyone.'

Danny shook his head, wriggled in his seat, and threw out his hands. But he did not comment, taking the empty cup to the kitchen sink when a call outside caught their attention.

'Where are you?' A woman's voice. Mara?

They glanced at each other.

'Here, love. Hang on,' said Kev. 'Come in.'

Dark-faced Mara appeared through the fly screen door. In her mid-thirties and ample-bodied, Mara had a ready smile when she chose to show it. In a loose-fitting flowery dress, her daughter Christine behind had similar clothing.

'Looking for your dolls and things, Mar?'

After rushing up the drive she panted, her brow hacked and moistened. She whacked the living room lounge with her hand. 'Save it. Shut up and listen.'

Danny stood to attention, perhaps because of Christine's attractive appearance, and her sneaky wave to him.

'Cops arrested Billy.'

'What for?' said Danny.

'How would I know?' said Mara. 'Could be bloody anything. Never been a problem before.'

'He'll be in the lock-up,' said Kev.

Danny's eyes widened. 'In those cells. After Henry?'

Mara swayed. 'We'd better go down there and give them a piece of our mind.'

Kev smothered his chuckle, respectful of Mara's spirit. 'I should talk to them, and we should take someone well-connected. We need a delegation.'

'No. We've got to go in strong,' said his son. 'That mob is out of control.'

He worried about his son. Prone to passions, he did not want to inflame them. 'Let me go, Mar, just me. If I can, I'll take Cheryl Sheila from the Council. We'll get to the bottom of this.'

'Bah. Not a chance,' she said, eyes narrowed, head thrust forward. 'She's a useless councillor.' She leaned, put her hand on his chest and hissed her words in his ear. Kev's eyes flamed and scorched disapproval. He turned away, picked up a cup and glanced at the lad. 'Getting some water, mate,' he said, heading for the door.

Christine and Danny eyed each other: what was going on?

'It's no time for fiddling,' called Mara as the fly-screen door slammed. Kev headed for the water tank when the kitchen tap worked fine. Danny sprung up, but she held him back. 'Let him cool down.'

'What did you say to Dad?'

'I said we got to do something to get Billy out without taking that sheila. Them cops have been attacking us for years. We gotta stay clear of informers.'

'Damn right,' he said as she picked at the lounge threads with one hand, the other searching for something unknown.

Mara leaned against the door frame. 'This town's had enough of bastard coppers. Time we made a stink, don't you think?' Danny raised a clenched fist. 'So tell your dad we're gonna shout about this. Ain't putting up with it anymore.'

Danny's eyes widened. 'What are we going to do, Aunty Mara?'

'We'll do something, don't you worry, and you can help. You've been to Sydney. What do you reckon? What'll we blackfellows do? Because we can do anything now – anything.

Chapter Eighteen

In the town lock-up, Billy occupied cell number two, charged with possessing an unlicensed firearm, resisting arrest, drunkenness and assaulting an officer, the last three a simple matter of the police's word against his.

'They're old hunting rifles,' he said after the police interrogators held up his bolt rifle like a trophy.

'Is that right? These fellas can murder someone.'

'So bloody what? A match can wipe out thousands. Now, get my lawyer.'

'Very well. Tell us where the rest of the cache is. You're darling wife tells me there's more where this came from.'

'Stop playing Silly Buggers. I'm not falling for it. I'm saying nothing.'

'Such a fine wifey. Rats on you at the first opportunity. You been knocking her around?'

'My lawyer. Now.'

'Not sure the phones are working, mate.'

With the prisoner silent, Farrell wandered the interview room, readying the same line of attack. 'What a little team-builder you are; keeping a dozen officers in work, a solicitor or two and a regular circuit magistrate. In any other town, we'd have two or three. Now we're looking for your mug army. We got you and Mara well covered. Don't think you can hide.'

'That's tripe, copper.'

'Clarkie. Take him to Gilgandra, in handcuffs. Leave by the back door. You can take the paddy wagon but don't bloody damage it. Farrell grinned. 'Lucky day for you, mate. New rules say we can't lock you up in a dead man's cell. Can't hold drunks here for more than twelve hours. So, we're taking you in the unpadded vehicle on the roughest road to Hades. After a session in Gandy, we'll find another town, another drive, and another lock-up. You should be sober by the weekend.'

Billy blew up. He swung his handcuffed arms across the desk, sweeping away pens, official papers, chairs and sandwiches. Clark leapt at him from behind, but the accused's strength and anger repelled him.

'Geoff. Come in here,' yelled Farrell.

Another officer raced in to wrestle him to the ground but pushed him off balance, he pulled out his baton and belted Billy over the neck.

'Argh!' He fell and rolled to one side, the cops standing over him, more batons at the ready.

'Enough,' said Farrell. 'Get him out of here.'

Billy mouthed a lion's roar, but when they dragged him out, he shouted abuse.

Kev and Mara walked to town leaving Christine and Danny before the television, surrounded by old magazines, second-hand lamps and faded cushions. An afternoon quiz show was her usual fare but Danny's presence stirred her. When he wasn't looking, she glanced at him, and couldn't help sticking out her tongue when she was caught gawking.

Danny busied himself taking cups, cutlery and plates into the kitchen, and depositing them in the sink. No rinsing or washing. Long accused of lazy habits, this was his way of getting off to an acceptable start.

'I'm going to Sydney,' said Chrissie. 'Mr Bourke says he'll give me a job.'

'Your mum won't let you,' he said.

'I'm eighteen next month. She can't stop me.'

Kev and Mara walked single file along the narrow track, a light breeze blowing through the scrub, the afternoon heat enforcing silence on them and the bush.

'You got the experience, mate. Talking to police, working for the union. I'm back-up. OK?'

He nodded and kept walking. She pursed her lips and fidgeted with her tatty waistband, tied to her girth. A young goanna gripped a tree truck with its claws and stared at them. He skirted it, and she waited for him to catch up.

As they neared the main road, her face twitched. 'Too much shit flying around. I got troubles coming out of my ears with so many kids, bloody drunks, and those pension police after us. I don't need all this.'

He put a hand to her back but otherwise approached the dusty intersection in silence.

'Chrissie is getting free-and-easy. She'll find herself knocked up before long. She's only seventeen.'

He glanced at thirty-five-year-old Mara and her worry lines.

'What are we gonna do?' she said. 'Billy's in trouble. Got the funeral on Saturday. Battles everywhere.'

'We better hope things calm down. We got to find friends and allies.'

'Be waiting a long time, I reckon. Where are they, eh?'

Alongside her again, he put his hand on her shoulder, the other taking up her hand, squeezing it.

'You're right, Mar. We got to be strong. You're something special. When you talk, people listen.'

'That so? You're the one looking for friends.' They walked again, following the last curve near the levee. 'I suppose you think the Bicentennial bloke was a friend. Is this why you're looking for him, asking silly questions?'

'Not like a black fellow, eh?'

Mara grinned, walking on until they neared the tarmac.

'He slept at my place the other night.'

'No!'

'When his car was missing, I sent him to Bourke's.'

'You did? Why'd you do that?'

'I shouldn't have but … What happened to him, Mar?'

'There you go again, asking questions.'

'Word is, you might know.'

'Don't be crazy. Nothing to do with me.'

'Except… ' he muttered before slowing his pace to gaze at the lorikeets.

Mara walked ahead, the bushes vanishing when they reached the park. From the solitary traffic sign, Evans Street ran to the left, the post office phone box within sight of the police station. They both searched for anything unusual around the cop shop.'

'My Danny worries me. He's been cagey about living in Sydney. I don't know what he does.'

Mara searched down the road, her back to the bridge. One of the Bourkes, or Farrell and his officers might be spying on them. An informer too.

Within the hour, they learnt that Billy had left town in a paddy wagon, destination unknown. Kev cursed. 'We'll visit the cop shop tomorrow, Mar. Without Billy, Henry's wake is up to us.'

Chapter Nineteen

Kev broke Cheryl's first commandment, avoiding Mara and Billy. Allowing for her mad idea of managing Mr Badger's Bicentennial museum, was asking too much of him. They were long-time friends and contributed to town life. With his Gundabarri project part of his days and weeks, he supported doing the right thing. Besides, their people had little enough without sacrificing friendship.

When Cheryl showed him tenderness, he admitted he was powerless to resist. She soothed his worries and promised to inquire after Mr Badger's whereabouts. Mindful of his Blacksmith blood, he would counsel Danny against obsessions.

'Son,' he would say, ' a man ain't a man when he's in gaol. Your spirit is taken from you, and without it, there is little chance of a good life. Murris are people of little means and see what happens when the Law takes a dislike to you. Jimmie was shot dead, my granddad. Anyone of us might perish in police hands.' Or something similar.

A man ain't a man in gaol.

Balli-al-mal.

I'll be careful what I say. After Henry'8s death and Badger's disappearance, Danny might ignore his advice. Difficult to tell when he took a deep breath and wandered outside. He stood on the river bank for an hour.

If something goes terribly wrong, it will be my fault.

Chapter Twenty

With Billy arrested, Kev and Mara had to organize the public gathering for Henry's send-off. So the next day, they faced the Police station's panelled doors of heavy oak, a structure built to hold off citizen sieges. Like a castle entrance, they belittled anyone entering, its scrapes, indents and lacerations evidence of the fearful Struggles of the Unwilling. Though no blood scarred it, they inhabited a ghostly fog of foreboding.

Balli-al-mal.

Place of the dead.

Upon entering, they spied Sergeant Farrell at the front desk speaking to his fellow officer. The head cop's eyes narrowed and lips tightened before he discovered a false smile. He put one arm on his partner's back. 'Constable Waverley. Some visitors.'

Kev faced them like a union delegate to the boss-cocky. On their property, he would be polite and direct, firm and almost friendly, although who can bargain while standing amongst the ghostly presence of the assaulted and abused? Though Mara stood by him, her body stiffened.

The junior cop reached for pen and paper, eager to appear busy.

'Mate,' said Farrell, 'go make us a cuppa while I talk to the general public.'

Mara gazed around the unfamiliar room before meeting Farrell's eyes.

The sergeant smirked. 'So, what is it?'

'Sir,' said Kev, 'there is something we must discuss.'

'The price of roses, the latest sports results? What'll it be?'

'Don't disrespect him, Farrell. You're talking to a man, not a dog.'

'Ah shut up, Mara. Shut your gob or I'll cuff you.'

'Please,' said Kev.' It's about the send-off.' He omitted mention of

Henry's name in front of the bloke who might have murdered him.

The sergeant's unshaven and sunburned face twitched like a rat in a bag. For the first time, she noticed the bruises. 'Funeral, is it? You want to, what, give us details?'

'Yes. Everyone's coming, and we wish to make it a day of dignity. Sir.'

'Right, put the info on this piece of paper. Write everything down and sign it.'

He slid the notepad over the counter. Kev approached and wrote the proceedings in his best handwriting.

The young constable stuck his head in. 'Two sugars, Chief?'

Farrell waved him away as Mara wandered the sparse room reviewing the Reward Notices and the waste baskets, peeping at the scratch marks on the cop's forehead, and a bruise on his neck.

After completing the page, Kev slid it across the counter. Farrell read under his breath. 'Eleven... service... Presbyterian... lunch... Henry... What's this? A wake? Irish.'

'In the reserve, where he sometimes slept.'

The Chief groaned. 'You want to conduct an event in a public park? Think again.'

'Right. But the Council is OK with it, the Church too. And...'

'And?'

'And your lot should stay well away,' said Mara, 'if you know what's good for – '

'Considering,' Kev said, hand on Mara's shoulder, 'there'll be no trouble. People are still, sad with ...with what happened.'

'Listen, you two. I've had enough of your demands. We're police, and when the law is broken, we'll pounce. Drunks and parasites watch out. But the truth is mateys, I got the Commissioner on the phone telling me to look after you lot. Be kind to the family. Be kind to the friends of. Be kind to piss-ants. Be kind to Kev, and be kind to blind bats and bloody dingoes. We're bursting with kindness.'

He gripped the counter, his face strained. 'So, have your little wake, but we're close by. Any weapons, any troubles, any bullshit, then we'll clean yous up, quick smart.' He let the words sink in. 'We shoved it up Black Billy, and he ain't demanding much at the moment.

'We're onto your lot. We got information. We know about you, Mara, what you're up to. Don't think you can get away with it. Love-

Me-Do Week will be over soon. And you, Kev, your Uncle Tom routine doesn't fool me. But OK, have your grog around the local shithouse. But don't give us any trouble.'

'So,' said Kev, after a suitable silence, 'you will stay away from the park?'

'That's what I said, didn't I? Don't push the envelope. Now, get out.'

Once outside, she turned to Kev. 'Did you see his face? Filthy. What's he been doing to our Billy, eh?'

He chuckled. 'By the bruises on him, what's Billy done to Farrell?'

She grinned. 'What he said about pushing the envelope? We didn't write no letters.'

Big news swept town: Mayor Peak's dog, little Giff, had been shot. Blown away. Old Dickie, Council Garbo, searched the mayor's driveway after noticing his bin missing from the footpath. Making the effort to fetch it, he discovered the stone-dead mutt on a garden path. Dickie alerted Humblebum, so the two men were present when the *Advocate* reporter-editor-photographer arrived to record the loss.

> Citizens are in shock today as the Mayor's prize cocker spaniel was brutally shot by an unknown gunman. His faithful friend for five years, and lucky charm for our first Tidy-Town entry …this cruel act …
>
> The Shire Clerk, Mr Roger Clifford, found the victim on a routine visit to the Mayor's home. A 'malicious and cowardly murder committed on his property. The perpetrator will be apprehended. This kind of violence leaves everyone vulnerable. No one can feel safe.'
>
> The matter is now in police hands.

The article included a photo of the scene, with an 'X' on the site of Giff's demise, Dickie later pointing out his boot on the photo's right edge, the first time he appeared in a newspaper.

Fame comes at a price, he thought, relieved suspicions hadn't fallen on him. If they thought he killed the dog, he'd find himself in Henry's cell. But Humblebum arrived soon after, taking command, contacting the *Advocate*, and chatting with him while they waited, pumping him for details. It came in handy when the administer briefed Hobby Jones, the town's all-round journalist.

Reading the news later, bemused or horrified, fellow councillors and all townspeople who loved dogs, or at least pretended, raised their eyebrows over morning toast before passing the butter, spreading the jam, and adding two sugars to their tea. 'Who would do such a thing?' 'That fellow's always near bad smells.'

Condolences arrived at the Council Chambers, hung in a row behind the Mayor's head like a line of Christmas cards.

'Who shot him?' said Peake. 'Who?'

His administrator reckoned several suspects, all blackfellows, but he said 'Best not to think about it, you'll only get upset.' His fingers danced on the desk while he stood behind him.

'I'm distressed, alright. I'll strangle the bastard who did this.'

Every day the cards hung over Peak's head reminding him of his loss. He tugged at his hair, scratched his scalp and twisted his locks, and by Friday, a bald patch appeared on the mayoral head. His secretary skirted around him collecting hair from official documents. After hours, she carried a small vacuum cleaner to suck strands beneath his desk and caught in his drawers.

'For God's sake, Tony, stop it,' said Humblebum.

'What?'

'The hair pulling. What's with the –?'

'Split hairs, everywhere. Nothing for …for anything.'

'Mate, why not take time off? This business about, you know… Leave everything to us. Go to Sydney. Relax on the beach, play the casino, see the musicals.'

'There are so many matters at hand: the roo factory, power problems, the Tidy-Town entry, this museum thing, and the Abo unrest.'

'They're not important. Think of your health. Take time off. Rest time. Fun time.'

He put both hands behind the mayoral back, easing him out of his comfortable chair. Peake meandered around the room, palms sweating, while his administrator draped his jacket across the seat as if taken by another person.

'Go on. Don't worry.'

He wavered, one hand clutching his head before twisting away. 'I will. Yes. OK.'

Humblebum threw out his arms like a conductor for the *Blue Danube*. 'Alright, boss. Everything is under control.'

First the Peake, now the trough.

Chapter 21

At the Presbyterian Church, Kev welcomed people arriving at the funeral. Townies like Cheryl, Marco, Danielle and Susan joined Patchtowners who crossed the bridge, Henry's families, and the river-dwellers who usually kept to themselves. Mara and he sat with Ellie and Rose, wife and mother consoled with a dignified send-off.

Throughout the proceedings, his thoughts perched on a precipice, perhaps by memories of Bess's farewell a few years earlier, or with Danny's untimely return. In the hot, noon air, standing outside the church, he stood aside, preoccupied that people felt that any disturbance might break him in two.

During the service, the mother and wife stayed close to his thin, warm body, shedding tears, bearing life's pain in every whimper. Knowing the two women were unfriendly to each other, he sensed so much might go wrong. Had his comforting brought them any closer to the heart of the matter, or were they so torn and worn, their kinship so threadbare, that their spirit frayed to nought?

Here's Mara's speech, the one she gave standing beside the cemetery's cement wall near Henry's grave, the one no one expected.

'We Murris have had enough. Police killing Henry. Been murdering us for two hundred years. No one's stopping them. Not the Council; they're a useless mob. Not the government. They closed their eyes again, using smart words, and making empty promises. They're talking about a Royal Commission. More lawyers coming our way. They have been killing us for a long time, and poor Henry's done nothing. So, this arvo, we're going to have a shindig at the park, for Henry. Let them see we care. Show them cops we ain't afraid. Will you come along, eh?'

With loud cheering and an awkward blend of clapping and weeping, the presiding minister's hand combed air, not knowing how to prevail. Mara held up her hands, so the mob's attention stayed with her, the religious official left standing by the coffin in case Henry rose and walked.

'This Christian fella been telling us to go home, to finish up. It's not right. It ain't enough. We're gonna have a wake in the park. Them politicians' fine words don't mean nothing. His mum's got no money to see her through. So we made a collection, me and the mob, a bag for each. I'm giving it to them. Emmy. Rose. Come here, girls. This is yours. Give us a hug.'

With heartening cheers over the grave, Mara had stolen the show, the minister speechless. She'd come from nowhere, spawning four kids, given Welfare a mighty run-around, and started up dances in the public hall without notice. Now her words shone through the gloom. From the dimming embers of her people's spirit, her slow-burning heat, smouldering on Patchtown tinder, becoming a defiant firestick carried through mulga and dogwood, lighting all within hearing distance.

That week she had a raging realization that with Billy arrested, and Kev distracted, she must do what needed doing. Undoubtedly, one had the fire, although he could never realize it, nor open the way. As a man, he had the strength and venom of the brown snake, often found on the searing pitch of a football field. Kev was a kangaroo, going long distances to find water, forswearing battles with snakes and demons to nourish his people.

She embodied the demon: willful, malicious, miraculous and unstoppable, a spirit of heroic proportions who formed, dissolved and reformed, surpassing all around her. There would be a commemoration, and her speech ensured that everyone would come along.

By early afternoon, the Patchtown mob reached the park, leaving their battered cars in the shade and by the toilet block. Others came on foot, rode horses or bicycles, or else relayed in Dickie's Cortina. Billy's river-dwellers sniffed the air around the willows by the fish traps before emerging from the levee, moving from the shady trees to the red-and-green picnic tables. Other Murris, mostly station hands and drivers, arrived with their supplies.

A few respectable townies came too, Ellie and Rose in funeral black, given condolences. Other women wore their best floral dresses, fancy shoes and necklaces, most of the men in clean shorts and colourful shirts. A few boys had their faces painted with white ochre.

Glen, Danielle and Susan stood on the footpath until Mara waved them forward. 'Come on. Join us.' Once everyone had gathered, she held up her hand for quiet.

'This is a time of sadness, people. We're here, you're here, in this park, for Henry. I knew him as a boy, a little scallywag swimming in the river and stuff. Well, today, we're gonna show them cops we're the ones; we're not giving them a chance of causing trouble. We got our pride, ain't we?'

'Yeh,' said the many, together.

'We got some tucker and some music, something for everyone. We got campfires, and we're staying here.' The cheering reverberated under the slight eucalypt canopy. 'Because we know respect. So, let's get on with it.'

They would have this wake, talking, drinking, eating, playing and paying attention to each other. Winning fraternity; yes, and dignity. It was Mara's miracle.

By late afternoon, the Patchtown mob poked and turned sausages with sticks over fires, rolling them on a galvanised iron sheet. Others leaned against trees dotting the park, hands in their pocket or fags in hand, eyes half-opened to yesterday.

Children clustered near the men splashing tomato sauce on bread, adding the steaming hot meat, handed to them before carrying more to the women. The youngest ones clung to their mums or chased each other around the shrubbery, giggling and squealing.

With their sausage-on-bread in hand, the older children wondered about the strange stirrings created by bongos and guitars, the adults clicking fingers, waving their butts and dancing. Mara shepherded children to rugs behind a shady tree and hounded the dogs away.

Three hundred people tendered in fading daylight, eating, in quiet conversation or passing the football at the fringes. Horses and dingoes were patted, guitars strummed, bongos in rhythm, oddly parked cars spread about, aboriginal flags draped from branches, picnic blankets laid out in the shade, and flattened cardboard used for seating.

Respecting the dead, breaking through the gloom.

Glen talked to Christine about the marvels of George Bernard Shaw, Charles Dickens and London's Chelsea where music rocked, markets flourished and dope was alluring. But her eyes searched for Danny.

ABC technicians stood on the opposite roadside, under Mara's rules banished from proceedings. Silence for a sound technician, cameramen and journalist, though the chaotic, gypsy-like gathering was as visually alluring as fish-and-chip wrappings. So, after their last shots, they put away equipment before heading for the Shearers Arms.

Danny had other ideas. Curious about their heavy battery pack, cameras, microphones and black wiring wrapped around technician's waists, he intercepted them. They chatted about the machines' functions and capabilities, their buttons and levers, the whirring and hissing their number-one hit. Examining their equipment, he soon won an acquaintance, discussing the machine's sound qualities, vulnerabilities and the various microphone types. Their conversation continued until the sun fell behind the Post Office roof.

He stayed solid, saying nothing about recent events, just as Mara insisted. He brought his new friends a barbequed sausage on bread as Kev's hand-waving reminded him to hold his tongue.

Nearby, Tambo Johnnie's soft guitar played. Billy's friends poured warm beer into plastic cups, later collecting flagons from the Unity Hotel. From tree branches overhead, five aprons faced the pub, each one having a single letter printed on it, collectively spelling H-E-N-R-Y.

As daylight turned red, a leather-cheeked drinker with a painted forehead, pointed across the road, his white shirt acquiring a pink hue. 'That's him,' he said. 'He dobbed Henry.'

Others gazed through the late afternoon haze, past the discarded cups and cigarette butts, to a man on the Unity's upstairs veranda. In khaki shorts and singlet, Mr Martin's brother was the pub's joint owner, a man who said little but disliked rule-breaking and ruler-breakers. The two Martos were bastards, but OK bastards because their patrons largely complied, and even enforced the rules. They did not insult his clients worse than calling them 'stupid bastards.' With its new outdoor BBQ area, most days the mob ate in peace. But many suspected they informed the station about Henry's phone call.

The Martoes dob? Them?

Two cops stationed on the footpath outside ceased their conversation, looking upwards, Marto unsighted. The figure on the balcony merely stretched his arms and clutched the veranda columns.

'Bastard,' called a Murri casting his beer bottle towards the pub. It bounced on the park's grassy fringe and rolled harmlessly into the gutter. From his high perch, Marto pointed his shoulder, arched his head forward and aimed at them with an imaginary rifle. The unsighted officers watched the men in the park turn away when another song struck up.

In the cooling afternoon, everyone relaxed and warmed themselves by the fires. The evening grew sweet, mellow and promising, Mara's fighting words evaporated into the pale, ebbing sky.

Quite a few people asked Danny about the new music in Sydney, the Redfern's Murri pubs, the leaders and the new ideas. He told them about the demonstrations on the city streets. He marched too, or so he boasted.

Nearby, Danielle and Susan bickered about something, when Kev came along. 'Mind if I join you? You two OK about being here?'

'The pigs won't do anything silly,' said the music teacher, 'not after a funeral.'

'Johnny's playing guitar. Help yourself to some tucker.'

'Shouldn't we go?' whispered Danielle, but grabbed by the shoulder, she was led to a fireplace.

Dusk turned the evening mellow until the blood-red sunlight revealed every hint of air-born haze. A pinkish stupor numbed them, the day heading for an agreeable night around the campfire. They claimed the park for Henry.

Across the road, a black Holden beeped its horn. Several heads poked out of its windows, calling 'Clear out, you black bastards.'

Mara threw up her hands. 'Come over here and say that. Come on.'

From the corner of her eye, another pair of headlights swung around, their light dancing across people and trees, the car hidden in darkness before an explosion of dust caught everyone's attention.

Kev heard it before he spied it. Having little interest in roaring engines passing down dark side lanes, he turned only when it bumped the curb and landed on the park's fringe. 'What the –'

In the evening light, a man launched himself from behind the wheel. 'It's Billy!'

'Brothers,' he shouted to the gathering mob. 'Sisters.'

A great cheer arose, and a few loud whoops, followed by laughing well-wishers. A youngster said, 'Uncle Billy's here,' to which he held up his arms, feet parted. Making space for himself, so everyone faced him. 'Those mongrel coppers locked me up in that cell. Henry's.'

It sent a wave of shame and apprehension around the park. People hung their heads, groaned, and even clawed the sky. It shook them.

They'd do that? That.

No doubt he expected outrage. 'They carted me around Dubbo, Narromine and bloody Wagga in an tin can. Damn near killed me. What do you say about them cops, eh? What? What? What?'

He grabbed a spoon, and hit the table's metal surface, creating a blunt beat. Others took anything at hand, beating on bottles, picnic tables, tins, and more spoons in hand; joining in, providing them an unlikely solidarity in near darkness.

Chomp. Clomp.

Clomp.

Clomp. Chom. Clomp.

Their drumming continued before breaking into defiant cheering, intervening calls and general backslapping. They gathered around, leading him to a park bench where he received his lamb and tomato roll, a bottle of beer at his elbow.

Kev's frown turned to a slight smile before peering over several shoulders, hearing the sharp voices of concern, and the tetchy conversations that he hoped would soon ebb. If everyone settled into the agreeable rhythm of strumming guitars, he could relax.

A strong light beam quivered overhead. From where? He noticed shadowy figures darting between the streetlights, unrecognisable people in black spreading out across the road. The dark, bulky outlines carried weaponry. Flash memory of old cowboy movies, the Alamo, or space aliens with bulbous eyes and spiky ears.

Police! Kev thought.

Truncheons and shields were visible in the gloom, people around him taking stock, and the party hubbub closed down. Light beamed into bushes like a roo hunt, except they were the target.

Farrell promised. He permitted it. Witnessed by Mara.

We have the elderly here. And children.

His hands held his head. Henry's wake, sanctioned but not sacred, the dark knights opposite.

'This is the Police. Clear the park,' said a megaphone voice. 'This is an unauthorized assembly under Article Two of the Crimes Act.

Disperse, or you will be arrested.'

'No way,' said Billy. 'No way.' A loud cheer followed. 'Go on. Arrest us, you bastards. You've no right. Stand, mates. Don't let them through.'

The mob cheered again, louder this time, many with fists clenched.

As his brigade gathered force, the uniforms advanced in well-drilled steps, before rushing, pushing and shoving the people blocking their path.

Kev burst through disbelief, moving forward, not to Mara or Billy, not for his people, not to oppose, not for the gathering. His eyes searched for Danny, his boy near the frontline.

No. Kev lunged towards the line of confrontation where the melee's first blood spilt. He grabbed Danny with the wavy black hair, his son, Bessie's son, turned him, and pulled him away, his boy reluctantly falling back from scrummage.

'Come on. We got work to do,' yelled Kev over the mayhem.

It was something he said to him over the years: 'We've got work to do,' even when he was three years old, until the time he left home. So, his resistance faded, and they retreated, desperate for shelter.

"No" to Blacksmith blood.

"No" to balli-al-mal.

The advancing police overwhelmed night, the first Murris standing against them slipping, falling, pushed and battered towards submission. He could hear the curses, the screams and grunting behind, the casting of implements and weapons on bodies, the pain and intercepting anger. Chairs, bushes, baskets and bicycles were abandoned, overturned, broken or mangled. Children screamed and whimpered.

'Over here,' said a black helmeted figure.

In the darkness, he spied a cavernous shell, a black hole amongst the shadows —the Commodore! The one with two wheels in the park, the driver's door open. Ducking in during the tumult of the charging conquistadors, the heavy hooves of the advancing cops, the skirmish and Murri retreat, metres away. The batons thud, the muffled cries, dust and clenched fists of victims with the gruff, growling determination of the prevailing.

Danny clambered in the back seat, leaving his dad the smaller driver's space, both pulled the doors closed and pitched themselves to the floor. Kev reached out, fumbled and secured the front door locks.

'Lock them. Lock them.'

The clashes outside; thuds, desperate running and scuffling, the chased and the pursuers, the hunters and the hunted. Someone bumped the car. The car body swayed the force of bodies absorbed by the Commodore's silky suspension.

'Farrrk.'

'Give out. You. Hands.'

Someone escaped by pushing off the bumper. The baton swished, and its victim fell on the road, groaning. A short tussle, and, 'Black bastard.'

Handcuffing. Metal clicks.

Another thud. 'Move it.'

Nothing more, except the muttering and groaning of someone being beaten. Other Murris scattered towards the river or scurried into dark laneways. It was all over in a few minutes.

Despite the quiet outside, Kev and Danny held position. Sprawled on the floor in equal silence, Kev's discomfort turned to cramp. His shoulder blade threatened to dislocate itself, and the hot, sharp pain in his rheumatic fingers made his eyes water.

'Sarge. Over here. Got more.'

'Got?'

'You know.'

Someone knocked on the window.

'You, in there. Come out.'

They didn't move.

"No" to balli-al-mal.

The cop pulled at the door handles. 'More, in here.'

'Bloody ABC is here. Keep them busy, will you?'

A resolute thump on the Commodore's windscreen.

'Aaaaah,' roared the officer.

'Give her a bloody wallop, Casey.'

He ingored the hollow conversations, occasional yelling and an faint altercation before silence persisted. After an interminable time on the car's floor, the darkness enveloped them, both alone in their thoughts, but terrorised.

.

PART THREE, Chapter 22

Get Rid of It

After a few reclusive weeks of chaos, confusion and resentment, Danny entered the living room, the fly door slamming behind him. Dad. The town is overrun.'

'What?'

'Cops. Not the old lot. The fucking Riot Squad are here. Farrell's been sent packing. The cop shop's crawling with uniforms.'

Kev sat up. It was his day to man the Op shop. 'Should I go to Vinnies then?'

'Fuck that. Don't go anywhere near the place. That mob's a bunch of racists.'

'Mind your language, son. We got enough troubles without swearing and abuse.'

'Yeh, well, the new uniforms carry bloody great sub-machine guns. People in town are cheering.'

You sure? Have you warned Mara?'

'I'm going around now.'

'Be careful. There'll find any reason to stop you.'

Danny was already at the door before he turned again.

'Oh yes. That's the other thing. The Commodore. We've got to dump the thing.'

The fly door slammed, and he was gone.

The next day he was at him again. 'The car,' he said at the breakfast table, 'If the cops come here, they'll say we stole it.'

Kev nodded without saying anything. He only spread butter over the toast, rising to bring a pot of tea to the table. 'But first, we have to let things settle down.'

'OK, but … this Riot Squad is like an army, at least until the heat hits them. I wouldn't drive that car anywhere.' Danny added jam to his toast, remembering the night the police attacked the wake. Painful memories for both of them; his Dad, because he was the one who negotiated with Farrell, and Murris trusted him; and him, because he was pulled away just when he committed to Billy and his fellows.

For Kev, the car saved them from disgrace and arrest; from being put in front of the court, convicted and gaoled. Only by hiding in the locked car, and laying low, until the crickets drummed, and could they stick up their head. Their bodies glued to the vehicle's vinyl, the boy's shoulder still in pain.

When Kev raised himself, his right head struck the steering wheel. His ear in pain, his face wet with anxiety, he spied the fractured streetlight and the dying embers of campfires. Silence reigning. No cops, no Murris, or passers-by.

Below his chin –hey – silver keys dangled from the ignition.

'Bud. Let's go home.'

Danny scrambled into the front seat, wiped his face with his arm, and scowled. Both hands gripped the dashboard. Some kind of disgust appeared in his son's face. He allowed himself a grim laugh, fixing himself behind the wheel, turning the key in the hope of a purring engine.

Deliverance. A deep throated puurr.

The Commodore hummed and coughed, he hoped the sound didn't resonate across and beyond the park, down the streets or over the river, alerting others to their escape. Putting the vehicle into second gear, eased forward, the clutch poised.

Minimum revs.

Ground crackled and scrunched under the wheels, rolling over grass and twigs. A sudden bump brought it to the road, tyres crackling like fried eggs. He feared the whole world would wake.

Like a ghost in search of quieter haunts, it floated the dark passageways, stole beneath the street light, and passed stands of wattles and shrubs.

On the levee track, the marshy bank loomed. Out of sight, his Dad braked, turned sharp right and put the vehicle into first gear beneath the overhead bridge. Anxious to not endanger the river people holed beneath the iron edifice, he slowed again, wound down the window for fresh air, and steered them to the other side, home a short distance away.

Danny said not a word. his silence persisting as they approached the cottage. The boy's stare verged on sickness, his appalled face angry and confused.

What's the matter with him? Thought Kev. We escaped. Weren't arrested.

Something twisted inside him. But whatever it was would have to wait.

The next morning, he wondered how Billy afforded a late model Commodore. His job didn't pay much. No surprise when his son said 'If the cops find us with this, they'll say we stole it.'

The boy downed his tea and shuffled to the lounge. 'There's a nasty smell to it.'

'What?'

'The car. In the boot.'

'Needs cleaning out.'

Danny slunk into town on unspecified business. After warning others from going, he wondered about the attraction. Given time alone, he went outside to admire his prize, though he asked himself how Billy drove the same model car as the Bicentennial official. Coincidences don't happen in detective work, so Billy's car might be Mr Badger's.

Different colours, but …a scratch will show

 what's beneath.

Within minutes, he had the answer: under the black, a dense grey undercoat, and scratching further, he found the original white.

'Holy –'

Billy offered payment to fetch the stolen vehicle, or at least, one acquired in the worst way. Might this shiny car be a motivation for murder?

'Flaming Hell.' Holding it is a criminal offence.

Mr Badger handed him money too. Though only a stranger asking for a little forgetting, Billy's attempt to recover the VL endangered them.

Billy couldn't afford a new vehicle, not even a Mini. No one amongst us owned a new-model Commodore; and if they did everyone would know about it. To buy a "new" car there meant a vehicle less than three years old. Our second-hand town knew first-hand what it was to be third-rate. Mr Badger's museum proposal beggared belief: his car alone told them they should be thankful for government mercies.

Kev neither liked nor disliked this Bicentennial bloke, even with his impatient way of going about things. The official spoke to him and offered a few bucks for a bit of privacy. Catherine provided him with a tape recorder for his words, and Cheryl promised him a job running the project if he stayed away from "trouble."

He shook his head, reminding himself to be wary of exchanges.

If anyone found the VL in his garage, questions would be asked, and rumours relayed. People would make up wild stories, or worse, accurate guesses. What if they asked about the familiar and mysterious odour coming from the boot? What would be his explanation?

Without the key, what could he do? Sometimes a secret's best kept. Besides, he would never smash up a decent car. Not Kev. Damaging the rear end would be wrong, selling the beast illegal. How do you sell a car with a pong?

Perhaps he didn't want to know the contents, preferring to inspect the driver's domain. He opened and peered past the front door. He could feel Mr Badger's presence. It was his car surely, a flash one for a high official. Hopping into the driver's seat felt like violating the man's authority.

He resolved to keep the Commodore a little longer, as he couldn't park it at the police station and leave a 'Sorry' note on the dashboard. If he or Danny drove it around town, it'd be noticed by a nosy motel manager or any number of people with little to do.

He'd find a solution. This miracle must have been given to him for a reason. It saved

them from arrest, disgrace and goal, leaving him free to find the missing Cliff Badger. If he did so, it would be like minding the car for him.

If only the bloke reappeared.

But if he went to Bourkes, he might be dead.

It's not Billy's, so Danny's right; we've got to get rid of it.

Chapter 23

In October and November, anyone visiting Kev could have seen the Commodore poking from his garage, its black colouration providing faint camouflage. After the events though no one walked up their bush driveway. He was disgraced, and Mara warned people to stay away, leaving him time alone to admire the car's sleek headlights as a shiny testament to their deliverance.

After feeding the chooks, chopping wood and another session talking to the whirling tapes, he took a bucket of soapy water and scrubbing brush and cleaned the dust from the vehicle's bonnet, windows and front chassis. Later, on his seat by the chookhouse, he delighted in the afternoon sunlight deflecting from the headlamps.

A beautiful car.

By now, Cliff Badger might be bullet-ridden, buried in scrubland, or sliced into pieces and thrown in the river. Nothing heard from him. Farrell and his fellow coppers left town without fanfare. No Council or mayoral farewell, and the Bicentennial grant was secured without accounting for a lost representative.

Kev shook his head.

Maybe he's locked in the boot!

Surely not. It's too dreadful a thought.

Cheryl said Mr Badger "was" careless, like she assumed him dead. The new police probably gave him no thought. Nothing in the papers, nor any news about the disappearance of a Bicentennial figure. Coppers hadn't posted a single Missing-Person sign.

What happened to Cheryl's inquiry?

No-one cares.

By late November, the old cops were dispersed across the state to hide embarrassment. The new lot, the TRG or Tactical Response Group, possessed a fancy name but wasn't interested in policing. Sydney's CIB, formed for high-profile disappearances and murders, found the city back lanes more alluring, and financially rewarding.

'Bigger payoff than touring the outback,' Danny opined.

The year drifted to an end, only Christmas to see out before the weeks and months of Bicentennial events and ceremonies. The nation's midnight fireworks, exhibitions and festivals would lead to Australia Day's Tall Ships parade, more sparkle and lights, concerts and a First Fleet re-enactment on January twenty-six. Everything else might be forgotten.

How could he celebrate, holding a stolen vehicle in his garage, its owner likely murdered? Only if Mr Badger returned would everything be OK.

God, help me find him.

With the TRG patrolling the streets, he did not seek company, in or about town. He quit Vinnies and returned to volunteer work at the hospital, on the outskirts, where no one bothered him. If he kept to himself and disturbed no one, people would probably forget after a while. This way he spent more time recording, cleaning the machine heads, and doing house repairs before the next storm threatened. Dust and water make mud, and there is enough of that already.

And Danny? For the last few weeks, he missed his boy's face, his jokey voice or his easy and boyish ways. As far as he could tell, he hung around Mara's, enjoying some hunting, fencing jobs or drumming with a rough band, anything except come home.

When he did, no conversation was possible over loud Metal, Midnight Oil, and AC/DC. According to him, only losers liked country music.

He despaired. Perhaps it would be better if his son returned to Sydney, or Newcastle, or a growth town far from the troubles. With a busy job, he wouldn't hang around pubs and meet 'bad types.'

One night, he walked in, threw down his bag, fell into the lounge and turned on the TV. With their trivial conversation, eventually, it slipped out. 'Got to drive to Sydney tomorrow. Be back on Tuesday.' He jumped up and went to his room.

Going to Sydney, six hundred kilometres away. How? Why?

When he returned later that week, saying nothing, Kev took the initiative.

'Next time, say hello to Billy, will you? And say nothing about the Commodore, right?'

'I can keep a secret.'

He would not demand knowledge of his son's every move; nor humiliate him, their conspiracy, keeping it in the garage, the one thread holding them together.

With Billy in various city courts, and Mara shunning him, at times like these, he sought Cheryl's comfort. Not anymore. Since the cops stormed their wake, she absented herself, cancelling Sunday services, only appearing in the *Advocate* under "Council Business". No more talk of him running the Bicentennial museum, and no mention of Mr Badger. She did not seek him out at Vinnies, or the hospital where he worked when she met patients.

Called the Medical Centre, the hospital was a converted barracks left over from the war, a couple of iron and wood structures without use until they added curtains and windows, cleaned out and installed supplies. The adjacent shed became the garden house, and a parking lot was constructed outside Ward A. Three nurses managed the place without a doctor most days.

Since the arrests, Mara kept to Patchtown, the kid's broken toys, repaired and waiting. She avoided him, probably because he asked too many questions. With Henry's death, Badger's disappearance and the police raid, no denying it, Billy drove his vehicle into the park, and the day he disappeared, she sped past the motel.

The car didn't need a chauffeur; it needed an owner.

Why did he invade the wake that night with a conspicuous Commodore? Why did she make bare-faced denials as they walked to the phone box? Ted had nothing to hide and nothing to gain from his confidences. Since those events, the cops, new and old, questioned no one about that night. Why?

Lastly, what did he mean about keeping her 'under control'?

In the garden shed, he found courage cooked with curiosity when he spied her standing in the car park outside the Casualty ward. He abandoned his shelter and headed for her.

Seeing him approach, she met him stone-faced. 'Who's this,

Dickie?'

Kev stopped and leaned on the rusted railing.

She remained by the old Cortina, Dickie beside her.

'Lad,' he said, dipping his hat to a sometime shearer.

Pleased by the attention, his old comrade smiled and tipped his battered headgear but did not hold out his hand. 'Mate, taking up gardening again?'

Smiling before a frown overtook it, he turned to her. 'Where you been, Mar?'

'Where you been, eh?'

'Funny place to be standing around.'

'Saw your boy, a while back,' she said, changing the subject. 'Driving a hot-looking Falcon.'

'Must be a fence-and-gate job,' he said, ignoring "hot."

'But you don't go fencing with a flash car.'

Kev gripped the railing. 'Cars. Cars. Everyone's blathering about cars.' He took another breath knowing he was in danger of stammering. 'You were seen driving Mr Badger's car, Mara. The Bicentennial bloke. You were.'

'What are you talking about? Who told you this rubbish?'

'You were seen.' Though his words were lame against her denial. 'Mr Badger slept at my place the morning you drove the Commodore through town. I want to know "why," Mar. Tell me where you left it. That would help.'

Her scowl suggested she would bite his head off. After saying more than he once dared, more than he should, more than he might with anyone else if she did assault him, it would no longer hurt. He listened, realizing that his last question implied he did not know the car's whereabouts.

'Kev, times like these, you don't want to know, right? I didn't drive anyone's car I shouldn't have. That's the truth. Whatever happened to Mr Badger, he deserved it; sticking his nose in where it isn't wanted. Just you remember, I didn't take any car. And I don't go stealing them either.'

She's hiding something. Telling me to keep away, like some kind of threat. She's feisty enough because when someone threatens her, she always carries a hammer in her bag; insurance she calls it; the only insurance she ever owned.

Kev took a deep breath and withdrew.

If this is what she wants.

It won't stop me looking or sticking my nose in. Yet …

What if she finds out I garaged the VL?

What if Mr Badger went to Patchtown, found the car, and took on Mara's gang? I'd put a few quid on her winning.

If she drove the car, how did Billy come by it? What happened between his first arrest and arriving at the wake? When and where did he take possession? He stayed quiet on all these matters. No one but the cops knew where he'd been taken.

Once the Cortina left the hospital car park, he sat on the workshop steps. He no longer trusted Billy, and Mara no longer trusted him. With his promise to Cheryl broken, she no longer took an interest. He would not and could not return the Commodore to Billy.

He sighed. Danny was his only friend.

Chapter 24

From the first morning after their escape, Danny said to his Dad, 'Get rid of it.'

'I will. Just you wait,' he said, and the next day covered the VL's bonnet with a tarpaulin so anyone coming up the driveway might not notice. If questions were asked, they would receive evasive answers or fanciful tales.

Danny fumed. 'We can't keep the stupid thing. It smells.' Yeah, his Dad always wanted a fancy car, who wouldn't? 'For Pity's sake, people know we ran that night. If they know how we evaded the cops, we'll be dobbed.'

Dad said he was only minding the thing until the right time. He believed in fate but also the narrow path of Hope.

Kev collected the eggs and considered visiting Mario's general store that morning, but survived on tea, damper, eggs and honey, sitting under a tree and reading an old magazine. With a cool breeze coming off the river, and his Astrology, novels and Readers Digests piled in a corner between the lounge window and the first bedroom, maybe he'd never go to town.

He chuckled. It's been a while since he dug past the towels and pulled out his Arthur Upfield tales.

Which one? *Murder Must Wait* or *The Widows of Broome*? Inspector Boney. Clues! There might be evidence of Mr Badger's whereabouts in the car.

He threw down a magazine and rushed to the garage.

I should be uncovering something not covering. If I take a closer look who knows what I'll find?

He moved the old milk crates, magazines and other half-forgotten treasures out of the garage to gain space.

Good. Now the whole car will fit in.

By afternoon, he started up the vehicle, listening to its rich, throbbing engine before carefully moving it forward. Foot on the clutch, he couldn't help revving the beast.

Wow, impressive.

A roomy interior included a stylish dashboard, plush seats and air-conditioning. Driving that short distance into the cleared space thrilled him.

What kind of people own these cars?

When it bumped into the cardboard he positioned against the wall, he braked. Jumping out, he found the bumper bar firmly against the cushioning, the back end fitted tightly against the garage door.

Better. Should please Danny.

He washed and cleaned the three garage windows, two on the riverbank side. Sticking his head inside with renewed satisfaction, he took in the Commodore's alluring textures, curves and colours, his hands running over leather and vinyl. Intoxicating, though the interior's stale sweat mixed with sweet and salty aromas. A discarded Coke can and cardboard containers from McDonald's lay on the backseat floor.

None of them are from around here. The first Macca's is two hundred kilometres away.

He found a dirty sock, a trampled brown cloth for the duco, and a familiar, crusty substance on the back window.

Shifting to the front seats, so many people had already sat in the driver's seat, four he knew: himself, Mr Badger, Mara and Billy, and maybe more. The dashboard and passenger seat had been given an admirer's rub and scrub, with a small screwdriver jammed against the windscreen. Everything else was stuffed in the glove box: a Sydney Street Directory, a crushed state map, scissors, chewing gum, drawing pins – ouch – a couple of pens and a toiletries sponge bag.

To be thorough, he opened the bag, though he felt silly looking into someone else's private possessions.

Soap, cloth, and — a handgun!

Holy mackerel.

He pulled out the cowboy-like gun. A replica? It's heavy.

He put his nose to the barrel, sniffed it and opened the casing.

Lord! One bullet is missing.

He whipped it back into the bath pack.

It's been fired, and I handled it. My prints are on it.

I won't tell Danny.

One bullet fired. The Bicentennial official must be dead. Or what?

If I remove my hand prints, I might be removing the killer's.

If I leave them, it will be construed as "proof" that I murdered him.

Nothing for it. For Danny's sake, I'll clean the gun. I'll dump the car. If we're discovered with this little beauty, the spotlight will turn on us.

We'll be hunted down like Jimmy Blacksmith. But the disgrace will kill me first.

Chapter 25

Dad has his head in the clouds, thought Danny, hovering around little things, distracted by the tape recording, his thoughts and ideas amounting to nothing. With Mr Badger's disappearance and the crushing disappointment of events, the VL Commodore became an obsession. Like a respectable townie, he believed he might have owned a sleek late-model.

Fat chance. He's never been the same since mum died.

He admired Billy most of all. On his first city run for Bourkes Garage, he stayed with him in Sydney. Met the big mob. They respected him for defending his country Murris, standing his ground, word, going to gaol, fighting the cops all the way. Mara too. She had more guts than his dad, that's for sure; collected money for Henry's wife on the bridge, and stood up at the Council meeting, contemptuous of Cheryl Sheila. With her takeover of Patchtown, her rebel spirit spilt around the district. The fence-fixers, part-time shearers and other black fellows took notice.

That night of the wake, he wanted to be with the other men, scraping with bastard coppers. His dad always ensured no one from his family landed in trouble.

He's stuck in the old, timid ways, not ready for real action. He doesn't understand that if I were arrested and thrown in gaol, it wouldn't matter. We're in it together. He's afraid of balli-al-mal. We defy it.

His dad was obsessed with the pink-assed Badger, of all people, a Sydney bigwig. The guy's dead and gone, nothing surer.

The night of the Council meeting, he learnt that Mara and her mob hounded the Bicentennial official out of Patchtown, the bloke scouting for sex with Chrissie, or anyone else he ran into. Disgusting.

I'm not telling Dad. It'll only complicate matters.

He wanted to say to him: What about caring for Henry and all Murris? We're poor, proud and scarred, not some bureaucrat from the big city.

But he couldn't say it, and bit his lip on his nights home. Instead, in the comfort of his childhood bed, a waxing moon shone through the bedroom window only weeks before Christmas. When the cool air that drifted off the river disappeared his thoughts and the dry heat kept him awake. He wiggled and twisted on the sheets. His hands rubbed his flush face. He sweated.

It's futile talking to Dad. He's got fixed ideas.

Yet, he had to listen to him, his words sincere, quietly spoken, without anger. Infuriating. His huge silences tugged at his heart, making his passion wane and his self-belief evaporate. In face-to-face talks, his dad intoned his mother's memory, the rippling lines on his forehead a measure of his compassion and experience. They wept, so he put aside his beliefs for the sake of his parents and all who came before him.

Patchtown offered another solace. Mara welcomed him around the campfire and hugged him. They sit outside on the old lounges from the tip, poke the fire, drink a little, laugh and conspire to do everything to win justice, no matter what. The police were the enemy; the government too: magistrates, politicians and all their hangers-on. Mr Badger was all talk. Bicentennial money will never go in Murri's pockets. Little wonder he got his comeuppance from Billy.

Whoever knocked him off deserves a medal.

With her encouragement, he determined to stay away from the Unity's do-nothing drinkers, instead, visiting the rival Shearers Arms.

Damn the Unity.

Damn the cops.

And damn Dad.

* * *

The town's second pub attracted a different clientele: men from the kangaroo factory, motor mechanics, contractors and shopkeepers, and even a few schoolies and truckers, all talking rugby league, horses and pool. He'd fit in.

A South Sydney supporter from go-to-woe (and there was plenty of woe), he liked talking engines and car models. They divided into the Holden or Ford tribe, and go-hide if you talked Toyota.

The Arms sponsored a touch-footy competition, and looking for sport, the guys in "Rogue's Corner", the self-styled Hard Boys, drew him in. Led by Pete Bourke, Paddy's son, he could see a bit of fun in them. They liked a practical joke, an occasional flutter on the nags, a few beers, and a day out. He could outrun any of them, so he stepped forward.

'How about it? I can run the legs off any of the others.'

Long-faced Con eyed him up and down, without saying 'But he's a boong.'

Danny absorbed his glare and pulled away.

'Hold on,' said Pete. 'Reckon you can play like Simmo?'

'Maybe.'

'Come on, lads. Give him a go.' He smirked at the lad's fine physique. 'We want to win a few games.'

'I can do that.'

'There'll be a fee,' he said.

'What?'

'A round of beers for the Hard Boys.'

Pete's word won the day. He joined the team, and weeks later qualified as one of them. He worked for Paddy running 'hot' cars between cities and the larger country centres. They eliminate a vehicle's identity by knocking off the engine plate, giving them a coat of paint, and wham, a new car is born.

Bourke and the Hard Boys had similar ideas to Mara: the police were the enemy, to be evaded, avoided, misled, and, in some cases, paid off. Unlike her though, Paddy Bourke had the old cops under control: fooled, charmed or favoured, they needed him for vehicle repairs, hot tips, favourable arrangements and occasional license.

It would have stayed "cool" if events hadn't ruined things. Henry's death-in-custody disrupted business when the new mob moved in. With the media in town asking questions and inviting comments his workshop needed to start again. With twice the police numbers and all strangers, it would take ages to become familiar. In the months ahead, they needed to keep their comings and goings unnoticed. With a Murri on board, they had an extra source of information, putting them in better shape for the changed circumstances. With the new copper's threatening presence on the streets, they might poke their noses where they're not wanted.

'If we want to stay in business,' he told the Hard Boys, 'don't be smart-asses.'

Paddy's steely gaze of enforcement froze anyone's soul, and his stare lingered longest on his son. To "measure up", he had to be hardened.

Pete offered his own rules. 'We're the Hard Boys. We never dob. Golden rule. We're making money. Doing nobody no harm. Sticking together, right? Have a lot of fun. Get laid, go revhead. But never, ever dob.'

All present nodded. Never rat on a mate, on Paddy, or the Hard Boys. Danny too. He would never dob on his Dad or Mara or Billy. Though the Bourkes would love a late-model Commodore for trading purposes, no one must know he kept one in their garage, including the Hard Boys.

Chapter 26

Kev settled into a routine without Mara, Billy and the others. He went to town weekly and twice a week helped around the hospital as groundsman and general handyman, sharing friendly relations with the nurses and the ill. He enjoyed cheering up patients, cleaning and sharpening garden tools and reordering the shed. Over lunch, he shared a cuppa in the staff annexe called 'La Canteen.'

He stayed home with Skipper and the tape recorder most days, striking up amiable conversation with either, the machine more attentive. His recording reminded him of Catherineof Canberrs, a figure for something better, something kinder. No doubt he wished Bess was still with him, that he was younger and more educated. Though rich with memories, they carried regrets too. But if others valued them, he would record all he could remember or tell without fearful retribution.

Each morning, he removed the bath towelling from the red and grey recorder, placed it in the centre of the kitchen table and took a seat with his back to the light. Before and after, he made notes.

Switching on the machine, he talked, hesitated, and spoke again, glancing at his writing pad or watching the tapes turn. Within those walls, he teased out the past, made sense of things and reflected on himself and his family, and recalling the old ways.

Speaking Gundabarri was easy enough, though explaining how the language worked challenged him. He pronounced the old expressions, their intonations, nuances and meanings, sometimes in sentences.

'Madda means "take." Maddang, "I give." Being opposites, together, as Nadda, is "trading." You might trade a goodaroo or, what some call, the nulla-nulla; or the bundi or shield, for pushing away missiles. We'd use them to jump up, and push away, like in a game, playing around.'

Later, his voice trailed to a moan, the recording capturing rough, furious sounds, attacking the microphone.

'Raining outside. Hear it?'

The machine's electronic hiss recorded pelting, beating and striking the fibro walls and galvanised iron roofing.

'On top. Too much noise. Enough.'

Clunk.

Afterwards, the storm relented ... cl-lunk.

'That. Is a dry storm. (A little laugh.) It's raining dust, knocking scrub and sand about. No massive lightning, mostly wind. Better now. I'll have another go.'

For a while, he didn't speak, sitting under his homely roof sniffing a faint dusty aroma, in a place surpassing all storms.

He jerked. 'My ceiling again. Still rattling.'

Every time a storm attacked, wet or dry, the house breathed. The wind would suck air through the manhole and other gaps, letting in fine dust or water seepage. Even then, insects sought safety inside his walls, so all his biscuits were stored in old tins left over from earlier times.

A year ago, he wrapped a brick in gift paper, fetched a hook from the shed, and screwed one into the manhole cover. Using rope, he hung the brick as an anchor. Suspended above his bed, the Christmas wrapping cheered him though he had to move the bed in case the brick dropped.

When the storm relented, he commenced recording again.

'Might be a time to talk about the river, about the fish traps the anthropologist bloke wrote about a long time ago. Good job he did. Don't know if I can add much.

'Upstream - that's different. Gundabarri has names for all them river bends Biowin, Buckcunyah, Billibumbo, Cudgina. There are more, though I can't name them all. Maybe old Elsie can help.

'On the first bend, you can still find people's bones sticking out there. Our people massacred out Carnival Creek way, killed trying to escape, swimming the river. Shot dead.'

The tapes hissed and crackled like eggs and bacon in a frying pan. Kev sat there, staring, shoulders drooped. Skipper lifted his head, alert to his master's statuesque frame, rising to his front legs in anticipation. When he stared back at him, he settled down.

'Have to work slowly sometimes, because I can't find the right words. I go back a long way, imagining I'm around the campfire again, hearing them fellas talk to me, listening to the old men.

'This Gundabarri. Not many speak it now, so you might not believe me. You might think I am lying, making it all up. I'm not.'

Kev took a deep breath, let his head drop, and released air.

'I'm leaving town soon. Talk to old Elsie. She might put me right. Her language is better than mine.' He rubbed his hands together as if dark matter stuck to his palms and would not rub off.

'This storm could ruin the tape, for sure. I'm finishing up.'

Keeping the recorder in running order, meant wrapping and unwrapping it in a plastic sheet, and storing it in his cleanest cupboard well above the floor. He vacuumed around it too and cleaned the cupboard with a dry-cleaner's cloth. He soaked a finer one in plain alcohol before finding the recorder's inside reaches, all the surfaces he dared touch.

So far, it worked. The machine gave him only minor battery and head pressure problems. He struggled with modern electronics. Despite everything, he feared his machine might break down. If he could not fix it, his project would be over.

Catherine wrote two letters to him, recalling their first meeting and chats about the upcountry rains, when the swollen river broke its banks, spreading across the plain. In reply, he joked that when his cottage flooded he only stayed dry under the water tower.

In her second, she thanked him profusely for his recordings, and said he made a "great advance" on their knowledge of Gundabarri and its speakers; no one had given them so much. She and her academics were eager for more.

That dust storm also wrote a letter, its fury reminding him of the night police charged him and his people in the park, at Henry's wake, advancing on his mob without notice.

Storming.

He could not wipe away memories so they sat on his shoulders most nights, beating on his ears. Billy and the others suffered because of those skirmishes, arrested and beaten, women and children cursed and terrified, including Henry's wife and mother. He tried forgetting, for sure, but a bitter taste lingered, even as he sipped his milky tea, no sugar.

Chapter 27

When Danny returned from Sydney, he asked his dad again, 'When are we getting rid of it? Isn't the Commodore Billy's?'

'I don't think so,' said Kev.

He wanted to let the matter rest but Danny insisted, 'We can sell it.'

'No. It's not right taking money that's not yours.'

'Not right? A stolen car is sitting in our yard. It's using our space.'

'I'm thinking about the next move.'

'It'd fetch a couple of thousand.'

'No, son. We're not like that.'

Danny thrust an arm to the air and paced the room. 'Jez, Dad. We can't sit about any longer. This ain't the old days. It's hot, I'm guessing. The cops might nab us, anytime.'

His dad turned to him, face haggard. 'Look, I haven't told you but...I scratched the duco and found white beneath the black.'

'So, it *is* hot.'

'No. Well, maybe. Perhaps Billy bought the VL from someone else. I don't know. You stayed in Sydney. What did he tell you?'

'Nothing; except he wants his air-conditioning back.'

'You didn't tell him about ...'

'No,' said his son.

'Fact is, Mr Badger drove a white Commodore. The same vehicle.'

'Him! Shit.' Danny bit his lip. 'So how did Billy ...?' Realising his dad's suspicions... 'Him, murder the bloke?' He let out a whistle. 'You think ...'

Kev didn't say what he thought. His head spun and his hand brushed his scalp.

Danny collapsed on the lounge. 'He wouldn't.'

They both took a deep breath to recover their wits. Kev sat with his son to address the other matter. He took a deep breath. 'You're working for the Bourkes, aren't you?'

Danny wiped his hands against his new jeans. 'So?'

'They're trouble, mate, that's what they are.'

'You wanted me employed.'

'Those filing tools I found at the tip, remember them? They're used to remove the engine plate on stolen cars. What would your mother think? You could be in gaol before long.'

'Whiskey?'

His dad's eyes sank. The two of them stood in the room, backs to each other, lost for words. How would he explain? How could he tell his son about his detective work and the fingerprints on the gun wiped clean? He had been sloppy and could not afford another mistake.

Blacksmith blood is a curse.

Danny too kept his thoughts to himself. Some of his school friends had been arrested on the day the police raided the wake. But not him. 'Were you across the road or … where?' one said as if he must have run from the men in blue.

For months now, the odd-named Tactical Response Group had invaded, inhabited and overwhelmed the town, pounding the streets with repeat rifles in three-hour spells in dark uniforms. It was summer, for God's sake. They sweated like pigs in armour.

Townspeople's common bickering was pronounced suspicious, daily given a hard time by the police. Any fracas around the pubs and clubs would bring cops waving truncheons and semi-automatics, prodding and pushing disputants down the street until residents ran like rats through the narrow alleys between the shops. Lockdown, they called it.

With the ongoing harassment, Danny wanted his dad to dump the vehicle in the outback's endless expanses. In complete secrecy, a skill Murris knew about only too well. Give them air to breathe.

Nevertheless, he was tempted to ask Pete Bourke how much they could get for an as-new Commodore but held his tongue. He'd keep quiet a little longer. But something must be done.

'You've told no one, right, Dad?'

'Right.'

'So, we dump the VL?'

Kev nodded. If anyone found out about this, there'd be plenty of talk and the TRG would arrest them for car theft. Soon enough, they'd charge them with murdering Badger. If they returned the Commodore with or without the handgun, the cops would still suspect them. "No-hopers" in police eyes, they were ripe for a round-up, a tour in the paddywagon, conviction and prison. After all, the TRG were in town to whack troublemakers, and with no blood on the truncheon, a murder conviction would provide them with credibility. Might earn them a medal or two.

His dad was the last person to talk to Badger and being painfully honest, he would admit it to someone. From someone to someone else until they'd be charged with breaking any number of laws, and risk Henry's fate.

The court magistrate would readily agree: judged guilty.

Danny thumped his skull. They must protect themselves, Mara and Billy too. But what if one of them murdered Badger?

Danny fell on the cushions, his face as pale as a Gubba's.

'You alright?' said Kev.

All right? Nothing was all right. 'Look, if you won't sell the beast, dump it upriver. No one will ever find it.'

'We will, but not with our ancestor's bones. There's a better place.'

Chapter 28

With the slam of the fly-screen door, they left home after midnight. The roosters panicked, and the stern-faced Barking Owls flew from the scrub over the moonless river. With his better eyesight, Danny would drive the Commodore.

The car loaded, Kev beat away regrets while his son started the engine, letting it purr in gratitude. Easing the beast forward, only millimetres from the garage walls, they avoided the leopard bushes by turning sharp right to the driveway. His dad hopped out and swept away the tyre marks in the sand with a casuarina branch until they entered Gumby Road.

Taking another gravel way, they headed away from town and the river. A minor track around the tip, took them south, bypassing residential lights. No cop would be awake at this hour, or so they hoped.

Riding the anonymous grey surface in an ocean of black, only their parking headlights illuminated the way. Passing several kangaroos, eyes alert, a few other animals sprung up and hopped into the bushes. A goanna scurried to safety from its warm dust bath.

'Like being a thief,' said Kev.

He disliked the secretive night movements characterizing many country towns: the liquor and cigarette hauls, the drunks with their grog disguised in brown paper bags, the sheep duffers, car shufflers, and the marijuana hauliers using the Sydney back roads. He abhorred breaking the law. Hiding evidence and stealing cars didn't sit well.

Regrets.

Conspiracies.

It all carried a sense of disgrace, going against his every fibre. About to dump a new Commodore, and a gun fired in anger, with a familiar, foul smell coming from the back, it nagged him. Could

Badger's corpse be in the boot? If it did, he be guilty of one more crime and free from one more burden.

To protect Danny, Mara and Billy from the police, from balli-almal, he pushed the thought to the back of his mind. They might have moved the Commodore interstate or disguised it with a myriad of stolen vehicle tricks-of-the-trade. Or firebomb it. Removing the engine number would delay the authorities. But he would dispense with the VL his way. In the webs of forgetting and remembering, they were heading for Phil's Hole, a past unknown to his son. One way or another, Phil would be there.

* * *

He met Phil Nichols many years earlier, in the neighbouring district when his boy still suckled from his mother's breast. A bloke in his sixties, he had considerable years on him, turning up unannounced, taking up Yantalah Station in poor country.

Locals were suspicious. You would never grow much out there. Not enough feed for sheep or cattle either.

Bit of a loner this guy; comes to town once a fortnight, less when it rained and the roads became impassable.

It took time to find out about him, and Kev found out before anyone. Only natural, collecting food, gear and supplies, wrapping them in a tarp all stuffed in the boot.

The car betrayed him. He owned a custard-coloured 1964 Holden FJ. You needed to be well-off to own a vehicle in those days.

Back then, a new model excited him, though it didn't impress the town's 'better' families when he didn't join the tennis club. Weeks turned to months, and the locals within a hundred kilometres of scrubland decided to ignore him and his worthless property. They decided the car was just another way of getting attention. They recognized pretenders. So, when Kev showed an interest in what lay beneath the bonnet, Phil responded.

'A beautiful piece of engineering. Two-point-one-cc, sixty-nine horsepower at 3800 rpm, water-cooled four-stroke, six cylinders. It'll do a quarter mile, standing start, in twenty seconds.' He turned his head in admiration and ran his hand along the mudguard. 'Brand, spanking new.'

'Have a radio?'

'Yep. And a speaker. Cigarette lighter, ashtray, glove compartment, speedometer, petrol gauge, heat indicator.' No doubt about his enthusiasm.

They soon learnt another shared interest in Heaven and Earth, in Astronomy. Phil knew the heavens as well, or better, than him. Star charts hung from his walls, a small book collection on the dining table. At night, sitting outside on a leather lounge, surrounded by bushland, they viewed the constellations to the sound of crickets, dingoes and hooting owls. Sometimes, they walked into the mulga, away from the homestead light. A few 'roos would panic, and dash through scrub.

Positioning his telescope under lamplight, they focused on the skies for hours in darkness. Times like these, he recalled boyhood stories when he and the old men left the mission for a week, going walkabout, as some say.

One night, he wondered aloud: 'Where are the fields, the crops or gardens? Or cattle. He had fertilizer, didn't he?

Phil grew cagey. 'Keep your mind on the bloody job,' putting an eye to the telescope again.

Kev shut up. No point annoying him.

For months, Phil didn't talk about his farm or his work out back. Though fit enough, he said he wouldn't stretch the hours to make the country productive. As a former miner, his retirement venture would be a garden, penned chickens, and a small workshop, a million acres left for the roos, emu and dingoes.

Not that Kev farmed or ran cattle; too hard and unforgiving, though he noticed the bloke bought fertilizer one week and collected fuel the next. He gave it quiet thought.

With fertilizer, you can make explosives.

As a retiree with a generator, the bloke worked in the night cool, the chemicals more stable. With a mining lease, he might dig for opal, silver or gold. Men grew secretive about mines.

Hostile to his curiosity, Phil was not necessarily greedy or desperate, but kept the information to himself, lest others move on him. This far out of town, he could detonate explosives. Bigger ones would be harder to keep secret, especially when black fellows still wandered around properties like they owned them. The better one's bare feet would feel the Earth vibrate.

He sought fraternity after a couple of weeks, and settled back to their easy conversations, mostly. Talking about the weather would be safe, but not always.

'When the heavens open up five hundred kilometres upstream, the rain saves us,' said Kev, the river formed in Bathurst and Chinchilla's back hills.

Sitting on his verandah, the panorama of scrubland before them, flattish country, a curious mix of blue and grey as far as you cared to scan. A few unspectacular rises too, but Phil's place sat on a lower rise, the view good enough to dissuade anyone seeking higher ground.

'Flooding; massive, bloody floods,' said Phil, taking a breath of outback air. Kev grinned and said nought. 'Did you know, you dig deep enough, you nearly always find water? So much, you need a million years of pumping to make a mark. More water comes from underground than above.'

'You reckon?'

'The Great Artesian Basin, mate. When your Bible talks of the flood, where do you think the water came from? Breaks from beneath, shoots out in springs and the like. Ka-boom. Water from below. Could happen any moment. It's all there, you know, from underground.'

Rain brought inundations; made the Great Flood, water pouring from the heavens, according to Kev.

'From underground, mate. Deep below,' said Phil, eyes fixed, and fist pointed down. 'As the Earth cools, all the water mixed in rock comes to the surface, making seas, oceans and lakes. It's geology.' He didn't think so, but Phil wasn't finished. 'Or else the Earth sucks, and swallows us up.'

Kev poked and jammed his stick in a floorboard gap. Sure, he thought, bore water came from below, though it didn't amount to much around here. He couldn't think what to say to this scary, half-crazy guy. The Bible only talked of God's creation. Noah's Ark saved people from flood, the water from the heavens. In black fellow legend, the spirits came from the sky, from all around us. With the space and planets and stars, science and religion sat together. Blackfellow religion. Christian religion. Science. For him, water fell from above. Below is where the evil dwells; black or white spirits, from a darkness that dogged his kind.

'What's the matter?' said Phil, screwing his eyes, his mate red-faced. 'Out of sorts?'

'Hmm. Right.'

He enjoyed this man's company, and with his silence, he would keep it that way.

* * *

Danny carefully negotiated the corrugations, swerving around loose rocks and common ruts, progressing the sandy track, a bare glow to the east. In the night's cool airs, they pushed past a disintegrating gate before moving up a gear on firmer soils, heading for the derelict property.

Kev's lips pursed. After Henry's death and Badger's disappearance, his and his son's future were as uncertain as Phil's had been. Fatalism scorched their spirit, though he and Danny had different ideas about how and why this happened. Cliff Badger though, left no note, explanation or hint of his whereabouts. Simply paid him twenty dollars to tell no one of his overnight stays. Inclined to keep his word, he suspected the Bicentennial official might be dead, perhaps locked in the Commodore's boot. But if he told anyone, it would bring disaster, for him, the boy and all Murris. Blacksmith trouble.

For a month, Phil stopped coming to town, and Kev puzzled meetings missed, whereabouts unknown. Strangers came and went in country towns; and many went to considerable effort to display their indifference. No phones out there. A bloke like him came to town without tennis commitments, community meetings or any other obligations; he only came for supplies, and that counted against him. If he displayed no interest in townspeople, they would do the same to him.

Having not seen him a while, he borrowed a motorbike and steered his way along the gravel highway before turning on Phil's track, passing high clumps of dogwood, pulling up low, sandy rises, crossing rocky puddles and skirting slippery, clay patches. Took most of an hour.

At the farmhouse, Kev yelled his arrival, though the noise of his unhinged bike would have alerted anyone. The two-bedroom bungalow had an ample veranda down two sides, a wood and iron structure open to scrutiny from the clearing, an unattached bathhouse and laundry nearby.

Finding the house unlocked, he walked into the living room where everything appeared normal, though not quite. Below an upper window, a layer of dust covered the near coffee table. He ran his finger over the surface; last week's rain and wind left its mark, so no one had been here for a while.

Where is he? Either he's abandoned it, or …

He went outside, heading for the galvanised iron shelter, some way past the pit toilet, spotting two empty bags dried on the peg line.

Must be a storage area nearby.

The fertilizer!

If he made explosives, it would be at least a hundred metres from the fuel depot.

With stains down one side of the garage, and a minor track disappearing into the scrub, he dived into the saltbush, discovering a wooden bench with glass jars, string, rope and a stump seating. No metal.

There would be tracks, he thought, though any footprints had been obliterated by last week's rain. Going to a distant wheelbarrow at the base of the nearest slope –there! A hole in the ground, a ditch, wider than a truck, with no end in sight.

Too big for a well.

Coming closer, his eyes adjusted from bright daylight, the descent at an angle against a rise. Curiosity turned to dread. With another step, he spied a set of rough-cut path. Not really a mine, more like an inexact adit. Never heard of a mine with steps into it.

Rock and gravel were piled around the coolabahs.

Need explosives to make this.

Kev stood stone still. Out west, you entered a place and walked up steps, never down. He always walked up an embankment, stepped up to an office, or into a shopkeeper's home over their business. Walked to the Courthouse, to the cop shop, to the boss-cocky's verandah (or as far as you were allowed), even for some shearing pens.

But walk down, into darkness?

It meant nothing to Phil. A miner started his day stepping into the Earth's pitch, out of sight and wearing a light. He descended tunnels undaunted, spiralling into the eternal without a car, a journey to gold, silver or some imagined treasure. Like any of his fraternity, he accepted that every step might be his last.

Kev detected an abyss, remembering another set of steps to a cellar below the old grain store. Old Kennedy, years back, used to imprison aboriginal girls, keeping them to satisfy his lust.

He jerked to attention, directing his torch inside, seeing muck, broken wood and jagged rock. He moved forward, the cavern closing on him. Ahead, a rope led to the pitch so he followed. After a few more, the air chilled, cold and dry like an ice chest.

With a bend ahead, he shone the torch further, spying a strange, soft grey shape, something recognizable. At the rope's end, a shrivelled hand clutched a rope, unmistakably fingers and a thumb clenching.

Phil. Must be him.

There's nothing much left.

He gripped the jagged rock and leaned against the wall, letting his head rest, dizzy. His stomach in his mouth, he vomited and retched.

Afterwards, he returned to the grizzly remains, looking to a single aura of light across the shadowy steps, a sickly cascade.

He left Phil where he found him, in bits and pieces, in darkness.

Months later, no one asked after him or sought him out. Ashamed of himself and the town, he told no one. What could he do when no one listened to him or believed his witness? As it was for his kind. So in many outback centres, their motto was "never talk" about unsettling affairs, not where others listen nor let events upset business-as-usual.

Practical forgetting. Proper forgetting.

Now he stood before Phil's Hole again, his son by his side. They would run the VL into the cavern, snuffing out the memory of Mr Badger's prized possession.

Bury it, thought Kev.

Bury it, thought Danny.

With one last glint from the car's stainless-steel strip, Kev watched the Commodore enter the adit with a red-and-grey halo.

On the first crunching drop into its depths, the suspension rode well before – bang, the floor hit and pushed sideways. The next proved steeper, the underbelly ploughing against rock and gravel, its rear rising skyward, back wheels sliding into darkness. The car screeched, slid and thumped on unseen steps, threatening to crash. The brakes applied, the Commodore eased in until halted– thump, the vehicle swallowed in black.

Kev felt a technician's regret. A beauty lost, all around him the eucalypts reached for the stars. He rubbed his cooling body, only the dim tail lights suggesting the vehicle's existence when they too faded.

The driver's door groaned, and a chaotic light danced through the cavern as Danny emerged. The two men gathered mulga and acacia, creating a bush screen across the entrance. Wordless, they tied successive layers with mallee stakes and small rope packets, disguising the site with three native bushes taken from his nursery. In a few weeks, unless you knew Phil's Hole, the Commodore would never be found.

Never.

Because they worked in easy cooperation, Kev wanted to hug his son, to congratulate him for using traditional techniques with a new purpose. In collective efforts, he hoped they shared a future together.

It could not be here, not in conspiracy, not where Phil blew himself apart, his remains scattered over the cave walls like stars in the heavens.

An indecent burial.

Danny traversed the adit without dread, or the burden of history, possessed of youth and masculine strength. The anguished cries of yesteryear and the cruel twists and turns of misfortune eluded him. He entered night without fear, without knowing or caring what came next, without the caution befitting his people.

Phil had been fearless too, and the Earth took its revenge. He dabbled in darkness, amongst the bubbling underground spring waters, against God's command.

You don't dabble with Dynamite.

He feared for Danny. Perhaps disposing of the Commodore was futile. Putting the matter behind them, like collective forgetting, might not block out evil, but lock it in.

PART FOUR, Chapter 29
It's All About

Chief Warren called a squad meeting in their cramped police station's tiny offices despite the prevailing wall of heat, and unreliable air conditioning. He expected everyone to present in a spotless uniform, order and discipline his motto.

'Straighten the tie, detective,' he said to Cassidy as he entered the staff area. 'Chris: remove the pin from the lapel. We're not a charity.' He swung around. 'Listen up.'

He surveyed his squad arrayed about the filing cabinets, desks and chairs, glaring at those leaning on the scuffed walls. 'Shortie: turn up the bloody air-conditioning.'

Geoff Short adjusted the rattling yellow unit poking through the wall, and everyone relaxed.

'Righto. We've been here a few months. Had enough marching around town?' A few smirks and jostling before the boss' scowl cut the din. 'Had enough sweating it outside pubs?' No acclaim this time. 'Enough carrying weaponry and cooling down the natives in this shithole?' Chuckles and laughter. 'We scorched Main Street, and every other bastard holding cold beers? Well, we've had it easy.'

Warren glanced at his notes, and might paced the room were it possible. 'We received a brief to lockdown this place, and men, we've done it, right?' The squad mumbled, tempted to say "sure we have." They'd spent weeks patrolling the lanes, parks, schools and shops, breaking up petty fights and stepping on toes. Nothing much to speak of.

'Mateys, it\s time we swung into town policing. Remember theft, graffiti, licensing, motor vehicle accidents, neighbourhood arguments, and missing persons? Thought you'd left the plod, eh? Well, for now, we TRG have nothing better to do than police this rathole while the pollies promise the world to the general public, at least until the election is out of the way.'

The men cackled. Johnnie Crowbar even let out a hoot, the boss' stern look silencing him, and others on the landing.

'A special case arrived yesterday. A Bicentennial official, Mr Clifford Badger, disappeared not long before we camped here. Went missing, unseen in Sydney or elsewhere.' Warren picked up a sheet of paper. 'On August twenty-second. Last seen at the Council meeting on the night of the twenty-first, when he had a difference of opinion with, guess who, Billy the Revolutionary, chief rioter, the one causing the ruckus now in the Big Smoke.'

Astonished glances to fellow officers.

'That's not all. It seems Councilor Sheila also attended, and she is Badger's ex-wife. Huge secret this. Town don't know about it, so we'll bust her. They divorced nine years ago, so they didn't exactly get on. Put that in the mix. Topping it off, Madame herself informs us on the quiet, her hubby called on Kev Trust the morning of his disappearance. He's the other riot leader. Boom. Next day, Cliff Badger disappears.'

'Whoa,' his men roared.

'Wham, bam, thank you, mam,' said another to laughter.

Warren let the hubbub die down.

'Shush!' They did. 'Kev lives alone in the scrub, upstream from the bridge. Thin, weedy guy. Not often seen. He's the one who organized Henry what's-his-name's funeral, and the park wake, and a shit-fight that followed. Killed-off the local coppers.'

He paused for effect. 'Now, here's the thing, might have a murder on our hands, and if we cleaned up this mob, a media-feeding frenzy. With all the who-ha about the Bicentenary and this damn Royal Commission, the blacks plan to disrupt Australia Day. Full-scale terrorism. Direct from headquarters.'

Warren held the floor, lingering on his men's faces. 'Could be a hell of a lot happening under our noses.

'Yep. This is TRG territory. It's our job, and I mean *our* jobs, on the line. We've got revolutionary Billy mouthing off in Sydney, surrounded by his pro bono lawyers. Nothing we can do about them. We got Cheryl big-tits Sheila on Council, helping us out and covering her arse. We got

Princess Mara of Patchtown, don't forget her, with her gang of boofheads. Lastly, Kev. Lives close to town and is the last man to see Badger alive. That's right, all info care of good ole Sheila.'

Quick side-glances; heads rocked.

'So, who's our Head Honcho? Kev? He is a friend of the other two, and, he's the quiet one. And get a load of this.' The Chief showed a rare smirk. 'He has the hots for Councilor Sheila. Badger's ex-wife. Might be motive.'

Meaty stuff. Raised eyebrows everywhere. Shortie elbowed Cassidy as others laughed, giggled and tittered.

'Hold on. Whoa. Understand that radicals like Mansell and Dodson are mouthing off about Gaddafi and guns, revolution and revenge. On January twenty-six, expect trouble. They're preparing for a black uprising. It's up to us to ensure it doesn't happen.'

Everyone nodded, the cool-heads keeping their arms folded, and pursing their lips.

'Our first task is to seize weapons from the blacks. Detective Hanna, interview Kev. Badger visited his place the morning after the Council meeting. While you're asking questions, check for anything hidden in his shack. He's a bit of an organizer, possibly Badger's murderer, so keep your wits about you.

'Go after Princess Mara too. Find what she's hiding. There's something very smelly out there.' The men laughed at that as most of them drove out that way and spied only disgusting shanties. Warren absorbed the kudos. 'Tell her straight: we're investigating a murder. Check her whereabouts. Put the wind up her.'

He turned to Cassidy. 'Cass. Comb the scrub country and hit all the black haunts. Confiscate weapons and find people doing shooting practice. We've got to disrupt them. Arrest them. They need weapons, transport and money for their dirty deeds. They'll keep Badger's car. Find it. A white VL Commodore. If the blacks are behind his disappearance, chances are they'll trade dope for cash and weapons.'

The air-conditioning conked out. With sweaty bodies jamming the room, the Chief removed his hat and loosened his tie, despite his demands. He rubbed his balding head with a handkerchief as his unsightly underarm drew sly winces.

'All right? This ain't a holiday. All rosters are unchanged. Let's move.'

With their dismissal, Cassidy approached him with his cap underarm. 'Chief. Why is the Lebo dong the interrogations?'

Warren waved his hand. 'Mate: you're the one searching for weapons, not Hanna. Think about it. He looks a bit like them, right? Let him chase this Cliff Badger. Who cares? He might land some info. Might be helping *you* find the guns.'

Cassidy's downturned lips matched his stony face.

Warren insisted. 'Forget it. If Hanna can't force their hand, we'll send you in. Let the Lebo do the softly-softly.' Cassidy warmed a little. 'I've every confidence in you, my friend. OK?'

'We'll see.'

'You mean, "Yes, sir." Say it.'

'Yes. Sir.'

Chapter 30

After posting another tape to Canberra, Kev spied his son in the Shearer's Arms Beer Garden with young Pete Bourke, Con, and Ginger Taylor, Paddy's enforcers. Not a pleasing sight, although he acknowledged him with a wave.

'Dinner at six-thirty.'

He turned on *Country Hour,* and while he peeled potatoes and cut carrots, sang along with *Good Old Why Does It Have to Be (Wrong or Right)*. Tossing the veggies into his misshapen pot, he sprinkled salt to the rhythm and added tap water. Fetching steaks from the fridge, he pounded them with a tenderizer and rolled the beef in a cloth to keep off the flies.

Like Bess did.

He lit the gas as *Saving My Love For You* played over the currawong calls when the lounge room light came on.

'Hey,' said Danny, 'some light.'.

Kev worked at the gas flame. After he put the pot on, the potatoes' starchy aroma filled the air and rising vapour frosted the adjacent window. Lifting a frying pan with one hand, he spooned a pat of butter on the sizzling oil, the other turned down the flame.

'Playing touch-rugby tomorrow. Me, Pete and the Hard-Boys against the Meat Works.'

'Hard Boys? You mean Bourke's lot.'

'It's only footy, Dad.'

Sitting at the dinner table, his son spied jerky torchlight sweeping the landing.

'Look.' He pointed his fork towards the driveway. A dark shadow passed across the wall, Kev thought. Ain't police, so he remained seated, though his son jumped up, and positioned himself near the old cupboard.

Mara's pretty face pressed against the window pane, and both men relaxed. While he eased into her line of sight, she stepped inside. 'You blokes got to help me. I ain't asked before.'

Refraining from a belly burp care of his earlier drinks, Danny put his hand over his mouth. 'Yeah?'

'What's that, Mar?'

'What's wrong with you two? I'm crook with worry. Chrissie's missing, and you two are asleep.'

Kev came closer. 'What do you mean?'

'What are you two staring at?'

'No. I'm asking: What's happened to her?'

Her eyes narrowed as she addressed Danny, who maintained his stunned mullet mask. 'What do you think, boy? Where's my girl?'

'Sit down, luv. Please.'

'Please me, Kev,' she said poking him in the chest.'Who's been whispering things in her ear? Who's been making suggestions?'

'Hang on. How are we getting her back? We'll help you, Mar. Danny, where will we find her?'

Danny bit his bottom lip. 'Sydney. She told me, a month ago. When she's eighteen. You know, "old enough."'

She paced the room wearing a dirty scowl. 'She couldn't do it on her own.'

For her, his imprudent words suggested likely guilt. With one hand clenched, the other swept a long finger over the table top, eyes fixed on him. You could tell she wanted to pummel him, despite their different size.

Something held her back. None of her gang came along, but out of respect for his Dad, she only turned her back to him.

He put a hand to her shoulder. 'Mara. Need a heart-to-heart, eh. We can work this out. We'll get Chrissie back.'

'Ha.' She scowled, still considering her options.

With the faintest nod, he directed his son to sit, encouraging her to do the same. She rejected it with a shudder.

'Listen, you two. Chrissie's my flesh and blood. She's been giving me trouble for years, but no one's going to take her away. And you. You're still sniffing around for that no-good Badger. Time you learnt the truth. He circled our shacks that night, offering her fifty bucks to cut the blanket. Goes and takes her behind my back, and no guessing what might have happened. She's too young. Down by the blasted snake pit, and she laughed.'

Danny fumed.

'I found him. Whipped out and gave them a piece of my mind. Took my bloody hammer, she thought it funny. Could've damn near thrashed her. Badger too. Oh yeh, we upset him. Had my boys holding lumps of four-by-two. He ran. Real fast.'

Mara laughed at the memory. Bitter, black laughter.

'Didn't kill him though, because we guarded the bridge. Scared the shit out of him. Made the bastard swim the river, past the fish traps and all. Pointed the way. We helped him.'

'Mar, he slept on my veranda, remember? But what happened to the car? That VL found its way to others. And you drove it.'

'You're a smart bugger, Kev. Doesn't mean I killed him. We dumped the mongrel Commodore outside town and left it. Didn't want that rubbish coming back, me thinking what a fine time he'd have being lost like a dopey donkey. He deserved a thrashing.'

'A thrashing?'

'He was an alley cat, after my girl.'

'So where did you leave the car?'

'Out near the tip, of course, where trash belongs.'

'Hmm.' Kev grinned, and shook his head, knowing anything could have happened to it, there or thereabouts, a bedraggled, bruised Badger ill-prepared for someone's revenge.

He left my place, heading for town, so how come no one reported seeing him? He probably didn't know the tip's location.

Should he believe her? Did she met him later use her hammer? Did he intercept her, clash, and use the handgun in the glove box? Would she?

'Anyhow,' she said, 'why are you doing favours for Missy Cheryl? She's a traitor.'

'Favours?'

'You got my note, didn't you?'

They stared at each other.

His son winced. 'I didn't …'

'Didn't, what?'

'Danny, your father ought to know. Listen here, Kev, That Sheila is

Badger's ex-. They were hitched. Probably, still cutting the blanket.'

'Married?'

He took the blow well if you didn't count the stiff shuffle of his feet beneath the table or the awesome silence that burnt time to a crisp.

Mara expected anger, but between them was a haunting. 'Come on, you two, things need doing. I've told you my Chrissie's gone missing. Are you gonna help or not?'

He lifted his head. 'Without a car, Mr Badger would go to Cheryl's place.'

'Mate,' she said, rising from her seat, 'your Dad's playing Detective Boney again.'

Kev put his hand on her shoulder. 'We'll find her. Danny will.'

Mara winced again, refusing to sob. 'Yeah, well ... Said she'd take a bus to Lake Cargelligo, to her grandma's.'

'She talked about going to the city a month ago,' said Danny. 'Plenty of Murris around Blacktown and Redfern.'

Her eyes narrowed. He sounded too certain, like he knew more than he was telling. But instead of anger, the type many feared, her face fell in a heap, her skin falling into dark folds. He saw her go from mother to granny. In her thirties, the years took a toll, but without the glory of tears.

Kev held her hand, and hugged her long enough to be embarrassed.

'We'll let Danny search for her. He'll find her, Mar. Don't worry.'

He gestured his son to make tea. 'We'll have a cuppa, and he'll go in the morning.'

At last, Mara sat on the lounge. He drifted to his boy in the kitchen. He leaned on him, moving close to his ear. 'You took her to Sydney.'

His wrist went limp, and the teapot fell to the floor.

'Ouch! Dad –'

'Get down there, son. Find her, and bring her back. And no more working for Bourke's.'

He remade the tea, his hands feeling disconnected from his body. He fumbled with the spoons, couldn't hold the cups, unable to pour sugar into the bowl. Carrying the fresh pot into the lounge room, he placed it before his dad and their guest and retreated to his bedroom.

I thought I did her a favour.

He liked Chrissie. She gave him that look and a cuddle. He thought everything would be OK for her. Mr Bourke promised a job. It's what she wanted, her as pigheaded as her mum. Besides, she'd start her working life soon enough.

I'm running hot cars to the cities. Fine by me; long drives, plenty of thinking time. Listen to the radio, and it makes me money. The boss only had three rules: don't stop, don't speed, and don't touch. You only stopped for fuel. Speeding risked being nabbed by coppers. Anything in the boot, or under the seats, is off-limits. Drive to the chosen spot and hand over the car. Done. The vehicle, and the goods. All OK by him, even when his Dad disapproved.

I'm not stopping.

He'd stick with the Hard Boys, play footy, drink and enjoy a joke or two with Pete, Con and the others. They got on: it was a matter of putting a few-bob on the nags, hanging around the pub and talking big.

Not just chat. These boys do it for real. After being snubbed by the Mayor, he wanted to teach Peake a lesson. The fat, ugly bastard; 'toad' they called him. So, they shot his dog in the face. Blown away. The Mayor fell apart. Unbelievable. When suspicion fell on Humblebum, we laughed louder.

Every day, we're fooling the cops. Love it. Stupid bastards see nothing. We're transporting cars, dope, cross-bows, anything, under their noses. Pete's old man is smart.

Me, not stay at Bourke's Garage? Dad's got to be kidding.

Paddy ran more vehicles through town than ever; from Brisbane, Adelaide, Gold Coast and Broken Hill. The Hard Boys moved them to Sydney, Bathurst or Canberra, wherever they fetched high prices. The new, out-of-towner coppers knew nothing, he reckoned. Sooner or later, he would offer them a few favours. He suspected the new mob might make things easier. Besides, Danny and Pete were familiar with every bit of country, every street and every rusting piece of cast iron. They appreciated him.

Me, not working for Bourke's Garage? Dad's got to be kidding.

Bourkie said he found a job for Chrissie in Sydney, all the work she needed.

Working for him is money in the pocket. If the Bourkes made loads of cash from everything they did, so what? Chrissie had no idea about surviving the city. They'd train her. Bar work. No problem.

Dad's old-fashioned. Look at the old, green soda siphon beside the lounge. Its elaborate cut glass and silver pressure unit is like something from outer space. Some silly, glossy metal thing from Planet Delta. Disgusting. Displaying a useless old bottle. St. Vinnies wouldn't take it.

He had been different once. When he first returned from work on the Lachlan, his father joked with him, reckoning he was the better rifle shot.

'Oh, yeah?'

Danny grabbed the soda siphon, pointed at his dad, and fired.

Squirt! Got him.

Squirt again.

His dad held up his hands.

Surrender, already?

No, he was urging caution with his precious memento. That acknowledged, the siphon put aside, they took up battle again. He launched a paper plane and a few odd Smarties into the kitchen. The water pistol came in handy.

Squirt. Squirt.

His dad sprung up, wrestled him to the floor, and rolling free from one another, laughed themselves silly.

These days, he's so earnest. Or something else. I can't find in the word. He spends hours cleaning the mantelpiece, vacuuming around the tape deck, dusting his old soda siphon, polishing his shrine. He restored a useless radiogram, kept old books and magazines, the stained Mixmaster and blender, stuff bought at St Vinnie or found at the tip and returned to working order. All junk.

He felt as mad as hell about his Dad's pride in it, living in poverty and he didn't recognise it.

When his turbulence ebbed, he abandoned his room, returning to the kitchen, noticing Skipper lifting his sorry, brown head, his Kelpie ears pricked up. Skipper leapt from the lounge, and paced towards the back door, barking all the way. The door thumped. The old, green soda bottle rattled.

Chapter 31

The door banged and a window shattered.

'Open up. Police.'

They tensed, and their eyes widened. Skipper kept barking.

'Wait,' called Kev. 'I'm coming.'

'Answer, or we'll bust down your door.'

Danny grasped the kitchen stool while his Dad no more than leaned forward on the lounge, saying, 'It's unlocked.'

The door swung away, the first cop sheepish at the threshold. A second barged in, announcing, 'Detective Hanna.'

Kev rose and shook the man's hand as Danny froze. Mara was nowhere to be seen.

'How can I help you, officer?'

Two cops behind their leader made a menacing laugh-wall.

'Shut up,' said their boss without turning his gaze from his Subject of Interest. 'We have a few questions for you. You are Kevin Trust?' Kev nodded. 'Then, I believe you met Mister Clifford Badger on the day he disappeared.'

Kev sat down with his son and invited the officer to join them, explaining his early morning surprise. 'He had injuries, nothing serious. Looked like he ran through the bush, got scratched down his arms and legs. A bit wet and bloodied.'

'Beaten up?'

'Unlikely. He never told me what happened. Mostly, he ate at the kitchen table. In the end, he more or less asked me to forget it.'

'And you say, he left?'

'About eight o'clock or a little later. He lost his car somehow so I advised him to go to Bourke's Garage. I hoped they would find it or fix him up with another. He appeared in a rush.'

'In a hurry? But his Council meeting occurred the night before. Did you attend, Mr Trust?'

'Not at all. I'm in bed by ten.'

'So, why would he hurry?'

'I guess he wanted to clean up. He liked to dress up like most city folk. Return to his motel I supposed, or else find someone who'd supply him with fresh clothes.'

Hanna took notes eyeing Danny as he wrote.

'Quite a story,' he said. The cop put down his notebook and took a sip of his host's tea. 'Here's my scenario, sonny Jim: you are romantically inclined to Miss Cheryl Sheila, and this Mr Badger is her ex. He appears on your doorstep, a rival, so this is your once-in-a-lifetime chance to knock him off.'

Kev's brow creased, crested and flew away. He fell back into the lounge. 'I am much too old for that sort of thing, Detective.'

'I think you're lying.'

Looking to his son, he threw out his hands. 'I am trying to help you find him. But if you don't believe me …'

A kerfuffle halted their conversation when Fibro smashed outside, Mara yelling and cursing her captors. 'Got her,' said a distant voice.

Two men stationed outside wrestled, jostled and pushed Mara to the landing. Officer Short shoved her, and she accused him of poor ancestry, biting him on the arm. Pushed through the door, she cursed again, though no longer resisting. The cop moaned and examined his wrist.

'Let her go,' said Hanna.

'I'll damn well charge her for assault,' he roared.

'Settle down, officer.'

'Mar, behave yourself,' said Kev.

She stood bold, game, and ready for a fight. Eventually, her shoulders dropped, she wiped imaginary shackles from her wrists, and rubbed down her arms, still smarting from the cop's gorilla grip. Fixing on Hanna, she scowled, before easing herself into dignified defiance. Physically, she overshadowed no one in the room, although she equalled Hanna's height.

Kev invited her to join them at the table, her, still eyeballing Hanna. He stared back, not letting her gaze defeat him. 'Please Mara. You gentlemen, take a seat. You are welcome here. Mara too. She comes and goes as she wishes.'

'Through the window?'

'If she wants.'

Several cops leaned on the wall.

'So, what's your pressing problem, lady?'

'Her daughter has disappeared,' said Kev, nursing the old green soda bottle in his lap. 'We're trying to find her. We are all worried.'

Hanna glanced to the other officers, assuming a deliberate diversion or ruse. When neither of his Subjects of Interest pleaded, he said, 'You should report the matter to Missing Persons.'

'Yeah, sure,' said Danny. 'And you might be Santa Claus.'

He let that pass, though his eyes narrowed.

'Mr Trust, you talked to this Bicentennial official last. After that, no one has seen him. Don't you think that is highly suspicious?'

He rubbed his upper arm, the soda bottle on his lap. 'Officer, this is a country town. I admit meeting Mr Badger. Others might have seen him but aren't telling you.'

'Why should I believe —?'

'Get real,' said Mara. 'What's Kev got to do with this? He wakes up one morning and finds this stupid bugger on his veranda. I'd throw him out on his arse, quick smart. But Kev gives him breakfast, and you guys want to hang him.'

'Alright, Mar. The detective is only doing his job.'

Hanna's face squeezed as he divided his attention between the three. His hand dropped from his cheek, he almost smiled. 'In which case, you won't mind if we search the premises.'

'You need a warrant for that,' said Mara.

'Please,' said Kev, 'take a look.'

'They'll trash the place, Kev. The bastards will trash it.'

And they did.

Chapter 32

Every year or three, townspeople, station hands and squatters converge on the town hall for a special day. Dressed casual or formal, everyone is invited, and you don't need a dance partner, eat fairy floss, place bets on a nag or carry homemade jams in a basket. People come and go, morning and afternoon, alone or in small groups, purposeful and polite, sometimes tense and nervous, disinterested or hurried, yet entering and leaving via that same plain, white door. They might say a few words to each other, tip their hat, smile, or shuffle by to avoid eye contact.

It was local election day. Cheryl stood outside in her best floral dress and cowgirl plaits, handing out How-to-Vote cards with a poorly reproduced black-and-white photo of her younger self. Above it, in dark blue, 'A Sheila for Mayor,' and below, 'Vote One: For Law and Order and Progress.'

Phillip Bowler, National Party MP, threw his considerable weight behind the "independent" candidate, visiting town before touring the sixteen centres within his million-hectare electorate in a cocky's light aircraft. Ruddy-faced, and stuffed in a grey suit, he appeared every inch a man of ample means. Topped with his signature- Akubra, on arrival, he lumbered forward to kiss his candidate.

For the next while, he handed out voting cards with the grace of an angel, every angle of his gifted jaw photographed by an *Advocate* part-timer photographer. With a State election only months away, his entire body worked up a re-election smile in drought conditions. His weighty problem made him sweat even on local government results.

Across the road, Mara stood under shade wearing blue jeans and a blazing green blouse. She never voted, plain to her that elections were nonsense. Politics never altered a thing. No one ever helped her mob. Others went to polling booths and attended election gatherings, and not one of them looked her in the eye.

But something changed. Instead of steering clear of the voting game she hovered around town hall like a bee to honey. Perhaps her speech at Henry's funeral renewed her confidence, and, on the night of the wake, her anger. Maybe revolutionary Susan said something. Who could tell?

For Mara, politics now meant shouting over the others, being listened to or letting them have it. She could do that.

'Hey, Cheryl,' she shouted across the street. 'They trashed Kev's place. That's Law and Order for you.'

The candidate smiled, having already planned on interruptions. Step One: hand a voter a vital How-to-vote card. Ignore the heckler.

'That Mr Badger's missing. He's your old man, right. Where is he? What sort of sheila are you?'

Step Two: Lean to Phil Bowler, an Honourable Member, and whisper in his festering ear. He raises his eyebrows in disbelief at such ungracious behaviour. So the MP, an important man, hands his leaflets to a nearby helper.

'Got nothing to say, eh Mrs Badger? People can guess why.'

Step three: She gives him a peck on the cheek and he toddles off in the direction of the police station. Game over.

Further down, Kev held a bag or package across his chest. Under the struggling Jacaranda, he eyed the town hall much like people stare at a distant train. Unlike Mara, he voted. Had done so in every election since the nineteen sixties when Aborigines were the last Australians to win voting rights. He considered it his duty to turn out for himself, his family, the union, the church and his people. Bess joined him from the start, walking hand-in-hand to the voting booth, letting everyone witness what dignity demanded.

But not this time. No Bess, no confidence, and a harrowing sense of betrayal.

Along the length of Barrier Street, after Henry's death and the police attack on the wake, he only saw 'others', all those townspeople who said nothing, did nothing and offered nothing to alleviate the pain. They were silent when the sirens wailed, a community welcomed the

TRG outsiders like saviours and ostracised Murris with their calls for Law and Order. How could he vote when Cheryl manned the town's only election booth?

Remembering and recording what others worked to forget, he held his recordings to his chest. His hard-fought recollections would set tongues wagging and see eyes accusative, should they learn of it. Retribution would surely follow.

He believed memories, stories and legends helped people heal and forgive, but the small-minded welcomed a strong-willed punisher beating the living daylights out of anyone raising unwelcome ghosts. He prayed his witness did not betray, lie or mislead anyone nor leave him and his family vulnerable. He plumbed the forgetting and brought so much into light, leaving others to learn from it. When so much had happened around him these last few months, prudence suggested their prompt send-off to Canberra. Cheryl stirred up discontent about his people when they needed support and calm reassurance. Her public accusations of riotous behaviour, attributions of blame and the entertainment of concocted rumours worsened matters.

'Law and Order and Progress.' Her words. They divided people and drew the worst in others. Poison, prompting the old suspicions about Murris, supported by the likes of Phillip Bowler, MP. She joined the punishers. She cast aside Kev's notion of everyone getting along.

That day, Cheryl Sheila clutched her pamphlets like a weapon. Arms on her hips, she spied a slim figure approaching the Post office. With her salty curiosity, or perhaps wondering about the chances of reconciliation, its desirability or the necessity. She let Kev drift into the distance.

When he reached the Post Office he joined the queue, when young Marlene recognised him. 'How are you?' she said when he reached the counter.

'G'day, luv. Have you heard anything? Chrissie's missing.'

She searched sideways and poked her head forward, grabbed his hand, and pulled him closer. 'It's terrible. She's in Sydney-Trouble. On the game.'

'Eh?'

'In Granville. My cousin saw her.'

'Ah ... thanks.'

She smiled, glad to be of help, though being On-the-game was nothing to boast about. He nodded, fist by his side. 'Danny's down there now, trying to bring her home.'

'I can make calls from here sometimes. I'll call him. Gimme his number.'

He scribbled Billy's Sydney phone number on an old receipt, handing it to her.

'I'll talk with him, Mr Trust.'

'You're grand, Marlene.'

He checked and handed over his parcel, watching his precious tapes disappear down the old grey chute, heading for Canberra. Doubly pleased she offered new hope of finding Chrissie, and with his package safely dispatched to Catherine without challenge, he backed away. Turning away, he crashed into Cheryl.

Kev and Cheryl walked along Cassowary Street, free of conversation. If anything, he trailed, and she twice paused to let him catch up. He wondered why she sought him out after avoiding him for so long. While he probably hankered for reconciliation, he must have also felt suspicion.

'I have a few minutes,' she said, once inside her home, offering him a seat.

He said nothing at first, keeping his counsel, or plainly lost for words, silence his way of coping with the demands of superiors, her message so far: don't waste my precious time.

With arms crossed, he felt light, like hot air on a dry day, perhaps sensing their relationship was a mirage. From times spent tinkering with electricity, he searched for a spark, a current of information that might led to Mr Badger. His lifetime of persistence, caution and curiosity, including his frustrating search for the Bicentennial official, amped his anxieties. She blocked him from voting at the Town Hall voting booth, so what did she want now? What might he understand after this?

In her loungeroom, she said, 'Life's hard,' adding, 'for you.'

In reply, he did no more than rock his body before stilling it.

She spat the dummy, her arms stiff, fingers flayed. 'I told you to stay away from them.' She flung her campaign hat on the table. 'Now, they think you're part of it.'

'Part of what?'

She got up and walked to the kitchen like she'd forgotten something. The light flicked on, even when there was daylight between them and their meanings. A familiar tinkle of ice fell into glasses, she emerged with two whiskeys on the rocks, pushing one before him.

'Alright,' she said, sinking the whiskey, 'My secret's out.' Glancing at her, lowering his eyes again, his hands clasped the glass, without drinking. 'Cliff Badger's a bastard. Married to him for six years. My mistake. So, when he turned up with his Bicentennial money, I thought: it's my turn for a reward. The boofhead thought he's God's gift.

'When he stuffed it up at the Council meeting, I went to his motel room, unsure whether I'd console him, or get stuck into him. We had a drink or two, and I got stuck into him.'

'You hit him?'

'Not really. I gave him a piece of my mind, told him he's a selfish bastard, and he could stick his money.'

He sat up.

'And?'

'He kicked up a fuss, threw a few things around the room and pissed off.'

'Did you see him again?'

She shook her head.

'So ... where is he?'

'Wish I knew,' she said, 'so, we'd get through this safely.'

They did not eye each other for a while until she took Kev's hand.

'Listen. I could be mayor next month, as long as his disappearance doesn't blow up. We all want to find him but there's only so much we can do. How would it look if the head of Council were associated with a missing Bicentennial official?'

"Disappearance"? "So much we can do"? Was she hinting at rewards for his disappearance? How could he believe her when she cried out for bloody law and order?

'You're looking for him, aren't you? Have you found the car?' He clasped the glass. She slumped into her leather lounge. 'Everyone's looking for it, the cops too. Not surprised he lost it. Cliff was so careless about things; totally unreliable.'

She said Mr Badger "was," and "careless." What else does she know? When he left my place, seeking out clean clothes, and if he didn't return to his hotel room, he must have imposed on her. Her opportunity, her chance of getting stuck into him. She had rifles hanging on her wall. Maybe they argued once too often.

'I'm not sure I care anymore,' said Kev. 'I've got Danny to worry about.'

Plus Mara, and Billy, and Chrissie.

'He's a good lad.'

Her words. "Good lad?" Someone else said the same thing, and it wasn't reassuring.

'Anyway, no way around it? I mean …is he involved?'

'No,' he said, too quick.

His shoulders stiffened. Cheryl fidgeted with her empty glass, his untouched. The sound of a passing vehicle built up, climaxed, and receded. A dog barked. Surely, anything Kev said after this would enmesh him in a web of lies.

If she murdered him, I'm a threat to her. If she finds out we secreted the car, would she use her rifle on us?

'For the last time, I'm telling you: stay away from Billy and Mara. If you have any info that would help us find Badger, tell *me* first. You'll feel a lot better.'

His shoulders caved in, his Pepsi T-shirt hung from his frame like wet clothes on a line.

He jumped up. 'Goodbye.'

Just like that, he walked out without another word, his numb legs walking on air. Out the front door, down the garden path, past the open gate, to the solitary footpath. God knows what she made of it.

When he finally found sense again, when his brain allowed small thoughts to pass through the tall grasses of anxiety, he was sitting on the levee, a warm breeze brushing against his cheeks. He stared at the stranded fish traps, the rocky network of interlaced stone pockets filtering the flow, delaying the fish's passage downstream.

In earlier times, a thousand of his people and surrounding tribes conferred here, the great meeting place where they provided food while the tribal groups made agreements on hunting, sharing and ritual.

Old Man River witnessed all the events of those years, each passage of water a memory swirling about the traps. His tapes readied their release or might be speared into extinction by murderous events, fractures and betrayals.

He beat his fist on the levee.

Damn.

He'd lost Cheryl's friendship, perhaps Billy and Mara's too. Fortunately, the river flowed wide and shallow in a dry year, the sun bouncing off its surface like jewels. Its serenity whispered something about trust, something about courage, about his long journey to the sea.

Cheryl never says anything about herself, he thought. She encourages others to talk about themselves. She only admitted her relationship today when it threatened her Council ambitions. She asked about the car but nothing about the terrible raid on my home. Billy asked me about the car too. Now, she confirmed the cops are also interested.

She'd tell them about today's meeting.

She would!

A twig fell from his fingers. His jaw tightened, and a tear fell from his eye.

Doesn't matter anymore. The car's gone. I still have Danny.

Chapter 33

In the RSL's air-conditioned expanse, a tribal chant overwhelmed the poker machine's rattle and din.

'She-ila.'
'She-ila.'
'She-ila.'

Shopkeepers, publicans, station owners and their wives, including Paul Martin from the Unity, Jimbo from the roo factory and Paddy Bourke, all wore victory's smiles. Cheryl Sheila and her backers stood at the Black-and-Gold bar, dark red carpet underfoot, receiving the crowd's adulation.

She won, with more votes than any other, and no one asked about that Bicentennial Official anymore. Dead in the water. And this time there'd be no demanding, whining, dog-tired Tony Peake. He had gone fishing, or more likely, searching for a Gold Coast property. The mayor's job would be hers, so they shared around the Cold Duck and pink champagne, a few blue-and-white streamers thrown across Cheryl's bow, a new elation surging through alcohol-enriched veins.

'She-ila.'
'She-ila.'

The lady took acclaim in her stride as the crowd spilled into the gaming area's colorful displays of cowboys, gangsters, pop stars, pirates and aliens. Stepping onto a steel chair like a circus tiger, held by Humblebum, even the ring-a-ding pokie-players fell silent.

'We've the winner,' she shouted. 'We've won. We can do anything.' Wild cheers arose, many of the clientele beating on tables and splashing their beers, the knockabout players already becalmed and impatient.

'We're going to clean up our town, make it shine again. It'll be one hell of a place.' The barman paused at his tap, one hand still reaching and shuffling glasses behind the bar. 'And you know what a little birdie told me? Our Bicentennial year will be a little beauty.' With this unexpected announcement, this hint, the gathering let out a slight applause mixed with disparaging commentary. 'This place will build its way to progress: a new police station, new firehouse and museum. With this Council, we're going places.'

Louder, reassured applause this time, Cheryl's steady eyes surveying all below her

'On a personal note, I want to announce, some have guessed this, that Mr Roger Clifford and myself are engaged to be married. Yes, we are.'

'Whoa! Whoa!'

Everyone loves a wedding, especially when it brings together a prospective mayor and Council manager. When she stepped down, people beamed. Husband and wife-to-be. Her supporters whooped and waved their hats. What a power couple, Humblebum, a man emerging from the shadows.

'Thank you. I am so pleased to serve our district. As diverse as our councillors are, I think we can all work together. And it is agreed – '

Cheryl grabbed the microphone, 'Agreed, that we party tonight.' She pulled him to the bar and threw down another Glenfiddich.

In Pokie Arcade, a woman in a lemon-coloured dress and pointy black shoes yanked the Elvis World lever as the spinning figures of 'the King' — lean, ample and Los Vegas — flickered before her eyes. Her thin frame and long brown hair stood out beside the wide-bodied pensioners with beer and cigarettes in hand.

With her hard stare and pursed lip, she slid off her stool and glided towards the party like a stingray in a working-class tide.

Marto from the Unity Hotel pointed her out to Humblebum. 'How did she become a member?'

'The pink-arsed one? She'd get lost in a caravan.'

It was no idle comment. Ever since her friend Susan spent more time with Mara and her piano, Danielle retreated to her air-conditioned Viscount, with its television and tape deck, everything needed to maintain insanity. On most days, the neighbours heard the harmonious Melanie, Righteous Bros and George Harrison, the same elongated, dreamy tunes played so often they took on an air of menace.

I want to t-ell you
I feel hung-up
but I don't know why.

The same tracks repeated as this was all she brought with her after her late appointment. Discovering the local music and tobacconist store sold Country and Western heroes or numerous Christmas or special-occasion compilations, her musical collection was fixed and determined, much like herself. Left with her caravan tunes, tea and chocolates, she freed herself from the obligations of visiting sickly folk demanding her attention in every part of the district. Glen couldn't be lured inside when she needed him, so she comforted herself with a sound wall, his repeated offers of hashish rejected lest it unhinged her.

Social work became optional when she realized the Welfare Inspectorate took no interest in our faraway town. She only signed off her Housing Commission commitments on Mondays, and that week waited until she spied Mara buying goods from Marco's grocery. She drove to Patchtown and took photographs of unsupervised children on the pocked road outside the shanties as evidence of inadequate care.

On Friday afternoons she stood by the hospital's docile patients as they talked their heads off or stared ahead with insane smiles. It suited and comforted her as she needn't make inane conversations, which proved to herself she hadn't been reduced to idiocy.

That night Danielle kept close to the colourful gambling machines as Cheryl worked the room offering complements and amusing anecdotes to townspeople of her ilk. Humblebum pointed to desirable company, to the people who mattered, like the local pharmacist, property owners and solicitor. She could do that.

The mayor-to-be came nowhere near her, she left Pokieland for the mauve dining area where she shared hard looks with the elderly. Stalking Cheryl, the mesmeric spell of the Righteous Brothers carried her past the stone-faced or gleeful, drawing closer, eyes sublime, shoulders stiffened until she bumped into Cheryl.

The mayor-to-be turned. 'Oh, hello. Pleased to see our social worker this evening.' The caravaner said nothing. Cheryl's faint smile held position. 'How are your duties?'

'I spend a lot of time at the hospital.' Her eyes darted around the room. 'But you said something about people you'd rather see gone.'

Cheryl raised an eyebrow. 'Did I?'

'Yes.'

'On a night like this …' Her eyes drifted skywards, perhaps under the influence of the whiskey. She half-lifted her arm and waved. 'There are one or two hopeless cases.'

'Mara, for starters,' said Humblebum overhearing them.

There were shrieks of delight from the nearest acolytes.

'This is the only place safe from her type,' opined the town pharmacist.

'As long as the prescriptions keep rolling in,' said the administrator, attempting humour.

Danielle grimaced. Madame pharmacist's prescription drugs were the devil's work. Those chemical companies sold snake oils and useless tablets. All those doctors were raking-in money. Her clients swallowed them for blood pressure, arthritis, lung conditions, diabetes, and all manner of diseases. Feigned or favoured, she reckoned them without benefits, in fact, an excuse to be sick and ill and always on welfare, her opinion firming as she spent more time in her caravan.

'Miss Sheila. May I talk to you in private?'

'Sure. I've got time for our social worker.'

He tugged her arm. 'Watch her. She's a strange one.'

The mayor-to-be swayed, grinned and turned her back to the others, stepping close to the squeaky-voiced Danielle. 'What's this about?'

'It's about Mara.'

'Mara?'

'You want to be rid of her, don't you?'

Chapter 34

Paddy Bourke's workshop was a fixture, one of its largest buildings in town, a cavernous, galvanized iron structure built on a concrete slab some twenty years ago. With damaged cars, tools, oils and vehicle parts illuminated by a line of suspended fluorescents, he cut three skylights so its dark corners shone.

The building was entered via a narrow driveway between Fitzie's Hardware and Madam's Dress shop, the alleyway walls lined with bazooka mufflers, brutish fenders and black car doors. At night, it was blocked by a two-metre tubular gate mounted with barbed wire.

On a cloudy day, the workshop's blue-grey exterior conjured an ethereal indefiniteness, the colours applied in a random way when Paddy was away. Its corrugated steel cladding formed an armoured appearance to a dubious inner sanctum. A white sign read: "Open. Ring the bell."

A sharp mind recognized he didn't like people poking their noses in. As the massive shed door was kept slightly ajar, anyone peeking in blocked the light, giving them a warning of intruders.

Paddy Bourke preferred talking to people over the phone, so they carried out business with the minimum fuss and the maximum security. To improve the indoor lighting, he insisted the back door be always open during work hours. With additional light and airflow, it improved his sense of well-being and allowed him to keep a close eye on the yard's cars. Handy too, when he required a quick getaway, though his castle had been breached only once.

His final alterations happened a few years earlier, a hole cut in the edifice to install a glass and timber office with a telephone installed, a sign outside reading: "All visitors, report HERE."

The arrangement, he called it, so anyone on the receiver must be brief. 'Just stick to the facts, whatever it takes to do business. If the call isn't friendly, hang up.'

Blinng-blinng. Blinng-blingg.
Pete Bourke opened the enclosure door, and answered, 'Bourkes.'
'It's Billy, mate. Put Paddy on.'
'I'll deal with it.'
'Listen, son. I won't repeat myself. Your, daddy, now.'
Silence, before a call for 'Dad' echoed down the line.
The phone crackled and reverberated before he heard steps.
'Who's this?' said Paddy.
'Don't your boys tell you anything?'
'You!'
'Don't worry, I'm not looking for favours.'
'Is that right?'
'Listen, here's a history lesson, bud. Your employee hit me for thousands for a red-hot Commodore. For a man in my situation, generosity never entered the picture. Instead of a Vee-eL steak, I got the pork chop. I want my money back or the vehicle in one piece.'
'I see. Of course, we'll help.'
'I'm not the dreamy kind, Bourkie. Sort this out. My dough back or the car returned. Start at the park. That's where it was taken.'
'You sure?'
'Listen, don't are-you-sure-about-this to me. Remember, we've got common interests about the place. I helped you, and its double time you did the same. Otherwise, things might turn very nasty.'

Bourke had been reminded he reneged on last year's deal. He promised to train two Murris in the mechanics area, and at the end, employ at least one. So, when he "forgot" the arrangement Billy did what no other townsperson had: he threatened him, and carried it out. No difficulty finding people who despised the Bourkes. Easy rounding up mates to pour sugar into his fuel dump, and slash tyres at no extra cost.

They weren't friends after that, more like business associates. Since the bastard became a 'big man,' Paddy cut a new deal to keep the peace, which brought advantages and disadvantages. Figure it out for yourself.

Bourke calculated the place didn't need more aggravation; too many skeletons in people's cupboards. Town unity mattered, even for him, so with unemployed men aplenty, he offered to hire Murris every second time, for tow jobs, moving vehicles, repairs, whatever. He took on Kev's son soon after, and that suited him. He would play the magnanimous man because his shady dealings needed to weave their way into civil life. There had to be a few bucks in it for everyone.

What about their "common interest"? How much did he know? Perhaps Danny told him something.

'I'll sort it,' said Bourke. 'Be my pleasure. Satisfied customers and all that.'

'When?'

'Oh, when? Should be done by New Year.'

'Why so long?'

'This problem is not easy, mate. It requires a bit of detective work. Last time anyone saw the car, it was in the middle of an ambush. A wonder the Royal Commission hasn't asked questions.'

He sensed Billy bristling at the other end. 'January. I'm coming through town about then.' Clunk.

Paddy held the phone from his ear and dumped it on its rocker. 'Pete. In here.' His son arrived in his greasy overalls, his long, slicked-back hair falling across his face. 'Billy's asking us to find the VL.'

Pete's grey lips tightened, and with his dad's silence, he forced a smile.

'Now ask yourself,' resumed Paddy, 'why is Billy calling us? He's in Sydney, right? If he asks favours, wouldn't he go to Mara or Kev first?'

'I guess.'

'So, why aren't they helping him? I don't like it. What's their game?'

'Well, they ...' His voice tailed away as Dad had his own ideas. Better to listen or land a smack on the face.

'Or Mara's got the VL hidden in the scrub. The cops searching too. Did you send Danny out today?'

A worrying question.

'Uh, ha.'

Paddy dropped his head to his fist. 'To?'

He winced. 'Sydney.'

'Crickeys. He's blabbing to Billy. Why in hell didn't you ask me?' He sensed an eruption and stepped back. 'One of them boongs has the VL.'

Pete's eyes widened. 'You think Danny knows?'

Paddy farted and rolled his head around the base of his neck. 'One of them does. But I don't see anyone spending up around town. Billy's asking us to fetch the Commodore. He must know Mara and Kev would have a better idea.' He bared his teeth. 'They were there the night of the riot! Kev and Danny weren't arrested. How come Billy doesn't trust them?'

Pete hadn't an answer but poked his lips out anyway.

'I reckon when Danny returns, you pump him for information.'

'About the car?'

'Spin him a yarn, how the cops are after his dad. He's our mate, so tell him if the police find the car, they're dead. So we'll help them, and pay him for the privilege. We're experts at disappearing cars, right? We've laid low for long enough. We gotta recover that vehicle before anyone else.'

Pete thought about it, and seemed pleased. 'So, we gonna grab the car and fuck him over?'

Paddy's eyes popped. He slapped Pete across the face and sent him reeling. He disliked swearing; it was something boongs did.

'The car is secondary,' he said. 'We got bigger fish to fry. So mind your language son. Mind it, real good.

Chapter 35

Another meeting, thought Cassidy, that's all we need. One piece of drudgery traded for another.

Inspector Warren ran his eyes over the uniforms, his thatched eyebrows demanding full attention or else receive his displeasure. Finding unflattering scribbling on back office walls last week, his tolerance frayed.

'What have we got, Detective Hanna?'

The officer stood up to address the men, all eyes on him. 'Interesting. Kev Trust confirms he met Cliff Badger on the morning of his disappearance. According to him, the already bruised and battered official couldn't, or wouldn't, reveal the reason for his injuries. He claims the guy lost his Commodore, a VL, current model, white, on the previous evening. He sent him to Bourke's Garage in hope of relocating it.'

'So?'

'Our other suspect, Missy Mara, was present at the Trust cottage. We caught her climbing out the window. When we dragged her back, she told us she's looking for her run-away daughter.'

That brought a hearty laugh, under his breath Shortie whispered to Cassidy, 'And he believed them.'

'I checked on the said, Christine Boorandji, and she is indeed missing. Kev blames her disappearance on the Bourkes.'

A few whispers percolated before Warren spoke. 'What about weapons?'

'Well, nothing much to report. We did a thorough search. The old fella has a licensed firearm for roo shooting. Totally unused. He is also recording the local aboriginal language for some Canberra academics.'

'Gawd. Not that bloody mob. That's all we need.'

'We held Missy Mara at his place while we ransacked– ah, searched — the housing estate across the river,' said Detective Hanna.' We confiscated three bolt rifles. Nothing more except a pack of badly behaved kids. I mean …with a dozen houses out there, searching them took all day. A bloody nightmare. Can't tell who's living where, or with whom.' His finger pointed sharply down. 'Upshot is, I suspect Patchtown's keeping a few more secrets. Plenty of young men going bush. If we caught them red-handed … As for old Kev, he's frail. I'm not sure he's our man.'

'Hold on,' said Cassidy. 'Remember, he's the last bloke who saw Badger alive. If that bloke went anywhere, someone would have seen him. If he didn't do-him-in, it could still be the son, or some little deal made with Mara's army.'

'You need a motive, and we don't have one. He never met him until that morning. As for that twerp, Danny, he was in Sydney at the time.'

'Motive?,' said Cassidy. 'Perhaps old Kev learnt about the museum plans. The blacks don't want the project going ahead because it'd ruin their revolt. Proof of progress. Missy Mara wants money and who knows what she'd do to double her pension? Either way, knocking off Badger is a winner.'

'As I see it,' said Hanna, 'we should be looking for the Bicentennial official, dead or alive. At least, find the body.'

Cassidy stood up. 'Christ almighty. He's already listed as a missing person. Nothing found. Obviously, on-the-nose around here. Motive, mate. Plenty of motive. Why was he bruised and battered in the first place? Who did that? When did it happen, and where? What were the consequences? Only Kev saw him. Opportunity, mate. Work it out, drongo.'

'Steady on,' said Warren. 'Anyone else got something to contribute?'

This meeting dragged on. The frontline plodders sweated it out on the streets in their heavy uniform, carrying weaponry, meandering its meagre shopping strip with its empty lots and hungry businesses. They searched every old tin hut outside town and found nothing.

In December's heat, they settled under shady awnings rather than expose themselves to the blazing midday sun and recovered at Marco's air-conditioned sandwich counter every hour or so. The Club they called, after the club sandwich, their day punctuated with aimless conversations, sometimes with locals, but more often between themselves. Townspeople dashed in and out of shops with only a nervous smile, a quick 'G'day,' an officer's only reward. Damned if they had anything to say.

'OK,' said Warren, ignoring the nil-response. 'Let me add some new information, and then summarize. In Sydney, Billy the Revolutionary is under surveillance. Seems he is moving in radical circles. While they're talking rights and precedent, he's yabbering about "blowing-it-wide-open." He's talking about collective action. All recorded in pubs and elsewhere. If this man returns, we nick him. Hit him for jay-walking, anything.

'Here in town, Kev has secrets but ain't telling. Cassidy: get in there and put the pressure on.

'The victim's vehicle hasn't been located. Is that the motive for murder? Find the Commodore, and we'll find out what happened to Badger. If he lost his vehicle, and went looking for it, chances are he found his government vehicle in someone else's possession. The scene of the crime is on wheels. So, where is it, what or who is inside, who stole it, and why? Has it been reconditioned, dumped, burnt, trashed, or what? Surely, we can find an oversized white cruiser.

'Eddy, twist a few arms, will you? Dewar. Hire a boat and go fishing for sunken cars. The river is down so it should be easy. Nothing will sink far at present.

'As for this dope, Mara, she's constantly in Kev's company. Is she humping him, giving him money, or taking lessons? Something's going on. Put a watch on her. Chris, that's your job. I want you following her, day and night. Note everyone she meets. When she takes a shit, you be there.'

That brought a laugh, and yeh, they needed one.

'What about the Bourkes?' said Hanna, legs crossed.

A few blokes stiffened with his question; that's no way to win promotion. Better to shut up, because if an investigation goes pear-shaped, guess who'll be blamed.

'Red-herring, mate. The bloke's fixing cars all day, and these layabouts want to blame someone else. Still, ask them whether they've seen Badger's car. One thing for sure, everyone here has something to hide.'

Warren tugged at the base of his nose with his thumb and forefinger. 'One last thing. Let's solve this before New Year. You want time off? Let's put these bastards in cells. Collect the low-life that knocked off this Bicentennial bloke, and bang, I'll sneak a week's leave. OK, get cracking.'

In imitation, Col Dewar pulled his nose, and waved his hand breezily. 'Easy. Nab them by Friday for sure.'

'Miracle on Main Street,' whispered Mattie Edwards.

'It's almost Christmas,' said Shortie. 'But for this Bicentenary, we'd be out of here. I got family.'

On the far side, Chief Warren called Cassidy with his wiggling finger. 'Don't forget,' he said. 'Give that fuckin Kev a real scare.'

Chapter 36

When Danny returned from Sydney, Pete approached him in the workshop, quizzing him about Billy and his love of cars. His patience frayed with the insistent talk of Commodores and Toyotas. Cornered near the grease gun, he reckoned Pete's interest, out-of-shape, poking his nose into the Commodore's whereabouts during their pay-day gathering.

The VL saved him from arrest but its possession always presented the problem of disposing of it later, more difficult when the cops were on the lookout. So, when they buried it at Phil's Hole, he considered his Dad a genius, despite what he said about how the best plans can go wrong. Such a worrier.

As divine protection, they left Bourke's files on the back seat, the ones salvaged from the tip. If the car was ever found, it pointed to the Bourkes as previous occupants, something his dad read in a detective novel. "Planted", a misleading clue, or trick the police used to convict Murris when they were too lazy to produce evidence. So Pete's insistence made him smile.

'You want to find it or not,' said Pete.

'Might be miles from anywhere,' said Danny.

'Your dad must ... Wait until the cops catch up, there'll be trouble and –'

'You, and trouble? I mean, you're the one who knocked off the Mayor's dog.'

'Yeah, but the Commodore is bigger news. Someone murdered that Bicentennial guy, so when they find the vehicle, and your Dad's got it, they'll say he did it. They'll lock him up and throw away the key.'

Sure, Danny knew the VL's location. But it belonged to Badger before Billy, and others before the Bourkes. They got rid of it to save everyone's embarrassment. He wouldn't tell anyone.

'Lay-off, Pete.'

'Hi-dee ho. Who are your friends? We want to help. We disappear cars. Who better?'

How come he keeps asking? What does he know about the disappearance? He grinned inside. He's a bullshit artist.

But the boss pretender gripped Danny's shoulder. Even when he took a step back, Pete shirt-fronted him. Being the same height, and not needing a fight with his boss, he peered down at the greasy rag stuffed in Pete's pocket.

'Who, is, your, friend?' Danny stood still. 'I, want, to help.' The bastard clutched his upper arms.

'You can help.'

He shook himself free. 'Lay off.'

'What if I don't, eh?'

'You're going all strange on me, ain't he, Con?'

The Hard Boy shrugged his shoulders as the others within hearing distance took an interest. His tormentor stepped up again. 'Your dad will be in gaol for years. How old is he, sixty? He won't be coming out before he's a hundred-and-sixty, except in a box.'

Danny pushed Pete away. 'You want a fight, do you?'

'Take it easy.' Pete brushed his greasy overalls as if smeared by something offensive. 'Don't get your knickers in a knot.'

He picked up a spanner and turned before him. His lips tightened, eyes narrowed, watching him. Showing a cocky grin, he put down the tool, collecting packets from the safe. 'It's payday.'

Half-sitting on the nearest bench, he once again became garage manager, as he liked to call himself, handing out envelopes filled with wads of twenty-dollar notes to all the Hard Boys.

'Guess, I can't help. A man tries.' He glanced at Con, checked his support, measuring out distance, appearing satisfied tempers had cooled. Collecting a satchel from the Cortina's bonnet, he lingered there. Ensuring Danny's fists were unclenched, he pulled out a second set.

'Major shipment this month. We're shifting station wagons and sports cars over Christmas. Remember, plenty of cops on the road this time of year. Don't screw up. No speeding. I hear some of you blokes play tapes at top volume. You think BMW owners do that? So, lay off the volume. Be light on the accelerator. Some of you guys want trouble. We don't.'

Pete let it sink in, before distributing the envelopes.

'Con. Yours.'

'Danny. You have a couple of Canberra trips. Have your Christmas there, if you want. Next job's after New Year.'

Taking his assignment, he stepped backwards, still facing the gang. Never turn your back at a pub brawl, and this was reminiscent.

Once outside, under expansive blue skies, Danny counted his wad of notes, putting Pete's outburst back of mind. With Canberra trips ahead, and Sydney a few hours up the highway, he planned to visit the pumped-up metropolis, to hardball Redfern with its unpredictable bounce and bursting energy. He'd watch his beloved Souths with his city buddies. Go-the-Rabbitos.

I'll stay with Billy. Not staying in Canberra.

Over Christmas, share a beer, talk footie and The Cause. Join the black bustle at the legal centre. Plenty of temptation. If things didn't work out, he could always come home. Country's easy-going ways, its people, river, open spaces, hunting too. He had the best of both worlds.

The thing with Pete? He'll get over it.

* * *

Cheryl Sheila and her fiancé, Roger the Humblebum, were Club regulars. On a pre-Christmas evening, she arrived in her plush, dark fabric dress, a light blouse, and padded business coat. The Council manager came in a grey suit, a blue shirt with a plastic flower in his lapel. They made a splendid partnership.

'Oi,' called police Chief Warren from across the room.

They, and half the club, turned to him as the mayor-in-waiting made her way to the cop-in-power, the administrator trailing.

Warren occupied the club's best table overlooking the rockery with three palms equidistant around a spluttering fountain. 'Been a bumper week?' he said to her.

'That's Irish.'

He laughed. 'Contacts. Progress is a wonderful thing. Moves in small degrees, and bingo, it all falls into place.'

'In your line, perhaps, Inspector. But for Council's success is slow and steady.'

'Meaning?'

'Confidential like, the Bicentennial grant is a given. When I announce the news, it will work like whiskey, producing a warm, inner glow in the gut. More work, jobs, people in the shops, etc.'

'The funds your …Baxter? Batcher? arranged.'

'Misarranged,' said Humblebum.

'Nine-hundred-and-seventy-five thousand dollars.' She ignored the reference to her ex-. 'Most of a million bucks.'

Her fiancé put his arm around her. She brushed him off.

'Subject to several conditions,' said the husband-to-be.

'Of course. No worries.'

Sheila seated herself, and placed her purse on the table.

'We'll need a Trust, with a committee made up of three Council members, one local aboriginal, and one Bicentennial rep. You should know, given Kev Trust is a suspect in a murder investigation, Billy is a certainty as aboriginal rep.'

'Stop worrying, dear. We'll manage him.'

'The minute he shows his face around here,' said Warren, 'we'll nab him. Plenty of ammunition. Mr Billy won't be troubling you.'

Chapter 37

Called a "drongo" by Cassidy in front of the entire squad, Chris Hanna fumed. Around the office, his bete-noir referred to "bleeding hearts" behind his back, and later, drew attention to him by exiting the toilet dragging a long stream of loo-paper by his desk, whispering "soft, so soft." No surprise when he stormed from the Command Room red-faced and angry, Charlie Dewar and the gang laughing.

Driving the patrol car too fast down Evans Street, he accelerated past shops, the tip and out of town on the southern track, flat country where a bend loomed like a bad joke. Not content to brake, Hanna pumped it, sending the vehicle into a spin. The dust flew before he hit a roadside post for six. When it came to rest in a drainage ditch, a grey haze blighted vision.

He would have lit a fag if he smoked and checked Police Property if he cared. Instead, he clawed the steering wheel as if strangling someone, probably Cassidy. A sweat broke across his forehead. Eyeing nothing awhile, he slammed the vinyl panel and tested the ignition. It restarted, so he revved it mercilessly before letting it purr until something like sanity dawned on him.

As the dust drifted, the haunting grey bush, decorous coolabahs and incorrigible boulders reappeared like a waiting audience. Using first gear, he mounted the road and gained cruise speed. In his first year in the Force, he recalled stealing onto the Mount Panorama circuit, dashing around and taking in the whiff of burning rubber. He was only a constable at the time, enjoying a copper's post-race privilege of reliving speedway glory. There was a good side to being a cop, but for …

Damn, stupid Cassidy. What he did was bad enough, but what he said about that woman, about this town. "Dirt, dust and dung. Three types of people here," he said, "except for that black bitch. I'd like to have her in a dark room."

In his fury, he wrestled with him before storming out.

Could've killed him until Dewar pulled us apart.

I did that. At the station. What was I thinking? Luckily Warren wasn't there.

The squad judged tough guys as those who never lose it. You "stir" all you like, especially deadbeats and no-hopers but not *be* stirred by fellow officers. He reacted, and that labelled him a softy, an easy beat, despite landing a good one on the bastard.

What'll the Chief say when he hears?

Chris Hanna drove back to town. Truth is, he liked this place. After meeting a few locals at the Shearer's Arms, he shared a lunch or more with some teachers, salesmen and shopkeepers, laughed at their ribald and droll jokes, played pool, and measured the town's erratic pulse.

He slowed the squad car as he approached the pub, pulling aside, leaving the engine purr, perhaps in consideration of those pleasant conversations, observing Danny Trust, Pete Bourke and his lowlife friends enter the side entrance.

Never seen them do a day's work. They like drinking and cooking up schemes.

Pack of louts.

Steering his damaged vehicle away lest others took an interest, the local park on his left, he couldn't help wondering: How does a wake become a riot? Missy Mara recalled the day, saying 'it was a massacre not a riot.' Something in the realm of Denmark stank. Riots happen in pubs, sure, or on the street blocking traffic or at massive demonstrations with militants, at panicked sports matches and the like. You get these in confined spaces or in intense encounters of opposing groups.

But at a wake, in a park?

He shook his head. Now Cassidy's fired them up with his us-and-them bullshit. We supposed to be of equal rank. A tight little circle. Now we treat almost everyone in this town is our enemy, or, at least, under suspicion. No surprise when they return favour. Just crazy.

He exhaled. Can't go on fighting Cassidy or anyone else in the

Force, even if Kev and Mara are half-decent. Taking sides would rip the squad apart.

When Warren demanded an explanation for his spat, he'd blame the heat, the bad tea, the stroppy locals, the difficulties, the stress, road conditions, and anything else that came to mind. The car's scratches and dents didn't matter to the boss; they were scars of honour in the relentless search for scumbags. Though Cassidy irked him, in the Force, you couldn't pick your friends.

Approaching the cop shop, he shifted into neutral, he let it ride past, for no reason apparent to himself. Letting it drift, towards the bridge, it's how life goes sometimes. On the other side, Patchtown, his recent raid, and ongoing surveillance of Missy Mara. What piteous sights greeted him: snotty-nosed children, angry boys and surly young men standing amidst refuse and rusting car parts. That woman at Kev's place, she was their queen. When she found out we raided her realm, she kicked back. The way she stared him down, fists clenched; it gave him the shivers.

His body slumped against the seating. He fixed his arms behind his head, defying chance, the car drifting on, towards the looming earthen levee, a red rag to a snorting bull. Grabbing the wheel at the last moment, applying the brake, he brought the battered car to a halt under the shadow of the great eucalypt.

Cooler here.

'Be right with you,' he said, his words coming from some mental periphery.

Talking to the tree, perhaps. No, the river.

His sweating hands pressed the dashboard. Temporary insanity. His arms tingled, his body sweated in the canned heat. Throwing his service cap over the back seat, he removed his tie, unbuttoned his light blue shirt, and sat disrobed.

Bugger the rules. It's too damn hot.

Jumping out of the car, he stepped onto the vehicle track beside the giant eucalypt, removing his shoes and socks at the river's edge. His trousers too. Left in his underwear, he rounded a fallen tree trunk flattened by storm, three or four branches reaching for life. Feeling roots underfoot, the water lapped his ankles. Passing a veil of bull rushes, he surveyed the ribbon reeds and slits of river and sky beyond, a breeze caressing his arms and neck.

Over his knees. Oh, yes.

Deeper, into the cool, brown waters. The sparkle and chill. Shiver. His feet sunk in thin, warm mud. Why hadn't he done this sooner?

He jerked his head around. Did I lock the car? Anyone looking?

Relax.

His quick dip would be of no interest to a soul. Who in the force would deny him?

As he entered up to his knees, then waist, his skin and body hair tingled, the sun burning his shoulders as the tree cover thinned. As the flow tickled over his calves, the river became firmer underfoot. The sparkling waters dazzled his eyes, and the warm air surrounded him like a Turkish bath. The churning cascades upstream overwhelmed his senses, the dipsy, gurgling waters hailing a deeper, chilly pond. As the rippling currents danced around him —

'Who's that?' said a voice.

He squinted. He could make out a figure downriver, a woman perhaps, someone dressed in orange.

'Who are you?' said the voice.

'Detect – It's Chris Hanna.'

'Holy Moses.'

His hand fell from his face, compelled to shield his lower body. With the sun shining across her shoulders, Mara observed everything worth looking at, a half-naked man standing against the sublime reeds. Bit of a hunk without his pig suit.

The river's loud and turbulent waters lapped her waist, the reflections dancing on her face. She leaned on a long stick.

He wore only black underpants, his hand shielding his face like some lost explorer.

She worked the fish traps, moving quietly around the stone complex, gazing into another rocky pocket, spear at the ready. Apart from making occasional repairs, she fished the expanse for easy pickings on cloudy days. The traditional rules might have forbidden her freedoms once, but so much had been lost, they presented no limit to her recreation. Tribal 'skins' were still acknowledged, and that kept them sane and respectful.

'Coming in, Moses?'

'Mara, is it?' He yelled across water as she occupied downriver, some thirty metres away.

She didn't answer him; just moved to the next trap, replace a rock, and look up again.

'You're a black fella.'

He took depth, water to his waist. 'No. I'm Lebanese.'

'You're a black fellow. Chops like that.'

'No. You're ...' His jaw slackened, and his eyebrows drew together.

'Sorry. None of my business, eh?' she said.

Chris Hanna dived into the channel, swimming upstream, before allowing himself to drift back, coming within a few metres, in deeper. Regaining his bearings, even at the deepest point, he could stand.

'You better watch out. You'll find yourself in the deep end,' she said, laughing.

Turning around, he swam upriver again, in strong, smooth strokes.

'Hey, stay away from the bridge.' He stopped, lifting his head out of the water and felt the current beneath him. 'You don't know what's been thrown over there.'

Treading water until he found the struggle useless, he allowed himself to float back to her.

'Come on. Over here. Make yourself useful. Help me catch a fish.'

Minutes ago, he had been drowning in dust and humiliation. Now he drifted into Mara's sweet waters, thrilled.

Chapter 38

The next day, Detective Hanna entered Bourke Garage's driveway less than confident. He had little to go on except his instincts, his suspicions, and Mara's word. When Bourkes' first popped out of Kev Trust's mouth, he gave it no weight. Yet she seemed to think very little happened without them being enriched. As the town's only mechanics and with its massive shed, there'd be shady dealings boosting their finances.

He assured himself he wasn't out to prove that bastard Cassidy wrong. Visiting the place was the boss' suggestion. It employed seven or eight men, a ridiculous number for a small town. His Hard Boys occupied the pub too often, and made money too easily, so at least some of their activities would be illegal, though nothing to do with the TRG.

But the utter lack of threat, months of meaningless patrols,and the demands of an ongoing Royal Commission meant the Bicentennial Official's disappearance might justify their mission. The bloke might be dead but Cassidy did not understand it the way he did.

Badger might have been murdered or just a missing-persons inquiry, he thought. I'm not trained to determine it. But Warren's attempt to inject purpose by involving them in policing puts us in conflict. No one in the squad signed up for that.

He grinned. Some officers expressed their boredom and discontent with grafitti scribbled on toilet walls at first, but spread to the back blocks, probably to ensure demolition.

The Bourkes. Focus, he thought.

He wilted with the prospect of setting eyes on an underutilized workshop cluttered with a million clues, and therefore, none at all. The owner would pretend an interest in the investigation but soon offer outright denials.

He could plant a few ideas calculated to lower their confidence, increase doubts or make them cautious. A few contradictions or misshaped words might reveal guilt sor at least provide another lead.

A cop's first instinct is to believe no one, yet Kev and Mara puzzled him. His politeness under pressure made him a master tactician or a brave innocent. Or a brave tactician or masterly innocent! Which? A mischievous local who kept his counsel on many matters, he guessed. The coincidence of the city-slicker landing at his cottage on the river, the home of a black radical (though she laughed at that), gave grounds for suspicion. How come an important public official stumbled into his place unless he were lured there?

If he were to be believed, he mused, the bloke would be equally helpful to me and Cliff Badger. And he had. If he knocked off the Bicentennial figure, he needed a murder weapon and the strength to use it, because Badger was a Rugby player of bulk. Kev was thin, weedy and any muscle he possessed withered.

He shrugged his shoulders; he couldn't tell.

Princess Mara was feisty enough. She lived in a ramshackle Housing Commission cottage. A shameful place. Yet she thrived amongst that crowd of thieves and desperadoes. Its surly youngsters eyed him as an out-and-out enemy, the elderly merely passive or intimidated. How much good came from that?

Now that he knew her as a temptress and feisty mother, he doubted himself. What she said. Her loyalty to him. Talking about the Bicentennial official's whereabouts, both of them pointed to the Garage where Danny worked. Incredible. Somehow, he hoped to make sense of the situation.

In this town, you repaired your car yourself, or went to Bourkes'. Bourke or Buckley's.

Having passed down his narrow driveway, the frontage widened. Approaching the workshop's oversized entrance, he peeped through the small gap.

'Who's that?'

'Detective Hanna.'

A greasy silence.

'Pop into the office. I'll be around.'

He spied a truck to his right, and a 1984 model Holden, with other vehicles in various stages of dismantlement. Bare steel framing walls, lights hanging from a high ceiling in rows, and, on the left, a chaotic array of car parts. Below, a line of storage compartments, perhaps for smaller components, and numerous open and closed toolboxes. Nothing unusual with the familiar aromas of grease, leather, polish and petroleum.

Alerted by boots tramping towards the office, he took his place. Peering into a darkened workshop hadn't helped. If he kept staring, it would only alert them to his suspicions.

'What can I do for you?' Said a ruddy, shortish man approaching fifty. His muscular arms and unkempt hair filled the reception enclosure.

'Routine inquiry,' Chris Hanna.

'Bourke, Paddy.'

A squarish, boney-faced man with uneven eyebrows, he wore deep blue overalls, barely used.

Waved towards an old table and bare timber seating against the shed wall, the Detective got into business. 'Sir, are you aware of the disappearance, a few months back, of a Mr Cliff Badger, the Bicentennial official?'

'Oh, Yeah. That fella. He was going to build a museum or something.'

'Yes. He drove a Holden Commodore, the current VL model I believe. You familiar?'

'Sure. Don't get too many late models around here.'

'So, what I'm asking is: did you see a white VL in the last few months? On the street. In your workshop. Repaired one, painted one, or sold one in that time?'

'No need to view the books for that. No way.'

'Think again. Because our informant directed Mr Clifford Badger to your garage on the day he disappeared. Are you saying he never came here?'

'No way.'

'Or perhaps while you were away. Check with your staff?'

Paddy ran his hands through his hair.

'Possible, I guess. Pete and Con will look into it.'

'Do you know Billy Matchett or Kev Trust?'

'We all know them. Billy's a bush lawyer these days, and Kev's ... I employ his son.'

'Is that right?'

'Nice bloke, our Danny. Is he in trouble?'

Too damn cosy.

'Where do you keep your cars, Mr Bourke?'

'Here and there. Ain't always got the workshop space.'

'So, one might appear and disappear without your knowledge?'

'Well, not if I have my way. I try to run a tight ship.'

'Tell you what, sir. You ask your staff about the VL. Inquire whether Mr Badger visited. We're tracking his whereabouts on the day. All routine. Happened before we arrived, and soon after Henry Freeman's demise. Remember that?'

'Him. Good riddance to him. Bloody drunken lout, he was.'

'Billy? Any contact with him?'

'Not really. Got little in common, you might say.'

'He's never visited you?'

'Nop.'

'Never repaired his car?'

'No.'

'You'll ask staff about the Commodore?'

'Sure. Always willing to help the police. We've gotta stick together you know, in town like this.'

'You beggar belief, Mr Bourke. You denied everything, offered nothing, and contributed nil to our investigation.'

Paddy took no offence, raising his hand in acceptance. With little left to say or ask, Hanna stared at his face. The stuff of leather, steel too. With his small mouth, shaven face, his eyes narrowed to every answer. Never smiled or scowled; as casual as can be. Kept the smallest aperture to his eyes, much like the workshop door.

He's lying.

After the detective left, Paddy thought, Who's talking to them, Billy or Kev? None of them like the cops.

Con and Pete stood around him.

'Listen you lot: keep this copper's visit a secret, especially from Danny. No loose tongues. You're under orders.'

They mumbled agreement.

'Pete; any luck with Danny?'

'Nar. He's not giving.'

'The Police are asking questions so they haven't found the Commodore. But they're searching. Putting the heat on us. The cop asked whether we've done business with Billy. I don't like that line of inquiry. Any association with him is poison.'

'What if Danny's informing? He's seen too much.'

'He's manageable, son. The cops are only sniffing. Main thing is we don't want them getting too close. I reckon Kev turning them on us, him and Cheryl Sheila. Maybe Danny is nosing around for his dad. Bad timing, because we got plenty of vehicles to move.'

The Hard Boys shifted on their feet. If someone in the gang betrayed them, there were consequences.

'Fact is,' said Paddy, 'we've gotta find that car. It has valuables. Jewels-in-the-crown, my friends. So, here's luck, there's a thousand bucks for anyone who –'

Paddy's eyes dilated, his mouth seized up, his pupils veered off-centre, face muscles tensing. Unbalanced, he slid and fell against the Falcon model, hand reaching out before he rolled to the floor, twitching, jerking and curling up like a dried leaf in summer's heat.

Pete rushed forward, arms flayed. His dad never liked staff or townies seeing his fits.

'Fuck!' said Con, thinking the boss was possessed by the devil, or having a heart attack, later remembering his parents talk of "pink-fits."

Paddy's jerked and writhed, hands pressed on tyres spilt about the floor, his breathing uneven. His face contorted so much, he pulled a drop sheet across him, but left him twisting and writhing. The others stepped back from the strange undulations and jerks, their boss as none had seen him.

Con's fingers to his mouth, he bit hard enough to draw blood.

'Get back.' He lifted his arms without purpose, the shroud slipping, he hauled the cover. The gang fell back or rushed to the toilet. Pete stood nearby with his hand to his cheek, unable to treat him or do more than remove equipment from reach.

After a while, Paddy's jerking subsided, with only a growl and an occasional gurgling emitted beneath the white and out of sight. Eventually, he pushed the drop sheet aside, a foam substance oozing around his lips. Paddy swished Pete's hand away; water too rejected, he struggled to his feet. Dazed, he moved to the hand basin by the door, washing his face, neck and shoulders with a wet cloth. Afterwards, he gazed into a mirror, rubbing his cheek and arms.

The Hard Boys were witless, barely able to look at one another.

When Paddy returned, his wrists itched, yet he stood before them again, sniffing readiness, the event unacknowledged. Nothing demanded or expected.

'Let's see, the cops, put the heat on Kev. We'll nail the bastard. Billy too. No one's going to find the Commodore except us.'

'Kev's the one, I reckon,' said Pete.

'Billy left it in the park, so, Kev is the one They must have it, or know who has. They wouldn't waste it; he never wastes anything. He's hiding it. It's right under our noses.'

An air of relief, even cheeriness, spread among them. Even after his fit, he worked out things faster than anyone. He solved problems by sound, smell and touch. He got results even if it meant wielding a wrench, screwdriver or grease gun at someone's face. Paddy was a genius.

'Pete: check Billy's movements on the day he and Badger had a punch-up. Find out what happened. Remember, any time we meet cops, we mention Kev.'

They waited for Paddy's next utterance.

'While Danny's in Canberra, we work on Kev. Just Kev.'

Chapter 39

Crouched over his dog-eared notebook on the kitchen table, Kev wrote a Gundabarri phrase in pencil, an eraser at the ready, and pronounced it repeatedly. He peered around the place, his mind searching for the right letters and markings, Skipper at his feet.

After a deep breath, he thought, this won't be easy.

Acting above your station once daunted him but after he worked for the union he realised himself. As an Official, he talked to his fellow shearers so they understood what needed doing. Like in the army; giving instructions. Now he committed to this business because of Catherine and her Canberra mob. They had confidence in him.

Since he mailed his last tape, he realized Gundabarri had not been 'spelt out.' So, he took the job on. Once he overcame the problem of the lettering to bring words closer to the best pronunciation, he recognized that written on paper the language might be learnt at home or in school. That surprised him.

'Obvious, isn't it, Skipper?'

To the song of his scratching pencil morning passed peacefully until he heard a grumpy, grinding engine on Gumby Road. He expected it to fall away but instead, the vehicle changed down a gear, suggesting a truck turned onto his drive. When it came to rest and two doors opened and closed, the new arrivals made their way to the landing. By the time their footsteps scraped the step, he fronted the door.

'Hello,' he called, seeing two men, one of them, Danny's employer.

Something happened to him, he thought. Everything alright? He turned out his hands as if to say "What's this about?"

Paddy glanced at his companion, Con Demitriotis. 'He's fine.' Almost smiling, Bourke stretched his body like he was newly out of bed. Putting his hand to the wall, and one foot on the boards, he was coming no closer.

Fifteen years ago, this prickly man rammed Dickie's tow car off the road on the other side of the bridge and drove his rival into receivership. Poor Dickie lost everything, only saved from destitution when he won a Council job. He lived on the other side of the river ever since.

Now he stood where Badger once slept, shadowed by a green-and-white motor.

'I've come about a matter.'

'Business?'

'We've got a few things in common. Gotta stick together. We have things to protect, things to share. Cops are a problem, right?'

He let him draw a chummy picture at his leisure.

'Like Danny. He's a good boy. Works well for me. Very friendly with the boys. So helpful.'

'What's this about?'

'He says you'll lead us to the Commodore VL. Seems you're the only person who can.'

Kev sucked his top lip.

He wouldn't.

'You are the man about town, mate. A volunteer plenty; everyone likes that. And now,' he said so melodious, 'I need your assistance because … He stopped mid-sentence. 'It's like this: I left some valuables in the boot. Sentimental value, you understand. Billy drove off with them. Careless of me, I know. He didn't know anything about them; innocent as a newborn.'

He might have admired the mechanic's patter if he hadn't used Danny's name like a casino chip. The rotten odour from the back of the Commodore couldn't be valuable to Bourkie unless … it's a body!

Paddy's rugged face appeared menacing under the landing shade. 'You understand what I'm getting at? I'm not interested in the car. I want to recover my precious things. The car's all yours. Your son as much as said you'd take me.'

'I see. How did you come by the car? What kind of things are they?'

A rare grin. 'Sentimental valuables. I won't insult you by offering a reward, though, why not? Five hundred bucks for your help …easy money.'

'What about Billy? Surely, he's the one to talk to.'

He smirked. 'Ah, poor fellow. He misplaced the VL that night in the park when you drove away with a beautiful new vehicle. And why not? Late model. Air-conditioned. Powerful engine.'

Kev shuffled back, his heel striking the wall. Bourke already knew too much, or was he guessing? 'That car might be dumped in the river,' he said. 'Your goods would be ruined, top to bottom, and no use to anyone.'

'Not your style, mate. Besides, I am offering you five hundred bucks for the location, tipped in water, firebombed or hammered. Uncle Paddy will handle everything, no questions asked.'

He waited, and so did Kev, a heavy silence borne with impatience.

Finally, his visitor took out a fag and asked Con for a light. Once it was lit, he settled back. 'Con is so helpful.'

With that, the boss stepped on the landing. 'I'm grateful for him but losing patience with you.'

'I'll ask around, Mr Bourke.'

'Nar. I think you'll assist me.'

'I will.'

'Not like this, mate. Not like this.'

Kev's face told his enemy more than enough. Paddy threw his fag on the floorboards and ground it in with his cowboy boots until the remains slipped between the boards. He reached into his pocket and took out a silver lighter and a packet of Redhead matches.

Striking a match, he watched the flame settle into a steady burn on its thin slither of wood, and flung it at the cane chair.

Kev moved quickly to smother it, using the nearest rag to prevent the seat from catching fire.

Bourke lit another, this one he tossed onto a newspaper pile beside the door.

'Damn you,' said Kev, turning and he smothered that too.

And another, held in front of his face. 'I'm not normally this clumsy,' casting the flame at the window curtains, although it fell in the woodpile.

Amongst the scattered logs and kindling, he extinguished the match. 'Stop. Just ...'

Paddy grinned, the man's eyes so excited. 'So, Kev, help me out. Or see what a common lighter can do.'

'Not a chance. Get out of here. Out,' forgetting he might call on Con's thuggery.

'That's unfortunate, matey. There's trouble if you think you can run a racket yourself. Think I'll let you threaten me? Think you can turn the cops onto me; pin Badger's murder on me?'

'What are you talking about?'

'Bit late, sonny Jim. Better give up before your place goes up in flames.'

With his jaw grinding, and cheeks rippling, he examined the cottage like a hack building inspector. 'Will burn well. And I don't care who's inside.'

Kev swallowed. 'You've got this all wrong.'

'I've never been more right. You take me to the Commodore or you'll lose everything. New Year's Day. Should be fun.'

Kev remembered how much he disliked tow trucks, and he didn't like green either.

That night, Cassidy's men broke down his front door. The unlocked one. That made an impact. Charlie Ward smashed and climbed through the back window, Crowbar swept aside chairs, scattered and hammered cups, crockery and plates like he played the xylophone. Plenty of noise, action, darkening his senses.

Raids should be quick and loud according to Cassidy. Entry by smash-bash-and-crash, before the poor bastard wakes up. Grab the scumbag before he has time to think, shove him across the room, and pin him against the nearest wall. Put your hand on their throat and the bastard's eyes pop. Extract the guilt and get out of there. If she's a black sheila, dig where no one else dares. Always works.

This isolated suspect received the treatment, the same as everyone else. It produced the same reaction too: the sleepy, wide-eyed crim searched for a way out of chaos, cacophony and calamity. Cassidy laughed.

'A blackfellow in pajamas. What next?'

Back to the wall, clutching a blanket, his eyes narrowed, but his mouth quivered.

A disfigured face pushed against his. 'Gimme the low-down, Kev. Now.'

Turning his face from his inquisitor and his black-faced cohorts, he expelled sweaty fear.

'On what you did to Bicentennial Badger.'

'I told –'

'You told Hanna-spanner a pack of lies.'

A swift slap across the face, and a kick in the groin, darkness preventing any defence. He buckled up in agony, Cassidy peeling him open again, bringing his face close, observing the pain on his face, smirking.

'I'm telling ya, we're serious. Tell us about your gun-toting army, or we'll fuck you over; Billy, Mara and the rest. Where are the weapons?'

He said nothing, sliding to one side, and curling up again, fearing another slap and kick. Or worse.

With his boot against Kev's back, the cop demanded, 'Come on, mate. Give me something. Give. If you're so innocent, give me something.'

Kev searched past, perhaps in hope of seeing an angel, but instead, spied more cops in dark clothes, with blackened faces leering at him; with torches in hand, the house off, altogether a sideshow's Ghost Train of Horrors.

'Why? I –'

'Boy, oh boy, fella. We ask the questions around here. No time for introductions. What do you reckon, boys: did Henry what-his-name say "Please" or "Thank you" before being dispatched?'

Their laughter bore down on him, only encouraging his inquisitor. 'Bet Henry begged forgiveness for his sins, eh? On his knees praying for his hide, because he didn't have much time left. I only wish I could have helped him.'

Cassidy's comic routine must have relaxed him because he fell on the nearby lounge, lit a cigarette, sucked deeply, and let the smoke pour from his lungs.

With a bruised shoulder, crotch and arms, Kev checked out the damage. Coughing violently, clutching a blanket, he didn't attempt comfort.

'Understand, mate,' said Cassidy in darkness. 'We're here for the town's protection. Rough times. Unless you gimme-some-shelter from my boss, you're doomed. So is your son.' Kev stiffened. 'Yeah, Danny. He's been a bad boy. Chances are we'll have him in gaol soon enough. Any time, really.'

Kev wrapped his arms around himself, though he couldn't refrain from closing his eyes and lowering his head.

The cop leapt from the dark, holding Kev's head by his ears, pulling forward, bringing them nose-to-nose. 'Thinking time, mate. Don't hold out. Think quick.' He chuckled in short fits, before pulling back.

'I guess we should wait a bit.' He looked over his shoulder to the men with darting torchlights. 'We clocking overtime yet?'

Laughter rippled around the room as Kev shuffled his legs to fight off the cold.

'You'll catch the flu lying on the floor, fella. Who can tell what condition you'll be in by tomorrow? I ain't no medico. What can I do if you fall sick or try to escape? You could be hurt; you could die. In this dark, you could have a nasty accident. I can't be responsible. Chances are you're on the grog. Kidneys fail. I'm no doctor.'

Cold fluid dripped down his face, whether blood, sweat or snot, didn't matter to him. Further down, his trousers soaked up his fear, the salty urine rising. That bothered him.

Give them something, he thought. Something.

'Come along,' said Cassidy, grabbing his shoulder, then his throat and mouth. With both hands, he slammed him against the wall. Thud. He leaned to his face and placed his hands against his throat. The pressure intensified before his hands moved up and down, oscillating between throat and face.

After a while, his removed his hand, using a finger to draw a sharp line across his windpipe and flesh.

Oblivion.

It was enough.

'The car.'

'What's he saying,' Cassidy asked the other cops? 'Speak clear, mate.' His face drew closer, the tobacco breath flooding his nostrils. He examined him for every sign of fear, a true perfectionist. 'I am listening.'

'Mr Badger's …was …a VL.'

'Bugger you,' answered Cassidy, and shoved him hard against the table.

'Same as Billy's,' he blurted from his wretched position.

'The VL. They're the same.'

'Same? They drive the same model or *is* the same car?'

'Is, same.' Kev tasted blood in his mouth.

'Good boy. Good boy.'

Cassidy paced the floor to take in this new information, leaving him gasping, coughing and rubbing about his throat, his hand glided over his bruised contours. His chest and neck ached. Propping himself, a sharp pain made him fall back against the matting. In this state, he felt as wet as stepping from the shower.

His torturer reappeared. 'So what?' he said, standing over him. 'The Commodore was stolen by your mate. And what? Did they fight over it? Kill him?'

'He ... bought it.'

Cassidy grinned like a car salesman. 'You mean, your mate, the revolutionary, says to Mr Rich Sydneysider: "Here you are, mate. Have a few hundred bucks for your Bicentennial car. I'll take it off your hands. We've been buddies for days. A little fight on the street doesn't matter." Uncle Bicentennary says: "Thanks for the dough. Me vehicle is all yours."

'Sounds sensible, doesn't it, boys?'

He put his back to him but swung around again. 'Fuck you.'

A boot crashed into his thigh.

'Arrh,' cried Kev, his eyes smarting. 'Off Bourke. He bought it ... off Bourke.'

'Hello. Him again. We're playing Pass-the-Parcel, eh? Let's see: The vehicle is sold to a garageman, and Billy the Revolutionary buys a luxury Commodore, as you do. It disappears, and no one's seen it or the official since.'

Cassidy considered it, still grinning. 'Kev. You wouldn't be telling me fibs, would you? More likely you murdered him and sold it on. Where is the corpus delecti? What happened between you and him?'

'He must've ... took the money and ...'

'What a story? Mr Badger is the Happy-little-Vegemite who takes a few hundred, and says "I'll retire on that." He's alive and well and living in Cuba.'

Another kick in the guts, and his eyes watered. His body begged for breath, vomit rising, leaving him sprawled on the floor, Cassidy retreating to the next room. Men talked and whispered, occasionally laughed, expletives free-flowing before his tormentor returned.

'Don't be sad, Kev. Maybe, we've been wrong about you. We're gonna slip out now and make some enquiries. Don't go away, mate. Don't leave this house. Your phone calls will be recorded.'

His parting words were not enough. He picked up the soda bottle, juggled it with both hands and pretended to lose grip. Regaining it in his fist, with all his strength, hurled it across the room. Smash. His wife's gift exploded.

'Remember, we'll have another little chat real soon. And …Merry Christmas.'

Chapter 40

Kev wrapped his cold arms around himself, his injured wrist pulverized where he protected himself from Cassidy's kicks. Conscious and curled up on a gritty, soft surface, still and uncomfortable, his skull throbbed, eyes wet with tears, his beaten legs burning when the slightest pressure brought certain retribution.

The blows.

His ribs had given way like sticks. His consciousness in a moonless realm, pain is its own kingdom. He dug like a worm and scratched like a wombat, his body in an earthen hollow. With shallow breaths, his arms against his chest, his cheek pressed to a coarse surface. He smelt dust and animals, his skin clammy from toe to scalp.

The persistent aching.

Pain's kingdom surged.

My legs.

He bent his knees in search of peace, warmth, comfort and circulation. In return, pain seized his chest and legs, cold and plain.

My lounge. Haven't brushed it in weeks.

Gritty, dull contours imagined behind his swollen eyes. Mara's dolls torn, ragged and dumped.

Am I crippled?

A leering Jimmy Blacksmith looked down on him from a branch, a swaggering wild man in glee.

Now you know, he cried. You're finished.

That was the full fear; his limbs searing, muscles tight or crapped.

I can take it. Nothing's new for an old shearer.

In truth, he couldn't open and unclench his right fist; wouldn't flex. The cuts, abrasions and bruising, parts disfigured, familiar in shearing sheds when things go wrong, or the hours bent.

Nothing new.

A purple-blue tsunami washed over him, shuddering, a body angry for itself, shook him from one side of existence to another, Jimmy Blacksmith above in murky darkness, laughing. This is what it's like.

A second wave, a malevolent violet-grey wake of self-disgust. Revulsion. Pissed himself. Alone. Grasping his coarse blanket, he hauled it across his back, over his neck.

Jesus help me.

But he didn't. Airless, eyes moistened, salty tears rolled over his lips. A warm liquid leaked down his leg. Gasping and drawing back, his head dropped on the cushion, departing unwanted consciousness.

At the cop shop, Cassidy sat in the boss' seat and swirled in front of Detective Hanna. 'Results, mate. Put the frightener up those scumbags, and watch them squeal.' He pointed at Chris. 'Kev Trust held out on you. Billy drove Badger's car. His Commodore somehow became Billy's. So, I got in touch with the last police Chief, Farrell's his name, and he's fairly sure he entered town in a Commodore, a dark colour, not white.'

'So?' said Hanna.

'The previous coppers never made anything out of it. The VL must have been repainted. A spray job at Bourkes, although any bugger can do the job nowadays. When these boongs go bush, they've all the time in the world.

'Kev is a liar, and Farrell confirms it. He's protecting his buddy because signs of their shenanigans will be all over the vehicle.'

Hanna shuffled in his seat, refusing comment.

'It's a link with Badger's disappearance. Those black radicals will murder someone for the price of a new vehicle.'

Chris shook his head, lips downturned.

'It's the squeeze mate,' said Cassidy. 'A firm hand on their throat. Apply the pressure until they squirm and worm and confess. Love it.' He searched officer faces to see whether his words hit the mark, inviting replies.

'I said it earlier,' said Hanna, 'Kev Trust thinks the Bourkes might have murdered the Bicentennial official.'

'He would, wouldn't he? One of the two is our man. Either Kev or Billy knocked him off. If we put a tail on them, it might spoil their revolt. Bang one or both behind bars and I bet the rest couldn't run a chook raffle.'

Hanna swung away, hands in the air.

'You're a bad loser, mate. I got the info, not you. Simple as that.'

As Hanna did not respond, Cassidy sneered. 'Hey, be happy. If we locate the car, we'll enjoy a week off.'

'A paint job implicates the Bourkes. Besides, we've no evidence linking Badger's disappearance with a black mutiny.'

'OK. If we could only find the frigging Commodore, we'll soon see about that.' Cassidy pushed against the wall, sending him and the chair to the room's centre. 'What have you got on Princess Mara?'

Hanna wrinkled his nose and narrowed his eyes. 'Apart from J-walking and swearing mightily, nothing. She dashes into the scrub now and again so she could be wise to us.'

'Up to no good in the bushes,' said Cassidy, swivelling a full circle in his seat.'Anyway, Kev holds more secrets. Either Badger left his place that morning or he didn't. But it doesn't explain how Billy repainted the car days later.'

'The Bourkes.' He had to say that much.

'You're obsessed. Get a life.'

Chapter 41

In the pale light morning, Kev trudged down the road with Skipper trailing. With the earth at his feet, he countered his lung pain with shallow breathing. Another metre passed with his head hung down, rocks and stones avoided like bad memories. Barefooted, each post marked progress without triumph. With an arm against his chest, he dared not look ahead.

Poor Danny. Bastard cops said they'd hurt him, and meant it.

He limped down the rough track bathed in warm, dry air, no longer pinned to a wall by uniform, nor pressed to the floor by a copper's knee. He stepped left, right, to the junction where gravel gave way to tarmac. Once a brisk ten-minute walk, it took most of an hour.

There! Someone ...It's Ted, chatting with them river-dwellers outside the motel.

Ted spotted a lone figure, an ordinary man in pyjamas. At first, he thought it might be some mad bugger, another fella gone crackers in the sun. But his laboured steps, stiff movement and vacant stare said otherwise. His old mate.

Must be him. Something's wrong!

He scrambled across the road and down the track to meet him. 'Look at you. You're a beetroot in pyjamas. Casualty for you. Good God!'

At the Hospital's front desk, Kev spoke first. 'Might be a few broken ribs.'

The receptionist gasped, recognizing the swellings, the bruises, the difficult physical movements, his face drawn. Besides, it was kindly Mr Trust, their gardener.

'Hell's Bells,' said the Head Nurse. 'What happened to you?'

She fetched a wheelchair. 'I'll take him through.'

Later. she questioned him as other staff gathered around.

'I'd rather not say,' he said as any movement or violent thought brought pain.

But Suzy Conroy insisted. 'I'll take it to the police.'

Humoured, he laughed in agony. 'That's just it.'

'Oh, Mother Mary,' she said, then cut his pyjama top to ribbons. 'Them. To a man of your age.' She waved the others away. 'We'll put on bandaging. Doctor Panetta will be here tomorrow.'

Mara and Susan invaded the wardroom in dull light, Mara greeting familiar patients before him. 'I won't hug you, bud; it might kill you.'

The room burst into laughter, and that hurt.

'I heard,' said Susan, her hand touching his shoulder. 'The cops, wasn't it?'

Cocooned in his warm bed sheets, sedated, he sensed their presence as they surveyed his battered face. Mara wept.

'Keep this from Danny,' he said. 'He shouldn't worry.'

She held his hand as Susan leaned to. 'We'll get those bastards. And Welfare at us too. They are after her kids.'

Mara raised her hand. 'Nothing new, eh Kev? You rest easy. No social worker's gonna take anyone away. We're staying right here.'

He emerged from the haze many hours later, struggling against the bedsheet's stiff embrace. His body sweated sweet puss and acetous drugs and a sickly odour like rotting vegetables. With white walls, starched pillows and passing nurses, the angular sunlight blinded him.

Is it morning or afternoon?

A nurse pushed in a silver tray of glinting, scraping, chiming cutlery with tea and biscuits, cornflakes and toast.

Hmm. Breakfast.

After his plain fare, the disturbances fell away. Blue skies and waving eucalypts outside his window, the silence within. Sharp light cut to a blazed glory like The Coming itself. His hand ran along the crisp sheets and in the absence of smarting pain, he winced and spluttered.

The next day he struggled down the corridor and phoned Billy.

'Billy?'

'Hey. Who's that?'

'Billy? It's me, bud.'

'Kev. What are you doing?'

'I got to tell you. The Police. They've been around my place.'

'What? Over Christmas?'

'They beat me up, Billy. Made me tell them things.'

'Bastards.'

'They made me.'

'How do you mean?'

'I'm in hospital. I had to give them something or I was dead.'

'What have they done to you?'

'Don't matter. They know you drove the Commodore the night of the raid ...That car was Mr Badger's.'

'What!?'

'The Commodore you dumped in the park. It was Mr Badger's.' When Billy said nothing, he repeated 'Didn't you know?'

'Bugger me, Kev. My Commodore? I bought the little beauty from Pete Bourke.'

'The cops will be asking questions. Have you been raided?'

'It's bloody Christmas, Kev. Those guys never miss a holiday.'

'Just as well. But ...I'm sorry, OK?'

Billy said nothing, wondering again whether the line had dropped out. 'Mate. Danny's in the backyard. Will I put him on?'

'No. Let's keep it between us. He shouldn't worry.'

'Sure.'

'I'm sorry. Everything's going wrong, ever since we lost Henry.'

'Yeah. Them cops are out of control.'

No need for further gibber-gabber. His throat was dry and sore. 'Stay together, Kev. I'll deny owning the car. There are no photos. From now on, there is no beautiful VL. I must have imagined it.'

'I had to give them something.'

'It's OK. Pete sold me that car. Bugger me, how in hell did they come by it?'

'The Bourkes sold it to you?'

'Uh, ha.'

'You drove into the park that day.'

'Of course.'

A jumble of voices at the other end. 'Hey,' he shouted. Git –'

The line went dead.

Kev had to think. If the Bourkes supplied Billy with the Commodore, how did they come by it? Badger clashed with Pete or Paddy he guessed. Either one of them, but not both, he suspected.

Perhaps he is buried behind the workshop. It's too awful to think of the body stored in the boot all this time. Might explain why the key is missing.

One of the Bourkes has it! Or Billy is making up stories. If they sold it to him as is, wouldn't he wonder what was going on?

Damn. Danny is living in his flat. He'll question him, wily-like.

Kev's hand reached for his exploding head.

Nothing I can do, about anything.

He assured himself he could keep the secret of where they dumped the vehicle. Danny though? Staying with his 'uncle'?

He sighed. Staying in Sydney was better than being here, as Cassidy couldn't hurt him. But the police in the city might.

He had to consider it: Would Billy kill Badger? They fought on the street and clashed at the Council meeting only the day before. Could it have led to murder? Or did Pete's gang knock him off? Given the recent visit, Paddy's threat chilled him. Why would he or Pete stop now? His "goods" must be code for Badger's corpse.

Like Inspector Boney, he reflected on the subject at lunch. He chewed over the problem as he received lashings of sympathy from hospital staff. Billy's cousins visited him too, without offering legal help. The young blokes occupied the 'shop' until Uncle Billy returned.

Denny Carboni, town chemist and condom queen, offered him her sympathies. 'They oughta put a stop to it,' she said. 'The place is going to the dogs.' Dickie popped in with a million theories on who, why and how this-and-that happened, reckoning Cheryl harassed anyone who stood in her way. Most shopkeepers and cockies supported her, though the cops might serve or frighten them.

Marco came in, checking out his credit worthiness, he guessed. He elaborated on his growing business in sandwich-making for detectives, offering to take a sweet pickle revenge, Kev declined, as any poisoning would see the shopkeeper put in gaol.

A few bowling club members arrived with chocolates, coyly saying, 'We want you to have them,' to make up for two years of silence. Past friends and acquaintances of him and Bess.

You'd think I suffered a heart attack.

The Pommy teacher, Glen, muttered about *One Flew Over the Cuckoo's Nest*, *Easy Rider*, *Chinatown* and all that, a conspiracy of the rich and powerful, the dumb and the dumber, he said. When he learnt of events he fired his air rifle through the boarding house ceiling. 'Better than putting my boot through the TV,' he said.

No sign of her. Irreconcilable differences, he suspected. Busy with her mayoral duties.

With a few more days in bed, he formulated nine tales of what might have happened. Tired of visitors, though consoled and sore. He faced facts: Cassidy and Bourke were dangerous men. No one could stop them. Striking out in anger like Jimmy Blacksmith spelt defeat; and though Billy and Mara could be willful, determined and bloody-minded, it was not his way. Besides, the police and the Bourkes help each other, and both had firepower.

Hiding in the hospital delayed things. They'll be after me the moment I step out of here. They want the Commodore. I have to decide.

Chapter 42

'The whole town talks about it,' said Marco.

'You mean him?'

'The cops have been hitting him around. My God, in his home, they kicked him in the guts until his ribs broke.' The taller, balding bloke shook his head, though everyone expected a conversation in his store. 'He's a wreck. His face is terrible.'

'Police are out of control.'

'He fooled them though. Walked from the hospital after breakfast. On Sunday.' The hard-faced listener poked out his lips. 'So much trouble,' he said. 'Never had it before.'

'Too right,' said Paddy, grabbing a Coke from the fridge and tossing two dollars on the counter. 'I'll pray for Kev.'

Back at the garage, he threw his fizzy drink at the corner wall, shattering the bottle. 'Pete. Ginge,' he yelled, 'Get yourselves in here.'

The two out the back squeezing blackheads and sharing girly magazines so the arrival at the workshop's back door took longer than expected.

The boss had his hands on his hips. 'Come in, you silly buggers. The cops bashed Kev, and now the bastard's gone bush. We've gotta move.'

'Been shooting and rooting, ain't we?'

'God Almighty. Don't you guys comprehend? They are after the VL. If they find the car before us, we're cooked. If we don't locate it –'

The phone rang, and he broke away. Even on New Year's Eve, they gave twenty-four-hour service.

'Yeah?'

'I've found the Commodore,' said a voice.

'OK.'

'So, no need to keep searching.'

'We can fetch the vehicle for you, Billy, in town or nearby. No problem.'

'Bourkie. My friends told me to grab it myself.'

'You are getting me confused. I'm offering assistance. You're down in Sydney, mate.'

'Never mind where I am. I'm hearing things about you I don't like.'

'Like?'

'Lay off Murris, Bourke. You've got form.'

'I'm shaking. You're scaring me.'

'Shake in your boots, Bourkie, because I have a few lawyers in my service. Got the Royal Commission wanting stories. The media's lapping up my words. Better be damn careful or I'll make you the story.'

'Billy. You got me all wrong. Nothing happening here. I'm only doing my business, staying out of trouble.'

'Keep the peace, bud, because I'm coming to town.'

'Good. You'll need a car. Always ready for helping. Satisfied customer and all that.'

'I reckon you're keeping something from me. Just stay away from Kev, or else.'

'My word. He knew about your car for ages. What do you think he's after?'

No reply.

'You there?'

'Sure. And lay off Danny, or we're after you. If you talk to anyone about the VL, make sure it's me.'

Before he answered, Billy hung up.

Paddy dropped the phone before strolling back to the boys, and putting his hand on Pete's shoulder. 'Matey. You sold the car to him. Now he's curious, nosey and demanding.'

His son stepped away from his grip, suspecting his other arm might swing at him. His dad made him squeeze Danny for information and hadn't helped. He and the Hard Boys already did the heavy lifting; they deserved more respect.

'You got some making-up to do, son.'

'I know what I'm doing.'

'Is that right? You can't tell shit from a hamburger. Look at the situation. Kev gets roughed up by the cops and half the town saying he's a son-of-the-soil. How about that? People are getting all sentimental about him. I shed a few tears myself at Marco's to keep him sweet. I warned that boong to give back the VL. So, now he's gone bush. If he thinks he can hold out on us …'

He held up his fist. 'Hell, Pete: those two annoy me. One's a bloody bully, and the other's a do-gooder. And you sold the Commodore to Billy.'

'So?'

'We could land in Long Bay Gaol. Our goods are locked in the boot.'

'No one fucking told me.'

Paddy whacked him in the neck, and he reeled against a chassis, hand to his cheek, eyes smarting. He moved closer. 'Listen: we're going to find the car, so stop pissing around.'

Pete didn't answer. Ginge either. Better to say nothing when his dad stood over them.

'Billy's coming to town. As sure as Hell, he's gonna collect the Commodore. He knows where to find the beast.' His dad's hand squeezed a spanner like he was ready to whack something or someone. He marched away, and back again, grimacing. 'We'll tail Billy. Once he leads us to the VL, you boys do whatever it takes.'

Pete wiped his hand across his face.

Whatever-it-takes, he thought, torturing a smile.

That's my idea too. Yeah. Dad usually wins.

He bit his lip. Whatever it takes. Like Schwarzenegger or Dirty Harry.

Grabbing a nearby rag, Paddy rubbed his stainless-steel spanner, and held it up like a trophy. 'Now you'll earn your keep, son, because what I promise, I deliver.'

Chapter 43

After Christmas, Danny join the Sydney exodus to cross the Blue Mountains, singing and miming to his driving rock 'n roll, his VW dashboard vibrating in sympathy. 'My, my, mmmy,' he sang over an ecstatic, female voice, his feverish hand tapping on the steering wheel, his head nodding to the beat.

Grand music.

Homeward bound after his Sydney holiday, with all its sweet memories. Instead of busing-it, he drove to Bathurst to visit a few buddies and continued on the next day.

Man; what a fantastic time. With the dough I earned at Bourkes, I have this red VW.

After he bought it, Billy threw him fifty-bucks for retreads. It gladdened him so much, plain his dad's friend became his 'uncle.'

'Stay cool,' said his hothead mate at his departure.

'Why not come with me?'

'Got something going for New Year, Danny boy. Thanks for the offer.'

So, he turned his back to the city's inglorious Bicentennial celebrations.

Invasion Day.

No. I'm going home.

To summer's heat, outback plains and cold beer, some shooting and fishing, idle cricket, a swim in the river, the odd bet, hanging around Mara's campfire. Mag and yarn with the girls from his school days.

Billy reckoned he'd found Chrissie too.

'Where is she?'

But he's a cagey bugger. Gave me no details; no arrival time, no return date.

How could he arrive the bearer of happy news? If he disappointed Mara, and Christine didn't come soon after, he'd have a mighty price to pay.

Uncle Billyo. Gotta love him though.

On Boxing Day, they borrowed the video machine from the Legal Centre and watched the Rabbitoh's last Grand Final win, the whole gang rooting for their heroes on the back landing. Sizzling BBQs.

Billy taught him the good fight, but warned: 'It's an all-in scrap sometimes, like league or show fights. You go in hard, mate. Hit them where it hurts. Only, you got to use your brains; don't volunteer your chin. Two-hundred years, our hands tied behind our backs. Now the Bicentenary, celebration of their continental loss.

Henry ain't celebrating.

His concerns were not about politics, or football. He wasn't sure what it meant anyway. All about elections, parliament and politicians, but none of that made sense to him. But they deserved better than unemployment, disease and living in dumps. They were here first.

Billy's ideas were sharper than Dad's.

One day.

With the Commodore ditched at The Hole, they could get along again. Things would improve. Working for Bourkes, he could hold his head high. Being a Hard-Boy gave him pride, even if they were a bit over-the-top. His Dad and Mara should turn a blind eye.

More car-moving jobs. Easy money. Cash in hand.

OK. Dad doesn't want me there, but there isn't much work in and around town. He understands. Besides, I've brought gifts.

Man. When I arrive, I'm making an entrance.

Beep-beep. Be-e-ep.

When Danny's red VW braked, scrapped and tore into the main street's crumbling surface, it guaranteed the Hard Boy spied his arrival from the Shearer's Arm's verandah.

'A bloody Volkswagen.'

'You're joking. What a rust-bucket.'

The Hard Boys laughed at the sight of it.

A rust and dust "Beatle" with a lame-duck's horn, engine at the wrong end, and shaped like a half-moon; a jalopy. Couldn't be owned by anyone from town, everyone wanted a Ford or Holden. A few brave souls risked credibility talking about Toyotas. No one possessed a VW.

'It's a girl's car.'

A thought jerked the collective muscle: we'll have a little fun with this one.

They rose, beers in hand, leaning over the footpath railing. A Volkswagen is a laugh, when driven by a blow-in, light entertainment. As the joker put on a show with his city-slicker toy, throwing up dust in their eyes, they had a right to take-the-piss. Lousy parking too.

'She needs driving lessons.'

As they approached the car, out popped Danny.

'Struth.'

'Bloody hell.'

He carried a shiny steel implement in his callased hand, a screwdriver in the other, heading towards them.

Con spied him with weapons in hand. 'Bastard knows.'

Pete pulled out his blade, his eyes locked on the new arrival. He thrust out the hunting knife he used to skin and gut 'roos.

Danny's stride fell away. Standing midway, exposed, he instinctively lifted the wrench to his chest.

A few drinkers caught sight of the confrontation. A fight?

Danny's face clouded. 'Can't you see?'

'I can see, alright. Now, piss off.'

'What?'

'You're not one of us, dickhead. Piss off.'

The tool dropped from Danny's hand and Ginge stepped back rather than forward, suspecting a trick. So did Pete.

'Bugger off, boong. You're all washed up, like your dad.'

'Yeah. Nick off, unless you'd like a shit sandwich.'

Danny's face contorted, hand rubbing against his leg. His eyes darted this way and that. 'You …you bastards.'

Pete smirked. 'You're dead meat, Danny; like Henry; too big for your black boots.'

Stepping back, Danny retreated nearer his VW, the Hard Boys laughing themselves stupid, poking out tongues and making rude signs.

Pub customers gathered around windows and doors enthralled by the prospect of more than usual. Although they pointed knives at young Danny, there was nothing they could do, and nobody wanted a knife in their belly. Besides, it made sense for him to beat an undignified retreat.

'Hey, fellas,' said someone behind, a caller from the pub offering a distraction.

With their backs to the pub, the Hard Boys refused to turn away, retaining their defiant stance. More drinkers peeked around the door, pushing their way outside. Old Harry Messell waved his thin finger calling out, 'Mean ole Paddy's boys.'

'Bugger off, you lot,' said Ginge.

'Yeah. We're talking business.'

'What's the knife for?' said someone from amongst the crowd.

'Keep your noses out of this.'

Danny stood at his car door.

Finally, he looked around, sensing enemies behind, when –

'Copper!' A few drinkers dashed away. Others shuffled backwards, pulling their head inside or feigning casual conversations with daylight, leaving the lads exposed. Pete sheathed his blade under his jacket, between trousers and belt. Danny retreated to his vehicle as red-headed Terry scanned the corner for more uniform.

'Something the matter?' A familiar, plain-clothes cop, standing a few metres from the pub entrance, expressionless, alert, eyes narrow, his posture suggested his right to step on their turf and trample all over it. His stare fell on the gang near the gutter.

'Back off,' said Detective Hanna.

The Hard Boys returned to the footpath with contemptuous sneers. It was no time for trouble after Paddy's orders. As for the lone officer, he couldn't take on four of them, and calling for backup wouldn't earn him friends at the station.

From the pub door, old Harry called, 'Devils.'

Chapter 44

Danny fumed. That fuel in his tank drove him down Gumby Road, but his brain seized up with anger. Poison anger. Rogue anger. A sense of betrayal that saw him grip the steering wheel like he was ready to fight.

What's got into them? I've done nothing to them. Been away, so … Am I fired? What the hell was going on? Shit, shit, shit.

Turning into the driveway, instead of seeing his familiar shack, henhouse and river bank, he saw the town fire truck and a few men scurrying around a lazy smoke. They drifted across their way, and further in, his home appeared intact. But on foot, he found ashes past the front door, burnt wood, cracked fibro and the buckled ironwork, their garage in cinders.

From the steps, the unaffected front door expected someone to knock and be welcomed; a mockery of the reality. Everything else was broken and crumbled, the black and grey roof, walls of the bedroom, furniture, beds, mirrors. The men hosed down small fires spread in the surrounding bush, trees still smoldering. The garage consisted of twisted iron sheeting and skeletal poles poking out of the ashen rubble like barbequed ribs.

Noticing Danny's arrival, fireman Ted raised his hand, yelling: 'Your dad's not home,' the others taking note of him before resuming work.

Danny put his hand to his head. So, why this? What for?

Only minutes earlier Bourke's gang rejected and humiliated him in front of everyone. Is this what Pete meant when he said "you're too late"? "Too big for your black boots"? He turned around sharply.

The Commodore! Pete wanted it so badly.

What'll dad think?

Slapping his hand on the VW's roof, he approached the fire-truck, pressing his hands on the paintwork.

It's punishment.

He stepped up to the henhouse where the rooster and hens lay dead, confronting a hairy, singed form, slumped against the wire fencing.

Skipper!

His hand reached within patting distance, hovering over the carcass, seeing the mutt's scorched nose and a small bullet hole through its brain.

Rising from the remains, he staggered to the fringe, ignoring the raw heat, avoiding eye contact, the place smelling of singed feathers, hair and flesh.

Only one person would kill Dad's pet like this. Pete. Of course. His way of telling him so.

For reasons unknown to himself, he walked to the river bank, rubbed his scalp, staring downstream to that bridge and those fish traps, onwards to tender infinity.

Them. Paddy and the Hard Boys.

Only way our place would catch alight.

He kicked the sand.

Ha! The kitchen's intact. But where's dad?

When Teddy took a break with the other firemen, Danny spied the rust-red fire truck and his vintage VW like lost causes, both vehicles the makings of a museum. Worth a laugh, but with the cottage's back frame teetering, two firemen fetched a long steel rod and gave it a final push.

Collapse. Down went Kev's 1964 monument, a shack build by his hands from timber, bricks and framing he salvaged; a home provided for a pregnant Bessy.

No whooping, laughter or celebratory pats on the back after demolition. Arson embarrassed them. Their buddy, Kev, his garage and much of the cottage, burnt down, his house ruined, his son in shock.

All three men realized the stakes greater than they could calculate. But what could they say after Kev's assault and escape from hospital? He outsmarted the cops and they wanted payback.

The fire started in the garage, and spread. They sniffed kerosene.

No idle chat this time, having the boy there.

The town's firemen would not prattle on about this in front of him. They would talk about the cop's savagery later, the threat to Mara's children, the assault on Kev in his home, and Henry's death in custody another time. By now, most of the town learnt what they did to him, even when the *Advocate* did not report it. The fellow volunteered so much, the fellow who believed in getting along? If the out-of-towner TRG did this, what else would they do?

A keen footballer with a talent for drawing, he was Kev's angel boy. How much could they tell a young bloke the truth without burdening him beyond his years, without making him as angry as hell. He might go off and do something crazy.

At last, Teddy approached. 'What do you think? Was it them?'

Danny identified the culprits, no problem; a couple of Hard Boys raced in, did a sloppy job, quick and dirty. In and out, all matches and guns, then back to the pub for celebrations. When he appeared so soon after, they panicked.

'Yeh, it was them.'

So, it *is* the cops, thought Ted.

'Where's Dad?'

'Matey. He skipped town.'

'What?'

'The police put him in hospital.'

Danny's jaw dropped.

'He didn't want you to worry, so he –'

'Where is he?'

Ted shrugged his shoulders. 'I reckon he's gone bush. They'll never find him.'

So, he would be homeless, fatherless and righteous.

'If I were you, I wouldn't bother reporting this to the coppers.'

Danny dragged his hands down his face.

His dad assaulted by cops. Paddy and the Hard Boys burnt down their home. Yeh, he understood what he meant. Don't inform the cops about what they already knew; they'd only laugh at him. Given the town elected the two-faced Cheryl Sheila as mayor, what's the use of telling people something they don't want to hear?

Aar r r r r r r r r r r r r r rrrrh.

His cry drawn out like a solitary dingo's.

Not at Ted. Not at anyone. Yet, Pete must have dobbed his Dad like he said he would.

No dobbing, he said in front of us. Demanding our loyalty.

Betrayal.

Danny sprung up, and paced ground like the last Tasmanian tiger fighting extinction.

Ted put a hand on his shoulder. 'What are you going to do?'

Danny swept the arm away. 'Just bugger off.'

Grabbing the pig-knife poked in the log, he jumped in the VW and drove away.

I'll deal with Pete and the Hard Boys myself.

Chapter 45

New Year's Eve, Sydney

Redfern is Sydney's loveliest suburb, downbeat, down-to-earth and down market, heating up over summer, the street tar bubbling black day by day, the evening cool giving permission for celebrations and disagreements spilling to the streets.

Closer to the city, parkland Domain and the Cross neighbourhood, younger patrons, fueled by alcohol and recreational drugs, sometimes lost civility, made skirmishes ending in theft and hard-arsed knifings. More traditional and natural enthusiasms occurred nearer secluded harbor coves.

When Billy and the others rose from their beds at three am, they prepared to invade harbour shores. Under a naked light bulb, they loaded their provisions and drove the short distance from Redfern down the Art Gallery Road into the Botanic Gardens. Their black faces grinned when they passed the unmanned police roadblock to claim a plumb location around Lady Macquarie's Chair. With a glorious panorama, camped on the grassy slope before the New Year ship's parade.

He clenched his fist. 'Dare to struggle, dare to win.'

In jungle fatigues, he probably stood out as the other picnickers dressed in the urban camouflage of blue jeans, T-shirts and overcoats. Unloading equipment by torchlight, the two men and two women pitched their K-Mart tents with supplies inside, leaving space for sleeping beauties.

They won the best location for a New Year's celebration. From here the re-enactment of Captain Phillip's 1788 landing would be followed by the tall ships parade, speeches and partying, fireworks, carousing and more; everyone inebriated, careless and disarmed. They overlooked the Harbour Bridge and the Sydney Opera House

They were armed with food, drinks and blankets, all the city's jewels before them: the dark, sparkling waters, its bushland parks and numerous secluded bays. They imagined the time when their people paddled bark canoes past Pitchgut to confront the strangers and their massive vessels. Their distant relatives would have been amazed, dazzled and intimidated by the white devils in their ghost boats with red uniformed soldiers, bellowing sails and spidery ropes.

Billy adored this spot with its 360-degree views from Sydney headlands to the city skyline, the arched bridge and the gleaming Opera House between, the lush Botanic Gardens to the left, the shimmering bays and bushy heights beyond, some parts almost unchanged for centuries.

'They should paint it black,' he said, a blanket over his knees.

'Nineteen-eighty-eight. I love New Year's night.'

As Coral smiled, he put his arm around her.

'Unfurl a banner, you blokes,' said Kylie. 'Let them know.'

'It can wait until morning.'

'Bloody slacko.'

'I'm catching some kip now.'

'Me too.'

At first light, Billy awoke to the aroma of onions, toast and coffee. Sticking his head out of the tent, Coral lit their two gas stoves, preparing breakfast.

'Got some champagne, m'lady?'

'Tea and damper. And here's the caviar.' Coral handed him thick, buttered toast with brown muck.

'Hmm. Fish paste.'

'Almost as good.'

Later, the crew completed their Protest Lawn, marking out a generous area for themselves, space with signs saying 'We were here first', 'Land Rights Now' and 'All Immigrants Go Home.' They brought a thousand fliers. 'We'll hand them out soon.'

With a burner boiling water and a checked tablecloth spread out before them, their domesticated tent embassy opened for business. Their mob were staying, all day, all week, all year; taking turns after the dumb-arsed re-enactment.

'Break out the sausages and eggs.'

By midday, more revellers filled the peninsula, many in *Genesis* and *Bon Jovi* T-shirts, carrying huge tape decks and beers by the crate, their picnic baskets full of food, champagne and pillows.

'Where's Yogi bear?'

The men wore golfer shorts and plain shirts, the women, jeans, dark green dresses or tight black slacks with red belts. Although midsummer, it didn't stop them from wearing leg warmers, scrunches and butterfly clips.

The big-hair-look caught Coral's attention. 'Must be the Paddington mob. Bloody trendies. Take a geek,' she said nodding in the general direction, having the grace not to point. 'It's a jewellery shop with legs.'

As the day advanced, radio-tape decks blasted out disco, or themes from *The Dukes of Hazard* and Astro Boy. Countdown's Greatest Hits competed with *The Goodies*, *The Young Ones*, and *Kenny Everett*, the wall of noise rendering the harbor unsightly. 'Hells bells, what a racket! This place is madder than a brown snake,' said Billy.

'Wait 'til it gets quiet and dark,' said Coral.

'Yeah. A favourite,' said Ky. 'Beer, chocolate and a romp in the tent.'

Billy smiled but his mind turned to another matter.

I've got a Commodore to collect.

Wait 'til Coral runs her hand over the bonnet.

PART FIVE, Chapter 46

Return Service

'Welcome back,' said Chief Warren to his squad. 'You're just in time for a Bicentennial New Year.' Most men enjoyed a holiday grin but those who held the outback fort, like Crowie and Shortie, scowled. 'You guys had a week at home while the rest of us didn't. Well, "Hello" again. We've got no Badger, no car, a few guns, and no Kev.'

'No Kev?' said someone from the back.

'Yeah. Someone put him in hospital before leaving us. Now he's hopped it. Gone bush. Well done, Cassidy.' The officer opposite held his tongue, though his jaw protruded. 'Well, what have you got to say?'

'Kev cracked. We followed standard procedure and when we find him again, he'll confess everything.'

'Ah, I love the voice of confidence,' said the Chief, letting an unholy silence fill the room. 'We ascertained Billy took Badger's car to the wake. Had it repainted. They had a punch-up the night before. They had another altercation at the Council meeting, so he is a prime suspect. He drove the Commodore into the park where he did his mad-bugger routine, arrested for riot. The previous coppers dealt with the black blubber and his city lawyers but no one saw the link.' He surveyed the room again and stepped forward. 'So, get around the district. Talk to people. Ruffle a few feathers. Find him, the guns and ammunition; more than anything, I want the bloody VL.

'I want more info on Kev and his gang. Where's he gone? Who took him? Who's he been talking to? That way, we'll find the car. The Bicentennial revolt and Badger's disappearance are linked.'

A week's leave refreshed most of the squad but not Warren. They recognised his speech lacked its usual punch, his face hacked and sunburnt. Chris Hanna volunteered to stay over the summer but the heat and lack of progress on this case hadn't affected him.

Bloody dopes, thought Edwards. The two of them must be bar-B-Qed by now.

'Christ,' said Warren. 'The Bicentenary starts tonight. From New Year's Day, our black cousins are planning a stink, Chief Billy among them. Word is, it happens on Australia Day. HQ's telling us to make a breakthrough. With a revolt afoot, we reckon Badger was target practice. So, any ideas?'

'We could find out more,' said Cassidy, 'if we offered rewards. The low-life around here will sell their mother for a few dollars.'

'Your opinion. I want concrete means and material results.'

'For a pack of fags, their kids will tell us what mum and dad said over dinner. First port. For the cost of a flagon, I bet the river-dwellers will also pitch in.'

'OK, go for it. Stretch the budget.' Warren removed his Service hat. 'Lastly, for all you happy holidayers, a few nights ago we found arrows in the station door. A crossbow fired from across the road. No messages, just a little piece of bastardry care of the niggers. So bloody well keep your wits about you. Some of these buggers fight dirty.'

The men exchanged glances, sure and certain it would be no fun having an arrow in your guts. Using primitive weaponry was a low act, giving the Task Force a new way of meeting misfortune.

'That's not all. While you were away screwing your wives, poor old Detective Hanna and Crowie collected another body, a farmer impaled on his backhoe. Name of Harris. Ugly stuff.'

'His wife is missing,' said Crowie.

'God knows why the bloke would farm over Christmas or husband a crop at all,' said the boss, crushing his hat in his fist. 'The wife's either ran away after murdering him or been kidnapped. The town's a maggot of rumours. Every stupid bugger has ideas on who's been knocking off who, and we're included.'

Squad members eyed each other, shaking heads, lips downturned. What was Warren rambling on about?

'Anyway, the thing is, the black radicals are on the cusp of their anus,' he said waiting for applause. 'Show this place we make and stick to the rules. Next couple of days, it's lockdown. Let me spell it out: anyone points their arse at you, arrest them. If someone causes trouble on the street, cuff them. Strike hard and hit first. Carry your guns, and scare the shit out of any disturbing influence. We might raid the Unity or the Shearers Arms, the teacher's residence, park, office or caravan kingdom. We're warning troublemakers.'

A few faces grinned. This is what they signed up for.

'But for Heaven's sake, do not, repeat, do not fire your weapons. Only a mad bastard's gonna take us on. We got muscle. We use back up.'

The squad admired standard procedure, even on Sundays. Having weaponry handy always scared the natives, and if not, the stupid buggers deserve everything that hit them.

'Refrain,' said Warren, as an afterthought, 'from ramming doors except during an operation. The deal is, be everywhere. Be there in force, show them what we've got. Take into custody at the first resort, not the last, whether they're smashing bottles, pissing in the street, loitering, cursing, whatever. Let them know the Law is boss.'

Although the squad appeared satisfied, a few bums shifted in their seats.

'Antsy, ain't yous?' he said. 'We've still got to find Badger, Kev and the car. So, Hanna, put it to Mara; unless she coughs up information, Welfare will take her kids. Everyone else, damn well find the car. We need a body.'

The Chief slammed his fist into the palm of his hand, picked up his crushed hat and headed for a squad vehicle.

'Bingo,' said Cassidy leaning on his desk. 'Target Kev, Billy and the Commodore. Knew it.' Hanna took a deep breath and shook his head. 'And that bitch, Mara. You got the best job.'

He waited for Hanna to lose it but his object of derision only grit his teeth. He turned away, run his hand through his hair, and hoped the dandruff spread.

The bastard's not the same since he raided Kev's.

'I still reckon we're after the Bourkes,' said Hanna as casual as could be. 'They keep coming up. You need equipment and experience for spray painting. What's the bet, he's running hot cars?'

'Leave it out, will ya. Who cares? We're TRG. We're after murderers, radicals, anarchists and agitators. We're after black conspirators, gun runners and the like. Billy the motor mouth has a history. Odds on the others are co-conspirators.'

But Hanna hadn't finished. 'Who's to say Bourke isn't working with them; supplying and feeding them? Think he'd knock back quick money? If we can put Bourke out of play, the black radicals will lack a conduit. He must be part of it. Could have knocked off Badger. Maybe he is hiding the Commodore.'

'Mate, you have too much imagination. You already visited him. Didn't bother telling me. And what did you find? Nothing to tell?'

'He's all bluff and denial. His workshop is cluttered but nothing is going on? He employs at least six people.'

'So, he's as cagey as they come. Ain't a crime.'

'Are you listening? We've assaulted Kev Trust and I'm supposed to threaten Missy Mara. We're busting into people's homes, harassing families and finding nothing. It's not right; we're wasting resources.'

'You need a break, mate, a little sunshine and a shag. You're a toffee: dark on the outside and soft on the inside. You gotta be hard all over.'

Chapter 47

Cassidy, Edwards and the rest of the TRG scratched their heads, stomach and waist from a flea outbreak at the station. Bad enough with nine men cramped into a room designed for four, and worse when everyone moved to the back area to allow the fumigation guys their afternoon's work.

Two squadmen occupied a cell each for the next few days, keeping indoors and raiding the fridge, so news of the fire outside of town did not reach them.

Warren laughed. He told them to patrol the streets more often, make presentations in the school, do exercises and stay away from bad women. Mercifully, he resisted puns about 'the itch', 'little buggers' or 'producing evidence' so they thanked him in absentia as he used The Club facilities to fraternise with the better class of locals.

The squad did not appreciate his suggestion that they join a panel-beating course when they returned to the city as the budget did not extend to using Bourke's every ten seconds. So what if rough driving and attacks by local delinquents resulted in more dints, bumps and scratches on the patrol cars?

In the absence of anything useful to do, his men scribbled messages on the station walls and loitered in Marco's air-conditioned shop by his refrigerator or at the sandwich counter. They took long lunches and emptied his shelves of Vegemite, chocolate biscuits and Smith's Crisps, with tea an afterthought; everything on-the-tab as NSW Police Force paid their lunch bills. According to Dewar, their presence kept thieves from entering so they deserved a fatter sandwich.

'Three corn-beef and tomato on rolls,' said Cassidy. 'Another two with double ham, and a free Chiko roll. Anyone want pickles?'

With uniforms clustering around him, Marco wiped the steel bench, sweeping away breadcrumbs near the meat slicer, long enough to annoy them.

Edwards whistled a gee-up, a hurry-on, the shopkeeper moving to one side, opening the cooler, taking out the cold meats and butter, reaching into the Fruit-and-Veg section for the overripe tomatoes.

'Dagos making sandwiches. At least they're learning,' said Eddie.

'Lots of mayonnaise, will ya,' said Dewar.

'It's Marco. My name is Marco.'

'Mate, don't get your knickers in a knot.'

The shopkeeper slid behind the glass casing, buttering the rolls, and preparing ingredients.

Why they do this to Kev? he thought as he sprinkled Bicarb of Soda from a salt-shaker. He grabbed the slice of bread with one hand, bent closer under the sandwich counter, and dripped saliva over the beetroot.

There. Nice and moist.

.

Chapter 48

January, 1988.

Danny drove in circles for an hour before he returned to the cottage ruins. He salvaged his thongs, swimmers and towels, chucked them into a plastic wash basket, and added the clothes least damaged by smoke and falling debris. In the kitchen, he found tinned spaghetti, biscuits and baked beans so he tipped them into a bucket and loaded the VW.

With the bedrooms gutted and blackened, the air smelt of lime and kerosene. Buckled roofing hung over shattered tiles and broken masonry. With the water tank collapsed, soggy newspapers and magazines littered the floor. The cottage would crumble after the next rains, or the next dust storm.

Was this proper forgetting time, or time for revenge?

Without the energy, desire or strength to answer questions, let alone ask about Pete Bourke, he longed to curl up in some remote hut or an abandoned station made for misery.

I can't search for Dad. Not when I left me to the cops when I told Billy when I …

Shaking his head of vexation, he imagined himself falling into the depths, washing away his troubles. Or be snared in those fish traps like glowing algae blooming to justice. The river invited it.

Breaking open a can of warm beer instead, he took a sip, then another, gulping the rest. Throwing the can aside, he hopped in the car. Starting the engine, he let the VW thump and purr, ready to fly over the bridge in search of Mara's comfort.

Would she want him trundling into Patchtown with his new wagon, blowing his horn, ripping up dust, and showing off to Dickie and the younger ones? He might have told them about making money with the Hard Boys, joyful times in Sydney, and Chrissie's imminent return. He would have been a hero.

But I didn't find her. I poked around Parramatta, but at the address, some burly bloke twice my age told me to clear out. Truth is, Billy found her.

Me, boasting about driving illegal cars? What a fool I am.

His clammy hands felt useless and disconnected. Hoping for some miracle, some idea, some peace, some thread for reconciliation, only reminded him of his dad's terrible fate. He had defied him, held him in contempt, and abandoned him.

I left him to monsters.

Stamping his foot in the VW's cramped confines, he noticed two cans of paint on the veranda. Placed there for another task, he fetched them for himself, like prizes, putting them in the boot. He had no use for them but liked having a bit of his dad. Plus, the colours. Their potential.

Yet, his last survey of the cottage and surrounds confirmed a wreckage and a reluctant farewell. No Skipper. No home.

And no Dad.

Despite the paraphernalia and memorabilia lost, perhaps because of it, he recalled his mum and dad, the play, the meals, the times, the prospects. He remembered Pete Bourke and the Hard Boys.

This shouldn't happen to anyone.

He shook his head, and fell against the VW's seating, the vinyl groaning. His leg knocked against the metal beneath the dashboard, a gassy odour drifted into his cage. If the fumes filled the interior and snaked its way into his lungs, gas would provide a merciful end.

His stomach churned.

Can't go to Mara's place now.

Emptying himself from the vehicle, hot, dry air washed around his self-disgust. Tapping his hands against his pockets, searching for his tobacco pouch, he found them empty. Walking to the riverbank like he turned his back to his funeral, and followed the river bank until he reached a eucalypt with its limbs hanging over the water.

The brink. He stepped in. One step, two, face expressionless, he sat down. Plomp, covered up to his waist, sitting on grit, sand and mud.

Who cares?

With a warm breeze sauntering around his face, he twisted sideways, dipped down to a lower depth submerging his whole body, his hand clutching silt, released himself, and rose again. He might drift, float and ...

Who cares?

Pushing out, he bobbed about in watery space like an astronaut, softness all around, sounds muffled and the water lapping his sides.

Adrift.

Bucking down again, he pulled himself deeper until his hands clawed the sticky mud, his open eyes seeing murky greys and brown matter float past.

Springing upwards again, his head burst from the water. He gasped air, rolled to his side, and swum downstream, grit and water in his clothes.

What Pete said about Henry. What they did to me, to us ...I should have known. I've dumped him in this whole mess.

He clambered up the embankment to a grassy patch, stripping off his wet trousers, shirt and T-shirt, almost naked under the sun. Hand-wringing each item, he laid out his clothes, setting them lightly over grass and twigs where they'd catch the heat.

He taught me this when Mum insisted on using the clothesline.

Napping, his head swirled on indecision, dreaming in warmth, gifted slumber before he woke again in shadow. In late afternoon light, he scanned the riverbanks, spying two figures downstream, holding hands. He took a short breath, ducking for cover.

Two lovers, he thought, hot-blooded. A secret meeting?

It isn't right, gawking at other people. But ... I want to, you know.

Not far away from him, there were fifty reasons to sticky-beak. He strained his ears to hear their rising and falling phrases, their trepidation and pleading, like a song.

The man's voice deepened, softened; hers, sparrow-like, to-and-fro, their voices drifting across the waters and dissolving.

So quiet.

The two embraced, moving under the willow. Danny rubbed his eyes, clearing away silt from his face. He couldn't help imagining, though he heard only their faint urgency, an occasional laugh and a sweeping breeze working its way over the rippling waters. In such hush, he wondered so much could happen between man and woman.

By the time the two reappeared, the sunlight roasted his legs. He saw again a dark-skinned woman and a lighter-skinned man.

The bloke turned his direction.

Danny ducked again. 'No.'

He retreated to the vehicle with haste, he rubbed himself down, throwing the towel over his head, breathing in sweat and sticky things. His flesh prickled, his heart beat faster, hands perspiring. Dwelling undercover a while longer, he swept it aside.

It's Mara with … that cop!

Them, hot and bothered behind the willows, so passionate.

Disgusting.

He could have screamed, but instead, he wept.

Chapter 49

Danny drove his VW up the river levee and parked it in full view of the town, the pubs, the bridge and fish traps. After New Year's revelry, discarded bottles, plastic bags, broken glass and cardboard littered the park, the river dwellers sleeping under the willows after the cops hassled them.

I'm making a stand. Up here, where everyone will see me. Here I am, coppers, come and get me. Where are the Hard Boys? I'll haunt the lot of them.

As the drinking season continued, the smelly embankment people gathered near Danny's perch, seeing him in purple outrage. They edged forward like they might have found a messiah, someone unlike themselves who made a loud and bold pronouncement. Shafted by townspeople and the Authorities, they understood everything through their silence, only whispering to him their advice: you better watch out.

Atop the levee, he and his red VW would be an embarrassment to every citizen, a reminder of what was wrong with their town. Drunk and sullen Danny, son of Kev, their easy-going, getting-on handyman, the bloke beaten up by cops for no reason.

They had their home burnt down without censor, Kev, the fellow who helped out others, was hounded as an unlikely suspected murderer, an outcast. He was confined to the hospital over Christmas, nurses and doctors appalled by the police bashing, and everyone learning of it ashamed. While most kept their head down lest the same happen to them, Danny made a drunken last stand at the Alamo.

With the river in his veins and *Midnight Oil* in his heart, he embodied the madness at their doorsteps. When townspeople spied his VW-red-moon-rising high against the evening sky, they likened him to an ogre in leery lamplight. Others thought him a spectre in a nineteen-fifties horror movie or a crazed astronaut flitting around his lunar capsule with a flaming kerosene lantern.

By day, he drew curious, down-on-their-luck souls into odd, idle conversations where he said little more than 'Yeh', 'Gotcha' and 'Bud'. They filled in time rolling tobacco, turning the pages of cast-off colour-in books and folding paper boats, the wrinkled river people promising to place them in the water to float downriver-hope. They wondered whether Moon Man had lost or found his way.

Most townspeople stayed away, a few who approached said, 'Is are you doing, mate?' 'You lookin' for your dad?' 'You're going crazy, boy' and 'Where is he? Where's Kev?'

'Go away' he said, or else he ignored them.

'You're only making trouble for yourself son,' said Detective Cassidy. He could have arrested him for something, but he couldn't think what. And anyway, why bother with town crazies?

'He's flipped. Can't have a sensible conversation,' he said back at the station.

'It's weird. He's so keen on being seen when his dad's in hiding,' said Dewar. 'Go figure.'

Danny made a point of explaining nothing because he couldn't explain anything to himself. Who cares? I know nothing about his whereabouts. They can't make me.

Henry's death broke friendships and kinships, but who didn't know that? Everyone rejected, stories twisted and perverse. But what did he know? How stupid would it look to pretend? With nothing to give, and no one to trust, he found proper-forgetting time.

Drinking helped. With a flagon or two a day, summer wobbled along its predetermined January path, red moon rising, crimson earth fading, each night Danny taking another swig of cheap grog so the world turned down another notch.

'Nice and sloppy and dreamy,' he mumbled sitting over the levee; 'creamy and steamy and loopy; slobby and sloppy – and stupid.'

As long as he did not move too far or too fast, the world didn't turn on him. He could sit all day watching the river flow. From inside his moon ship, the river's beguiling eddies fascinated him, people wandering its edges waved at him, and while children poked sticks in the water, the bridge's rattling wooden planks sang a tune.

Pete burnt down our place. So we'll build another.

Revenge? Can't be bothered. I am so stupid.

A car passed overhead, and his belly rumbled.

'Are you, hungry, Mister Bridge? Or too much grog, is it?'

People trampling all over you. He scratched his ear. I oughta talk to them fish-traps. Good tucker down there. But they were not listening the river too old and indifferent to a red moon rising.

Where are you, Dad? Where are you?

PART SIX

Chapter 50

After Kev left the hospital, he considered the isolated Murri outposts of Buckley, Boobindah or Goodoogah where he was always welcome. Many townspeople were unfamiliar with the residents and did not care to know they had a clearing used for football and a destiny of isolation and unemployment.

Unlike the rampaging Jimmy Blacksmith, he did not suffer a nationwide manhunt with a reward for his capture dead or alive. So he shared a cottage with an old mate for a few weeks, chipping in with a few odd jobs like tightening the clothesline, replacing door hinges and fitting extra hosing so they could water the veggie patch.

The place did not qualify as a town according to the Town and Country Act of 1945, nor was it dignified with a dot on a map. It's single, dusty road had identical houses on either side with a bore where it petered out in saltbush. Equidistant from each other, the shacks were built on unfenced land adjacent to a mulga highway to outback Queensland.

Kev sat on the unsecured brick steps of a fibro bungalow that day, surrounded by dust, rock and untended shrubbery. He might have thought to water them Geraniums but Dickie tracked him down, giving him all the news about Danny, the fire, and Mara's misgivings. According to her, Billy enjoyed the high life in Sydney while the town's legal services fell apart. Spurred on by Danielle's complaints, the welfare wolves threatened to remove her children, and who could stop them?

Mara wouldn't let that happen, he said, no matter how many snoops they sent. She advised him to stay away from town, recover, and wait for her signal. Dickie being Dickie, he promised to look after Danny, protect him for the next few weeks when things were liable to worsen.

'What does she say about Badger?'

'She thinks everyone's a Detective Boney now; because everyone believes they know who done it.'

'Who did it,' he corrected.

Kev accepted his promise and her advice, reckoning Dickie found him too quick. He would move to another settlement, one to leave him guessing.

Less the private eye now, he hid from detectives, the Bourkes, and Dickie too. After all, with the police, Cheryl and the social workers turning the screws on Mara, his whereabouts might be her price for peace. Cops like Cassidy forced him to implicate Billy even when he despised betrayals. They could do the same to her.

His phone call to Billy also gave him pause. He knew the Commodore belonged to Cliff Badger but before that one of the Bourkes nicked it after Mara dumped it at the tip.

Was it true? Billy thought nothing of disguising the truth, telling tales or full-blown denial, the telephone an easy means for the sins of omission. His contempt for Cliff Badger matched his love of cars. A new vehicle would have been a tempting prize, in normal circumstances, unaffordable. In his anger and his rage, Billy might have sacrificed Badger for some imagined glory. Yeah, he struggled with his allegiances when offered material benefits.

Of all his lost or wounded friends, Cheryl possessed more reasons than anyone to knock off Cliff Badger. She welcomed, defended and accommodated the TRG. Never said a bad word against them. Since Badger's disappearance, she oscillated between dumping the topic and feigning concern for his whereabouts. After harsh words with him that night, and two rifles hung on her wall, she was familiar with his habits and foibles; it added up. His Bicentennial folly almost ruined her ambitions. Of all people, she was best rid of him.

By now, so much of him had taken a beating. After his assault, he wanted to escape the threats and deceptions. He doubted the loyalty of Billy the Brave, Mara the Indomitable, Cheryl the Ambitious, sweet Dickie and amiable Ted. In those times, who was left to trust, and what was trust worth when it could be beaten out of you?

Compelled to help people who were in more trouble than they realized, Kev did not climb mountains, issue commandments or turn water into wine; he quietly skirted differences, gave respect and sought the quiet waters of fraternity. With mouths to feed, men to succour, women to favour, and children to rear, no one thought much about saints, conciliators and peacemakers.

Nursed, fed and cared for, he walked out of the hospital because he wanted to avoid harassment, for himself and everyone dear to him. In the backcountry, we believed he was safe. He would always make do, helpful no matter where he lived, believing in his God-given ability to set everything aright. As an unwitting source of trouble, when events went wayward, he disappeared like morning dew in a desert.

Danny will be protected by Dickie, thought Kev, but better still if he returns to Sydney.

Mara has troubles aplenty. God knows she's grown tougher those last few years, and Dickie would stick by her. For all Billy's hot-headedness, he bounces off walls; and when he came off bruised and battered, so too would the wall.

Could any one of them be a Jimmy Blacksmith and take out a Bicentennial official in anger? His grandfather snarled once, savaged and murdered people but found himself slandered, hunted down and slaughtered.

The gubba came to town with unasked-for money for a cultural centre no less, without consulting the local Murri or townpeople. He imagined a sterile building holding spears and woomera down by the fish traps. This government man bore gifts whilst celebrating the occasion of their Holocaust, and he expected acclaim.

Kev reckoned Paddy Bourke killed Mr Badger as he left his place in no mood for opposition. If he arrived there making demands, and they clashed, against the Hard Boys it would be an uneven fight.

As a small boy, he witnessed Paddy's father tear through the mission station on a police motorbike, firing a semi-automatic from the sidecar like a buffalo hunter. Two of them shot their hunting dogs and put holes in the water tanks. They shot twenty or more animals, the kids vulnerable, panicked and crying.

The fear stayed with him. It stayed.

Chapter 51

Rather than walk the river bank on a hot night, Danny headed for the park benches where he immersed himself in despondent council lighting. Surrounded by abandoned beer bottles, plastic wrapping and sticky paddle-pop sticks, he held out his hand to the spiky understorey of acacia so it might make him bleed.

With street lights in the distance, the road empty and still, not a dog barked this Sunday evening. So he rested his head on the grey table top as the fearless cicada calls rose and fell. His ears filled with their drumming, his hand gripped the wine flagon as a nearby couple struggled with words and clothing. They cuddled up in the warm air, hotting up under bushes, their fumbling and whispered intimacies all too audible.

He loathed these people with their sweet breathy tones, especially when they cut-the-blanket so close to virgin him, another reminder of his failure.

'Show some respect for Henry,' he said, though, after a pause, their tender efforts resumed, collapsing into "ohs," "arrrs" and giggles.

He wished the demon wind would blow them away.

'Everyone's forgot you, Henry. Even Dad.'

He thumped his forehead; hit himself again with his fist, knocking out painful thoughts, bad memories, leaving it red and sore.

Poor bugger, him.

The lithe lover's groans continued, so he lurched to the park's edge in leaden boots. When his head knocked against an outstretched branch, he grabbed it, shook and throttled it until the dead leaves rattled like a tinsel sleigh. His gut ached. Staggering to one side, he fell on the cold grasses.

Being young is bad.

A fellow wanted to try out the drink, the fags, the girls, his dad warning him against all three. In those years, it wasn't difficult getting a mate to hand over a few beers from the bar, and later share the foamy grog on the riverbank. He particularly liked sherry, its sweetness sent fire down his throat, though he reeled, almost passed out, making the other lads chortle.

Who cared?

The wretched figures living around the river looked on in silence, then and now, moving in and about their shadows, they created a tender illusion of safety.

I won't end up like them.

I'm twenty-two. No rivals to fight, no woman to curse me, no welfare people harassing me. Dad didn't give me lessons on women. He pretended I was a champion and left me to it.

No more than a few older women tried it on.

Henry was handsome. He would strum country tunes, make a joke or two. The girls loved it. He could be mellow, even after beers, maybe better, always with his angelic face. He knew all the lyrics to Merle Haggart, Johnny Cash, Slim Dusty. Sang with a sweet, deep voice. After he sang a song, he remembered saying to him 'You should join a choir.'

Everyone laughed.

My words repeated around town, weeks later, resurfacing in the pub.

Henry huffed. 'I'm no angel.'

For years after, the lads called him "Angel". It took a long time to be forgotten though his mum used the same name sometimes. He wouldn't be marked as a sissy or lover-boy, though, with his dad in a job, eased matters. His mum ran her hands through his hair when he returned for dinner; Henry didn't have that.

He gulped his nameless, aimless grog, and flung the empty bottle to ground. It skidded, bounced and knocked against a post.

Who cares?

Later he snoozed in the back seats, wrinkling his nose at a persistent odour attacking his nostrils. On one elbow, he crawled from the car and clambered to the boot.

That smell; it's the paint.

The two battered cans rescued from home had their lids loosened. With paint spilled over the edges, they congealed and hardened on the vinyl flooring. A mid blue.

He grabbed the cans and placed them on the embankment. Levering open the first with a large coin, a wondrous Azure conjured the sweetness and light of unbound potential.

The other can contained a lustrous black, so definite and defiant. Not a colour, remembering his Art classes. Black was light denied. Without. Like Murris.

Fetching a strong twig, he stirred the paint so the oil blended with the gorgeous pigment, producing a thick, flowing substance.

By the time he finished, a question rose and jagged in his throat: What would he do with them? The first pot sang so high and hopeful, and the next, so deep and without? He couldn't slap them on the lumpy levee bank, because the old bull would buck, snort and shake him off. The town walls had eyes, and cops were everywhere, looking for rats to catch. Wouldn't visit Patchtown or their cottages, though they always needed a lick of paint. Something closer, he thought. The question buzzed around his head like a persistent blow fly until –

The VW!

Falling against the mudguard, he laughed himself stupid.

My car in azure blue, red and black. What better?

As an angry kid, trouble discovered him, routinely locked in the empty school bookstore with only coloured pencils and paper. He could have been whacked, rebuked, or given "lines." But no, they stuck him there for the hours, lessons missed. When the bell rang at day's end, the door would be unlocked, so he would go home with his drawings under his arm.

His dad noticed them when he returned from shearing. Sitting in the lounge room with paper, paints and brushes, they drew people and places, saying 'Fabulous, bud. You're an artist.'

On the levee, Danny held the paint-stick aloft, letting a few drips fall to ground.

Like wagging school, but with endless time.

Now he would paint, and paint, in lusty black and azure blue, all over the VW's red exterior. He imagined pictures, and by painting them he drank his way through the week.

Yeh, that's proper forgetting.

Chapter 52

That evening, Danny met Dickie across the road from the Unity Hotel, sitting with him on the park bench, both men silent for a time. With broken bottles and fish-and-chips wrappings near, he smelt beer's sweet, sticky hops and greasy fat oozed from discarded food.

He kept a close eye on his VW but Dickie ensured the Corolla stayed closer as he needed the vehicle for work. Mara often seconded it and took Patchtowners on excursions to a Murri outpost with a bit of shooting, picking him up at day's end. At night, it carried people to dances. It was hers as much as his.

Must be his night, he thought, though he crossed the bridge alone. Feeling bad after the troubles he's had.

'Your car … it going well?' he said, his head swaying. He lifted an arm like he was about to make a point, but…

The lad's thoughts were beyond fathoming, so his question went unanswered.

'Get a charge up,' said Danny, thrusting the flagon.

Dickie folded his arms and would not talk about anything, in case it made things worse than ever.

'What's the matter?'

Dickie swished a bug from his face.

'Jeez, man, think you've got it bad? I'm the one with no job, no friends, no money, no Mum. And Dad's up and runned.'

'He ain't. He's staying alive.'

Dickie broke his silence, so Danny pointed at him. 'Got you, man.'

He would rather not discuss his Dad. Couldn't look for him. Or face him. Not like this. While I had fun in the city, he thought, the police nearly killed him. The Hard Boys played me for a fool. He took another drink before settling down to vice-like tranquillity.

Later, he broke away, stretched his body, and moved from his companion as if someone or something called him. But his weight pulled him sideways, and losing balance, he grabbed the next bench and slid stomach first onto it. His weary eyes detected tufts of grass and a cement slab as he wretched. He clung to the timber-slatting, maneuvering himself to the next seat where he took another swig to clear his mouth.

'Jeez, no,' he thought, remembering Mara kiss and cuddle Pretty-Boy from the Riot Squad.

'Eh?' said Dickie, hovering over him.

'Where's Mara?'

'Dunno.'

'I saw her and the cop doing it.'

'Eh,' said Dickie

'Yeah. Down on the river she ...'

Dickie turned his head away. Things were bad enough without accusations, insinuations and mad imaginings. The social worker, Danielle Pike-Jones, complained about Mara too. Said she threatened her. Claimed she suffered abuse from her clientele, her so stressed, oppressed, and plain distressed; relief from duty was the least the authorities could do. On the edge of a nervous breakdown, they said. Depression, with ever-sympathetic Mayor Sheila backing her up. They pointed to Patchtown and the wild, uncontrollable kids living in unsanitary conditions.

'Who would want their kids brought up like that?' she said. 'How's poor, young Danielle supposed to cope with their histrionics, day in and day out?'

Dicky shook his head and slumped on a log.

'Mara was with him,' mumbled Danny.

'That's not right, man. Don't go saying that.'

Danny meandered away. He couldn't bear staying any longer. 'Damn you, Dickie.'

He lurched to the BBQ near the bins with their rotting food and used containers, threw aside torn paper and crossed the park, closer to the levee. Dickie followed, and for the first time spied the new red-moon-rising, Danny's VW, with its fluid brushstrokes splashed across its bodywork like a voluptuous tattoo. Over the bonnet, the doors, roof, everywhere, black, pinks, purple and azure blue, even on the hubcaps.

He whistled, clambered up, and ran his hand over the bonnet. There were black boulders and spears, a mid-blue river and jumping redfish. The car door had chunky houses with onlooker's heads. He stood on his toes to spy the giant, concentric circles covering the roof, from the air, they formed a bulls-eye, like saying, "Go on, God, take a shot."

'Crickeys.' Dicky swept his hand over the car's wheel guard, showing guitars and drums, before circling the entire vehicle, wondering at each picture of river, fish, bridge and boulders.

'Fair dinkum Danny, you're an angel. An angel.'

Danny bucked.

Not that again.

He turned his back.

Saying that to me. He's Dad's friend; he should know.

He rushed past him and grabbed the door handle but struggled to open it.

'Damn you, Dickie.' He clambered into his seat.

Unbearable. To be reminded.

Turning the ignition, he revved his VW. He couldn't stay lest Dickie haunt him with talk about his family, his failures, talking about Chrissie, the house burning down and all his disasters.

Switching the lights on and revving the engine, he let out the clutch, taking off in his red-moon-rising, a sticky sweat across his forehead. Bumping down the rampart to the barren parkland, his vision blighted by thinly sliced nightmares, he hunched over the wheel. Escape the winds. In his carnival dodgem car, he steered in a circle, swerving around shrubs, around and around a tree until his lights shone straight at Dickie.

Shake off the winds.

Dickie scampered away to save himself as the VW veered left and dropped over the guttering onto Barrier Street. Wheeling tight right, and straightening, he located town, the Unity Hotel, all reminders of his school days bathed in weak and friendless light.

Hate it.

Veering off road again, he broke from the park's grassy verge, and past the noisy lovers.

Hate them.

They taunted him like he was some stupid loser, them, in parkland bushes smooching, grinding and whispering to each other, groping and fidgeting and mucking about.

Stuck in first gear, his untamed steering ripped into the turf, gravilleas bashed, the car accelerating past the picnic bench, two people dashing to the wasteland.

'Whhoo. Whoo.' This was more like it.

Ground control. Hating Planet Earth.

He dodged the comet roses and asteroid acacias, and dashed on and off the road's broad space to an insulting emptiness. His VW tore over every tar-black metre down his time-tortured bumpy road to the humped levee, and lumpy bridge, the looming iron-and-wood passageway to another universe.

Cosmic winds.

High over the luminous fish traps, the way to the Broken Hill ahead, through the Milky Way, and he'd be gone.

No. Not to Mara's. Not Dicky's. Not to Dad's friends.

He steered his spaceship left, taking the access track to the underpass, with the shooting stars above.

Enough. Not enough. Far enough. Damn.

He braked at the river's edge, beneath the overpass and road, on clay, stopped, he levered open his tin-can capsule and tumbled from the door. Sprawled on the ground, the world all askew, night sounds crashing on him, the cool air hitting his face and surged into his lungs. He chuckled.

When darkness joined him, he heard the gurgling waters, and imagined the fish-trap's glow. Surrendering to the weighted world, he laughed to wash away any hope of madness. He beat the winds away. He might have found the relief of sleep but another car trampled over the high wooden planking, making a dull, musical clatter.

You hungry again, Mr Bridge?

Sliding himself up against the car body, arms free, he reached for his tobacco pouch. Taking some out, he rolled the sticky stuff in his fingers, licked the paper closed, surrounded by the floating familiarity of the river's murmurings and the crossing's crusty friendship.

Dickie won't walk all this way. He doesn't like the dark. Yeah. He's a scaredy cat; without electric lights or an army of candles, he freaks.

Replacing his tobacco and papers, he lit the fag. He could still make a cigarette. As long as you can roll-your-own, said a bush-philosopher, you were OK. Can't? Then, you're a hopeless case.

Must have been something Billy said.

'Well, well,' said a voice in the pitch.

Pete! Pete's voice.

The car passing overhead must have turned down, switched off the engine, its passengers come on foot. His weary brain reckoned the vehicle headed for town.

He searched around.

'It all ends here, Danny,' said Pete. 'Your number's up.'

'Another drunken boong.'

Con, to his left.

'Hey, blackhead. Still hoping for a girlfriend?'

Ginge, to his right. And shadowy figures.

'You blokes can't hold your drink. None of you boongs can. Look at … at that Henry.

'What a wally.'

Danny threw aside the fag and drew out his pig stabber.

Three of them. I'm not fit for running. 'Piss off. Just …'

He backed to the car.

The Hard Boys laughed.

'Call that a knife?' said Pete, pulling out his 'roo blade and. holding it to his face.

'This, is a knife.'

The others shook with laughter, imagining him as *Crocodile Dundee*. With Danny cornered, drunk, and outnumbered, he dared not issue commands to them.

Satisfied the odds were neatly unbalanced, Con leaned against the bridge's base, Ginge scratching his head.

Pete turned his weapon, thinking it shone. 'Hey, babyface. Where's your dad, now? Can't help you, eh.'

Hate him. For the humiliation. For toying with me. For destroying our home. For persecuting Dad. For holding a gleaming blade to my face. The devil himself.

A breeze swept under the bridge, and the frightened leaves tumbled underfoot. Pete held his knife high before his demonic eyes, twisting it in hand, his teeth glowing.

No more.

Danny rushed him, energy surging through his legs, his arms, neck, backbone.

Straight at him, blade or not.

Who cares?

Black night.

Who cares?

He charged, not calculating his enemy unable to thrust a knife when above shoulder height.

Get lucky. Danny crash-tackled him. Like footy. Sent him flying. Smashed him, yet expected a knife in his guts.

All black.

Who cares?

They hit the ground. Thump. His thin form scrambled to Pete's chest, his arms banging against the elbow and skull.

Hate him.

A scream.

Pete hadn't sliced or diced him.

Where was it. Arms free?

He rolled sideways. Instinct.

Still alive. Get up, and find Ginge and Con.

Struggling for footing. Failed. His hands clawed darkness.

Someone there? Beside him.

Danny struck in darkness. A hack. A tearing. Bone scrapped.

He thrust again.

Arrrrh. Arrr–

The sound of drowning, of sinking in overwhelming waters.

The others? Pete's knife?

He pulled back until he hit against the VW, dropping a knife dripping blood.

It was black, black. Nothing in hand.

Where are they?

Spying something for his defense, he picked it up.

Pete's knife. He stood against the car with a large blade, seeing before him a quivering, grunting body issuing a ghostly, half-yell. Pete's death throes.

He swept his hair aside.

The Hard Boys could still stab him, belt him up, shoot him and throw him in the river like a dog. He jumped to his feet and held up his enemy's weapon.

'Who cares,' he screamed.

Con and Ginge ran. They scampered up the rise, past their car, and joined the empty road into town.

'Run. You bastards.'

Blood pumping from his Pete's neck.

The body still, it amazed him. Relieved at the sight of his blood-soaked victim.

Dropping Pete's knife, he spread his hands against the VW and exhaled. Groaned.

Black. 'Bloody hell.'

'Danny?'

It was Dickie, in an incoherent night, circuitry buzzing in his head. From the darkness, footsteps scrunching on twigs and dried leaves. Who turned up the volume?

Turning from the corpse, sick and nauseous, his face paled.

'Danny?' Seeing a sprawled body, the blood, he bit his lip.

Would the Hard Boys be back? Would he be thrown in a cell and tortured?

The bridge collapsed on him, the night swallowed him whole. Blood flooded his brain, his memory lost. He groaned like a wounded crow.

It's done, he thought. Who cares?

Yet all his forgetting would soon be remembered.

PART SIX, Chapter 53

Finale

In a syrupy world of disrupted images and passing thoughts, triumph, fright, and disgrace rose and fell in Danny. Under his grey blanket, his shaken body squirmed and struggled with memories of uniforms pushing, shoving and pulling him from river to cell. Arrested, and caged like an animal.

As his dad told him, you're not a man in gaol, you're a sack of stuff, a thing not a heart, mind, stomach and brain.

From the time the cops arrived beneath the bridge, he belonged to them. They propelled him against the VW, dropped him to the ground and dragged him from a turbulent underbelly. Jostled into the paddy wagon, dumped on a floor and hauled past blackened doors.

Him, the murderer.

Battered and abused, he passed through echoing chambers into Vegemite-brown corridors. Stripped, numbered, photographed, fingerprinted, stared at, spat upon and manhandled in and out of nameless enclosures, and after, settled behind welcome bars left to whirling, sickly sensations empty of content; and a persistent voice whispering "You killed Pete Bourke."

Some dog-eared skirmish without the solidarity and decency of a fistfight. A drunken brawl where hate found its mark. His weapon tore into Pete's neck before the knife plunged into his guts. Con and Ginge cried like useless babies. They ran out and down Evans Street, leaving him in the pitch, the body jerking and grunting and falling silent.

Cell Number Four. Under an itchy blanket. He twisted and

struggled, a voice repeated "You killed Pete Bourke."

The door swung open, 'Get up.'
No waiting. 'Up.'
A strong arm pulled and rolled him over, a torchlight spearing his eyes.
'Switch it off, damn you.'
Sticky sweat dripped from his back. His guts and head ached.
'Come on, chum. Pronto.'
Shielding his eyes, he struggled to find ground.
'Turn it ooo-fff.'
He thirsted. Brain and body reeling, a smoky brown light danced around him. With one foot planted on the cold floor, the cop's grip fell away, them, standing back, beyond reach.
Yeh. Stand back. I'm the one who knocked him off.
'Hands. Out.'
He complied.
They can parade me through town if they want. Through the haze, sweat and confusion, one thing reverberated: I killed Pete Bourke.
Yeah, the cops fell back when I faced them. They looked edgy, contemptuous and nervy; in awe of me. That cop struggled to fit the handcuffs over my wrists.
They led down a bare corridor, around corners, past a plain brick annex, his keepers knocked on the next door.
'Come in.'
A Pine-O-Clean odour permeated the squarish, concrete bunker, a table at its centre. Two steel doors, one to the cells, the other to who-knows-where. Two cops in grey suits sat before him; the ugly one, and the other bloke, the one he spied with Mara. They indicated he should sit opposite. Two uniformed officers blocked the exits. A microphone hung from the ceiling.
'Detectives Hanna and Cassidy present with the accused, Daniel Keith Trust.'
What? No one in our town talked about "those present," "the accused," and wouldn't pronounce his entire name.
I'm "It," bastard coppers. A thing. I don't even have a number. Address me by my proper no-name.
'You are Daniel Keith Trust?' said the ugly one, adjusting his steel

chair.

Was 'it' familiar with Daniel Keith Trust?

'Uh ha.'

Mara's lover took over. 'Daniel: you realize you are accused of murdering Mister Peter Bourke last night.' He examined the papers before him '... at the base of Hollingsworth Bridge.'

Hollingsworth? Ain't been called that for years.

'That you stabbed the said person after an altercation.'

Alter- what? 'It was his knife.'

'Meaning?'

'Hey. They cornered and threatened me.'

Hanna glanced up, head down again, writing in his notepad.

Perhaps he's still sleepy. Or too shagged.

'Jeez,' said Cassidy. 'Trash like you always tell the same story: 'they attacked me,' 'he knifed himself brutally.' Buster, you dragged me away from my holidays. I was at Surfers Paradise yesterday. Be twenty years before you'll see a beach.'

Mara's lover lifted a hand, pushing back his hair. 'Can I call you, Danny?'

'No, you can't.' His head throbbed.

'About last night. A witness who backs you up. Thing is, we want to learn why you and Pete had such a difference of opinion, shall we say? You were his friend not so long ago.'

What a miserable question, from a bloody know-nothing know-it-all?

'Maybe,' he said, to annoy Pretty-Boy.

In his wretched state, a firm denial took too much effort. Anyway, his Dad told him to admit his mistakes, and though it made a kind of sense, practising it proved difficult. "No use denying something," Kev would say. When things tensed he would raise his shoulders and open his hands, and invite his thoughts. And that bought time.

'As we understand it,' said Detective Hanna, 'this links up with the Badger disappearance. Heard of him?'

He rubbed his aching forehead.

I made a mistake. Yeh, but so did he.

'This Bicentennial official disappeared, what, four or five months ago. Like your Dad said, before you came to town. Nothing to do with you, only, his car, a white, VL Commodore couldn't be found. The bloke went missing, but the vehicle shows up again, this time with a coat of black paint.'

Danny kept his eyes on the table, noting a dark scar, like someone ran a blade along its surface. He placed his head in his hands.

'I believe you are aware of where we'll find it. Thing is, you wouldn't know about all the other stuff. You stayed in Sydney. As far as we're concerned, you might have driven the car not realizing it vital evidence in finding this Badger bloke, dead or alive.

'Help us, mate. You're in a heap of trouble. You're gonna need more than a lawyer.'

He glanced at Hanna.

'Twenty years to life. You're in deep shit, unless you assist us,' said Hanna.

He examined the other one's dried-up face, cracked lips and small eyes.

He's the one who put Dad in the Hospital!

He wanted to leap across the table and squeeze the life out of him, but said, 'The Bourkes attacked us. They burnt down our house.'

The ugly one's head swayed. He tapped his fingers and broke into a little tune. 'Reckon we might need traditional techniques.'

'Wait on.' Baby-face turned to him. 'Danny, your Dad told us the Bourkes worked on the car. Is that right?'

'Pete repainted it.'

'And you drove the VL?'

'Yeah. The Bourkes painted it, and I drove it.'

'You took it to?'

He glanced up at Mara's lover, and sneered. His eyes searched again for the scar on the table, running his finger over the surface.

'Well?'

'They filed off the engine number, and we hid the thing.'

Chris Hanna craned forward. 'Hid the Commodore?'

He nodded.

The ugly one sneered.

'Yeh. I'll take you there.'

He slouched back and let his focus slip away. *This way I'll keep Dad out of it. When we go to Phil's Hole, they'll find Paddy's files on the back seat. They'll blame me and the Bourkes.*

Billy wants the Commodore, but the cops can have it.

Chapter 54

Twice a week, travellers rode the Sydney coach across the Blue Mountains, switching at Orange, cruising the flat scrublands to the arid lands beyond.

Dirt roads, dirt towns.

The long haul through the mulga plains saw the bus crawl over Hollingsworth Bridge around noon, lingering atop to provide imagined tourists a bird's eye view of the principal sites. Locals might inform strangers that heavy vehicles must slow lest the ancient relic succumb to age and gravity.

After crossing, it rolled past the park, cop shop and pubs to the parking bay near Paddy's Garage.

Last off, Billy stepped on Evans Street, suitcase in his hand.

'Hey.'

'Eh?'

He told no one his schedule, his means of transport or his arrival day, although the easy 'Hi,' gave lie to it. With his feet barely touching ground, the bus door slammed behind him, pulling away millimetres from his back.

As the coach engine roared away, other passengers milled with their friends. He grinned at first before it dissolved when he spied Paddy.

The garageman tipped his hat. 'Only passing. Didn't expect to see you.'

He stared at his reception party of one: a fellow expressionless, cold and mute, focused on the arrival's chin and mouth.

I told him I'd return in New Year, but …

His reluctant associate attempted a smile but his lip drooped. 'Come and have a drink. I…' He choked. His face paled, and his eyes equivocated.

Miss Denny, a local primary school teacher, came to his aid. 'Oh, Mr Bourke. So sad to hear. Is there anything I can do?'

'No. But …come to the funeral, would you?'

She nodded, touched his shoulder and slipped away.

'What's going on?' said Billy.

'Come with me. We have things to talk about.'

Led down the lane towards the workshop, Billy stopped. 'This is far enough.' He would not go inside and leave himself isolated and vulnerable to the Hard Boys.

Paddy Bourke fiddled with his finger like his wedding ring stuck. His face twitched. 'Sit,' he said, indicating a bench. They discussed "the situation," Bourkie confessing that his son died in a car accident, yet, finding the Commodore for him would be "doing-right."

'Pete sold it to you. So, we'll fetch it.'

'Thanks,' said Billy in a quieter voice.

'Truth is, he forgot our gear.'

'Gear?'

'Yeah. He left them in the boot. I should collect them before …'

The bereaved petty crim was crashing his VL recovery party.

'Perhaps Ginger could do it. Save you the trouble.'

'Sure. But … I don't want anyone, any of his things, going astray.'

'Ah, ha.' Billy wondered what could drag him away from his dead son. It stretched credulity.

'I'm going tomorrow with the Patchtown boys. We might fit you in.'

'OK,' he said, 'but …' His face rippled in despair, brows genuflecting. 'I've only got today.'

He smelt a rat. 'I'll be frank, mate. You and I aren't exactly the best of buddies. If you want to go now, I set the terms. You behave like a man in mourning.'

With his head down, the bereaved father bit his lip. 'Your way. Sure.'

Billy's eyes narrowed. 'We take the old Cortina.'

Yeh, a weak beast with a reliable engine. On the return journey, I'll have my VL.

They would be roasted on a hot day, even with the windows down. I'll check for hidden firearms in the boot, glove box, under the seating, everywhere.

Rule number one: no weapons.

Rule two: no weapons. And watch your back.

Within an hour, they loaded additional fuel in the car so Bourkie wouldn't do anything stupid. When they reached The Hole, he would find out about his "goods," come what may, the most dangerous time, as his rival might try something to keep the "gear" a secret.

Paddy's facial twitch pleased him.

Once they planted themselves in the Cortina, 'Straight ahead,' he said.

'What?'

'Push the accelerator until the other side of Wanngandi.'

His unwelcome partner knew the way. That suited him. He figured his rival's local knowledge compensated for his ignorance. He worked the town and outland settlements but did not loiter on the dry plains and their labyrinth of dusty by-ways. Apart from the odd kangaroo shoot, he had little interest in overnighting in-the-sticks.

Half an hour later, they turned off the Broken Hill road. The unsealed southern track, well-formed at first, became rough and treacherous. He leaned against the seat, arms outstretched, yawning, barely glancing at his chauffeur's rugged face. When he expected to collect the car earlier than expected, and head for Sydney, why make conversation? The thought of being with Coral and the others…

Won't she be pleased?

He held a grim awareness that a man with down-turned lips and a lousy smile line wasn't humanity's cream-of-the-crop.

'Remember,' he said, wagging his finger, 'Follow my directions. We stop short, park, and you give me the keys.'

Paddy said nothing. For once, he drove without saying a word. Not rushed or jerky but smooth and careful, lodged in the appropriate gear, nice-and-easy on the tin-can's 1200 ccs.

Bloody disturbing when he's in mourning. He drives like a Sunday school teacher.

To calm himself and fray his opponent, he might have turned to top-volume radio rock-n-roll. But scratchy reception and the disc jockey's carping voice made music unbearable. He'd sat in two buses for eleven hours, a midnight, departure, accompanied by crying babies, blaring transistor radios, and leaky windows going over the Blue Mountains. His clothes smelt and his back ached, content with the thought of recovering his Commodore.

What a beauty.

It was the only newish car he had ever owned, and it had cost him a few thousand.

Bourke pulled over. 'Where are we going? Flanagan's?'

'Close. Phil's Hole.'

'You mean Old Frazer's. So, we'd better check out the station from the hill. Know it?'

Billy nodded. 'We'll park past the dry lake. Find a vantage. See if anyone's coming or going.'

Now it bothered him that Bourkie knew the terrain, though he approved his caution. A younger Bourke stole cars on the Great Western Highway and suffered at the hands of a bastard magistrate, Billy too from big-noting himself at the wake, so they shared a common motto: Never Again.

At the rocky bend before The Hole, he made him hand over the wheel, parking the vehicle himself hard against the dense mulga, facing it outwards for a quick escape. Two massive grey boulders provided them with shade after the Cortina's throbbing heat.

'That car is a bloody oven.'

'Over there.' Bourke pointed. 'We'll survey the whole property.'

Following the contour, the vegetation cleared to an elevated ledge with extensive views across the plain. He spied a dry lake to the right, following it for half an hour without him noticing. The road disappeared into sparse grassland and mulga with a striking pink-grey haze along the horizon, Sometimes evidence of fires, more often they were a phenomenon beyond explanation.

On the ground, the afternoon light marked out the scrub country by its lengthening shadow. A hot breeze pushed in their faces, a low-whistle of wind passing beneath them. He wanted to make his way down, Paddy already peering down from the lookout.

'Shit.'

'Uh?' He peered towards a few huts and a station-house amongst a thicket above a dry creek bed. If you stared hard, and with a good eye, in the shadowy light near the rise, other buildings became apparent.

He moved back from the ledge. 'Keep down.'

Billy watched his dead-still co-conspirator, in concentration. 'Any activity?'

When the wind relented, voices like chatter. He scratched his neck. Taking a peep, he didn't notice anything at first, straining to define buildings or people, as the afternoon light played tricks, and with his weak eyesight he was unsure what lay beyond.

'You see?' said Bourkie.

'Yeah.'

'Is this the place?'

'It's Phil's Hole, ain't it?'

'Might be people ahead.' He nodded. 'Hang on. I'll fetch the binoculars. It's too bloody far from here.'

He glanced at Paddy's retreat and turned to the scene below.

What in hell did he see? He wasn't sure about the voices; perhaps he imagined them. If there were, recovering the car would be delayed, possibly requiring an overnight stay. Not a fine prospect as the cops in town would be watching out for him. Identifying strangers from this distance, hearing them, or detecting what they were doing; impossible.

Could do with a closer look.

Standing up, shielding his eyes, he remembered.

Damn. I left the keys in the ignition.

He broke into a sweat.

With people down there, would he pull out without him?

No. He wants those "goods." Even with his son dead?

He shook his head.

Hang on. We didn't bring binoculars!

Paddy had a minute's lead through the mulga. To escape the cops in the Cortina, he swept aside the brittle branches and glanced behind for Billy, knowing it would be an uneven fight if it came to it.

Billy's a strong bastard. But I spied cops at the homestead. Gear or not, I'm out of here.

Reaching the Cortina, he launched into the front seat and searched for the keys.

Ha! In the ignition. No hot-wiring required.

I was this close. But the bastard coppers beat me.

Has to be them. Two vehicles with blue stripes.

If they find us, they'll pin Badger's murder on me. Pete never told me what happened.

He started up, let the engine hum for a few seconds before pushing down the clutch, and eased from the sandy base.

Billy raced down the slope, spying the bastard revving and rolling the car through the sandy fringe and on the track. Once he passed the first bend, he'd be untouchable. With the Cortina pulling to the track, the engine's low grumble strained to push through. Seeing it struggle to escape, he gave his every effort.

Only fifty-metres.

Is it stuck?

By cutting the corner, and dashing through mallee, he would jump out and stop him.

What I'll do to him.

Engine fumes. Dust and sand flying. With a set of boulders ahead, he was close to blocking him. Paddy rocked the vehicle back and forth, cursing until he broke free, but already Billy leapt on the track where a thicket narrowed the way.

Freed from the bog, the Cortina drove straight toward him, into the narrow gap without a hint of halting, the driver with one hand out of the window, a gun pointed his way.

Shit!

How did he come by that?

Billy fell back as fast as possible, clambering behind the nearest bushes, banging his head against branches and rolling on spiky ground.

As soon as he dared, he stood, watching the Cortina move away, the weapon apparent.

He wouldn't. Didn't have to.

He was out to run me over!

But he might have shot me too.

His indecision allowed the Cortina to plough through the last sandy patch, accelerating away.

He ran down the track and stared at the receding vehicle passing over a mound.

Damn. The bastard wouldn't have fired; it would have alerted others.

He slumped to the ground. I could have stopped him.

Paddy escaped; a Bourke-in-mourning, yet still had enough time and wit to save his skin. He scooped sandy soil in his hand, and in disgust, cast it aside. Seeing ants running over his palm, their underground home exposed, he scraped them off, dancing around like a bandicoot. His arms were scratched, his back too had been ground against rock and mulga. Now his hand stung.

'Damn.' Fifty kilometres from town. For an overweight bloke in his forties, his prospects were dire. He'd never walked that far in his life, especially in summer when ants were roasted alive.

The bastard has left me to the crows.

Finding a place behind a boulder, sand and sweat clinging to his neck and face, his mind turned to the situation.

Must be people, already arrived. If they are, they'll be the kind that scares Paddy. Cops. Nothing they'd like better than discovering me at the scene of the car dumping.

Pete's in the morgue, and Paddy came out here. So, how valuable are his goods? Why the cock-and-bull story about recovering them 'for Pete's sake'?

He searched for shade, dusted himself off, and listened again for voices, footsteps, trucks, bikes, or helicopters. A distant horn.

I'm doubly stuffed. No car, summer heat, no food, no water, and bull-ant police crawling all over the place.

Limping back to his vantage point, he peered below again, eventually identifying three vehicles with the common blue stripes of patrol cars, with numerous figures moving through the mallee. Grabbing some shade behind a boulder, he took a while gathering his wits.

Shit. Heaven yesterday. All hell today.

How am I getting out of this one?

Chapter 55

Paddy Bourke drove at a furious pace, gripping the steering wheel, eyes fixed on the sandy track, his foot tensed on the accelerator, lifted or compressed with cool calculation. Negotiating every bump and curve on the pathway to town, from the rough station tracks to the graded, dirt roads between towns, the Cortina progressed under darkening skies. Grinding and bumping over winding track, the dashboard rattled, and the sump thumped against hard clay and rutted corrugations.

I've lost everything: Pete, the gang, the trades, the lucrative fences. The cops are onto us. Because of him.

Paddy's juices erupted. His blood boiled, and as water hadn't touched his lips his tongue became as brittle and sharp as shattered glass. His temples bulged and without a meal all day his breath was like rotten gases from a rusted tin can.

I'll crush him.

It's only natural.

He glanced at the pistol bouncing like popcorn on the passenger's seat. Concealed around his waist, his reassuring little number fooled Billy though its lethal power was only good for a few metres. "Pop" he called it.

Handy. Pointed it at a few unsavoury types before now.

He sneered. Releasing one hand from the wheel, he clenched his fist.

I'll wipe him out.

He dealt with the smart-arse bush lawyer, left him to die in the desert or surrender to the cops. Hadn't needed "Pop."

This time, I'll corner his mate, and blow his brains out.

If he checked his contacts and tracked the offenders, it would be easy enough. Yet, no one should suspect him, most of all the target. So, he could not scour the landscape asking after a known person or follow him in his green tow truck. Suspicious from the start.

Rule One: no witnesses.

After all, Pete's dead.

His neck strained.

Rule Two: be tidy.

Righteous acts required dealing with passions, ace high. He hated as well as the next guy, but over the years, tidiness and method became his saving graces. With engines, differentials, axles and car repairs, method trumped all. Fixing people didn't stop them being identified by their face, fingerprints, body shape, and weight.

Too untidy.

Knocking off anyone near their house, place of work, with the public in sight, provided evidence. The cops would have it on a plate. Only losers left telling signs.

Rule three: no evidence. Shooting people wouldn't work as it involved a bullet, always leading back to a loser who fired it.

That's not murder; more like suicide.

'Nothing worse than people suiciding,' his priest once said. 'When you have the love of Christ behind you.'

Yes, I'm Joshua of the Old Testament; only want revenge. Simple, revenge.

Amen.

He admired cold-bloodedness. Leaders possessed it on the footie field, and far beyond. The best names in gangsterism. Churchill. All them generals. The goods were important, money too. The car-shifting game might be finsihed up, but this, this was a family matter.

His eyes narrowed.

I'm a bloke sticking up for his family. Nothing wrong with that.

After all my losses: Pete, the stuff in the boot, the dough, the business; I can take revenge, all at once. I'm super-normal. Yeh, this is better than anger.

He swelled and grew and almost burst from his seat.

An unbridled smile beamed across his leathery face.

Bigger than Simmo.

Any father would want revenge for his son's death. Only natural.

I'll be reborn. It ensures survival of the fittest. Me.

His desire embodied a kind of modesty. He didn't need to dash down the wing and score before a crowd. Never did. He liked fixing a car under the roof of his workshop; all cool and methodical. Murder was a transaction best carried out in private: when someone made his life hell, knifed his flesh and blood, and this would be the perfect trade. He didn't need anyone's acknowledgment, adulation or recognition, unlike footie players. This would be just another matter transacted; and afterwards, the till would ring satisfaction.

The father ran the son.

I'll make him an unholy ghost. I'll take him out. Bang. Lights out.

I'll do it for Pete.

Chapter 56

Billy swept dust and sand from his elbows and trousers, scrubbed his shoes for a hint of shine. Using his hankie to wipe sweat and grit from his face, he replaced his Akubra.

Now, I'm a presentable Abo.

He clambered down the rocky slope, he walked towards Phil's homestead straight into the cop's hands. As the country opened up his steady stride brought him to the patrol cars outside the homestead.

He called to the first man his sighted, 'Thank goodness you're here.'

In the late afternoon haze, Cassidy's eyes narrowed. A bushman in battered trousers, a dirty white shirt and a swanky hat snooping around in a God-forsaken landscape. A swaggering stockman without a horse? A real estate agent? A neighbour with a fifty-kilometre-long nose?

His jaw dropped.

Is that –?

The guy on their 'suspects' board for the last three months.

Glancing to the others, checking reinforcements handy, he confirmed the impossible with, 'Bugger me.'

The other cops turned to detect the cause of their fellow officer's curse, their interest in a tanned bloke in jeans and black shoes waned when time pressed for the Commodore's recovery from the Hole.

'It's Billy. A million miles from town.'

Him, thought Warren. He was supposed to be in Sydney. What's he doing around here? At this time of year? We have enough to do already.

The days of walkabout warriors in New South Wales were long past, but a well-dressed one striding towards them strained credibility. Just queer.

'Before you ask,' said the dusky sundowner, 'we were out hunting kangaroos. Weren't shooting protected animals.'

Crowbar stifled laughter.

'Hilarious,' said Cassidy po-faced. 'You're under arrest.'

'What? You crazy? You can't cuff me for telling bad jokes. I'm taking a walk in the neighbourhood.'

'You're trespassing.'

'Mate, I own this country.'

'Then try offensive language, suspicious behaviour, resisting arrest, interfering with a crime scene and swearing at an officer.'

'Listen, chum: I'm inviting you to give me a lift to town.'

The ugly one stepped forward and pushed him back. 'We'll see about that.'

The Chief intercepted them, his arm raised. 'Hold on. Wait up.'

He stared at the prisoner, sizing him up like a heifer fit for the abattoir. 'So, you're Billy? Glad to meet you.' He smiled. 'You've been seen driving a stolen car, a Commodore VL owned by the missing Cliff Badger. Explain that.'

'I'm not in a talking mood,' he said, dancing on the hot ground.

'Your associates hid the vehicle out here on your behalf. We've found explosive materials all around. And here you are, a million miles from town suggesting this is a coincidence.'

'Where's your bow and arrows, Tarzan?' said Cassidy.

'Oh. Here we go. Stitch me up, fellas.'

'You shouldn't laugh, matey,' said the Chief. 'Put the cuffs on him.'

Billy stood tall, with his legs slightly apart. He lifted his arms high, elbows out. He expected this, wasn't resisting, only giving them pause and him a chance to survey the place. 'Wait. What's this about explosives?'

Ha. The black bugger wasn't entitled to ask questions, only to receive their attention.'

'And you think I would …? Ridiculous. You gentlemen are kindly offering me a lift to town. After that, you'll release me.'

'You think so? After fighting and provoking the Bicentennial official. After driving his car here, there and everywhere. You're a prime suspect in a murder inquiry.'

'I'd like to help you fellas find the bloke, honest, but ever since he arrived trouble is our neighbour. I mean: how did it come to this? You boys messing with me when a Royal Commission's at your throat. Where's it going to end?'

'Ends here,' said Cassidy.

'Eh?'

'Ends here. You murdered Cliff Badger. You hid the body and then had others dumped the car.'

'Time you were confronted at your dirty work,' said Warren, shuffling on his feet.

'You're wrong. Deadset.' His eyes narrowed; he steadied himself for what might come next. If he had handcuffs on, they'd probably do more than take him to the car: they take him to town, to the cleaners, and park him at the morgue.

Balli-al-mal.

Then he noticed Danny behind Warren.

'Danny! Mate, what are you doing here?'

Chief Warren made a snap decision. 'Cassidy, take Billy to the squad car.'

Billy strained forward, yelling. 'Wait. Mate, tell 'em nothing.'

Cassidy and Crowbar dragged him back, although he shook off the ugly one's first attempt at cuffing him. When push came to shove, he kept his balance, arms out he lifted them level to his face.

'OK.' With his hands high Cassidy couldn't slam them so hard his wrists bled.

Once he was cuffed they walked the short distance to the vehicle. 'Easy boys. Don't worry, I'm coming with you. I like air-conditioned cars.'

Danny stood by Warren craning his head in Billy's direction. How in hell did he get here? Out hunting kangaroos? He shielded his eyes against the late afternoon sun and veil of dust.

Billy's smart. He'll say he's not much of a desert sorta bloke. He'll say he's never been to The Hole. And the Legal Service will help him out.

In the squad car, Billy asked Cassidy, 'What's Danny doing here?'

'You don't know? He murdered Pete Bourke.'

'What!'

'He –

Oh, my …"

Chapter 57

With Billy turning up at The Hole, and Danny leading them there, the three senior officers conferred under the scrub's thin shade.

'What do you reckon?' said Warren.

'Them? They couldn't lie straight in bed,' said Cassidy.

'It appears the car drew Billy back,' said Detective Hanna.

'We've nabbed a killer,' said the boss. 'With them and the Commodore, we'll find out what happened to Cliff Badger. Give it a thorough search, then …' He patted his forehead. 'That Billy's a cocky bastard.'

Around dusk, the Coonamble tow truck arrived to drag out the vehicle, it's floodlights pointed into the cavern so they could secure and pull the vehicle from the depths. That done, Warren and his men inspected it.

'This is costing us a fortune,' he said under his breath.

Hanna raised his eyebrows. 'Can hardly use Bourkes.'

The boss approached and rubbed encrusted dust from the bodywork to reveal a glossy black surface. A deep scratch with a coin revealed grey and white beneath.

'This is the one,' he said to faint cheers.

He removed dirt from the side window to take a peep into the gloom. As far as he could tell, there was no body or snakes inside; just the upholstery's former glory.

'Open the boot.'

Without a key, Shortie fetched a crowbar, brandishing it like a glamorous sword. Wedging a gap, he prised it loose, reeling back and dropping the tool.

'Ah, the smell.'

The other cops laughed.

'Get on with it.'

The boss had spoken so Shortie shielded his nose as best he could, digging into the space again, levering it with astounding force.

The boot sprung up.

He reeled back, this time clutching the crowbar, his other hand across his face. Warren approached, peered inside and spied a large, dried mass of flesh, human-sized, wrapped around a hair and bone structure, barely recognizable in the lower regions where insects, worms and invertebrates occupied its collapsed form.

The Chief turned his head and spat to ground. 'It's a kangaroo.'

Chris Hanna discerned the tufts of fur glued to the skin, other bits in clumps, light and fluffy, wafting around the boot on the slightest breath of air.

'Take it out and keep searching. And you,' pointing to the young Edwards, 'search the interior. I want more evidence this is Cliff Badger's.'

He stepped back, leaving the others to the dirty work. Wiping his forehead, this time with his shirtsleeve, his eyes darted towards Danny.

'Take a seat son.'

He did so.

Danny thought, the Cops have the Commodore and a dead roo so they'll find Bourke's files soon. Should lead them to the Bourkes, the car stealing and the missing Bicentennial official. Gotta spare Dad. Uncle Billy will save himself.

The search for the Commodore brought quick results, Edward first to jump.

'A gun!'

On the far side, he lifted it out with the aid of a stick, holding it high, Warren shining his torch on it. Crowbar grinned.

'Been used?'

Edwards examined the weapon without touching it.

'One bullet missing.'

One shot suggested they were dealing with an experienced assassin or a killer firing at point-blank range, either way, it was cold-blooded.

'Found a map,' he said, peeling a crumpled form between his thumb and first finger. 'Of the State. Can still make out pencil marks. And writing.'

'Must be Cliff Badger's,' said Shortie.

'The mileage?'

'Only 1400 kilometres.'

'In miles?'

'Dunno.'

'Yeah, fits. Gotta be Badger's car.'

'So, what is a revolver doing there?' said Hanna. 'You don't kill 'roos with that. If this is the murder weapon, wouldn't they hide the gun, chuck the map, and anything else to do with the victim.'

'Perhaps,' said Warren. 'But The Hole is the perfect dumping place. Never find it out here.'

'Only we did.'

The boss sniffed, taking his comment as a compliment.

'You pulled the 'roo out yet? Eddie, give him some help.'

The cop squirmed at his Chief's unlovely request. Lifting himself, he drifted into position, spying inside the boot. Together, they perched over the remains, Edwards abandoning his mouth cover, and with Shortie, lifted the decayed matter glued to the bone on a hessian base, and dragged the carcass away. To everyone's relief, it was thrown in the bushes, the next quarter-hour was spent sorting what lay beneath.

A body?

Dust-laden, junior officers sweated in their clothes, roo muck exciting flies about their hands and forehead. Edwards tugged at his shirt-sleeves, gore clinging to his lower arms. He swiped around his nose and face, the bugs returning within seconds.

'Don't get too cosy boys. The boot needs detailed search.'

Disgust crossed both men's faces, the boss' persistence pushing their boundaries.

'Over here,' said the boss, 'what do you see?'

With an oil rag across his face, he pointed to two stained bags glued to the ruined carpet. One appeared to be a velvet tie-bag, the other, a leather or plastic brief case.

'Open it, without ruining the evidence.'

Shortie took out his penknife and applied force to the lock. Throwing his cloth away, he met stiff resistance before the bag tore. He separated the two sides as the bugs harassed him. Crowbar arrived with an insect repellent, spraying the men's faces with aerosol abandon.

Shortie pushed him off. 'Go to hell, will ya?'

Crowie sneered and his mate turned away in disgust.

'What the –'

Warren held up a commanding finger, glaring at Crowbar before bustling in and searching the briefcase himself. 'Here. Pay attention. There are cloth bags at the base, more in the side pockets. Come on.'

The blue or red velvet ones were untarnished. Crowbar now took an interest. 'Jewels. There are rings and gems.' He grinned. His mate grabbed and lifted one to the light, pouring the contents onto his palm.

'Whoa.' A cluster of small diamonds. 'Worth a packet.'

'If they're real,' said the boss. 'How many pouches?'

'Don't know. Maybe ten. What's this?'

'Rubies.'

Though ignorant of their value, Edwards took a long look, separating each one with his fingers. The other cop searched the two black bags. 'Opals in this one.'

'OK. Enough. Put them back in the case. Seal them before Crowie gets ideas.'

'What about the square boxes?'

'I know these fellas,' said Edwards, formerly of the Drugs Squad. 'Standard hippy marijuana. Someone's making a fortune out of this shit.'

Warren scratched his head. If this was Cliff Badger's car, how did a used handgun, a dead roo, and all this contraband accumulate here? Was Billy fencing goods or running guns? And the explosives?

He pulled Cassidy aside. 'I don't know. What do you make of it?'

'Makes a great crime scene. But I can't think straight with these damn flies.'

'Yeah,' said an uninvited Crowbar. 'It's too hot.'

'Shut your gob, and concentrate.'

'I don't suppose this stuff has been deliberately hidden here,' said Cassidy, 'until they retrieved and sold them for weapons. Those two know about it. And here's luck: we got Billy at the scene.'

'So, why would Danny lead us here? Why does Billy walk right up to us?'

'Damned if I know.'

'Hey boss,' said Crowbar, 'look at this.'

He struggled over.

'The back seat. Files. Lots of them.'

'Bicentennial ones?'

'Nar. Tools, I mean, for scrubbing off engine numbers. Standard car theft. I can see the scarring.'

'Oh, great. Now we add stolen car dealing. Young Danny's keen on putting Paddy Bourke in the frame, even after he murdered his son. What frigging next?'

Shortie grimaced, their faces, hands and clothes stained with roo muck, the flies and nameless bugs attacking them. 'When are we getting outa here?'

With night upon them, the mosquitoes and more mysterious flighted animals arrived, this time focusing their bites on their necks and arms. The men were tired, dirty and sticky when Shortie fired his insect spray at their faces, necks and thereabouts. Here, there and everywhere he lurched with bared teeth, spotting still more insects on the butts, legs and hair, real or imagined. 'Bugs. Mossies. Flies. Spiders.'

The men reeled. 'F—- Get the — You.'

Warren wouldn't be bothered with them. They were gathering evidence aplenty.

'Cassidy. You and Crowbar take the prisoners into town. The rest of us aren't finished.'

Edwards groaned as Shortie and Hanna's eyes watered.

'Come on. There's a body somewhere. Find it.' He tore at his hair. 'We continue searching. If we want to solve this matter, we need a body. We need a bloody body.'

Chapter 58

On his trip to town, an oppressive stench of fatigued bodies permeated the patrol vehicle. After one of the worst tasks assigned to him in the Force, Crowbar scratched his legs, crutch and back while clutching the wheel. He growled and cursed the bumps, ruts, sharp turns and sudden appearance of roos hopping across his path. As bad as the farts up his nostrils and the setting sun firing shots at his eyes.

Billy sat beside him with his eyes closed suffering a criminal hangover as Danny snoozed in the backseat, pretending to sleep. He'd rather rest than be tempted to rip the neighbouring copper's arms off for assaulting his dad.

Cassidy had Danny Trust cuffed to the door, doubly satisfied he could also kick Billy's butt while issuing instructions to the none-too-bright Crowbar. With an oppressive hour's drive, he anticipated a cleansing shower while the prisoners shared their odours. So comforted, he could crow about their successes at the station later.

When the squad car swerved onto the Broken Hill road, Billy cheered. They headed for town when a few hours ago Paddy Bourke left him for dead.

'I love these new cars,' said Billy, 'engine power, soft seats, flash panel. When's the next recruitment drive?'

'Aren't you a smart arse.'

'I have me moments.'

'Well, keep your gob shut or your head will be hurting.'

'Don't you want to know more about the grand black conspiracy?'

Go for it, thought Danny.

'Well, tell us what you know,' said Crowie, 'and all will be well.'

'All *is* well. We've got a massive weapons cache: bloody beautiful AK47s and enough ammo to wipe out a thousand coppers. Come Australia Day: ka-boom. Your 'balli-al-mal' goes up in smoke.

'Our what?'

'It's Gundabarri for pig farm.'

Just as well Danny feigned sleep. Otherwise …

'Nothing you can do. Torture me and I'll sue you and the Force for millions. Jump on my kidneys and I am dead speechless. There's a Royal Commission after you blokes. My pro-bono lawyers will blow you out of the water.'

Danny pictured Uncle Billy with a grin on his face.

'Do you see, now? You can't go invading our country, hunt us down, take away our kids, and still have cheap labour. Not without backpay, and payback. Action and reaction, mate. Our time's coming.'

'Ha.'

From his position, Cassidy couldn't eye the bastard. He could only hear his words and see the back of his fat, dark head. 'Danny'd love to see his Dad, don't you think? Sad to see them separated.'

'Time will tell. Come the revolution, you can't make an omelette without cracking a few eggs.'

'So, what's Kev in your revolutionary ranks: mastermind or stool pigeon?'

'Good question. Fact is, he's too smart for you lot. Once he went bush, where are you going to search, eh? Cause you'll never find him.'

'We'd be happy for Danny to spend time with him. Would you like that, matey?'

'Bugger off, copper. He's learning but Kev knows.'

Cassidy kicked Billy's seat. Thump. But in the confined space, and as hot as buggery, he suffered a cramp with the second kick.

'Enough,' said Crowie. 'I'm trying to drive.'

I'll give him a lesson in manners, he thought, remembering the delicious satisfaction of interrogating Kev at home. First chance I get Billy receives a walloping.

Back at Phil's Hole, Warren's depleted crew pointed their searchlight into the adit, their generator low on fuel. With an exploded monster bulb already lost, their last one gave them one-eyed hope before exhaustion, darkness and a power failure turned out their lights.

Edwards went in first, his rotund, lumbering outline overlapping with his elongated shadow. In no more than a minute of cursing and huffing, he had a result.

'Whoa!'

'A body?'

'Yeh.'

'You bloody beauty,' said Warren, 'Just what the doctor ordered.'

'A hand.'

A hand, thought Warren? Lend a hand? Wants a –

'And corpse.'

The Chief rushed through the macabre light as his meagre torchlight jumped and swung. The officer ahead fell backwards.

Thud. Splash.

With Harry smeared with unidentified matter and surrounded by a putrid odour, the outside spotlight veered away, leaving them in the pitch.

'I dropped in… it's… ah, shit.'

'Give us some bloody light,' the Chief yelled,

Prone on splintered rock, Edwards shone his torch on his gnashed knee, sticky, brown mud glued to his hand and stained his shirt, one leg in more gunk, the other hand against the stone facing. Warren's weak beam searched elsewhere, spying something like human remains.

'Found it.'

'But …I'm …'

Harry shook with disgust, rolled back and whimpered against the rock wall.

When the bright light returned, he regained sense and used his boss for support. He rose and stood, cursed and stumbled towards the entrance. Warren ignored him, not bothering to issue orders to an idiot.

Outside, Harry rushed past Shortie, pushing off his service cap. When he bothered to pick it up he lost balance and his head banged the machine's switch.

All black.

'I thought …'

With only his torch for light, Warren stared wide-eyed at his find in the cavern.

'It's a bloody corpse. Give me light. Down the bottom.'

With the boss excited, Shorty rekindled the beam, powered at maximum.

'This will change things,' said the boss to himself. 'Now we'll find the murderous scumbags.'

The others outside were impatient for orders to pack up, for relief from the savage harassment of bugs, flies and mosquitoes. So the boss found a body ...so what; they sought rest, sleep and a decent meal.

'Bugger this for a joke,' said Shortie, his eyes unfocused, his neck and face scorched by the machine's heat.

Harry Edwards rubbed his hand with a dirty towel, his knee bleeding, his eyes dazed and his brows convulsing. Waving his arms about, he dropped to the ground and pulled a blanket on his head and wept.

Shortie jerked left and right as repulsive smells attacked his nostrils. Grabbing the aerosol, he pointed it skywards, spraying as he reeled and twirled. When the spotlight exploded, heat and shattered glass radiated. He raised his arm, dropped the spray can and fell to the ground, hot glass fragments on his lap.

At the cave entrance, Warren held out a disembodied finger like a trophy.

'Got it.'

Chapter 59

Around midnight, pop-eyed Warren washed himself in the motel room as quietly as possible as nightmare visions of caverns, exploding spotlights, roos on the road and decaying body parts circulated his brain. The squeaky water pipes might wake visiting reporters in neighbouring rooms, and they might bang on his door til dawn. So he lit a carcinogenic cancer stick and sucked.

I'm a cautious man, he thought, sitting in a foetal position. A champion of calculation, a coacher of coaches. I don't stand on ceremony. The officers are at my command. Yeh, at my call.

In the office the next day, he sat in his comfortable seat facing the wall. He would not consult anyone today, nor converse about the unanswerable. Instead, he opened and closed his office drawer several times as it jammed yesterday, or was it the day before? It seemed right to shake and correct it as a vexing conundrum played in his head.

'Seen. Not seen. The scene. Was it …'

After their charming outing at The Hole, and with all they discovered, nothing added up. He knew that. The thrill and horror of discovering the Commodore and the body was relived in strobe lighting as he picked out flies from his Coco Pops. At least he returned with the severed finger sealed in a clear plastic bag.

I can't believe I was there except for the smells.

No matter how much he washed himself, the cavern stench clung to him, and the thought of insect bites and men's collapse into idiocy chewed him up.

I changed my uniform. I showered. I scrubbed. I…

After yesterday's marathon, he slept fitfully, remaining in bed until nine to shake off demons. In the office, a black cat rubbed against his cuffs under the desk, or at least he thought it did. It gave him the shivers. He would have kicked it but Crowbar entered, and he hastily pushed the drawer closed.

'Sir?'

'What?' He slid his bowl of soggy Coco-Pops to one side.

'It's almost twelve. You're due at the funeral.'

Warren stared at his cereal. 'I swear this cereal tastes like shit. There were flies in the box, eleven of them.'

'Were …eleven?'

'I clawed them out. Counted them.'

He pointed to a row of tiny, dark objects arrayed on his desk.

'Twelve, sir.'

'No. Eleven. Exactly.'

'Even so …the funeral.'

'Is it eleven already?'

He peered beneath his desk, and spying no signs of a cat, fell back in his seat, shaking his head. 'Cats. Cereal. Criminals. Clocks. Commodores. Why do they all start with "C"?

'Like constables,' said Crowbar, trying to be helpful.

'If I catch them scribbling "c" over the walls …'

Crowbar bit his lip. He didn't want Warren talking about that, at a time like this. Besides, so many words started with "C."

'With chalk or crayons,' said the aimless Chief. Crowbar withheld comment.

'Worse if they chiselled or carved, sir?'

The Commander crossed his arms. 'Me, going to ceremonies, standing beside crims and offering condolences.'

'For form's sake,' purred Crowbar. 'Under the circumstances.'

He jerked. 'Forms? Don't talk to me about forms.'

'No, sir. I mean—'

'You giving me lessons now?'

'No, sir.'

'Well, get this straight. Someone put flies in my Coco Pops. If I find out it's you…'

The constable gripped the chest, about to disappear around the corner.

'Don't leave,' said the Chief. 'There's something else.' His jaw hung like a wet towel. 'The corpse. Have the samples been sent to the labs? How long before they're identified?'

His officer slid a few papers from one hand to the other.

'We just shipped them, sir.'

'Ship? Yeh? Right. OK.'

Crowbar retreated after the officers convulsed and hid laughter lest it offend the boss. They didn't want a post in the desert; there were no rewards for cold nights and bloody hot days camped by a disintegrated old homestead.

Shorty and Harry will go mad still stationed at The Hole.

'That box,' said Warren, pointing at the Coco-Pops, 'is evidence.'

Cassidy stuck his head in the room. 'I'm out for a club sandwich. Crowie, you coming?'

They made a quick escape, walking straight past Chris Hanna, in the next room no longer bothering with niceties. Most of the squad sided with him, Crowbar too. Yet the Lebo did not blink. He's too damn perky, thought Cassidy. Usually, he bites like a shark and barks like a dog. Something's going on.

At Pete Bourke's funeral, Chief Warren stood behind Paddy Bourke and the Hard Boys, letting the priest's sonorous cant pass over him. With other things on his glutinous mind, for the moment he stared at Pete's burial patch as Paddy circled with his employees trailing like a dirty rag. As a few directionless townspeople hovered around the camellias, Mayor Sheila and Humblebum joined him.

'Quite a carry-on,' whispered Warren.

'Trouble for mayors too.'

With his hat in one hand, Warren's other hand fidgeted with its edges. 'Longest assignment ever, after the Grafton Affair. Not that you'd know about it.'

True. Since late November, most of the squad believed the street patrols would be withdrawn, job done. After all the boredom, they'd move to greener pastures. 'Anywhere would be greener than here,' said Cassidy. Nothing much happened apart from local insolence, indifference, and public hostility.

With Pete Bourke murdered, and the Commodore recovered, they had intriguing clues and an unidentified body. HQ's theory about a black revolt made sense.

Must be a connection, though Warren, or why keep us here?

His fingers fiddled with each other.

The Royal Commission bureaucrats will arrive again soon though he wouldn't let negative thoughts enter his Zen mind.

The Force is a brotherhood. We won't be hung out to dry. We're solid. It wouldn't work otherwise. Everyone would go mad.

He was a tidy man. It irked him to see damaged patrol cars parked around the station. He would have to explain their state. The broken windows and graffiti too. What would the Commissioners make of the commentary on the loo walls? Even the flies in his Coco Pops amounted to chaos.

That Commission stirs public discontent. Central Office ordered us to demonstrate "charity" over the Christmas and New Year celebrations.

Charity!?

He was a realist. Last week's stone-throwing and the bow-and-arrow episode were sure signs of an impending revolt. 'Stupid, bloody radicals: they're getting sneakier every year.'

People turned and stared at the interruption. Even the Fatherstuttered.

Mayor Sheila and Humblebum stood back from the funeral proceedings, and Warren retreated with them, red-faced under his deep blue cap.

'You alright?' said Humblebum.

Warren wiped his brow. 'It's complicated.'

'You heard, I suppose …' he said, leaning in. 'We've collected body parts, bones, guns and explosives, all over the place. Could be we found the remains of Cliff Badger.'

Cheryl glared. 'I don't want that kind of rumour spreading around town,' as her links with Badger were common knowledge.

'You should be very careful what you say,' said the administrator.

'Nothing, like, fits.'

'People have fits all the time.'

'I got people guarding a hole in the ground.'

'Inspector; we have a council to run,' said Cheryl. 'We don't need more commotion. The Royal Commission's coming here. You should be careful what you say. And if you are, we'll be careful about what *we* say.'

'Trouble at Cadiburrabirribalong Station too. Don't forget that. A man's been crucified with a backhoe. His wife's missing.'

'The Carrolls are as mad as hatters,' said Cheryl.

He jerked to attention when Cassidy arrived.

'Here,' said the detective, 'Chew on this: a chicken and cucumber sandwich.

Chapter 60

The next day, Warren and Cassidy took their banana chairs to the cop shop's upstairs landing, adjusting their position to harvest a weak breeze off the river. After their recent victories, they were buddies again, enjoying a long chat about the Badger case and what it all meant.

'We're closing in on this one,' said Cassidy. 'Two scumbags behind bars, one a murderer, the other a revolutionary.'

'Danny and Billy. Only a matter of time before we catch the others.'

They relaxed and pictured their next cold beer at the air-conditioned club, never better than after their day at The Hole. Sparse sounds around the intersection brought them close to sleep.

A distant drumming served as a wake-up call, Cassidy's beefy body starting. Searching for sense and a source from under his regulation hat, he peered through the railings and the quivering heat haze, spying marauding ants crossing the bridge, and invading the parkland.

'Bloody Patchtowners,' said Cassidy. 'Take a look.'

'What?'

Mara's mob paraded beside the road, past the rose bushed, one bloke strumming his guitar, some others banging cardboard or aluminium pots to an odd timing. No banners. No chanting. No jumping up and down. Nothing scary. They weren't even loitering.

'Spanna, keep an eye on them. Over there,' said Warren, pointing below. 'See what's going on.'

Chris soon stuck his head out the door.

'Ensure there's no trouble. I've had enough for a bloody lifetime. Besides, we've no backup until tomorrow.'

Chris Hanna put on his hat and stepped away.

'Be a good boy,' said Cassidy.

Under orders, he passed through the station, fists clenched, heading for the town's only pedestrian crossing, sure that catching to the parade on Evans Street, she would be amongst them. Drawn there, but doing his job as he saw it.

Mara's stories vexed him. She hexed him. He wanted the truth about Kev and this Badger guy. Because he cared for her. He admitted it. Against his better judgement. If she had something to do with Cliff Badger's disappearance, he was roasted and toasted. He knew it.

What if she's toying with me? He couldn't stand to think about the implications. Caught between allegiances and romance (a word not used around the station), he could not acknowledge her as he wished, and nor would she, despite their red-hot trysts.

Be a detective. Deal with it.

Yet, when he reached the street, in his first act, he searched for her.

There!

She glanced his way, so he held back. She wouldn't want him coming any closer.

With her mouth tight and eyes narrowed, she turned away and barked out a few words.

Anxious, alright.

Who wouldn't fear Chris Hanna, in uniform, tall, hovering around her mob, looking for errors, misbehaviour, anything to pounce on them. Mara called him Boney Moroney when they were together. In the river, he had stood around almost naked.

Is Kev here? If he is, must I arrest or interview him? Could I?

Guess not. No instructions from Warren. No warrant. The mob would lynch me before another interrogation like Cassidy's. It might kill him. We're already holding his son. Hell! We know he'll try to visit Danny.

Mara described Cassidy's method and injuries inflicted, and Kev's time in the hospital.

Yeah, it sounds like him, the bastard.

Kev! On the far side. There he is.

Duty dictated he approach him, though the principle of discretion told him to leave until later, race back to his superiors or fetch reinforcements. His inclinations said otherwise.

Taking off his hat and throwing it against a wall, he removed his tie and stuffed it into his pocket. Unbuttoning his shirt two notches, he ruffled his hair and stepped off the curb. Crossing the road to the parkland, he approached the mob at the site of their humiliation only months ago, the event that triggered the Royal Commission.

He winced but soon breached the gathering.

'G'day,' he said, like a casual street meeting of a friend or acquaintance. Though no one answered, his path led to Mara, and having reached her without obstacles, he bowed deeply to her.

That brought belly laughter. A dishevelled cop bowing to Patchtown's queen. She briefly smiled. He bit his lip. 'Ah, what's happening?'

Mara stepped closer to him and his plump cheeks, puffing out her chest. 'None of your bloody business.'

The others laughed themselves silly, backing her with a few well-armed barbs. Some young men jostled him before Kev slotted between them, putting one hand on the cop's shoulder. 'Leave him, boys.'

'Only want to know,' said Chris.

Some of the mob stood back, expectant.

'Mara's daughter is arriving on the next coach,' said Kev. 'Come along, if you like.'

Hanna might have blushed. He took a deep breath and glancing at her before noticing Kev's stained, plaster cast on his left wrist and hand, with many names and well-wisher's signatures. With patchy, swollen areas on his neck and cheeks, his previous speech showed dark lines around his eyes. He limped rather than walked.

A minute later, a bulky tour bus pulled around the corner, a dusty green one with a Greyhound stencilled down the side.

Beep. Beep.

The mob rushed down the road, leaving him and Kev watching.

They gathered around as Chrissie alighted. They whooped and cheered her beaming smile. When she embraced her mother, every man and woman lit up. They would celebrate her return somehow.

'I should arrest you,' said Cassidy, 'while the mob's distracted.'

Kev took a breath. 'How's my boy?'

Chris couldn't look him in the face. His eyes closed. When they opened, he gaped. 'God! What happened to you?'

Kev had aged. He possessed none of the energy and spirit he recalled at their first meeting.

'Mr Trust, I'm sorry; I really am.'

Kev's mouth squeezed. Perhaps he thought the better of asking which event the cop regretted. Besides, what could he say when so much time and residual goodwill had perished?

'Look,' said Chris, sweeping back his hair. 'I can guess why you're here. The others will pounce on you, first chance. I won't let that happen. If you'll wait, I'll arrange a meeting with Danny. I'll get you inside without them being around. But it's difficult. If you come to the back entrance at two …the next shift is at three, so …'

Kev stared back and bit his lip.

'You don't have to believe me. It's all I can do. OK? Sorry.'

Kev put his better hand on Chris Hanna's shoulder, looking him dead in the eye. He nodded. 'Two, then.'

The meeting he'd never make.

Chapter 61

At the station, Warren placed his cereal packet at the back of his desk so he could watch over it. If anyone removed it, he'd catch the culprit. He remembered the officer who bought the Coco Pops from Marco's store, and Crowbar made a point of putting it in his locker, so one of those two or someone between tampered with the contents. He kept the eleven flies in a glass jar holding down the Commission's Interim National Report.

The fly-screen door banged when Chris Hanna returned from overseeing the Patchtown mob. Passing reception, he spied Cassidy with the *Daily Telegraph*. A few other officers had their feet on the desks. He headed to the kettle.

'Well?' said Detective Cassidy.

'Nothing to worry about. They're collecting Chrissie, Mara's daughter, at the bus stop.'

'Her daughter? That slut.'

'Bugger off, Cass.'

Hanna went to the small fridge and discovered it almost empty when Cassidy pointed at him. 'You're telling us fifty people marching down Evans Street, beating drums right under our noses isn't provocative?'

'I wouldn't think so. The girl's been missing for months.'

'After what we found at The Hole. When Billy boasts about his AK47s. After Danny knocked off Pete Bourke. With a body, explosives and a murder or two, you think they're not geeing us up.'

Hanna eyeballed him. 'First, we recovered a corpse. In fact, bits of one, and ancient if I'm any judge. And no milk. Why is there no bloody milk?'

He swung away, desperate for a sweet, milky tea.

'The chemicals got there by accident, eh?' said Cassidy.

'Old fertilizer, incapable of making explosives. Like this damn squad. Can't even keep milk in the fridge.'

'So what's Billy the Revolutionary doing there?'

'Who knows? He's not telling. But the Commissioner will ask why he's been holed up on trumped-up charges. No chance of a conviction.'

'Listen, Spanna-in-the-Works. We've recovered a fortune in opals, diamonds and dope from the Commodore, enough to finance a bleeding black, mother-fucking army.'

'And what if there isn't one? What if we're just imagining it?'

Cassidy sneered and shirtfaced his adversary just as the kettle came to the boil with a high-pitched whistle.

Warren struck in his head, saying 'Back off, you two.'

They faced off with grim, sweaty disdain.

'Last warning.'

Hanna withdrew with a full head of steam, and switched-off the appliance.

'Detective Hanna. Where's your service cap?' said the Chief.

Chris reached for his head. Cassidy laughed like a hyena until Warren grabbed a paper cup and poured cold tea on his head.

'Jesus,' said Cassidy. 'What are you doing?'

'You two are in the Force. We're on the same side. There's a damn conspiracy under our noses. They're wrecking our cars, firing arrows, and now they're poisoning us. Work together. Come Australia Day, there'll be Bicentennial blue murder.'

Cassidy retrieved a towel, dried his hair and picked out the tea leaves. Hanna stood in a far corner and examined his watch. 'Almost two o'clock.'

'Don't remind me,' said Warren.

'You two,' said Chris. 'How about lunch at the club? This job is getting to us. We need a break.'

'Bloody hide. Inviting yourselves.'

'Nothing is happening here. Go on. After yesterday ...'

'Ah, boss. I think you owe me a beer,' said Cassidy.

'What about Mara's gang?'

'They're lazy lambs, Chief. I'll keep surveillance.'

'Sure,' said Cassidy, agreeable to stranding him at the station on a stinking hot day.

'No, Chris. You're coming too.' Warren dragged him from his chair. 'We will be seen together, so fetch another cap. A cop with nothing up top, you know …'

'But – '

'No buts. Come on. I'm as hot as buggery.'

He stood his ground but his Commander pulled him to the door so the three men crossed the road, hopping into a battered squad car. When they drove away, Hanna searched the rear window for Kev.

Chapter 62

Kev leaned on the bridge's iron railing overlooking the river's tepid flow and the rock arrangements that constituted the fish traps. From there, he could glimpse the shops, pub, police station and a battered Falcon on Evans Street. Since Chrissie's bus rumbled over the town's bridge no other vehicle appeared.

Mara's mob set up lunch in the public hall but he preferred to be alone over the river. He had an hour's wait before the police's shift emptied the station when he spied Chris Hanna manhandled into a patrol car and taken away.

Kev's head fell into his arms.

Soon after, another vehicle approached him from behind. He took no notice until it stopped beside him, the driver's window wound down.

'Hop in, mate,' said Paddy. His great, green tow truck, its engine turned off, parked above the place where Pete died, where Danny knifed him, and neither showed expression.

Kev should have shuddered at the thought of seeing him, as he knew as well as anyone what happened, and why his son lost his liberty, locked up in a cell down the road.

'I'm so sorry,' he said to the bereaved, as it was always his inclination to console.

Paddy bit his lip, his face stretched but sterile. He swung the door open. 'Jump aboard.'

Kev's sight fell to the loitering brown stream leaking through the rocky foundations of the fish traps, his cautious mind aware this invitation might hold a sting. Hanna gave him hopes of seeing Danny, a current that might carry him to consolation and its calming waters. But with him carried away before his eyes, a fervent dream washed downriver to an inland sea, westward, to uncertain times. That old river coursed to where most ended, in an all-consuming ocean.

The fish that swum its depths were drawn into labyrinths where the barbs of spears drew blood. Paddy Bourke or the Police might do the same to him, except he had no obligations to the cops. They took from him all they could, his son and grandfather, taken to Balli-al-mal.

He owed the father sympathy after his son's death, lost forever at the hands of his boy, even if they burnt down his home. That was an iron and wood construction. With a life extinguished by his Blacksmith blood, he would show his respects for all those lost unwanted conflicts.

Paddy Bourke's overflow of hate would sweep him away as a river in flood swept aside Europeans who did not have millennia of experience with the land's wildest moods.

Despite this, Kev pondered the garageman's invitation, and in his usual manner, he took his time. With Pete's father in mourning, offering his sympathy would take enormous spirit, familial forgetting and a colossal remembering. He bled for the people he loved, for their losses, and for a Bicentennial official he met once. Pursued by police bullies, he left town for everyone's benefit.

So he put a hand on the door frame and swelled to magnanimity just when summer's heat bore down on him and the gravel crunched under his feet. To offer condolenceswith a battered body in the vehicle of his enemy, he surpassed himself.

'It's air-conditioned,' said Paddy.

Who would settle on cheap vengeance, that shortcut for those of little character, self-knowledge and wisdom?

The tow truck was poor bait but its open door begged for an all-father meeting of lost sons and worn souls. Paddy's false comradeship hid unspent wrath and the reckoning of a spendthrift spirit.

Kev must have believed Pete's dad bore more pain, so he thanked the river for its calming waters, the stars for time itself, and his ancestors for unbroken kinship. With a bruised body and fractured ribs, he lifted himself and stepped inside the shiny, mechanical frame. Pulling himself until they spied on another tortured face, he offered his body and soul to reconciliation.

A trap.

A holy tear.

'Ginge. Hop in the front. We've got to get Kev out of here.'

His helper moved to the seating blocking Kev's retreat. 'You never know when them cops might return.'

Starting up, he revved the truck and drove off the bridge and turned onto Gumby Road, the engine grumbling like a deep-throated bull.

'You're going to die,' said the garageman, spittle flying through the hot air.

In the time it took to reach the Council tip, his passenger did not speak; he only looked straight ahead. Paddy's first utterance stated his intentions, amounting to moral judgment backed by the force of weaponry that destroyed Jimmy Blacksmith. The name of "Trust" offered him no protection.

For his part, each unnecessary word compromised and degraded his lofty act. In plain terms, he rejoiced to walk into the bloke's arms as a gift from God. Jehovah savoured the spicy taste of Old Testament justice without long-winded speeches or a priest's unbelievable assurances. He drifted further from Danny, yet safely held at heart.

Paddy took the rough track to the tip, his shiny, green bull ploughing the scrub before he cut the engine at the clearing near the old water tower. When he wound down his window, a faint breeze in the crackling afternoon heat invaded the cabin. He squinted at the quivering landscape where a million indifferent insects, cicadas, bees, ants and moths flitted about the saltbush, dogwood and straw grasses. They hopped, crawled, munched, burrowed, fornicated and buzzed the earth's excitement.

Kev's two hands placed on the dashboard, he half-expected him to break into a hymn. God's gift to him formal and proper, as if mere sentiment would cut across his purpose.

No way. Ginge held the blocking position. His victim must have known this was a journey to his end.

Keep to the procedure. Cool as, when … the bastard prayed:

Our Father who art in heaven

Hallowed be thy name –'

'Shut it, or I'll stick you now.'

Giving me a prayer. I'll shoot him so he gets to Heaven twice.

For the garageman, death was a finality for someone else, someone who deserved it, someone who didn't understand the earthy reality of grease and panel-beating.

Paddy thought, he's doing nothing, saying nothing. This will be easy.

It was Paddy's first murder. Honest. He never anticipated such lofty criminality: the extinguishment of a life without mercy. Running cars, jewels and dope were his lines of work; stern feats of organization requiring discipline, payment and punishment. He warned people off, issued an occasional violent reminder of who ran the show, and generally took his proper place in the pecking order.

His victim had the gall to park himself on the bridge overlooking where Danny murdered Pete. He will never see his son again. It's only right.

After the funeral's trials, any man-in-mourning would drive to some unnamed coastal holiday spot, away from the heat, or else ally with friends and relatives for soothing times. He could not shake free from passion, nor lend it good ends. He would leave townspeople to laze indoors, leave the dirty tip scavengers sit by the river and share talk of plastic bottles, broken glass and mangled metal. Let the tradies sit in the pubs, the squatters guard their properties or shopkeepers take refuge in the club. They did not know his passion for righteous justice.

He gripped his thigh and twitched, as his blood reared. With no one else near: not a car, not a stray pedestrian, not one of Mara's lot were about, he would not give anyone cause to think their top scavenger had been abducted.

With Pete's death, the blow stung like a punch in the face or an alien invasion from an outer planet named Tobuggery.

No mercy. He envisaged murder for the first time, his son's death worthy of it. Nothing frivolous in a cold-hearted execution. With Pete's loss came the opportunity for the chill excitement of revenge.

He has to beg.

He tipped his rear-view mirror left and right, surveying the world behind him.

Not a soul in sight.

He could have grinned but …the bastard is silent. Better a prayer, though, both annoyed him.

All the troubles he's brought me. Let him wait. Let him dream of escape. Let him think "Pop" will be his end.

Let a little hope rise and …rub it in the dust. Let him know what wretched means.

Not for the first time, he had visions of burning bushes: the red-and-yellow of flames, an all-consuming fire with a crackling voice saying,

Do it.

Burning bushes, his son sacrificed, and God urging an eye-for-an-eye, a life-for-a-life with a eucalyptus aroma.

For Pete, his son, had been sacrificed before his time, in the dry country that cracked rocks. Where only the hardest survive without the bullshit of the three wise men.

Fire makes everything black. Black greasy engines, smoked, burning tyres, firebombed cars, barbeque-black seating, springs poking from the ashes like spare ribs. Bible black.

Hard men make perfect murder with a strike of the match, Kev consumed in righteous red-and-yellow. Charred beyond recognition.

'Get him out,' he said to Gunge.

Reaching into the glove box, he took his weapon in his right hand, while his helper dragged a rigid, weeping Kev from his seat to a cleared patch, his victim struggling for balance and footing.

He can't escape. What his son's done. He can't run. He's limping. Pete isn't. He's dead.

'Ginge. Leave the fuel here. Get yourself back to the junction, and wait for me.'

Ginger hopped in the truck and drove away as quietly as he could, common dust rising behind as he and the vehicle disappeared behind a mulga veil.

Paddy stood beside the fuel drum, with one hand in his pocket gripping the pistol, Kev a lone figure by a scarred stump, his brows knitted, hands pressed against his sides.

He waited for him to beg, but his victim's calculated passivity cheated him of that satisfaction, yet fired his determination. There would be no unseemly struggle; no skin torn, no blood stains, no knives drawn or objects cast around. Nothing out of place. With the bastard already battered and limping, his total control brought a surge of pleasure. Giddy joy.

He knows he deserves it.

'Strip.'

For you, Pete. 'Strip.'

Kev's face perspired in the intense, afternoon sun, his cheeks, salt-encrusted, his eyes set on the horizon. Though he didn't move, he sweated, his brow thatched, an imperceptible shake of the head struggling for self-possession.

Kev strip? He would never go naked in the open air, before his wife, or amongst shearers, all men. Nor did he possess the energy to stretch his tired and brutalized limbs for no purpose.

Paddy took out "Pop," and pointed the barrel. 'God damn you, strip.'

Kev turned towards him. 'Did you –'

'Me?'

'Mr Badger. Did you–?'

Paddy stamped his foot.

'What do you take me for?'

He lowered his weapon, his hand shaking. He advanced on his victim.

'I killed no one. That car was abandoned. Finders-keepers. What do you take me for?'

Circling Kev until he no longer faced him, he gripped the pistol, ready to pull the trigger or punch that sack of potatoes senseless. He'd have plenty of satisfaction.

The bastard wants to be belted to a pulp, and left here. With his stinking, guilty conscience, he's trying to save himself.

His sweat crusted in salt. 'You are good. Yeah.'

Paddy threw the gun aside. 'There. Make a try for it?'

Kev stood his ground, rubbing his shoulders in self-embrace.

'Go on. Got any guts?' He stepped closer, one hand pulling his shirt flaps from beneath his trousers. Moving in, he unbuttoned his victim's shirt, sneering.

I'm not his servant.

Nevertheless, he opened the fellow's chest to the dry air. 'Make a dash for it,' he whispered. 'Go on.'

But this bloke dwelt somewhere else, like an inscrutable guru in a world of hurt. It annoyed him. But he possessed more means of inflicting pain.

'That Badger. I reckon he did a runner. Cops running around, trying to pin a murder on you and me. How's that make you feel?

Kev broke into a jerky laughter, a chuckle. His loosened arms caused his tormentor to step back to the pistol.

When his laughter died and his shoulders folded again, Bourke moved back to release the last buttons with his free hand, the other in reserve. He struggled to pull the shirt from his victim's back. Failed. But with the world torn, ripped and conflicted, he said, 'We took his government car after Mara dumped it. I wondered what she was up to. Dead or alive, why should we care? Never saw him again.'

He pushed Kev against the stump like a disagreeable rag doll. By clamping his foot against his back, he ripped what he could from him, his victim screaming in agony, so he paused to see whether anyone else heard the cries.

He fetched his weapon. 'Damn you. Take off the rest or I'll kill you now.'

Kev lay on sand and grit, clawing in pain, groaning, eyes watered.

With his foot against his back, in his hurry, Paddy imbalanced, fell, clutching the gun. Twisting away in the dust, he jumped up, and kicked the ground. Turning his weapon on him, hand stiff, face sweating, he aimed.

Not the plan. Not the plan.

'Take it off.'

Kev removed the last vestiges of his shirt, held it in hand, and did not know what to do with it.

Bourke grabbed and threw it aside. 'Now, off with the trousers.'

Kev did nothing and said nothing. With Jimmy Blacksmith hovering above him, offering advice, grim-faced and leery. Back when he was hunted down and cornered, did his executioners humiliate and torture him?

Glory to the land, to the wretched of the Earth; this body was all he had.

'Mate. You're a peach. I was hoping the cops would finish you off.'

'You mean …'

'Look at you. They couldn't put you away. Somebody has to. I'm helping out. The fools reckon you're an agitator like Billy, preparing for the big revolt. The meek shall inherit the Earth, eh? That's a joke.

'And Cheryl Sheila. Hope you didn't fall for her. She's working for them.'

Unflinching Kev.

'Me, working for them? They worked for me more like it.'

Hands to his face, he wiped aside the caked dust. He moved around him, poking his gun into his back as Kev's arms dropped to his sides. Untying the belt, Paddy pulled his trousers to his knees with one hand.

'Take them off.'

He might have obeyed, yet his eyes searched his tormentor's without making sense of a fellow who would strip him of all dignity at the point of a gun, humiliate him for his foolishness, and tell him the Commodore story that might have saved him, Billy, Mara and Danny from calamity.

'Don't,' said Kev.

'Don't what?'

'It's only more trouble. You …'

'No trouble at all.' He just wanted to light the match. 'You never had a chance, mate. No one's gonna rescue you. The whole town would sell their mother if the rewards were good enough.'

I'm wasting words on him, thought Paddy. My red-and-yellow speak for me, for Pete.

'You disgust me. Bloody town saying, "Look what they did to Kev. Poor bugger's getting knocked about." All the time you were buggering us up.'

'I'm sorry.'

'Sorry? Sorry.'

He grabbed the petrol drum and heaved it above his shoulders. With the cap removed and the swirling liquid fighting his grip, he walked around Kev. 'What do you say now, eh?'

'Oh, God.

'Thy will be done

'On earth as it is in heaven.

'Hallowed –

He poured fuel over his back, his flanks, his stomach. Kev gasped for air, fell to the ground, rolled, clawed, attempting to rub away the fuel and rid the stinking vapour, crawling in sand and dust.

Paddy's eyes blazed, his mouth tight. Leaning forward, he poured more on him, the bastard writhing, choking, his hands wiping fuel from his eyes and nostrils. When he struggled to stand, he kicked him over. Crawling towards the water tower, one gasp and he collapsed to earth, unconscious.

'What do you say, now? Buggering me up. Buggering me up.'

He threw the can away, circling, reviewing the result of his labour.

Kev trousers trailed from one leg.

'Nothing to say? Nothing to say?'

He lit a match and threw it at the body. The flames caught, spread and engulfed him. His victim contorted, fell and writhed about the sandy soil, grasping and yelping.

Red-and-yellow.

Red-and-yellow.

Paddy stepped back, picked up the shirt pieces, and cast them into the flames. Taking a seat on the stump, he faced away from his victim. He itched, sneered and thumped his sides but felt no satisfaction More like a bond, an absence, a refusal.

Accept the willing tears.

Chapter 63

From his cell bed the same afternoon, Danny heard voices from the footpath below his lofty window.

'Hey, Danny,' said a young voice.

Chrissie!

Climbing his bed, he pulled himself up, one foot gripping the wall, two shadows on the concrete path.

'Yeah.' Having not spoken for days, his voice sounded wispy.

'Want some oranges, bud?'

Mara!

'Got some here.'

'Chuck them up, eh.'

A crumpling paper bag preceded a few pieces lobbed up. He caught the first –beginners luck. The next one fell back on the footpath, a younger voice smothering her laughter. Between giggles, he held it to his nose, savouring the citrus aroma. That zing!

'What's happening?'

'She's home. She's here.'

'Danny. Don't worry. We'll get you out.'

Uncle Billy found her, and brought her back. The old dog.

He slumped against the wall, eyes moistening, quiet now, thinking up his next words. 'Have you seen Dad?'

His voice was faint, barely reaching beyond his cell walls so Chrissie puzzled.

Mara called, 'Your dad's OK. He had to hide. He's come back.'

Tears welled from his eyes. He wiped them away.

'Hey,' said Chrissie. 'I'm coming up.'

With the sounds of shuffling bags and a few grunts and whispers below the cell window, he stretched, and peered outside, half-sighted by the wall's recess.

'Here,' said Christine.

At first, he only spied the top of her head with its curly hair. When a hand appeared on the ledge, he gripped it as she balanced herself on Mara's shoulders. At last, her beautiful green eyes captivated him, and they dipped into the other's being. He took her hand, admiring her forehead and lashes but by then she slipped lower. She fought for balance, glancing downward, before falling away.

With Chrissie in her arms again, Mara wanted to return home. So, after further talk, he waved them away, not so much out of understanding or a magnificent spirit, but partly because, Hanna and Cassidy argued in the corridor, firing accusations at each other. They growled, sparred and cursed the other, all trust departed.

The siren howled. On the horizon, a grey curl of smoke appeared from somewhere out of town. When Danny noticed it, that was you Kev, burning, sending signals; the curling, drifting body of smoke calling out to townspeople. His son couldn't read the signs, but years later, made sense of them, obsessed with that moment, the drift of smoke tracing millennia. In the dimming light, everyone was doing something, but no one cared for you, Kev. A dad, a husband, a shearer. A townsman.

* * *

Across town, Cheryl Sheila and Humblebum made love under a white sheet on a hot afternoon. Prone on the bed after, she spread her arms and licked her lips. Despite the outside light, she rolled over and groaned. He, half-asleep, failed to move.

She sighed. The roo factory's fired three men and the Bicentennial bastards are holding up the dough.

Humblebum's slumber persisted as she took herself to the bathroom, a favourite place for her to consider town matters. By the time she returned, a fire siren whined like a wild dog without dinner, or like one of those air-raid sirens from an old war movie before a Japanese fighter dive-bombed a hapless town.

Wer-hur-r

Werr-hur-rr.

It annoyed anyone about to sit down for their evening meal. But no one thought the battle is out there, shouldn't we do the decent thing? Everyone was looking after themselves, keeping their head down, and hoping for the best.

Who cared?

Mayor Sheila stuck her head out the window, noticing a drifting smoke over the neighbour's roof. 'Something wrong at the tip.'

It kept howling.

'Leave it to the bloody firemen,' he said. 'It's our turn for a holiday.'

She would have done so, except … 'Oh, shit!'

They dressed hurriedly, and headed for Evans Street, running into Ted outside the Travellers Motel.

'What are you doing here? Hear the siren.'

'You can go to hell.'

Ungrateful wretch. Talking to his mayor like that.

'You're in the Brigade. Where's the truck?'

But when he turned his back to her, Humblebum grabbed her arm. 'Come on.'

'Where's the brigade?'

She wasn't sure, yet suspected …

In a few minutes they banged on Bourke Garage's locked gate.

'Come on. Open up, for God's sake.'

Eventually, Ginger's leather face appeared under the lane's dim light.

'What?'

'The truck? Have you got it?'

'Yeah.'

'There's a blaze at the tip. What's the crew doing?'

'I dunno.'

The siren howled.

'What the – Do you know who you're talking to?'

The garageman was unfazed. 'What am I supposed to do? The truck's dismantled. The pump is broken, and the sump's in a bad way. The boss took a holiday.'

He turned to his lovely mayor. 'What do you think?'

'Let's go to the pub, and see who we can rouse. The fire might be out of control.'

They moved to the Shearers Arms, all dignity mustered. A near-empty bar greeted them; most of the men home for dinner, a few others down the road enjoying Marco's air-conditioning.

Sheila scoured the scabby surroundings, spotting the English school teacher. 'Glen. Aren't you a Volunteer?'

He did not move or turn towards her, absorbed in questions of gambling or global music.

'Aren't you?'

'To what do you refer, Madam? A Catch-22 or much to-do about nothing?'

'What the Dickens,' said Humblebum arms raised. 'Bloody foreigner.'

He turned to another townsman. 'Dickie? What about you?'

'Me? Got no legs,' he said with an obscene jolliness. 'Reckon all our rubbish needs burning.'

Steadfast, Sheila insisted. 'It's our fire brigade, ain't it?'

They had a fire; if only someone would go to the tip where they would have found Kev. But no one blinked, so she led her hubby outside.

'What a pile of garbage.'

'Easy on,' she said, 'Let's go to the fire station. Someone must have set off the alarm.'

They turned off Evans Street in the late afternoon's red-and-yellow light, but on arrival not a single light emanated, though the whiff of smoke carried by a westerly breeze wound through the stunted turpentines. A dust swirl cantered along the footpath, and a rush of blood hit Cheryl. 'I don't believe it. Johnno's supposed to be the Coordinator. Where the frigging hell is Marto?'

No sooner had her partner signaled puzzlement when she remembered. 'The bastard's on holidays.'

'Super. Holidaying in the fire season.'

'Typical Marto. Left his useless brother.'

Ever since Kev's wake in the park, Marto suspected one of the blacks would knock him off and steal his grog. So he nailed down every table and chair in the bar, leaving for God-knows-where, his brother as caretaker.

'What a bastard. Left town when his drinkers were thirsty. Where's the logic?'

It all added up in Cheryl's brain: she had enemies, betrayal afoot. With the roo factory in crisis, the Bicentennial were holding the money back. Mara spread rumours and Phil Bowler hadn't phoned since the election. He practically lived in Sydney.

'Let's go to the club.'

'For a drink?'

'No, fat arse. So we can climb the roof and see whether we're all going up in smoke.'

'And buy a cold one.'

As the grey smoke drifted about the water tower, Kev burnt. Your Kev, my Kev, our Kev, reduced from flesh to ashes when he demanded so little from the world.

Chapter 64

Mayor Sheila loomed like a cane toad in Warren's office when already cats and Coco Pops put him off beer, and the sight of cider drinkers and cocktails disgusted him. 'The town's unhappy with your treatment of Kev,' she said. 'You blokes hospitalised him, and now he's missing.'

The Commander's head rocked on its axis. 'How the hell am I supposed to find an abo who knows every piece of outback desert by its first name?'

Not content with demanding the absurd, she asked the ridiculous: would his officers join the volunteer fire brigade?

'Of course. Anything you say, m' Lady,' he said, hoping the irony not lost on her. What to do with this nervy, deranged bitch? 'We could ask Kev to lead the fire brigade. Solve two problems at once.'

Ignoring him, she claimed Kev's house had been burnt down last month, and a few days back, a brush fire at the tip threatened the school grounds.

'Well, somebody should report these things sooner.'

Once she cleared out he said to Cassidy, 'What does she expect when no one took the trouble to tell us? She has a nerve. Wants us working all night putting out bushfires. I mean, it's their dunghole. Let them fight their own battles.'

Kev had gone bush for weeks now but the Commander confided in Cassidy 'Oh, yes. I found out about his town visit. No one can keep secrets from me.'

Detective Hanna had been fraternizing with the enemy. Made contact with the suspect the day Mara's mob paraded through town pretending to be Presbyterians.

Gave him a bloody bollocking.

The Commander reckoned he had an advantage: he could wait for other people's mistakes. Like a Zen master, being patient was his trump card. No need for steam under the collar. Whether it was Missing Persons, Coco Pops, murders or wayward officers, Time and a snippet of information solved all problems. So, to the mayor's requests he replied, 'No use looking for a bloke when he doesn't want to be found. It's a question of priorities.'

He shook until it almost fell off. No one in this shithole understands, he thought, that our Missing Person fathered a murderer, and a young man died before they could act. Why should I care about Kev? There's no arrest warrant pending or otherwise, so I'll schmooze the mayor a while longer until we're out of here.

Before sh left, he said to her, 'I'll sent an officer up Brenangle way. Check out the place. Should hear back soon.'

'Look, mate,' she said, not content with his word, 'my community is worried. They want results. It's not only the blacks; it's the do-gooders, the unionists, schoolies, and his old mates. They drop into my office demanding miracles. They reckon you blokes knocked him off.'

He reddened. 'What a load of –'

'Mara and Billy are stirring things up. That lot will spoil the Bicentenary unless something is done.'

'Now you realize, eh? They were always planning to wreck it. In Sydney, this time. Any excuse will do. Admit it.'

The Mayor's hands fisted. 'For Pity's sake.'

Warren lifted himself until he stood over her. 'What about Mister Cliff bloody Badger? What about your darling ex-husband? You don't seem so keen on finding him.'

'Mate, what an accusation! It's plain unwarranted.'

'Listen, our squad struggle with this death-in-custody. Another bloke had a stake through his guts, his wife and child missing. There's the body out at The Hole too. Maybe it's him, maybe not. You come here and tell me a mob of blacks are out to kill us for knocking off Kev.' He threw down his papers. 'Who or what isn't dead, lost or looking for trouble?'

Mayor Sheila's jaw tensed. 'Town folks are worried, OK? They want me to find the town's favourite son.'

'Favourite son? Bloody hell, woman. Last month he was a pariah.

Now he's a hero. Give us a break. He's likely a fucking criminal. Murder's in his blood. He's been giving us the run around for weeks. He's related to that outlaw, Jimmy Blacksmith. Didn't know that, did you?'

Cheryl rolled her eyes.

Warren turned his back on her, lest he burst a boiler.

He confronted her again. 'If he wants to be found, he can walk in here any time, and we'll give him a pair of handcuffs for Christmas. I'd like to wring his scrawny neck.'

The Mayor said nothing.

'I'm no magician, woman. We've got a lot on our plate. They're sending inspectors our way …for an audit. An audit, for God's sake. Coded message, sheila. It's an excuse to shut us down, the whole bloody TRG.'

Mayor Sheila slumped into a seat.

'Well?' said Warren.

'So, you'll continue the search?'

'Tell your black friends anything you like; you always have.'

Two battered squad cars parked outside the cop shop acquired an off-white appearance. With their dust-laden wheels and lost number plates, their authority (and second-hand value) had taken a holiday in Siberia where at least it could be covered in snow.

Inside the soon-to-be demolished cop shop, Warren's men decided it best to stay indoors on sweaty days, play cards and reminisce about their hometowns.

By night, a gang of likely lads hoping for a job at Bourkes Garage, practised rock-throwing on their gallery of cells and the station roof, the night officers doing no more than throwing them back.

Beer bottles created better sound effects, so the local lads hurled them over the walls, officers scurrying away after an explosion of glass. If the cops dared take a patrol, the occasional live fire was required to scare away unwanted intruders.

With the heat bearing down on his men by day, Chief Warren assigned Edwards and Shortie car-washing duties. Perfect, he reasoned, as the younger ones liked splashing water. He reckoned it their chance to stay cool or let off steam. They could play like boys, and learn again what it means to start at the bottom. Besides, repairing the Falcons at Paddy's Garage brought up more harrowing issues.

Better to clean them up. They only needed a few rags, buckets of water, and a lot of elbow grease. The assigned men enjoyed a quick pistol fight with hoses to cool them down, and with a bit of splash and slap-dash, the cars came up half-clean. He reckoned that his men seen carrying soapy water past their windows lifted morale. With a supply of Coco Pops and savouries from Bathurst, he was content to bypass the town and its discontents.

Warren inspected his crunched, torn, smeared and scratched fleet from the balcony. Hubcaps missing and faded Duco on the bonnet.

'We're as tough as nails,' he said with no one present.

Passers-by had dragged fifty-cent pieces across the paintwork and pelted them with stones from slingshots, a suitable challenge for locals taking cover in side streets. January had never been so delightful. Pinching a Falcon's hubcap became a young bloke's badge of courage, a venture best undertaken at night, and later celebrated after at the Unity Hotel. The trophies were displayed on the Beer Garden wall, no officer worth the aggro to recover them.

The Chief claimed panel beating was not in his budget. He wisely instructed them to contemplate reality: 'We can't ban rocks, so, if you're driving through town, and you see them coming, put your foot down and Skidaddle.'

V-Vroom. They zoomed past the stone-throwers, and not one headlight smashed last week. Success. Save the lights, concluded the Commander, or else we'll have to buy Jumbo Car Conversion kits.

The state of the station didn't matter. So ever since the Coco Pops incident, the Chief only sighed when the Commission's preliminary report recommended its demolition. Unimpressed by the large "Captain C" painted in blue over the loo, Warren collected the calamine after a shift, ready to wipe it out. But the word "Captain" caught his imagination, and the second "C" might be for "Courageous".

Imagine that on a billboard, he thought.

On further thought, he scribbled over it: "Demolition Site. Have a go."

The next morning, he was beyond cheery. 'Anyone for breakfast? Plenty of milk in the fridge.' The few men present lifted their hand to suggest 'Sure, but …'

Away from his gaze, they used marker pens to add curses and commentaries on the walls from the back office to the far cells. Among those without expletives were "Snap, crackle and pop," "BYO Henry" and "Who Is Mr Big?" Cassidy identified himself as their hero-clown, spray-painting 'Eleven Flies, Twelve Nosedives" on the courtyard wall, saying, 'The boss can take a joke.'

Locals contributed too. Once confined to back lanes ambushes on squad cars, the young ones smashed station windows down the long side. Cassidy foresaw the danger and collected the fire extinguishers before anyone else. By locking them in the store room when they demolished the place, he would collect them for himself, the reward for his effort.

Damned if I'll leave them for thieves.

'Let off steam, boys. We're out of here soon.'

But when cowpats daubed the back entrance, Warren objected. 'OK, you buggers. I want to know who did this. I want them removed. Now.'

'No worries,' said his fellow officers, cleaning it up late afternoon.

Only Hanna wondered aloud: 'And the rest?'

'Easy, mate. They're pulling the place down anyway.'

That said, the men who ignored patrols took their shifts at Marco's, the club or more mysterious haunts. Those who lounged around the station avoided town whispers, preferring to make their own within the station's confines.

While adding milk to his Coco Pops, the boss made occasional inquiries. 'Can we do some work around here?'

Come Thursday afternoon, he inquired: 'Chris, what about the backhoe murder.'

'The wife can't be found. The parents are sure she'll turn up.'

'What's Missing Persons say?'

'Good news. They'll take the case if we call it an accident.'

And the body at The Hole? Confirmed?'

'Yep. Like I said, something from twenty years ago. But the town's as silent as. Seems Kev Trust visited the place around that time.

'He's got form.'

'No one's saying that.'

Warren fell back into his seat, waving his hands. He had asked Hanna about it; job done. Zen handover. Someone else's problem.

His officer pulled off his hat, swept his hair and returned it to his head. Useless bastard, he thought. He's lost all interest in Kev's whereabouts.

'Mate,' said the Chief, 'warn me if you see the mayor come this way. She's the biggest stone-thrower we have.' He read the *Telegraph*, swatted a fly and reached for his packet of CCs.

Chapter 65

Australia Day, January 26, 1988

With the crime scene at The Hole abandoned and the backhoe case put aside, the squad collected around the front desk, their broken chairs stored in the interrogation room. Hanna worked next door, the Commander reserving the last for himself. He drilled his men 'It's breakout day. Show them muscle. Maybe they won't bother us.'

Just then Humblebum walked into the station with a hubcap in hand. He placed it on the reception desk and announced, 'The water carrier reported a body under the tower.'

The squadmen groaned. Some buried their heads in their hands. But the Chief said, 'Knew it. They've started.'

With Bicentennial celebrations happening throughout the country, Warren expected trouble. The radicals wanted them flustered, on wild-goose chases, getting confused or ambushed. But he was a Zen master. 'Cassidy, confiscate the hubcap. Fellas, occupy Evans Street before the day heats up. Crowie, fetch everyone a decent sandwich. I predict a shit of a day.'

'But the corpse?'

'Hardly likely to walk away. We'll stake the crime scene after morning tea.'

Around midday, he and Crowbar headed out, armed and unready for the charred, stick-like form found by the water tower. Once they arrived, they identified only an unknown person incinerated.

'Dead alright,' said Warren.

'There's the deceased and the duly demoted,' said the wit behind him.

The Chief ran his hands through his ever-thinning hair. 'You're suited to washing cars, Crowie.'

Sweating under his stiff new cap, he took a closer look. From his shaded position, he screwed his eyes, noticing the persistent dripping from above.

That tank needs fixing.

Standing over the remains, he turned his excessive belly eastward, then south, before wiping his nose with his forearm. 'Another murder. The fire started here, and spread towards the school.' He kicked the ashes, if only to draw attention to the surrounds. 'This poor bloke's been lured here, set alight, and found his escape blocked. A few animals came along, but the meal ain't tasty enough.

Crowbar believed it, yet … 'Might be a "she".'

'He, she, it; who cares? Dumb bastard's been rubbed out.'

'What about suicide?'

'Nar. No one in their right mind would do this to themselves. Some black bastards took revenge on this bloke, sure as hell. Bet you, this is Cliff Badger.' Crowie scowled 'Anyway, seal it off. Fast.'

Twenty minutes later, he completed the job. 'Let's piss off. We've had our holiday. Missy Mara's probably giving Mayor Sheila her best Australia Day wishes this morning; she well and truly blasted Council all week. Our turn to give them troublemakers a hard lesson, now that their media mates are drinking cocktails in Sydney.

'Keep your eyes peeled. After we've shoved it up them, we'll drink to the Bicentenary.'

When they returned to the station, they burst through the back door.

'Take a geek of the mob.'

'The whole town's gone mad. They're angry as hell.'

Hanna looked to Warren. 'What'll we do?'

'Do? What we have to.'

The officers wore worried looks. They wanted to stay cool so the riot gear lay on their desks, hung from doors, with their shields and hats flung into corners. They hadn't acted as no one dared bypass the Commander. Cassidy took the phones off-hook to ensure no pesky calls.

'Must be a hundred or more outside. Stewie's keeping an eye on things. Marto's brother is protecting the Unity with his shotgun. He thinks they're after the grog.'

'We've just come from the dump. A charred body murder; and those boongs did it. They've gone too far this time.'

Edwards burst through the door. 'Black Billy's stirring them up again.'

'It's the fucking rebellion. Told yous,' said Warren. 'We've three dead in these last few weeks. I called this one. Grab your ammo. Put on your gear. We're gonna teach them a bloody good lesson. Here's a little tip, boys: if you point the gun at their face, they'll shit themselves.'

Edwards let out a whoop. On the boss' order, other men scurried to fit up in their gear, releasing shooters from the gunroom and distributing batons.

One officer stood stone still.

'Well?'

'You must be … I mean …'

Chris Hanna sweated as Cassidy stepped out. 'You're a pansy, Hanna. Been with the fairies too long. This is the riot squad, mate. We're under orders. No use handing out flowers like Bourke cop shop. They're probably eating them for breakfast right now.'

'Grab your bloody weapon, and be prepared to shoot,' said Warren.

He pushed the protective goggles and helmet into Chris Hanna's hands. 'Out there, now. We'll show those pollies how much they need us.'

The men formed a tight circle. Chris had a pistol placed in his hand and pushed him to the front. Objects thumped, thudded and clanged against the station door, angry people on the other side shouting: 'Where's Kev? Where's Kev?' With ill-fitting gear, he found himself pressed, a helmet squashed on his head, yet thinking,

Where is Kev? The time I invited him. If only I'd tried harder.

'Ready?'

Nods all round.

'Go.'

The scarred door opened, and they raced out, pushing and truncheoning people on the landing. The protesters, armed with no more than their anger and raised voices fell back, roared disapproval. Although officers knew a few of them, Hanna the most, the many faces of anger put them beyond recognition. The mob was beaten lower, reformed and pelted the cops with asphalt, sticks, rocks, boxes and anything that came to their hands, including exercise books and sandwiches.

With the unexpected onslaught, they fell back, holding the landing steps to the massive entrance door, the same one Henry entered and left without his life, the one Billy pressed on his arrest, the door Kev and Mara hesitated to cross, the one Danny feared until charged with murder.

The squad wore more than enough to repel them but the crowd's ferocity was born on a passion and horror of Kev's punishment and his treatment by Cassidy. He had been hounded and hospitalised, his cottage burnt and wrecked, on the run since. His son faced life in gaol. It wasn't right, and the townspeople knew it.

Balli-al-mal.

The TRG confronted the mob with itchy fingers. Given the order, they would shoot men, women, and children.

And Mara shot first, thought Chris.

With that, he swept off his helmet, and held his weapon aloft, his hands above his head. Unsure of what he would do, what he could do or what he might say, he searched left and right.

Some of the crowd recognised him. The cop who bowed to their Queen on Evans Street. A sweating, grim-faced cop – the one with dishevelled hair, and spoke to Kev when Chrissie's bus arrived.

Goggles and gun thrown aside, he waved to those behind. 'Don't,' was all he said.

The mob paused in confusion and curiosity at so strange an event. But their shouting rekindled when he did not follow up. He freed their voices –'Where's Kev?' – permitted to say 'Where's Kev?' as they already were riled and desperate. The bloke was speechless. What did he expect: everyone to calm down and go home?

Hanna stepped forward, arms raised, accidentally creating space for a few squeezed officers, making a broad line across the steps, armed and ready. Cassidy's gloved hand reached out and yanked him backwards, but he threw back his elbow and swept the arm away.

Seeing the two cops at loggerheads, the mob's eyes lit up. Their venomous whisperings continued until the chanting grew louder. 'Where's Kev? Where's Kev?'

Bruised and misshapen, Billy moved to the front. 'Where's Kev, you bastards.'

Hanna raised his hands again, when Mara emerged from the pack.

'Well, Chris?' she said.

'Chris?' said Billy, mouth agape.

Hanna dared not lower his arms as Cassidy might have led an attack or the Commander could have given a lethal order. 'Everyone. These guys have guns. Guns.'

'Murderers. You'll pay for what you did,' called Ted.

'No more bloodshed. Please,' said Hanna.

'You bastards killed him,' yelled Marco.

'I've thrown my gun away. I like Kev. I wanted –'

'What are you talking about?' said Mara.

'He's mad. He doesn't even know him.'

Chris capitulated. 'Yeah. Me. I hurt him. Might as well have.'

With this confession, they pushed forward again, outraged, with only she and Billy between them. They surged towards hapless Hanna, the other two trying to hold them back. They mob would have torn him to shreds but for her presence.

'Not him. No. The others,' cried Mara.

Billy swung around, mouth open. 'You? With him?'

Hanna raised his arms again. 'Please. I'll find him. We'll do it together.' With the derisive hoots and pushing, a mince pie bounced off his shoulder and broke into pieces. Warren glanced at Cassidy; squashed together, they'd soon be unable to shoot their firearms.

Warren fired his handgun in the air. 'Officer Hanna, get out of there. Decide whose side you're on before we disperse the lot of them.'

'Answer us. Come on,' Chrissie shouted. 'Where's Kev?'

Billy too shouted, 'Where's Kev?' the crowd's chanting renewed, the faceless men before them, guns in their hands. He thought of Sharpeville, Myall Creek and My Lai. Massacres. He wished Kev was here to bring peace, his brain exploding. He envisaged many dead.

Chris' eyes locked on Mara, pleading for help, screaming. They were burning the sun with their distress, her face his hopeful moon. She stepped up to him, and turned about. Cassidy could have reached out and hauled her away, so he stepped between.

'Brother and sisters. Brother and sisters,' she said. The shoving eased. 'Hey, you mob.'

People focused on the heroic black face. 'These coppers behind, they're useless, right?' The crowd cheered. 'This bunch couldn't start a picnic, I reckon. So, we'll find Kev ourselves. We'll find him ourselves, right?' Chris and Billy formed a protective ring lest the Force used force. 'When Kev's worried, where's he go, eh? Where does he go?'

Awash with doubt, the mob waited. They had no answer. The cops stared at each other through their goggles, some pushing them back for a better view.

'What does Kev do when he's worried? He's got a lot of worries, ain't he?' There were a few nods and mumbling agreement. 'Kev lives by the river, goes to our river, down by them fish traps. He sits and thinks like the ancestors. Washes away trouble. Away from stinking cops.'

The hubbub grew but Billy waved for calm. 'We're gonna wash away our troubles,' she said. 'We got Chrissie home, thanks to Billy. Nobody can stop us. We're gonna find Kev down on the river. He's kangaroo dreaming. Come join us, eh? What do you say?'

When the crowd only murmured and one shouted an objection, Billy stepped up. 'We've got no business here. Not dealing with guns and stinking coppers. We got business at them fish traps. They're ours, all of us. Kev's spirit is there. Yeah. It's what Kev would want. Come on, everybody. Let's get going. Australia Day, ain't it? It's our day too.'

When he descended the steps, the crowd parted. On the footpath, other joined him and headed for the park. Mara took a glimpse at a dog-tired Hanna, biting her lip, touching his hand and walking away.

Slumped against the door, Warren's officers stared in puzzlement and relief, wondering why their black conspiracy retreated to the river. Hanna followed as far as the park's edge, watching them make their way over the levee.

Mara, Billy and Chris brought the mob back from a precipice, away from a tragic conclusion. So they *had* seen Kev. Just for a moment, they embraced the ways of fraternity, of Getting Along, of marrying their spirit with Kev's.

Confined to a cell, and with a trial ahead. Danny was left to find his way.

Chapter 66

After Chrissie and Mara's visit, there followed that ghostly chanting at the station's other end. "Where's Kev? Where's Kev?" Like a distant football crowd.

In the endless idleness of the hot days in a cell, he puzzled life's misdirections and what seemed like the hand of Fate, even after this Dad taught him otherwise. With the return of the ordinary sounds of passing cars, wafting music, and the evening's sing-song conversations around knock-off time, he noticed every light breeze that entered his cell. From morning to noon to later afternoon, a rising heat saw him abandon his shirt and trousers to climb the westward-facing window for the lengthy sunsets. In the evening dark, stray headlights and cantankerous voices punctuated time. Rumbling thunder kept him awake but never brought rain.

His scanty meals were delivered at eight am, two and six pm, duty cops not bothering to strike up a conversation. They thought walking the length of the station was enough without having a chat with a murderer. With Billy taken to Bathurst and released soon after, life became orderly and dull, though the haze from his drinking bouts lingered. Whatever happening at the other end of balli-al-mal was another planet. Life's clutter ebbed.

With no grog and no washing up, he sobered up and only his hands felt itchy and idle. His visitors dropped by his cell window rather than by official channels. In his blind conversations with friends and acquaintances, he asked and answered questions about his dad, Billy, Mara, Chrissie and the others.

January clocked into February like a canoe floating under creaking bridges and past ramshackle towns, the lazy willows waving, the drifting current and its banks beneath the invisible plains. That long passageway of time broke into labyrinth channels crowded with reeds, muddy shores and water birds; quieter waters.

With the new school year, Miss Susan passed him a box of chalks through the cell window. With its blues, reds, yellows and oranges, he sketched the mulga fringed with the river's S bends across his two walls. He drew in thin lines, but as he gained confidence, he added a road disappearing at the horizon, a swelling bridge, toy-like cars and someone hiding in the bushes.

He scrubbed that, next inventing a picture seen from an exact position on his bed. In perspective. If a cop walked in, the drawing made no sense as it disintegrated into an incoherent jumble of colours and disjointed lines, the kind you'd expect from a lunatic or a murderer.

With the sun, clouds and levee crowding his walls, he added familiar things like Skipper, the fish traps, Mara, Billy, the football and kids jumping from the bridge. With the final addition of a VW and park benches, the confines of his cell dissolved. With a bit of imagination, hopped into the vehicle, drove to the horizon, returned to the embankment and took a short tour of the neighbourhood.

When he exhausted the black chalk, he sketched in blue and red, using thick lines drawn over the smudged wall suggesting a fog or haze from which God-knows-what might emerge.

They were better than his earlier paintings, with smoother strokes. The bridge straddled walls, and the fish traps spread across either side of the cell door, so when a cop brought his meal, they spied the kids jumping in the sky.

On a whim, the sun by day became a moon by night and returned as the sun the next morning. He rubbed off other parts when he thought of another picture with a fire truck with Mara, Billy and his dad holding hoses of white water shooting the sky in all directions. He reckoned he washed away balli-al-mal.

It was getting friendly like, inside, much like freedom.

On another day, he depicted him again, summoning the courage to compose his face. Drawn from memory. Sketching him, he wondered whether he reached into his dilly-bag mind. Staring at him, regretting his own hurtful words and thoughts, his eyes dug into his way of seeing and thinking and knowing. But if he still worried for him, it was "because."

By drawing the river, the traps, the road and the town, he journeyed to where he recalled himself. He, the killer, pleased, laughed so his self-loathing lessened and dissipated. Ever since he painted on the VW, something seemed right for him. Sure, tons of trouble ahead, but his dad would support him and Billy and Mara and Chrissie.

One day, he dragged his bed under the high window and lifted his weight until he spied the horizon. Not to hang his sorry self like Henry but as a reminder of the world outside: to the warm air, the local street activities, the early evening silence, and a whiff of dusty earth.

I'm mad, he thought, hearing the radio from the front office. Hushed voices too, reminding him of his last conversation with Billy.

'I'll be in prison for years,' he had said.

'Nah. Don't worry,' said Billy from the neighbouring cell. 'You are no more a murderer than I am. Claim self-defence. With a lawyer, wait and see. We'll make a fist of it.'

'No way I'll go free. I killed him. I won't tell a lie.'

No doubt Billy scratched his head at that reply, and a long silence after. 'Be sure to listen to advice, mate. He is the only one who hears everything.'

He didn't understand what he meant by it but still wondered about his miraculous appearance at The Hole. 'Why did you come back to town? The cops were after you.'

'Yeah. I wanted the Commodore. Paid money for it. Can't live off fresh air.'

'The car?' said Danny. 'Only the car?'

'One or two other reasons. I believe Marco makes a mean sandwich.'

They laughed, but it trailed off. After an interlude, he asked 'What do you think happened to that Bicentennial broke?'

Chapter 67

Australia Day, 1988

Lightning Ridge is close to the Queensland border, and as distant from Sydney as Timbucktu. No suburban nightmare, it had no shopping malls or elaborate signage, long labelled 'the outback'. A place suited for mavericks, this opal settlement's floating population enjoyed a night-for-day existence in molehills and pits with names like 'Lunatic', 'Pig', 'Bald' and even 'Badger.' Its occupants produced sculptures, backstreet bottle houses, deep potholes, mock castles, an astronomer's monument, and vagabond gardeners.

It celebrated Christmas every week if you counted the residents' short, sparkling pub crawls and Seasons Greetings bunting behind the bars. Thirsty diggers begin at The-Club-in-the-Scrub Hotel, move to the Glengarry Hilton and finally, to Rogues Corner in the Shepherds Inn. Afterwards, drunk and disorientated, they occupy idle shacks and caravans where they bedded down for the remainder of the night. The owners didn't mind; they reckoned discovering a dead body down an opal shaft much worse, and this saved them the expense and chagrin of a funeral.

'It's Australia Day, ning-dongs,' said Barry the barman, his place awash with liquor and customers.

They cancelled the underground mine tours because you can't expect anyone to be sober on January Twenty-six, especially in the Bicentennial year. Horses-for-courses, or to be exact, everyone indulging the Hairy Goats and Wheelie-bin races, the Thing Dig, and a flutter on the nags at the Ding-Dong Racecourse, with plenty of time to pull-a-leg and shout ya-hoo.

Things hotted up at night with fireworks, whoring and live entertainment at the licensed venues, everything from overdressed blokes masquerading as sheilas to lithe girlies imported from the Gold Coast wearing next-to-nothing, collecting money in their knickers. With the In-Tents events, the insiders continued drinking at the thermal baths, forbidden of course, except when dawn has a religious air.

'It's Australia Day, ning-nongs,' the Master of Ceremonies shouted through his crackling megaphone.

In the Shepherd Inn's Fruity Bar, pink ribbons decorated the stainless-steel taps, the deco walls with lime-green and orange streamers. Things bubbled along. In this mighty crowd, lads wore Bicentennial T-shirts declaring "200," and, in smaller letters below, "beers a day." Without straining the ear, some lusty swearing made the amber liquid blush.

There's Cliff Badger! Such a man in white-rimmed sunglasses, a polka-dot dress, and a top of two motorbike tyre slices joined together and tied around his chest. His nineteen-fifties birds-nest wig was secured with wire, crowned with a pyramid of eggs. Stepping on a small step-ladder, he almost crashed, steadied himself to stand atop the corner stage, his headgear precarious.

A roar from the crowd meant nearby drinkers clutched their glasses lest spoilt by men falling from his high heels. Badger's thin hips swayed to the sounds of *Hey Big Spender,* molesting his rubber because they slipped under his arm during his wilder gesticulations.

Turning to the audience, he pulled off his oversized bra and swung it about like a dead cat before being thrown across the bar. A tremendous uproar, banter, bluster and mighty mockery followed the performer keen-eying a random drinker. Picking up a German beer mug, the contents cast at the Calypso crowd, surprise becoming derision when a cluster of condoms flew through the air.

'Stick it, Clancy.' Plenty of laughter and horror.

Badger threw them a kiss, turned around and bent over causing his locally-laid eggs to fall from his head and splat on the floor.

A roar of hilarity.

'Gawd. Those legs.'

Barry, the MC dressed in a pink skirt and cowboy hat, took a deep breath.

'Miiiisssss Fanny May.'

'Potch, or opal? Come on nugget, let's hear it.' The mob shouted approval or abuse, roared mock outrage and beat their tables as Cliff

Badger returned to his companion.

'Superb show. Got a job for you in my pub.'

'You can shove that. Escaped your town, and that mad Sheila.'

'Our new mayor?'

'Gawd. If she deserves that, I should be Prime Minister.'

'Prefer opaling myself. Aint it grand, people scratch away in a deep, dark hole, looking for precious. You and a mate, underground, lamplight shining, clawing away.'

'And finding potch.'

'Or opal. Don't a beer taste perfect after unearthing lustre? Tastes like Justice.'

'Mato: you're a poet.'

They shared a laugh, took another sip, surveying the bluff, bluster and cursing around them, lads and lassies rubbing bodies and shaking hands, motorbikes arriving and departing, good-natured argument, and pint pots passed over heads, out windows.

'It's Australia Day, boofheads. We're making winners again.'

The Master of Ceremonies received a paper slip, but already holding the microphone and a beer, he struggled to read the judge's decision.

'What's the difference between having a beer and having a cold glass?'

He downed the contents and put his glass on the bar.

'You drink from one, and add more beer to the other.'

Few laughed.

'Anyway, the judges have conversed, convulsed and converged, taken all bribes, and decided tonight's champion. Written on this slip.' He waved a used docket close to a drinker's eyes, withdrawn before anyone grabbed it. 'By the way, the judge's decision is final. Anyone objecting, pays for the next round. Someone appealing, come my way and we'll exchange fluids.'

They hooted, beat their table or booed like true contrarians.

'The winner is…. the beautiful…. the inestimable… Fanny May.'

'Winner. Winner,' Cliff pumped the air, shooting forward to collect his prize: a scantily-clad, braless barmaid he carried past the mob. He placed her on the pool table's field of green and patted her bum.

When customers showed an unseemly interest in her, she planted her feet on the floor and winced (or was that meant to be a smile? :)

She checked her panties for donations and returned to the drinks cabinet.

Cliff reclaimed attention by throwing his hat across the room. With the crowd's acclaim. he waved, flapped his chicken wings, shook a leg and collected a carton of beer.

On return, Marto raised an eyebrow. 'You're making a habit of prancing around.'

Badger did not see what he meant and didn't care.

As the crowd settled down, drowning themselves in drinks, a few residents went outside to a newly-arrived donkey and cart.

He became pensive. 'We did a lot of digging and scratching around for bugger all.'

'Got us outa town though. The place is a nightmare. Dunno why I bother.'

'Yeh. But a man's got to return to work sometime. I'm itchy for Sydney, Brisbane or the Gold Coast. When all this Bicentennial whoo-ha's over, they're going to need people to win an Olympics bid or the World Cup. They're going to need can-do people. Someone to knock a few heads together, shove things along, a bloke who can pull down barriers, push the project across the line. Always room for Mr Majesty.'

'Working for pollies again? Our town isn't ready for those ideas.'

'Miles of room in the smoke-cities, government or business. I'm unlimited, mate. Plenty of developers will be knocking on my door. Kicking arse is universal.

'Remember Abe Lincoln's words about being knocked down and picking yourself up, and saying …err…I'll be back.'

Chapter 68

Postscript, January 2001

A new century, with Danny imprisoned for years on the words of Paddy Bourke, Ginge Ryan and Con Demsentious. He pulled a knife, they said. Threatened them twice before going crazy. Always hated the boss' son. Out for revenge, they said. As mad as hell.

'After killing Pete,' a Hard Boy affirmed, 'he said "A white for a black." Imagine, he was revenging a no-hoper Henry.'

Sure, the jury heard, Danny lost his mother, his father killed by a person or persons unknown, and a school friend died in police custody. No excuses. His violent, frenzied attack marked him as a criminal of the worst kind. He deserved the most severe punishment.

Time in the slammer sorting out his thoughts and feelings, figuring out how all this happened. At first, he hated his enemies, wanted revenge on the Hard Boys, and maybe a bit of sympathy too. There was things he hadn't seen at the time, and maybe it was asking too much of him to know so much. There so many distractions, interests and false friends that took him away from his dad, and when his dad was there, he ignored advice.

Billy's fame took him to new places, but by the year's end, public opinion hardened against him and "the rioters". All of them were agitators, undesirables and extremists, their word and the evidence on film, discounted more than Kmart special.

Even so, he wanted to know the mysterious hands that played havoc with his life, pushed and pulled him to a terrible destiny, and manipulated townspeople like pawns.

It took years, but the more he thought, the more he learnt, and the more his head became concerned with his people, Architecture and drawing, VWs, Souths, and the people he left behind like Mara, Christine and Billy.

Released from gaol, Billy met him at the Oberon Prison Gate. The landscape was his again. Pine forests and frozen air. Gritty roads and speeding cars. Hugs all around, given the strange "hi-five," before he spotted his old VW in the desolate car park.

'Whoa!'

Billy kept the Beetle all those years to remind Danny of his days on the levee. Perhaps he liked the beast too, though losing the Commodore so soon after he bought it made him wince. They were the two wild ones from the scrub, Billy apt to believe himself a lovable rogue, though he remarried a decade ago. with two more kids and a mortgage, he managed a dance troupe.

As Danny collected and sorted through his many memories of his dad, he recalled the paint job, hauling stolen vehicles around the state and his afternoons watching Souths. He recalled journeys through Bathurst and beyond, thinking of Uncle Billy's help, advice and notes passed on at his monthly gaol visits.

And the dough he provided for the VW's new tyres. His support during his trial and conviction, his years in the clink when he helped him choose a new way. Later, he secured Oberon's minimum security prison, where he worked outdoors.

Billy put the hard word on him, years earlier. 'Chum: what's it gonna be? You going to find religion or an education?'

Danny stayed quiet. But on the next visited, he settled on an idea. 'Houses. Drawing, planning and building them.'

Billy scratched his head. 'Sounds like Drafting or Architecture. I thought you'd go for panel beating.'

'Start from scratch, right? Making homes for people, homes for Murris. Places where they can be themselves, work, and ...'

From his first days of imprisonment, he realized you only made sense of things when you were in your right mind, in the right place, like his dad at home in the kitchen, recalling Gundabarri for those Canberra people, sitting with his tape deck.

After those first nights in the town cells with his coloured chalks, he drew signs, towns, rivers, roads, houses, trees and moons; things and places he magically recreated, all jumbled together. When he rubbed one drawing off and started again, he worked and reworked it until he found a kind of clarity. Architecture. Making every part of the building so people walk in and make the place their own. Not like a prison, confined and ordered about, given a number, told what to do, where and when. He possessed an imagination, a powerful glue that kept him busy and sane.

By the time he exited, he had nurtured a construction, a new umbrella for the soul, so when he and Billy sat on the nearest seat, they embraced.

'So proud of you, Danny. You got your life back, bud, with a future.'

'And I'd do well to remember it?'

He squeezed his shoulder. 'After reading your story. Made me laugh when you said "proper forgetting," I cried for your dad. Strange. Easier to believe in ourselves now. After all we went through. When he said things, it stirred my guts. Reckon we won't be happy until they accept The Invasion. Now, Mabo; well mate, there's hope.'

'Maybe,' he said, rubbing his neck. 'You paid the price, bud. We won't forget that.'

Danny bit his lip before finding his voice. 'That story took me where I've never been, led me by the nose. Wasn't like I thought it would be.'

'Never is. Who thought Mara would shack up with Chris Hanna?' He grinned. 'We all grew stronger. Had to. None of us are Jimmy Blacksmiths.'

He said nothing. With all those years in prison; he hesitated to speak or he might never stop, and then, what else would he say? He said so much already, but it was safely on paper where his pain remained at a safe distance.'

'Anyway,' said Billy, 'let's get you home in the old VW. With a new engine, it's a Time Machine. Vrrrm. Verrrm. Lots of friends are waiting, Mara and Chrissie, for starters.

'Can't wait,' said Danny. 'Do they remember me?'

The Author invites you to discuss *Start with C* with other readers at https://www.facebook.com/groups/788690365155249/

Post questions to the Author and leave a heartfelt review at KDP Amazon.

Australia's 1980s Common Usage Words

1788 = The first Europeans arrived at Sydney Cove, mainly soldiers, sailors and convicts.

A

Aboes = derogatory naming for Australia's Indigenous peoples.

Aborigines = common name for Australia's indigenous peoples. Most Australian aborigines refer to themselves as either Murris or Murris.

Akubra = major brand of country-style, or bushman's hat.

Arsey = or, as bold-as-brass, but also 'lucky.'

Arvo = afternoon.

B

Bicentenary = 1988 celebration of 200 years of European settlement, mostly by soldiers and convicts.

Balli al mal = designated as 'place of the dead' in Gundawarri, repurposed in contemporary times as the police station.

Banged up = in jail or imprisoned.

Bar-B-Qed = suffering from the heat.

Black Velvet = an obscene reference to a black woman's sex organ.

Boong = highly derogatory reference to an Indigenous person.

Boffhead = a foolish, but usually harmless person.

Billyo, or, To Billyo = a distant place.

Bollocking (UK) = angry words to someone who has done something wrong.

Buckley's Chance, or Buckley's = no chance at all.

C

Casuarina = a common Australian, fir-like tree.

Catch-22 (US) = from Heller's book of the same name. Contradictory regulations that make action or sense possible.

chalkies = a disparaging term for a teacher.

Clancy = reference to the poetic figure, Clancy of the Overflow (Banjo Patterson). Used here ("Stick it, Clancy") as the common man.

Coolabah = common, dry-inland eucalyptus tree.

Cobber = a friend.

Cotton-on - finally realise something.

Chops = the jaw.

Crackers = someone insane.

Cuppa = cup of tea

Currawong = a common native Australian bird, usually B&W, with a distinctive call

cut-the-blanket. Lovemaking, or shared desperation.

chookhouse = where the roosters and chickens are penned.

CIB = Criminal Investigation Bureau.

D

Daigo = slang for a migrant of Italian heritage, often generalised to other migrants.

dead-set = Really? (as a reply); certainly (if a statement).

dilly bag = a traditional indigenous carry bag.

dipsy = slightly mad

dingo = a wild dog, utilized and largely tamed by Indigenous people

dinkum, see fair-dinkum.

Dodson, Mick = a prominent 1980s Indigenous leader, later Labor senator.

dob or dobbed = inform on another of some ill-doing, often to the police or authorities.

Dosh = money. A variation on 'douh'.

drongo = a fool, an idiot. One worse than a boffhead.

Duco = a type of paint applied to a car's body work.

duds = working or non-descript trousers.

dunno = don't know

F

Fair-dinkum = 'really!' or 'Truthfully …'

Few-bob = usually any amount under a dollar, but sometimes reference to much more, an understatement, or sometimes gained by non-legal means.

Fish traps = Indigenous array of rock across a shallow river, used to delay and confuse fish so they are easily speared

Frigging = a swear word when you're not swearing.

G

Gimme = give me

G'day = Good day

Gander = take a leisurely look at something or someone.

Geek = only a short look at something or someone.

Garbo = garbage or trash collector, a local council employee.

Geek = like, take a geek, or a first look at.

Get square = get even, or take revenge.

Get cracking = to swing into action, or get the job done. Probably derived from the saying 'to crack the whip.'

Gubba = white man, used by indigenous people, probably derived from 'government men'.

Gone-bush = escape (usually from the authorities) to a place where no-one will find you, sometimes literally into the bush or wilderness.

Gaol = jail.

Gibber-gabber = lively, inconsequential conversation. Gonna = going to

Gundawarri = fictitious indigenous language.

H

Happy-little-Vegemite = childish happiness, innocent joy (frequent ironic usage)

Hit-for-six = to be hit hard. Knocked out of action, or out-of-bounds. A cricket term.

Hitched = married.

Holden FJ = dominant and popular car model of the nineteen-sixties.

Hooning = youthful, delinquent behaviour.

(as) Hot as Buggery = an exclamation of astonishment at the day's heat.

Hubbie = husband.

K

Knocked-for-six = knocked over, or like the game of cricket, when a batsman hits the ball out of the field.

Knocked up = To be pregnant.

Kori = an aboriginal person, a self-reference for Indigenous people on southern NSW and Victorian current use.

L

Layabout = a lazy person, usually unemployed.

Lebo = someone of Lebanese heritage.

Lip = smart-arsed remarks or disobedient statements. Giving lip.

Local rag = a local newspaper of dubious quality.

Little beauty = That's good, or, a good idea.

Loo = a toilet.

M

Mabo = Ground-breaking 1992 High Court decision opening up Indigenous land ownership, supported by a Federal Labor government.

Mag, or 'a mag' = a relaxed conversation between friends.

Mallee = A semi-desert eucalypt, usually low growing, with multiple thin trunks

Mansell = prominent Tasmanian indigenous leader of the era.

Mob = not a wild crowd, but meaning, 'that bunch of people,' coming from a 'mob of sheep'.

Mossies = mosquitoes.

Mug army = a bunch of fools.

Murri = an aboriginal person, a self-reference for Indigenous people in Queensland and northwestern NSW.

Ning-nongs = a name call, people who you think are plain silly.

Nop, or Nar = No.

O

Opaling = the activity of a single person, or small group, often amateurs, mining for opal.

P

Pansies = a derogatory term for effete men or homosexuals.

Patchtown = fictitious name of aboriginal public housing built outside of town, in reality, sometimes near tips or 'rubbish country.'

Peck = a quick, light kiss.

Paddy wagon = police vehicle for carrying arrested people and prisoners

Pinchgut = One of seven islands in Sydney Harbour.

Pink Fits = a generic term meaning anything from loss of temper to a schizophrenic attack.

Play School = a long running Australian TV show for 2-4 yr olds.

Plied = inebriated after a heavy intake of alcohol..

Pommy = an English migrant, derived from (argued) 'Prisoner Of her Majesty'.

Potch = the worthless material surrounding opal.

R

Rabbitos = South Sydney Rugby League team.

Redfern, a poor, inner-city Sydney suburb with significant numbers of indigenees.

Revhead = excessive car enthusiasts.

Rego = car registration, allowing the vehicle on road.

'Roo = kangaroos.

Rust-bucket = a third-rate car.

S

Scallywags = playful, naughty but harmless kids, or (sometimes) adults.

Schoolies = A disparaging term for teachers.

Shindig = a party, an occasion (US origins).

Simmo = a famous South Sydney (or 'rabbittos') football player.

Shafted = betrayed and rejected.

Shacked up = cohabited with.

Shandy = half beer, half lemonade. A 'woman's' drink.

Sheila = a colloquial term for all women, mildly disparaging, unless called 'a nice sheila'

Silly Buggers = mucking around but called to attention.

Slacko = a negligent or lazy worker.

Slack wire fencing = a fence wire with no tension, and therefore useless or abandoned.

Smart-alec = like the US 'wise-guy'.

Spiv = a petty criminal who deals in illicit, typically black market, goods. (UK)

Stir = provoke or annoy another person, usually with words. Can be hostile or friendly.

Struth = a surprised expression, derived from 'It's the truth.'

T

Touch-footie = A simplified game of Rugby league.

The sticks = out bush, a long way from civilization.

Two-bob snake = "two-bob" is two-shillings. "Two-bob snake" is a mishmash of the terms "two-bob watch" and "mad as a black snake".

Troppo = an unconstrained, unhinged person. A bit mad.

U

Ute = a utility truck, like a sedan but with the back altered to make a large container for tools, material and machinery.

V

Vinnies = St Vincent de Pauls, a charity outlet.

Vegie = vegetable.

W

Wagging (school) = non-attendance, without teachers or parents knowledge

Woomera = An indigenous tool or weapon. Also a place where the British tested their atomic bombs.

Y

Yabbering = meaningless or empty or uncontrolled talking, derived from feebleness, mental problems, perhaps alcoholism and extreme nervousness.

Historical Note for Non-Australian Readers

New South Wales (NSW) is Australia's first colonial state. Its capital is the famous coastal city of Sydney, and behind it, the Blue Mountains. The rural land to the west steadily grows more arid and hostile, known as the 'outback.' Its people are amongst the state's poorest.

Our Kev is a grandson of the infamous Jimmy Blacksmith (or Jimmie Gov'nor), an aborigine, or indigenous person, driven to the point-of-no-return in a remote country settlement. Jimmy murdered seven settlers in 1900, just prior to Australia achieving nationhood from Britain. At a time, many were fighting South Africa's Boer War, so national panic, outrage and revenge followed. Hunted down and killed, Jimmy was Australia's last person legally shot-on-sight. The great Australian writer, Tom Kennealy, wrote about it in *The Chant of Jimmy Blacksmith*.

The historical legacy is high Indigenous incarceration rates, and tragic deaths-in-custody that spurred the Royal Commission in 1987. Although action has been taken, the problem has returned with the popular lock-them-up-and-throw-away-the-keys mentality.

We can do better.

The Story Behind *Starts with C*

My phone rang one afternoon in Bulli. "Hello. Garry Mc here."
"The writer?"
"Yes."
"I want you to visit my friend in gaol."
A bit abrupt, but each to their own. "Me?" I said, wondering where the conversation was going.
My panic settled down when he introduced himself as an Indigenous representative for North-Western New South Wales.
"I regularly visit the prisons but the Oberon one is for a prisoner attempting to write a murder mystery. I am at a dead end. I have no idea how to help."
"And I do?"
"Of course."
I admitted my reluctance but was tinged with guilt as here in Wollongong we have writers who visit Indigenous prisoners for storytelling tuition, and this is supposedly my speciality. Yet I have never joined apart from entering a Prisoner Assist Raffle and winning. A volume of their stories is on my bookshelf to remind me.
This mob saved lives with their visits, or at least, gave them greater self-worth.
"OK," I said before I could stop myself.
Silence at the other end.
"You've never read a novel?" I said.
"In school maybe. But I've got no time for that. I read or write reports and leave the fancy stuff to others."
Another silence.
"You're the fourth person I've rung," he said with obvious relief, though I hoped someone else would be a better candidate, and it was not flattering to think I was fourth in line for this unpaid task.
"I hope the prison is close by."
"Yes. It's in Oberon."
The Author was probably not aware Oberon was king of the Fairies in medieval and Renaissance literature as well as the best-known character in William Shakespeare's play, *A Midsummer Night's Dream*.

Oberon seemed very distant, and the town of the same name was two hundred kilometres from home, over the Blue Mountains.

"That is a long way."

"Maybe, but I cover 40000km every year. I can drive you there the first time, and chuck in petrol costs for the next."

"I see."

"You must have friends in the mountains," he said.

"Sure," I said. I must and did, a dear old friend, Mick Childs and a few former employees who wouldn't jump for joy at a reunion.

"What's the author's name?"

"Vick Watson." * a pseudonym.

'And what's the crime?"

"Murder."

"So, an author with inside experience."

"Not really. It's a ding-dong case of injustice."

That is how I came to drive to Oberon with my new friend.

"Wants to be an author? Why?"

"It's rehabilitation. First, there was training as a draftsman and architect, and since then the idea of a novel invaded the brain. It wasn't my idea."

"OK, then. Just to be clear. I can give guidance only. Talk first, and thereafter, edit the work from home via the post. But even then, the prison authorities must accept my presence or it won't work."

"You'll find Vick a very willing learner, Gazza. There's plenty of petrol in his tank."

"And you'll make it clear that it is not my job to write it."

Yeh. Sure."

"One visit. And all the editing required, OK?"

I sounded like I was looking for a way out of the task. Another middle-class wanker whose thoughts as solid as a wet rag. But the visit turned out to be my first but not my last visit. I edited Vick's work from home for the next eighteen months and made another six prison visits.

Vick had perfect conditions for writing, a private location, a regular regime, and every reason to work on the manuscript. A willing disposition, and the Author's motivation second to none.

We had something in common. Brewarinna. An outback town

where Vick and I had overlapping experiences and acquaintances. I hasten to add hat my experience was over a week, theirs a lifetime, so I made myself a listener rather than a storyteller. This is his show.

We both knew Essie Coffey OAM (1941-1998) and Tombo Winters (1938-2004), wonderful people who led and enlivened the district. I had heard of Jimmy Barker (1900-1972), but he knew him when Vick was a child. I took the time to dig out transcripts of his interviews kept at the AIATSIS in Canberra and passed them.

The recordings made harrowing reading and probably served the Author's purposes as we find Kev too recording the past. It is these experiences that Vick channels into the novel, and why it reminds me of the searing honesty found in Elizabeth Smart's *I Sat Down and Wept at Grand Central Station.*

Starts with C is set in a nameless town, though it screams Brewarinna because both have rare fish traps and are the site of Death in custody events that led to PM Hawke's creation of the Royal Commission.

That said the unnamed town layout is quite different. The streets have different names, this town has different layout and very little about it says Bre. Perhaps Vick wanted it that way, to be not too close a reminder of the harrowing events that put him in gaol.

Still, we traded our stories of Brewarinna, his, Stephen's and mine, and this put us at ease with each other. Inevitably, the town's characters, living and dead, filtered into the Author's narrative, in a way that is realistic and affectionate. No one can be identified as this character or that, but there are ghosts here and there with longer and deeper stories.

Starts with C is Vick's story. He wanted to write a murder mystery and did it with a twist or two. Who'd have thought of a conventional opening so misleading? Everyone was sure Badger had been murdered months earlier when in fact no one had been. I was caught up in the plot as I edited it chapter by chapter. We didn't know who had been murdered, or by whom, and assumed the author was a conventional third-person until he became a first-person or someone similar.

I didn't guess it, did you?

The Brewarinna Fish Traps

For thousands of years, the Brewarinna fish traps sustained the Ngemba people, who shared the traps with other tribes including the Muruwari, Weilwan, Barabinja, Ualarai and Kamilaro, Kooma, Kula and Ngemba.

According to archaeologists and scientists, the fish traps or Baiame's Ngunnhu are said to be one of the oldest man-made structures in the world.

The engineering allowed the many fish to be herded and caught, so fish could also swim past the traps to spawn and continue the life cycle upstream.

Overlooking the ancient Baiame's Ngunnhu, stands the Brewarinna Aboriginal Cultural Museum, in the outback town of Brewarinna in the northwest of New South Wales.

Visitors to Brewarinna (or 'Bre', if you're a local,) can learn more about this special area at the Brewarinna Aboriginal Cultural Museum where expert guide, Bradley Hardy, runs tours of the fish traps.

And yes, the museum was my suggestion for a NSW Bicentennial Project when I worked on the Great North Walk Bicentennial Project at the NSW Lands Dept. What comes around, goes around.

An Extra For You

Here is an early short story, *Patting the Dog*, winner of the Peter Cowan Short Story Prize.

Patting the Dog

The State Premier liked me. He offered me a weekly train ticket. Love the trains, he said. Get out of Sydney. It'll do you good. Wran's my man.*

I went first class, student discount, half-price, handed over the money, calculating it was whatever the man behind the wire screen said.

Plan A. First train, Sydney Central, platform something, a light bag over my shoulder. Went to Goulburn, switching to another train. Hopped in happy. John Lennon said that death is like hopping off one train, and on to another. He was wrong.

My train-to-somewhere had 'First Class' written in pressed copper letters from the Nineteenth Century, my semi-compartment demarked, raised to comfort by a hot-coals foot-warmer. Luxury.

Hours later, the bush thinned, greyed and warned you to go no further, as if I had a choice. End of the line. 'Lake Cargelligo' said the sign. Trouble is, there was no Lake Cargelligo. Nothing but bush. They'd built the station here, built the town somewhere else.

When I found Cargelligo, the day had almost expired. Went to the pub for a beer, pie and bed. Told the owners I wanted to stay a night or two. You have a room?

I patted the dog. That must have been why.

They took me to a kitchen as large as a town hall with cooking pots the size of tankers. Shearers, she said. We cooked for shearers once. Those days were gone, the shearers too. The owners wanted to get away for the weekend. Would I look after their two kids? Free board.

I'm a long way from Sydney, I thought. Gone and gone.

I took the job, hoping there'd be no ghost shearers after midnight. Kept the kids amused, playful and bluffed, as if nothing were missing.

Two days later, I left Cargelligo and its shallow, grey lake, the bones of trees poking out of the water. By hitchhiking fifty kilometres across the plain,

I'd meet the Broken Hill line. Catch the train to Bathurst, then Sydney. Halfway, we stopped at a mission station town, its fibro houses running down both sides of its one and only street, fading into mulga and sand. There were two or three hundred people there, making it almost as big as Cargelligo.

What's this place called?

He told me.

But it's not on my map.

Guess not, he said, without apology.

So it doesn't exist. Or maybe those ghost shearers live here, all these black men and women, ragged and listless, floating between two ages, between two lines. You don't build railways to uncharted towns.

What if I'd patted their dog?

I reached the other rail line. Barely a settlement there. All around was flat, hot plain and more mulga. Looking along the steel tracks, I saw the Broken Hill train fifteen minutes before it arrived.

Like everything else, and everyone else, it headed for Sydney.

===

*'Wran's my Man' was the Premier's political campaign slogan.

The Author's Other Novels

Belonging

A doctor arrives in the legendary outback Gundagai, passionate about the new medicine and Lister's pioneering surgery. Louis Gabriel is fired with hope and ambition. But he is new, black and overqualified. Will he be top, or bottom, of the social 'pile'? Will he ever belong?

Based on the life of the eminent photographer and medico, we follow the real events and real dilemmas of living amongst Gundagai's colourful characters during Australia's adoption of a 'white Australia'. The story climaxes in 1901 with the Federation, the Jimmy Blacksmith massacres, the plagues and the murderous Boer War.

Vivid Press. Available from 16 Alanson Av, Bulli, Sydney Australia 2516, at A$25.50, US$19.50, free postage. Add $5 for signed copies or dedications.

Reader's Comments

…already up to page 80 - can't put it down.'

Lynne Sandberg, Sydney

…the text is very clear and readable. Dr Gabriel's story is actually a very good idea… and I think you execute it quite well. The medical scenes in particular are very vivid…

Zack Alexopoulos, Tutor, Sydney Uni

I was quite enthralled with the story …I got so I could hardly stop reading …the types of illnesses, diseases, misadventures, are relived vividly… The photos too …were illuminating… I succumbed to the National Library website and went through the whole 900 images!

Judy Newton, Sydney

…a very sure accomplished style with great feel for detail and idiom.' There is so much in it which is fresh and new.

Milorad Pavlovic, Editor, Writer

…the novel lovingly but unromantically recreates a fascinating slice of Australia's past …It is a great tale, and I would say the material for a great miniseries of say, the ABC.

Independent review, WordPress

I have just finished your book and am writing to say how much I enjoyed it. It was such an interesting story, and your creative use of the facts …were terrific. Also, the way outside events impinged on the Gundagai residents was so interesting. You evoked the resonances of the era beautifully. I enjoyed it, and will be recommending it to my friends.

Trish Walters, Sydney

Knowing Simone: A Political Romance

Victor Hugo is exiled, and France is led by an aging, repressive French Empire under Napoleon III. Marseilles anarchist **Patrice** is on the run, a 24-year-old with a false identity, meets **Simone**, 35, an ambitious Pyrenees mine owner in Gothic Lectoure Soon Patrice is caught in her erotic web, struggling with new identities that liberate and complicate their lives. He is obsessed with knowing Simone's mysterious connections to his father, Paris and Napoleon III's government. She is obsessed with developing her enterprise. But something else is going on. When threatening forces arise, they form an unlikely alliance against the National govt. Minister **Jessai**, Lectoure's Sub-prefect and their formidable allies. With dynamite in his hands, and the Minister s opening their new railway, Patrice is tempted with violent solutions. With duels, confrontations, riots, murder, kidnapping and a band of Republicans intent on reclaiming France.

Knowing Simone was five Star rated by the US Online Book Club.

'A subtly erotic, intense and heart-wrenching tale...' Muse22, Fanstory.

'Showing detail in time, place and purpose. Describing a community, a plan, a path and an intimacy. Surely this place must be graced by a song.' El Poetry1

1503, The Viviers Chronicles

The Series
From a poverty-stricken French village to Niccoli Machiavelli's inglorious Italy, Louis and Semla negotiate a treacherous age.
Vol. 1: **Blacksmith and Canon** Louis de St Martin and his bete noire make a pilgrimage where only one will survive. A Renaissance allegory.
Vol. 2: **Inheritance/ A Blacksmith's Lif**e Louis' love letter to Semla, a life transformed by rogue monks and soldiers, a saint's journal, and the mysterious innkeeper, Poldari.
Vol. 3: **The Reckoning** Louis and Semla traverse wild France, meeting the Cardinal who bids for papal power.
Vol. 4: **Machiavelli's Pope** Louis and Semla join Machiavelli in the struggle for the Papal Tiara.
Vol. 5: **Tales from The Viviers Chronicles** An anthology of tales told in the four volumes.
To be Published by Pamela Press, 2025 to 2027.

Blacksmith and Canon

It's 1503, contemporary to Niccolo Machiavelli, Michaelangelo, and Martin Luther. Niccolo is writing his ground-breaking *The Prince*, and Martin Luther's Protestant Reformation lay just ahead.

A blacksmith-storyteller, Louis d'St Martin, brought before a severe Canon Magistrate, is accused of three murders. But with one insight, and a wealth of experience, he strikes a bargain where only one will survive.

Memorable Quotes

Yet the milky light of our day put lie to our desires. In the shadow of walls the crystal frost remained, as the careless mist drifted over village rooves. Young Madeleine pulled a hood across her face. The archers kept their hands inside their downy pockets lest their long-stringed bows called for action. Black-legged sheep stamped their ground and moved in circles around their pen, and the ravens caw-cawed on the creaking gallows.

His eyes feasted on us when we were lean and hungry.

Yet here I am in Villefort less than dead. With this plume in hand, I am no longer a Viviers' captive flogged and beaten, nor the ragged prisoner in chagrin. With new-found regard I am made for deeds. Even as Spring finds me less hungry, gaunt, and sheltered under dignity, it does not make me happy or keep a fancy mind. I thought escape just yesterday, yet now this caravan glues me to a path.

I joined the others around the fire; four men aligned before me had heard more than I had liked, their faces ruddy and grim to the dancing flames.
'Do not do that again,' said Zendar, 'or her brothers shall be obliged to cut you.'
'Are you beaten?' said her brother Alberti.
'Perhaps,' I said. 'Or else I have met my match.'

Villefort folk stared at us from their windows joyless, not daring to move amongst us. As many knew full well, from the gallows hung the murdered not the murderer.

'I see your judgement bring fields of lavender to tears.'

... to be awake is to fear my sleep.

Now I see that You are no shepherd of the flock, as among us nowhere are you seen. You must be an orchardist asleep and snoring loud beneath the orange blossoms. Or are you idle by greening apples and sour quince? Perhaps you are fanciful and move among the blacksmith's forest owls. Why do we build cathedrals and go upon our knees to pray to thee when the devil asks for less?

I smile at the devil. Scowl at that blacksmith.

'Am I better company than dead men cut down by Judgement's blade? To dream and jostle sleep, and find myself in other's dreams remiss?...'

'You invoke the dark and hairy corners of ourselves...'

'If God makes poor women, men make poor gods.'

'...beauty sustains and nourishes the heart, reconciling us to the good and given.'

Sea Voices

En route to the Battle of Milne Bay, Private Hiroshi and his Japanese Landing Force are stranded on a Melanesian Island. They must survive hunger, violence, murder and corruption as Australian forces close in.

Hiroshi befriends an islander and learns their skills and ways of the world. It strengthens him against the competing demands of Commander Tsukioka and the manipulative Lieutenant Matsumi.

The five-hundred-year-old author invokes the power of unity while the Voice of the Sea sings for their resignation to Fate.

Despite his enemies without and within, Hiroshi summons confidence and intuition to find another way of their predicament that leaves everyone breathless.

Facebook Readers Sites

Start With C *www.facebook.com/profile.php?id=100063917890425*
Long-listed, Best Unpublished Manuscript Award, Whitsunday Lit Festival, 2024.
Knowing Simone www.facebook.com/profile.php?id=100028486285346
Belonging www.facebook.com/Belonging4/
The Year of 1503

Volume I: Blacksmith and Canon www.facebook.com/profile.php?id=100063946243470
Volume II: Inheritance/A Blacksmith's Life
Volume III: The Reckoning
Volume IV: Machiavelli's Pope
Sea Voice*s www.facebook.com/groups/577296254661388*

Non Fiction Works
Border and Soul -To Be Released, 2026.
Great North Walk
NSW Heritage Walks
Winging It, The Camino Journey. To be Published, 2025/
With Gusto (contributor, food theme, two stories). Not Available.
In Fifty Words, Coming Up for Air (editor, contributor). Available at KDP Amazon. Buy by direct bank deposit at Westpac, Australia Acct 313297, BSB 032020. Include your name, address, book title and email address.

Pilgrimage Spain

Colourful, narrative and prize-winning poetic stories from Spain.

Pilgrimage France

Imaginative and bold poetic stories from France. Colour pics incldd.

Buy at A$18, free postage. Add $5 for signed copies or with dedication Direct bank deposit at Westpac, Australia Acct # 313297, BSB 032020. Include your name, address, book title and email address. Email a confirmation at startswithc@aol.com

Inner Flash

The Author's Australian short stories, poetry and photographs. Colour pics incldd. Buy at $22, postage incldd by direct bank deposit at Westpac, Australia Acct 313297, BSB 032020. Include your name, address, book title and email address.

Pilgrimage Series (eBooks) Available at smashwords.com or buy direct from Pamela Press for A$3.99 each. Include colour pics, pilgrimage facts and advice.. Direct bank deposit at Westpac, Australia Acct 313297, BSB 032020. Include your name, address, book title and email address.

Pilgrimage Book One

-Chains of Enchantment; Manjarin, Cordillera Cantabrica, Spain; Belorado, Beating Time, Molinaseca, Biero, Spain, Spain; Pilgrim's Astorga, Leon, Spain; Marvellous Najera; These Birds Have Flown; Travel Alone, and Lost In Translation.

Pilgrimage Two

Meeting Spain's Ancient Pilgrim Towns

Including *Bermeo, Bermeo*, Bay of Biscay, Spain; *Indifference*, Los Arcos, the Rioja, Spain; *Burnt Out*, Belorado, near Burgos, Spain; *Pleasant Peasant Arzua,* Galicia, Spain. Include colour pics, pilgrimage facts and advice.

PilgrimageThree

Towns and Tales from the French Chemin, including St Domingo de la Calzada, Translating the Rooster Legend, Tribute to Decazeville, Stolen, Conques, From Charles De Gaulle Airport to, Pont St Espirit, Languedoc, France, Snippets: Espallion to Moissacm The Geography of Saints, Making St Martin.

Pilgrimage Four

Camino Frances: On the Road. To The Start, St Jean Pied de Port, Ostabat, Paye Basque, France; Manjarin and Acebo, Cordillera Cantabrica, Leon, Spain. Windmill Molinaseca, Leon, Spain. Never Asked, Bordeaux, Bayonne, France. Drive by Hooting, Santiago de Compostela, Galicia, Spain. To St Domingo de la Calzada, Rioja region, Spain.

Pilgrimage Five

Albi- The Power and– Albi, France; *Crave Love*, Pezanas, Herault, France; *Venterol Dawn*, Paye Drome, France; *What I Didn't See in St Nazaire*, Brittany, France; *Icehouse* Pont St Espirit, Languedoc, France' *Riveting Rugb*y, Nogaro, Gers, France; *Aigues Mortes*, Provence, France; *St Jean du Port,* France; *Worldwide Warning*, Bilbao, Spain.

Pilgrimage Six, Journey to the Ardeche

Includes *Rite of Spring, Pont St Espirit, Getting Around, And Merriment Tonight, Icehouse, To St Martin d'Ardeche, Well on the Way, A Beautiful Woman Around Thirty, The Making of St Martin, The Geography of Saints.*

***Pilgrimage Seven*, Along the Way**

Poems from the traveller's imagination, including *A Trouser Ecology, Icehouse, Pont St Espirit, Nogaro, ...And Merriment Tonight, Tribute to Decazeville, Venterol Bells, Stolen Conques, Conques, From Charles DeGaulle, Pont de St Esprit, Snippets from France.*

Garry McDougall is a prizewinning Australian author, artist and traveller, published and exhibited in many countries.
Join the conversation on Start with C at
https://www.facebook.com/profile.php?id=100063917890425
Other works by the Author include *Belonging, Knowing Simone, Inspire Pilgrimage, Pilgrimage Spain* and *Winging It.*
He co-founded the Bicentennial Great North Walk and was President of the Balmain Institute for seven years.
Longlisted for Best Unpublished Manuscript, 2024.
Winner, Art in Unusual Places Grant, Wollongong Libraries. 2022.
Feature Poet, Sydney Writers Festival, 2017.
Winner, Peter Cowan National Short Story Prize; 2015.
Winner, 'Highly Commended', Peter Cowan National Short Story Prize; 2013.
Numerous photographic, painting and mixed media exhibitions.
He is a proud supporter of Médecins Sans Frontières, UN Children's Fund and Wikipedia.

Ten percent of sales of Start with C go to the Indigenous Literacy Fund.

Published by Pamela Press. ©

Manufactured by Amazon.com.au
Sydney, New South Wales, Australia